NICK NAYLOR
POSTMAN'S DOGS

Postman's Dogs

by Nick Naylor

Illustrated by Nick Naylor

ISBN: 9798620222049 (paperback)

For Sue, my wife
For all the dedication,
support and the help of the mice

TABLE OF CONTENT

Chapter 1

LEARNING TO TALK DOG

Have you ever wondered why dogs are considered to be a man's best friend? Is it their unswerving loyalty, their blind obedience, or just the one thing that all of us seem to be missing: that ability to love unconditionally, without judgement? Even when a doggy has been cruelly mistreated, they still have that capacity to show love and forgiveness. You see, an Alsatian does not look at a Pekinese and think, "I don't like him because he's a Pekinese," He doesn't even recognise that he's another dog. He just sees him as another spirit who likes chasing balls and having doggy fun. That's how they see humans too! Doggies know no boundaries. They care not for fences or for whose property it is. They do not judge their owners. They do not worry if their human friend has a been bad in the past, is a boy or a girl, black or white or somewhere in between. Or even if they've come from outer space with green and purple spots. To them, none of it matters.

They couldn't care less if their owner is a King or a Queen come to that. An everyday person in the street will do just fine. They don't even care if they're successful, and they certainly don't ask to see a list of exams they've passed. The only thing that concerns them is that they share in that same doggy bond, that special connection that binds all living things. That is love, happiness and a waggy tail... and that's how Grandpa Bill saw it too.

Grandpa Bill had been a postman all his life and had spent most of his years in the small fishing port of Berrycoombe St Martin with his wife Alice and his two grandchildren, Alex and Niall. They had come to live with their Grandparents after their mother died when she got poorly. Their father, who was a fisherman, was away at sea for weeks at a time so there was no one else to look after them. Niall was seven and Alex was eight and three quarters (and as people say when you're that age, the three quarters makes all the difference). They loved their Grandpa dearly and had great respect for him. Everyone that they knew looked up to him and said what a wonderful guy he was, because of all the kind things he did for people and animals alike.

The customers on Bill's round said he was the bee's knees and would do anything to help them out, be it a tyre that needed changing, plants that needed watering, first aid administering, a fish that needed feeding or just a shoulder to cry on when times were tough – he was there. At Christmas Bill felt incredibly lucky to be thought of in such a way. People would give him bottles of wine, plants, choccies galore and cards with nice things written inside. Although he didn't really want to accept the gifts, he couldn't refuse as his customers insist he take them for being such a happy, helpful chap. Everyone said that his smile was infectious and his joyous mood brought a ray of sunshine into their lives. Bill didn't know what all the fuss was about. He just saw it as being himself, but he was glad he was able to cheer people up and spread a little bit of happiness as he went. In fact he loved his job so much that he'd even go so far as to say he'd do it free, if he didn't have any bills to pay.

Bill had another special talent too: that was his ability to talk to dogs. People were amazed how he did it. He said it was nothing special, that anyone could do it if they just sat and relaxed, then they too would be able to tune into their inner dog.

"They just feel the good vibes." Bill would explain in his thick West Country accent. However it hadn't always been the case. When Bill was a young lad, he was scared of dogs and a lot of other things too. One day he was out delivering the Church Green round, when the dogs from Hill Top Farm decided they were going to chase him.

It was one of those lovely days at the end of summer when everything seemed to be just right with the world: the sky was blue, the sun was shining and there was just a hint of a breeze. Strolling along in his shirt sleeves and shorts with not a care in the world, he picked through his bundle of mail for the next letter, which was for Hilltop Farm.

Opening the gate and closing it behind him, he ambled down the driveway to the farmhouse. Now this is not the beautiful thatched cottage that you might be imagining but some run down old bungalow with filthy net curtains, dead flies in the windows and grass as high as the washing line. As well as odd bits of rusted machinery and engine blocks scattered here, there and everywhere.

Drawing closer to the front door Bill heard the dogs starting to bark, when all of a sudden he had a strange feeling. He could imagine the dogs running straight through the front door, breaking the glass and chasing him up the driveway. With that odd thought lingering in his head, he quickly pushed the letters through the box and broke into a steady jog back up the drive just in case.

Before he was half way up, there was an almighty crash and tinkling of glass as half a dozen dogs smashed through the front door and came flying up the drive after him. Knowing he didn't have time to hang about, he broke into a sprint and, glancing over his shoulder, he could see the dogs closing on him. With one clean jump he leapt clear of the gate. With his heart in his mouth he watched as the dogs tried launching themselves over the gate to bite him. Safely on the other side, Bill looked on as the dogs barked and growled furiously, showing their teeth as they snarled angrily at him.

With all that noise going on outside, it aroused the curiosity of the farmer's wife who came out to see what all the commotion was about.

"What the hell's going on here!" she shouted over the noise of the barking dogs as she charged up the driveway in a fluster. The farmer's wife being a big woman struggled to run. By the time she reached the gate, she was puffing and panting, blowing like an old steam engine. Yelling at the dogs for being so naughty, she scolded and cursed them with names so rude that it even made Bill blush. Taking one of her slippers off, she hurled it at the dogs, hitting a Jack Russell square in the chops.

"Get inside, you lot!" she screamed pointing to the house. Sending them inside to cool off she tried kicking the dogs as they scurried past, but they were far too fast and nimble for her considerable size and left her thrashing wildly in thin air.

"I'm so sorry," she said, rushing up to Bill, all out of breath and red in the face.

'They just be a bit boisterous.'

"Boisterous," exclaimed Bill, who had been shaken by the whole incident.

"I think they're more than a bit boisterous!" he added, whilst trying to compose himself.

"I'm so sorry…they've never done that before!" the farmer's wife gushed, apologising.

"No, I don't suppose they have. Otherwise you'd need a new door every time I turn up," he joked, checking his bag to see that the dogs hadn't bitten a hole in it.

The farmer's wife then turned to survey the damaged door. From afar she cast her eye over the jagged panes of glass that hung in the frame like rotten teeth.

"The little sods… look what they've done!" she grumbled, looking at the mess that they had left behind.

"Ohhhh… I could kill those dogs!" she growled, rolling up her sleeves, her face all red with anger.

"I'm going to give them a good hiding when I get hold of them! Where's my slipper?" she seethed. The farmer's wife was quite a fearsome lady and the thought of what she was going to do to the dogs made Bill wince.

"I don't think you need to hit them. They were only defending their territory like dogs do," he said trying to calm her down, but it was no use. She was that mad she chased after the remaining dogs, flushing them out from in the long grass.

"Come 'ere!" she yelled waving her fist in the air, but the dogs were one step ahead of her and disappeared in the tangle of weeds and junk, giving her the slip. Throwing her arms up in despair she gave up the chase, knowing she was beaten.

"It doesn't really matter does it?" said Bill leaning over the top of the gate.

"Oh I suppose you're right…" she conceded, but just to make herself feel better she let out another burst of foul language. For a minute the air went blue, as Bill put his hands over his ears. Coming to her senses, she suddenly realised where she was and looked around all ashamed.

"Oh, do forgive me please," she begged of Bill. "It's a good job the vicar isn't about eh?" she tittered, looking rather embarrassed by her outburst. Then turning her attention to Bill, she enquired as to how he was.

Quickly glancing down at himself, he patted his arms and legs just to make sure he was still all in one piece. "I think I'm alright."

"Thank God!" she declared, leaning over the gate to give him a big sloppy kiss.

Now being as Bill was only a young man, and not used to such a public show of affection from a stranger, he suddenly found himself going all red with embarrassment.

"Ermm…Errr…" He stammered, trying to pull himself free from the headlock she had him in.

"I must be getting on now… I've still got quite a bit of mail left to deliver," he spluttered shyly. Hanging onto his post bag for grim life, he tried to get away from the clutches of the farmer's wife, but in doing so tripped up over his own feet such was his rush to get away.

As he ran off down the road he could hear the farmer's wife calling after him. "Mind how you go, love!"

Bill didn't stop to hang about. He didn't know which was worse, being chased by a pack of angry dogs or being kissed all over by a burly farmer's wife.

That wasn't the only time Bill had been caught on the wrong side of a dog. Not long after that he was delivering mail to the local Politician's house where Charles, a Spaniel, lived along with his companion Monty, a fellow golden-haired Spaniel. Charles was the oldest, most arthritic dog Bill knew. He wasn't particularly friendly on account of all the pain he was in. When Bill turned up, he would always growl at him and draw back his gums to show his teeth but, as Charles could hardly walk Bill knew he didn't have much to worry about.

However, on this particular Saturday morning in question, things went a little different to plan. Bill had only two houses left to deliver to when he came across Charles lying outside the front door of the Politicians's house. Now this posed a bit of a problem for Bill. Did he chance his arm, or a leg as it would be in this case, and step over the dog to deliver the mail or did he take it back to the office where he would have to explain to the manager why he had not been able to deliver it? Being as he was so close to finishing and did not want to go to all the trouble of going back, he decided to risk it and pop the mail through the letterbox.

Approaching Charles with hesitation, Monty came over to sniff Bill's leg, as it was well known amongst all dogs that the best smells were to be found on a postman's leg. Bill then asked himself if he thought it was safe to put the mail through the box, what with Charles being laid in the way.

The gentrified Spaniel barked back at him, "You'll be alright, he's asleep!"

"You think so?" Bill responded, unsure as to whether or not to believe him.

"Sure, he's as blind as a bat! Can't see the nose in front of his face, old boy!" Monty stated with an air of superiority. Being as Bill wanted to get home and didn't want to hang about, he took the brave decision to deliver the mail.

Making just enough noise to make himself heard, but not too much, Bill stepped over the grizzled old dog. It was then that Charles stirred, opening one eye and looked straight up at him.

"Ha, fooled you!" he crowed. Monty now began to laugh scornfully, knowing full well that the postman was about to get a good nipping. Seizing his opportunity Charles cocked his head and, without moving a muscle, opened his jaws and bit down hard on Bill's leg.

"Owww!" cried Bill as the nasty Spaniel clamped its mouth around his lower leg. After holding on to Bill's leg just long enough to get the taste of postman, Charles then released his grip to take a look at his handy work. With blood pouring down Bill's leg, there was a nasty cut where the dog had sunk its teeth into him.

"Mmmm… I always wondered what postman tasted like!" Charles gloated as the two dogs began to laugh wickedly at their own pathetic idea of fun.

"Why did you do that?" asked Bill in disgust as he tried to stop the bleeding with his handkerchief.

"Because being the chosen pet of a Politician, we can do

whatever we like and get away with it!" Charles gloated proudly. Bill shook his head with sad dismay.

"You've left you're true doggy nature behind you, do you know that?"

"Do I care?" Charles sneered, cocking his head as if he had the right to do what he wanted to anyone and get away with it.

For Bill the whole incident had nearly put him off dogs for life. But call it fate, call it what you will: life had a strange way of resolving the past. For Charles the naughty Spaniel, it came the following Sunday morning when his owner, reversed his car out of the garage and over Charles' favourite squeeky toy… leaving it to sound its last squeak. So, it just goes to show that you should always be nice to people!

Luckily not all dogs are as ill-tempered and mean as Charles and Monty and not all want to chase posties (like you would be led to believe). Most are pleased just to have a roof over their heads, a bowl of food, the occasional stroke and a bit of fun thrown in for good measure as well as someone to love: that's all they require. They don't need some fancy dog kennel to be happy or a diamond encrusted collar to make them feel better or even a designer doggy coat to help them fit in. They know that having a waggy tail is worth way more than anything else in the whole wide world.

Now I suppose you want to know how Bill came to acquire his special abilities of being able to talk to dogs, don't you? It didn't happen overnight…well it did, but I'll come to that in a minute. You see, being able to understand what dogs are saying requires a certain skill and that skill is kindness.

Kindness allows you to do all sorts of brilliant things for people as well as being able to hear what dogs are saying. It usually worked that if you did something nice for somebody, then they in turn would want to do something nice for somebody else. And there is also an upside to doing kind things. It makes you feel happy and gives you a warm feeling in your tummy.

Now I have been chatting far too long and I suppose I should tell you how Bill came to be able to hear what dogs are saying.

You see it all happened one Sunday morning. After having made a cup of tea and going back to bed for a lie in, Bill was distracted by someone shouting over the fence in the back yard.

"Patch, Patch, have you seen my ball?" Disturbing his lie in, Bill wondered who on earth it was making all this racket at this time on a Sunday morning? The shouting continued.

"Where did you last have your ball?"

Curious to see who was making all this noise, Bill got up and went over to the window. Sticking his head out between the gap in the curtains he scanned his neighbours' back yard, expecting to see two lads making all the racket. But there was no one except Auntie Joan's Airedale Terrier, Kurry, and Patch, a liver-and-cream Spaniel that lived three doors down.

Bill scratched his head, confused as to who it was doing all the shouting. Standing at the window for a couple of minutes, he waited to see if he could spot the culprits. But as his tea was going cold and he didn't want to waste anymore time, he went back to bed. Pulling the covers up over him, he took a sip of tea and let out a long, contented sigh.

"Ahhhhhh...that's better, nothing like a Sunday morning lie in, eh?" he said to himself, as Alice, his wife lay fast asleep next to him. Closing his eyes and enjoying the moment, his peace and quiet was once more disturbed by yet more shouting from outside.

"Kurry, Kurry, I've found your ball!"

Right! That's it, thought Bill, putting his tea down and stomping out of bed to tell off whoever was guilty of disturbing his lie in.

When Bill looked out of the window, there was no one to be seen except Kurry and Patch. From where he stood, they looked to be talking to each other. It can't be, thought Bill rubbing his eyes in disbelief. But there, below him, were two dogs stood on their hind legs, leant against the fence having a conversation.

"Are you going for a walk this morning?" One dog would ask the other, while Patch wanted to know if Kurry was going to the park this afternoon to chase squirrels.

Amazed by what he was witnessing, Bill rushed over to Alice and, taking her by the shoulders, roughly woke her up.

"Alice, Alice!" he cried desperate to show his wife the astonishing marvel of two dogs talking. Alice, not believing him, muttered something under her breath before finally getting out of bed to accompany her husband over to the window.

"Listen, look!" Bill enthused, excited by his newfound discovery.

Alice, looking rather displeased at her husband, turned to him. "What's so amazing that you've got to drag me out of bed at this time on a Sunday morning?"

Bill was slightly confused: surely she could hear the dogs talking too?

"Can't you hear them?" he asked.

"What? What is it that I'm supposed to be listening for?" She said rather impatiently, with her arms crossed.

"The dogs… they're talking."

Alice looked at him as if he had lost his mind. "Have you been drinking or something? You're not running a temperature are you?" said Alice, putting her hand to his head to feel his brow.

"No, no." He protested.

"Mmmm…" she sighed dubiously. "I think you should come back to bed and have a lie down," she insisted.

Bill wondered what was going on. If Alice couldn't hear the dogs talking, he wondered … was he going mad? Not wanting to look a fool, Bill decided to say nothing and pretend that everything was fine. But as he got back in bed he knew the truth. He knew that dogs really did talk to each other…and more to the point HE COULD HEAR THEM!

He decided to keep it a secret from everyone, especially all the other posties. He knew if he told people that dogs could talk, then everyone would laugh at him. But after a while, when the posties saw how brilliant he was with dogs – even the nasty ones, they all wanted to know what his secret was. Even his customers out on his round, when they heard about his special skill, wanted to know if he could come and train their dogs to be more obedient and not be so unruly.

So now you know, that's how Bill came to be fluent in 'dog'...

Chapter 2

A WAY TO A DOG'S HEART

Little Staffy

Bill's round stretched as far as the eye could see across the wild wind swept peaks of Exmoor and beyond. Each day his van could be seen making its way along the rutted tracks and ancient lanes that had crossed the moor for centuries. From high up on the lonely hills down the steeply sided wooded valleys to the small villages that clung to the cliffs everyone would be waiting on Bill, waiting for him to turn up with the parcels that they had ordered.

"Aren't you going to put some trousers on?" They would shout to him when he arrived wearing his shorts. Bill would give a hearty laugh and tug at the bottom of his shorts.

"When the snow gets this deep, I might think about it."

No matter what time of year it was Bill could always be found wearing his shorts. Even in the depths of winter when ice covered the puddles at the side of the road and the thermometer read well below zero he would still have his shorts on.

"Is there something wrong with you?" They'd want to know shaking their heads in dismay, but for Bill it made perfect sense. You see, if it rained it was far better to let your legs get wet as they dried out much quicker than a pair of trousers. For a postie there was nothing worse than having to sit in a pair of damp squibby trousers all day and besides he was always so busy that it helped him cool off. So next time you're wondering why your postman wears shorts all year round now you know.

Out on his round there were more dogs than you could shake a stick at, and that was saying something, as you know how much a dog loves a stick! All the farms had a dog or two or even five! Most of them were black and white Border Collies and Bill had got to know them all by name. He'd known most of them since they were pups, watching them grow from tiny balls of fluff into fully-fledged working dogs competent in the art of herding sheep.

Being able to work with a dog was a real skill. It took patience from both farmer and dog alike, with many years of hard work, practice and more than a few mistakes thrown in for good measure. Eventually, maybe after a lifetime of working together, the farmer and his dog became so well attuned with one other that they could tell each other's moods just by the way one of them was holding themself.

For a sheep dog, an excitable crouched position meant that it was ready to go to work. All you had to do then was give a few sharp whistles and a whole flock of wayward sheep could be gathered in off the moor in a blink of an eye. It wasn't just the sheep that a working dog had to watch over. They also had to look after the farmer too. Being a farmer was just like any profession: there were always troubles and worries to deal with, be it the weather, the crops, the animals or the family. But no matter what, his dog was always there for him. Even if there was no one else the farmer could to talk to, he could rely on his furry companion to lend an ear. You see a dog intuitively knows what's wrong with people and they know just how to help. Even if everything else in the world seems to be going wrong, there's nothing like a comforting lick on the side of the face to remind you that somebody out there loves you.

Bill had these same special skills too, but for him it went much further than just being able to communicate with a few sharp, shrill whistles and roughly grunted commands. Bill could actually talk to dogs. I mean he really could talk to them! For him it was just like you and I having a normal everyday conversation. Tapping into his inner dog had allowed him to do this. You see, the more love you have inside you, the shinier and kinder you are and the easier it is to hear what dogs are actually saying to one another. And did you know a canine conversation is far more interesting than a human one? Rather than talking about boring things like money or what colour curtains you should have in the front room, dogs talked about exciting things like where was the best place to slide down a hill on your tummy, which tree had the most interesting smells, or what was the best way to catch flies with your mouth open. Those were the real important things in life, not the silly things that humans worry about.

Each morning when Bill was out on his round the dogs would come running up to him all pleased to see him. It wasn't just the hugs and the tickles they came for though, Bill had a secret up his sleeve. Now nothing gets a doggy going more than something to eat and as all dogs think with their tummies, Bill kept a bag of dog biscuits behind the seat of his van.

All the dogs knew this and most of them were quite happy to sit and wait patiently to be given a treat, but some were far too eager and would stick their heads through the window leaving big muddy paw prints on the side of the van. Shooing them off, Bill made sure that only well behaved dogs got a biscuit and those that were ill-tempered, snarly and growly were not allowed a biscuit until they had learnt to behave themselves properly.

In return for a biscuit some dogs liked to give a paw while others liked to give a smile. A canine smile is an odd thing to see. To the untrained eye, it can look rather menacing with their gums drawn back and gnashers showing. However, the give away to a doggy smile is a waggy tail. If there's one thing a dog cannot hide is its tail, and a wagging tail is the human equivalent to a great big smile. The more a dog wags its tail then the happier they are and if they really thump their tail furiously on the ground then you know they are definitely pleased to see you.

As it was known that all dogs love a good sniff of the postman's leg Bill always found himself the centre of attention wherever he went. You see dogs just love smells. The more interesting, the more pungent, the more stinky and the more revolting the better! To a dog there is nothing finer than having a good roll around in the most disgusting smell it can find and rubbing it on someone. A festering stench is something to be savoured and as Bill's legs were long and hairy they made ideal conductors of doggy fragrances. The scent lingered on him and was carried everywhere he went. It was if his legs were the equivalent of a doggy internet, where messages could be left for friends and all they had to do in order to reply was brush up against him and let the news travel from farm to farm by the leg of a postman.

It wasn't just sheep dogs that Bill bumped into, but sofa dogs too. Now it might seem like an ideal life being the family pet. Sitting around all day, being taken for walks and getting treats at the drop of a hat, but let me tell you they work just as hard, if not harder than sheep dogs. You see looking after humans is not easy. It's a full time job. Unlike sheep who wander around munching grass all day and from time to time get themselves stuck on their backs, humans are far more complicated creatures. They have all sorts of peculiar quirks, odd habits and silly secrets and a sofa dog has to understand and learn how their 'owner' works.

Some humans are grumpy and grouchy and if there is one thing a dog cannot stand above all else is a sour faced, mean spirited person. You see our doggy companions are actually teaching us how to be more like them, to be more dog. For instance when a pooch gets a tummy rub we think that we are doing it to please them, but really it's makes us feel better without us even knowing it. And when doggies go out for walkies, it's not so they can just stretch their legs, it's a sneaky ploy to get us to meet other people, to chat, to make friends and, in some cases, fall in love. A doggie's main aim in life is to make people happy and that can't be a bad thing now, can it?

On Bill's round every dog had their own special character and funny ways just like their owners. There was Lottie, a longhaired lurcher who Bill bumped into most days. She had the most startling blue eyes he had ever seen. One was that striking that it glinted like a precious sapphire whilst the other was all cloudy and misty as if she had something wrong with it. But rather than making her look all odd it made her look uniquely wonderful, as if a whole galaxy of stars were floating in her eye.

Then there was Staffy, a short, stocky Staffordshire Bull Terrier who lived at Ash Tree Cottage. Bill thought his name was the most boring name ever given to a dog. He would have called him Big Shug or Chunk, or something with a bit of zing, something that was a bit more becoming of a dog of his stature. Now most people who saw Staffy were so scared that they wouldn't go near him, but the truth of the matter was, he was cutest, most softest dog you could ever wish to meet.

Each morning when Bill turned up at his house Staffy would get so worked up that he would cry with excitement, making strange whimpering noises like mmmmm… mmmmm… mmmmm…. Standing on his hind legs, he would peer over the top half of the open stable door and beg for Bill to coochy-coo him under the chin. Tickling him on the chops, Staffy would whine and cry so much that he sounded as if he were in heaven.

Some mornings when Bill turned up there would be no sign of him. His basket would be empty and the porch would be all quiet, but Bill knew exactly where he would be. Once a week his owner, Mrs James, would make pasties for all her boys and Staffy could always be found hiding under the kitchen table, waiting to snaffle the odd tit-bits and scraps that fell on the floor.

"Morning Bill," Mrs James called out of the window as Bill pulled up in his van.

"Got anything for me?" she asked. Bill flicked through the pile of letters he had with him.

"Looks like a lot of junk to me," he said, without even looking up.

"No parcels?" she enquired her voice full with expectation. Bill shook his head,

"Not this morning."

"Oh well, there's always tomorrow, eh?" she said, sounding somewhat disappointed.

"Say, would you like a pasty?" She asked him through the open window. Suddenly from under the table Staffy's ears pricked up. With the sound of scuffling paws on tiles he got to his feet to eavesdrop on the conversation.

"No I couldn't…' Bill replied stroking his chin thoughtfully. "I mean, what will your lads have for their dinner tonight?"

"You don't have to worry about them," Mrs James reassured him lifting up a rack of beautifully glazed pasties, still steaming from just being taken from the oven.

"Ohhh…" murmured Bill with delight. Meanwhile Staffy was leaning up against the kitchen cupboards doing his very best to make himself look as cute and adorable as possible with his pink little tongue hanging out.

"I'm here, I'm here!" he barked trying to get their attention, but Mrs James just ignored him. She didn't speak dog and to her it only sounded like an annoying bark.

"Get down!" she scolded him, telling him off. Showing Bill the pasties, she let him take his pick. "I've made you a cheese an' onion one especially for you…I knows how you like 'em."

Bill patted his stomach.

"I shouldn't really," He protested as he thought about his waistline, but Mrs James just smiled mischievously back at him.

"It'll only go to waste if not, eh?"

Knowing that refusing was a waste of time, Bill gave in to her kind offer.

"Oh go on then, I'm sure I'll work it off," he smiled, gleefully accepting the gift.

"I know you too well, eh, Bill Mathers?" she cackled.

"You can't refuse one of my pasties, now can you?" About to wrap it up for him, Bill told her not to bother as it wouldn't have time to get cold. Passing it out of the window to him Staffy looked on enviously.

"Bill, Bill," Staffy whispered trying to get his attention. Standing on his tippy toes, he strained to see over the kitchen worktop.

"Save some for me!" he barked.

"I'll meet you down by the gate."

Whimpering, his face all screwed up with excitement, he scuttled out of the kitchen and made his way towards the door.

Thanking Mrs James for her hospitality, Bill got back in his van and waved goodbye.

From the roadside he could see Staffy pushing the door handle down with his nose. This was a neat little trick that he had learnt when it was too cold for him outside and he wanted to go in and warm up.

Scamping as fast as his short legs would carry him he ran across the lawn towards the gate, "I'm here Bill, I'm here!" he barked, making sure that Bill wasn't going to leave without him. Pulling his van under the overhanging trees, Bill sat and waited and it wasn't long before he could hear the puffing and panting of Staffy rushing towards him.

"I think you need to cut down on those pasties, eh?" joked Bill, listening to the little dog wheeze from all the exertion. Taking a bite, Staffy watched on enviously as the flaky golden pastry shattered, covering Bill in a smattering of tasty crumbs.

"Steady on, save some for me!" Staffy pleaded, as a single pearl-like drop of drool dripped from the corner of his mouth. Tickling him around his neck, Bill offered him the pasty.

"I thought you'd never ask," Staffy remarked politely, as he sat bolt upright on his best behaviour.

"Careful it's hot," Bill cautioned him, as he tore off a corner.

"Don't worry it'll be alright," replied Staffy, eagerly shuffling around on his bottom desperate to have a nibble.

"You'd think by now she'd know how much I love pasties," Staffy moaned letting his thoughts be known on the matter. "I sit there all day, patiently waiting while she's busy cooking, and not once has she made me my own pasty. Do you know she has never once looked down at me and thought, you know what, maybe Staffy might like a pasty? Not once!" he snuffled, shaking his head in dismay.

"All I get is scraps!" he barked huffily.

"Well never mind, eh," Bill said, trying to comfort him.

"Here you are."

Holding out his hand, Bill offered the torn off corner of pasty for him. Staffy, with eyes as big as saucers, hungrily snaffled it from his hand in one go.

"Oww it's hot!" he yelped, spitting it back out.

"I did warn you…you should have waited for it to cool down," said Bill, telling him off.

Picking up the half-chewed pasty out of the dirt, Bill blew on it as Staffy did a little dance in the hope that it would help cool his tongue down. Taking pity on the over excitable dog, Bill dug out his water bottle from his bag and squirted him in the face, letting the water run down his chops and cool his throbbing tongue.

"Better?" asked Bill.

"Better," replied Staffy, ruckling up his nose and sneezing as he got over the shock.

It didn't take long for him to be feeling himself again and soon he was fidgeting about, in anticipation.

"Here you are…now steady," said Bill, holding the pasty out and blowing on it.

"Hmmfff…Hmmfff…Hmmfff," went Staffy, as he gobbled it down in one.

"You know you should really chew your food more," exclaimed

Bill, amazed by how fast he had polished it off. Showing his appreciation, Staffy thumped his tail wildly in the dust as he looked adoringly up at Bill. To Bill it didn't matter that his friends weren't human and that they had four legs and a tail. Being able to get along with everyone was what helped Bill to speak dog.

However, as loveable and cute as dogs are they do have one draw back, and that is they can get themselves into all sorts of trouble when trying to get their paws on a treat.

One particular dog in question was Ozzy, an Alaskan Malamute. Ozzy was a fluffy grey and white sled dog, who was the most chilled dog Bill had ever met. Spending most of his time laid out alseep in the yard, he was that slothful that he could barely raise the enthusiasm to get up to be petted. Every morning when Bill walked into the yard, Ozzy would give him a look that said, 'Really? Bothered?' And he could barely muster the enthusiasm to get up from where he was lying to take a biscuit.

Ozzy

On the morning in question Bill had arrived at Highfield Barn where Ozzy lived. The weather was blistering. The sun shone and the perfect blue sky was dotted with the contrails of planes heading west. In the van the temperature gauge read in the high twenties and sweat was beginning to bead off Bill's brow. With the windows wound right down and the radio playing, Bill tried to get some relief from the heat, but there was little chance of that. As the tar pooled on the roads the sheep who were sat hiding under the cover of the Blackthorn trees were glad that they did not have their woolly jumpers on.

Pulling up the driveway to house, the sound of crunching gravel woke Ozzy from his permanent state of inactivity. Opening just one eye, as two would have been far too much effort, he looked up to see who it was disturbing his sleep.

"Morning Ozzy!" Bill called out as he strode down the driveway to greet him. Ozzy blinked his big black eyes in recognition, but the very thought of getting up from off the ground was far too much even for him to think about.

Leaving the van unattended, Bill went round the back of the house to deliver the mail and while he was gone he got talking to Ozzy's owner. After a few minutes had passed and there was no sign of Bill, Ozzy's mind began to wander. Now it was rare that any thoughts ever entered Ozzy's tiny brain and thinking was normally far too taxing, but he had noticed that both windows were right down on Bill's van. Then, for only the third time that year, a thought suddenly passed through Ozzy's head.

"I wonder?" he thought to himself.

Now Ozzy knew that Bill kept dog biscuits in his van and since he was nowhere to be seen and the windows were down, an idea began to form.

Licking his lips he got to his feet, stretched and then strolled stealthily up to the van. Casting a sly glance over his shoulder he checked to see that he was not being watched. It didn't look like Bill was coming back any time soon. As he listened to them idly chatting away at the back of the house, he decided to stick his head inside the van.

"I know those biscuits are in here somewhere," he said to himself as he looked around. Cocking his nose to the breeze, he sniffed the air suspiciously, taking in a whole range of interesting smells.

"Mmm... biscuits?" he muttered, instantly recognising the smell. However, it was all well and good knowing that there were biscuits in there but that wasn't going to help him get his paws on them. Checking once more to make sure the coast was clear, he leapt through the window. As agile and nimble as a cat-burglar, Ozzy made it look easy and found himself suddenly perched in the driver's seat.

With his nose twitching he sniffed around for clues: under the seat, above the cab, down the side pockets and then… he saw them. There, in a big bag stuffed tight behind the driver's seat, was his prize. Grabbing the bag with his teeth he pulled at it and, as quick as a flash, he cleanly exited the crime scene as quickly as he had entered.

Once outside, he nosed his way headfirst into the bag eager to gorge himself on the stolen treasure. Ozzy was rather pleased with himself. It's not often that you get a whole bag of dog biscuits all to yourself, is it? It didn't take him long to polish off the entire contents and with a full tummy he thought he better make himself scarce, not wishing to get caught red-handed.

However, he hadn't accounted for his long pointy ears and when he tried to get his head out of the bag, he found that his ears were stuck fast. Panicking, he staggered round the yard trying to get the bag off his head. He tried everything. Rubbing his head on the ground, pulling at it with his paw, and biting his way through it, but nothing worked.

'Crumbs,' he thought, 'I'm in for it now. How am I going to get myself out of this mess?"

By now the cows in the field next door, who up until this point hadn't been paying much attention to what had been going, on decided to stick their heads over the wall to watch the hair-brained antics of the dog.

"Have you ever seen such a thing?" asked one of the heifers to the other. The cow, busy chewing on a mouthful of grass took a moment to think

"No, I can't say I have," she said, idly, while continuing to munch away.

"Bit of a stupid thing to do if you ask me," the other added, as they watched Ozzy stumble around blindly with the bag on his head.

"Typical dog, I bet it was thinking of its stomach?" one of the cows commented, as if she had seen it all before. After discussing Ozzy's sticky situation, the two heifers then went back to chewing the cud, leaving him to find his way out of the bag. It was then that Bill came round the corner.

"Pete, you've got to see this!" He shouted to Ozzy's owner.

Thinking something must be wrong, Ozzy's owner came dashing round the corner and was suddenly stopped dead in his tracks by what he saw. There he was confronted by the sight of his own dog wearing a paper bag on its head. Bent double with laughter, he was so consumed with hilarity that all he could do was stand and point.

"What a stupid dog!" he howled as he fell about laughing.

"How's he done that?" he wanted to know. Bill went over to Ozzy to take the bag off his head, but his owner wanted to take a photo of him.

"No, no, stand next to him Bill," he said directing him to pose next to Ozzy.

"But he'll be frightened, let me take the bag off him," Bill pleaded.

His owner wouldn't have any of it.

"Just one second," Pete, his owner begged of him, as he rummaged for his phone. Quickly before Ozzy could suffer any more distress he snapped a picture of Ozzy with the bag on his head.

"There!" he exclaimed, showing Bill the photo. By now Ozzy was feeling rather embarrassed by his actions and wished that he hadn't been so greedy.

"Help!" he barked from inside the bag. No longer able to watch Ozzy suffer anymore, Bill removed the bag from his head. Apart from feeling rather sheepish, Ozzy was looking a bit green around the gills, but then he had eaten a whole bag of dog biscuits all to himself.

"What's the matter eh, lad, eaten too much?" Bill asked. Ozzy burped and looked unsteady on his paws, as he staggered around trying to find somewhere that was out of the sun.

"I think you better go an' have a little lie down, eh?" Ozzy agreed with Bill and went to sit down in the shade of an old pine tree. While he lay there feeling sick, Ozzy had chance to reflect on his actions and wished he hadn't eaten so much.

Even though Ozzy had been a naughty dog, Bill couldn't help but feel sorry for him and went over to give him a stroke. Hoping that he'd learnt his lesson, he jumped back in his van and gave them a cheery wave knowing that Ozzy wouldn't be trying that again any time soon, not unless he wanted to feel sick again.

Chapter 3

THE OCEAN CALLS

Nelson

From their top floor attic window, Alex and Niall could see right across the rooftops and jumble of chimney pots out to the ocean beyond. In the summertime the small fishing town of Berrycoombe St Martin was busy with holidaymakers, ice creams and candyfloss.

Niall spent hours looking out of his bedroom window, watching the world go by. He had been given a telescope by his Grandfather. Alex, his sister had no interest in it, she preferred reading her books, but Niall was fascinated by it.

"Don't you ever get bored with looking through that stupid telescope of yours?" Alex asked him as she lay on her bed reading.

"How can you get bored with it?" he answered back, as if being asked a totally stupid question.

Through the lens of the telescope, Niall watched life unfold.

Some days, the clouds would scurry across the sky pushed along by strong winds and the sea would be all choppy. While other days it would be warm and balmy with hardly a ripple on the ocean. No one day was ever the same and that's what Niall liked about it. There was so much to see and do.

"Just look at it!" he said pointing to the ocean, unable to believe that his sister was not impressed by such a thing. Looking up from her book for a moment, Alex rolled over on to her stomach to glance at what her brother was so intrigued by.

"Mmm...," she commented before rolling back over again. Alex did not hold the same fascination for the sea as her brother. For him it connected him to something much, much bigger. Quite content to sit there, he was at his happiest when watching the comings and goings out on the ocean.

During the day, the small, one-manned fishing boats would spend their time close to shore, paying out line or laying pots for lobster and crab. The bigger boats, the trawlers, which Alex and Niall's father worked on spent their nights in the deeper waters of the channel while further out huge container ships made their way silently up and down the sea lanes. Niall wished he could live on one of those giant ships. He imagined all the amazing places he could visit and all the interesting people he might meet as it travelled around the world.

At night, after Grandpa had read them a story, Niall would sneak out of bed just to watch the coming and goings. All lit up with rows of lights, the container ships passed by as if floating in mid-air, like some giant spaceship. Half asleep half awake, Alex asked him what he was doing.

"I'm looking for Dad," he replied huddled against the window.

"You're looking for Dad!" she replied, mocking him. Granny and Grandpa had tried to convince their father to give up fishing for the sake of the children, especially after their mother had died, but their Grandpa knew it was pointless. He said that their father had the ocean in his blood and that was all he ever wanted to do in his life was be a fisherman.

"You'll never see Dad," Alex replied, as she lay curled up in bed watching him.

"I will."

"No you won't!" she argued, but that wasn't going to put him off. He knew that their father's boat was out there and carried with it a certain group of lights.

"It's that one down there," he pointed, pressing his finger against the windowpane.

"Where?" she asked, leaning out of bed to see.

"That one there, the furthest one on the right," he said confidently. Quickly rummaging under his bed, in amongst his boxes of toys and comics, he pulled out his torch.

"What's that for?" asked Alex puzzled.

"Dad's been teaching me Morse code," he said pulling his stool up against the window.

"Watch." Flashing his torch on and off, he tapped out a message with a series of dots and dashes. Then he sat back and waited for a response.

"What did you say?" asked Alex. Turning to her with a satisfied grin on his face, he told her, "I said hello Dad."

"When did he teach you that?" She wanted to know.

"Last time we were on the boat. I've been practising," he answered, all pleased with himself.

"Well, has he replied yet?"

"Not yet," Niall answered back. Alex slid out of bed to join her brother and, squeezing on to the stool next to him, they watched to see if there was any response.

"Nothing's happened!" Alex remarked, as if the lack of response proved Niall didn't know what he was doing.

"Wait! I'll do it again," he said, whispering so as his Grandparents downstairs couldn't hear. Repeating the message, he let the beam of light travel out into the night, across the silent ocean and then waited.

"Do you think he's seen it?" Alex whispered, snuggling up to him for warmth.

"Don't know," replied Niall, watching for a response.

"I'll try again." Then one of the boats flashed its lights on and off three times. Jumping off the stool, the pair of them leapt in the air.

"It's Dad!" they whispered excitedly. Realising that their Grandparents might have heard them, they put their hands to their mouths and gasped. Hardly daring to breath, they waited for the footsteps coming up the stairs, but there was nothing, just the usual noise of the T.V blaring away in the front room.

Niall tried again and once more and the little boat furthest from them flashed its lights on and off. In the dark of their bedroom they stood there waving to their father.

"It's nice to know Dad's out there even though we can't see him." Alex said, snuggling closer to her brother. For a while they watched their father's boat until it got too cold for them just sitting there in their pyjamas. Jumping back into bed they pulled the covers tight and snuggled down, their faces turned towards each other in the dark.

"Can you teach me that?" asked Alex, whispering so as they wouldn't be heard.

"Sure," Niall said, passing the torch over to his sister.

"What do I have to do?" She wanted to know. Niall talked her through it, giving her instruction as Alex tapped out the series of dots and dashes with the torch.

"That's it," he said, praising her skill.

"You'll have to do it next time." After teaching his sister the art of Morse code and chatting for some time, the two of became sleepy and dozed off, leaving only the lighthouse out in the channel to gently flicker away and keep watch over the fishermen.

It wasn't that often that Alex and Niall got to see their father. If he wasn't out at sea or mending his nets or fixing the boat or doing any number of the many jobs that needed doing, then he was usually asleep. So when the opportunity arose to see their father, they jumped at the chance to be with him. With it being always so last minute, Granny and Grandpa had taken to making a special thing of it.

They would all go down the harbour together and before meeting him Grandpa would take them to the ice cream parlour. There they could have an ice cream sundae, a knickerbocker glory or or whatever they fancied. The ice cream sundaes there were legendary. They came in a huge frosted glass bowl that looked like a flower with its petals opening. Inside it was heaped with all sorts of different flavours, topped off with fluffy white ice cream, red juice and chocolate sauce dripping off the sides, as well as fancy wafers to scoop the ice cream up with.

It was far too huge for one person to eat on their own, so the waitress would bring four long spoons out with her for everyone to tuck in with. Alex always said it seemed a shame to eat it as it looked so good, but Grandpa replied that he would gladly eat her share if she didn't want it.

Leaving the ice cream parlour to meet their father they walked down the quayside, paasing the Harbourmaster's office where Stan the Harbourmaster worked.

Seeing their father's boat moored up, Alex and Niall broke into a sprint along the quayside whilst Granny and Grandpa followed on behind. As the children passed the Harbourmaster's hut, Bill suddenly heard barking coming from the office.

"Stop!" snarled a dog, as the children raced by. "I said stop!" came the nasty bark.

Alex and Niall froze in their tracks, scared by the dog's terrifying bark. Bill was taken aback by the nastiness being directed towards his grandchildren and, peeking round the corner, found Nelson, a West Highland White, standing on duty outside the office wearing the Harbourmaster's cap.

Nelson belonged to the Harbourmaster Stan and was usually quite friendly, but on this occasion something had got into Nelson to make him rather disagreeable.

"What's the matter?" asked Bill, who had known Nelson since he was a pup.

"Do you know who I am?" Nelson snapped. Well actually, Bill did know who he was. After all, he had delivered his Kennel Club certificate when he was just a tiny ball of white fluff and, according to the certificate, his real name was Hillyacres Overlord the Third.

"Look, Nelson, there's no need for such unpleasantness," Bill said, trying to appeal to his better nature. Raising his paw, Nelson tapped the gold braid on the rim of his cap.

"See this?" he growled.

"This is the official badge for the office of Harbourmaster and, seeing as the Harbourmaster is not here right now then that makes me the official Harbourmaster!" Bill looked at him suspiciously.

"I'm sure Stan didn't give you permission to wear his cap did he?" he said. Nelson looked away, pretending not to hear the question.

"Can you see that sign on the wall over there?" Nelson barked grumpily, pointing with his nose.

"It says AUTHORISED PERSONNEL ONLY and you don't look like authorised personnel to me!" snapped Nelson, twitching his small nose at the sign.

"Look, Nelson, you know me. My son has that boat over there." Bill said, pointing to the row of trawlers moored up. "And all I'm doing is bringing the children to see their father."

"Ahh yes… that as may be the case, but rules are rules and I'm here to enforce them," he said, pointing to the list of rules on the wall with his nose. Bill quickly glanced at it.

"Seems like you've got that many rules, you're drowning in them!" he laughed. Bill knew that Nelson must have been bored and had probably spent the afternoon reading the regulation book, because he never spoke like that normally.

Bill, after having been at work all day, was getting hungry and was tired of all Nelson's rules. Bending down, he put his hand out for Nelson to sniff. The dog pulled back his gums and grizzled at him. Slowly and calmly, Bill put his hand behind Nelson's head and removed the cap.

"Give it back! Give it back!" barked Nelson, jumping up as high as he could to try and get it back.

"I think you're a much nicer dog when you're not wearing this," Bill told Nelson, as he stuffed the cap in his back pocket.

"That's my cap give it back!" he protested, but Bill ignored him.

"This belongs to Stan and I think you've pinched it."

Knowing he had done wrong, Nelson looked ashamed of himself. Bill tickled him under the chin to try and cheer him up. Now it's hard for a dog to resist being tickled because they love it so much, but this was proving to be a real problem for Nelson. As much as he wanted to give in and roll over on his tummy, his silly rules was stopping him from having fun.

"Grrrrr…Grrrr…Grrrr…," he went, as he struggled to fight against his true doggyness.

"Go on, you know you want to," chuckled Bill, as he tickled him some more and saw that Westie was beginning to crack, as his tail began to twitch.

"Oh it's no use!" Nelson blurted out. "I can't resist." His tail was now wagging like a windscreen wiper in heavy rain and, all of a sudden, he rolled over on to his back and begged for more.

"More, more," he demanded. Seeing Grandpa tickling his tummy the children joined in. Squirming about like an eel on the quayside Nelson asked him if he had changed his mind about letting Alex and Niall see their father.

"Yes…yes…" he said, as he rolled around on the floor giggling and pawing at the air.

Leaving Grandpa to go and get the fish and chips, Granny went to sit on a bench while the children ran along the long arm of the quayside and down to their father's boat.

"Ahoy, there mateys!" shouted their Dad, waving them on board.

Stood atop of the pier ladders, they called out to their father below. Climbing down they clung to the rungs as they waited for the just right moment to jump on board as the boat rose and fell on the surging tide.

"Are you coming out with me an' the boys tonight?" their father joked, nodding for them to join him and the rest of the crew. On the aft one of the deckhands was cleaning the boat with a hosepipe, while the other two were busy stacking crates down below ready for the fish and ice later on.

"I don't like your boat, Daddy," stated Alex.

"It smells!" she said, ruckling up her nose.

"I think it stinks too!" Niall added, agreeing with his sister.

"Well, that's what fishing boats do," he laughed.

"They're big, they're dirty an' they's smell!" Their Dad took after their Grandfather. He was a jolly chap and always had a nice smile for people and never seemed to stop laughing.

It was time for the boat to put out on the water. With a big sigh, their father lifted them out of the boat, watching them anxiously as they climbed the narrow rungs of the ladder back up onto the quayside. The electric starter motor beeped and the engine on the boat spluttered into life.

By the time Alex and Niall joined their Grandparents on the bench, they were already busy unwrapping the fish and chips.

"Ahh…just in time," Bill commented.

"Mine's the one with the sausage," chirped up Niall.

"There, that one's yours," said Granny. The fish and chips smelt wonderful. There was nothing better in the world than sat by the seaside eating fish and chips out of the paper. What more could anyone want?

Tucking into their tea, they watched as their Dad's boat pulled alongside them. Giving them a toot on the horn, he waved to them and they waved back enthusiastically.

It was just then that Bill felt something brush against his leg. Looking down he saw, to his surprise, an apologetic Nelson sitting politely by his feet.

"Now then Nelson what can I do for you?" he asked, looking down at the Westie.

"I was just...err...wondering... if...errr..." Nelson spluttered timidly.

"C'mon Nelson spit it out lad, I've got my tea going cold here," Bill said.

"Well..." Nelson began, as he sat down in front of him on his best behaviour.

"I was wondering if you could me spare a chip?" He barked ever so politely. Bill looked at him while he thought about it.

"I'll let you have a chip on one condition," he said.

"Name it! Anything, anything!" Nelson yapped, eager to please.

"Well, you were rather nasty earlier on, weren't you?" Nelson looked down shamefully at the ground.

"From now on you have to promise me you won't be mean and nasty to anyone...and that's not just to me and my family, but to everyone. Do you understand?" Holding up a chip in his hand Bill made him swear on it. Nelson stood up on his hind legs and, to show that he really meant it, he gave a salute with his paw.

"I hereby swear that I will no longer be nasty and will be a kind dog from now on!" barked Nelson sincerely.

"Good lad," said Bill, accepting his apology and tossing him a chip. Then reaching round, Bill pulled out the Harbourmaster's cap from his back pocket.

"Here, lad, here you are," he said.

"Really?" barked Nelson. "You'll let me have it back?"

"On the condition you stop being nasty and no more of these silly, petty rules!" he reminded him. Then placing the cap on Nelson's head, Bill gave him a salute. Pleased to be receiving his cap back, Nelson puffed out his chest and stood to attention, giving his best salute in return.

"Awww...doesn't he look cute with his ears sticking out from underneath the cap?" said Granny, expressing her delight at Nelson's adorable nature.

"Can Nelson have another chip?" asked Alex, seeking permission from her Grandfather.

"Course he can, he can have as many as you want."

Dipping her chip into the tub of curry sauce, Alex presented him with a chip. Nelson couldn't believe his luck. Gobbling it down as if his life depended on it, he let out a huge burp and everyone fell about laughing.

Plonking himself down in between Alex and Niall, they both took it in turns to feed him chips. Now doggies are not really supposed to eat chips, as they're not very good for them, but seeing as it's not everyday you get to feed a West Highland White wearing a peaked cap, it really didn't matter on this occasion.

Chapter 4

A HUMAN'S BEST FRIEND

Pugsley

It was dark as Bill pushed his bike up the alleyway that ran between the houses. Overnight the fog had crept up from the channel. Swirling along the streets, it wrapped itself around lamp posts, blanketing everything in a thick, white muffled silence.

Upstairs Granny was momentarily roused from her slumber, woken by the clunk of the gate as her husband made his way to work. Meanwhile snuggled down beneath the covers Alex and Niall had not even stirred in the slightest. They were still snoring away dreaming happy dreams of playing on the beach or rock pooling or whatever magical adventure it was that they were on.

The clock beside Granny read a quarter to three. Now to most people that was the middle of the night, but to Bill he just thought of it as early. To him there was something quite magical about being the only person awake at that time on a morning.

Each morning Bill would cycle into work. His bicycle was an old postal bike. It had a rusty frame, a worn leather saddle, pull lever brakes and a big wicker basket on the front for carrying mail. Flying down hills, he raced along the back streets, zooming past rows of higgledy-piggledy cottages and smart town houses as well as shops selling buckets and spades and candyfloss. Going as fast as he could, he sent a shower of sparks flying as his pedals scraped the ground. Then from out of nowhere he heard a dog bark.

"Morning Bill!"

Slamming on his brakes, he came to a halt. There, sat on the pavement outside the paper shop, was a rotund little Bulldog. Pugsley was his name and he belonged to Mr Peters the newsagent. Bathed in the glow of the lights from the shop, Pugsley waddled over to see him.

"Any chance of a lift this morning, Bill?" The Bulldog asked.

"Sure, hop on," He replied, patting the basket on the front of his bike.

Now Bill had known Pugsley for years. Each morning, when he called to pick up the papers for the people who lived out on his round, he would find Pugsley barking out orders at all the paper-boys and girls. Being a Bulldog, his pedigree was used to herding cattle, so organising a handful of unruly paperboys and girls came naturally to him. Pugsley's main job was to make sure that all the girls and boys had the right bundle of papers and that everything ran like clockwork while Mr Peters was busy serving the customers that came into the shop.

Like postmen, newsagents were also up at the crack of dawn and another one of Pugsley's many jobs was to fetch breakfast from down at the harbour. Mr Peters and Pugsley enjoyed nothing better than a grilled mackerel fillet for breakfast. When the fishing boats came in on the morning's tide, Pugsley would be sat there waiting patiently for them.

The fishermen would shout 'hello' and toss him up a fish from their boat, wrapped in an old bit of newspaper. Pugsley would catch it in his mouth and kindly leave his money for them in a plastic bag on the dockside. His soft jaws were ideal for carrying things and so he would scamp back home with the parcel in his mouth. The trouble was that Berrycoombe St Martin had far too many hills for a short legged Bulldog and so, on his way home Pugsley would find himself all out of breath.

After the morning rush was over, he and Mr Peters would sit down to enjoy a well-earned breakfast together. Mr Peters was very strict about cleanliness. So much so that he insisted that Pugsley always wore a freshly starched napkin around his neck while eating and that all the knives and forks had to be washed at least twice before they could be used. Sitting down at opposite ends of the table together, Mr Peters would cut up the fillets with his finest silverware and place it down in front of Pugsley in a gleaming silver bowl with his name on.

Before tucking in, Mr Peters would hang a closed sign up on the door outside and put some soothing music on the radio before sitting down to eat.

"We are not animals!" He would declare, tucking a napkin into Pugsley's collar and pulling the chair out for him to sit on. Pugsley loved Mr Peters very much.

Mr Peters had never been married and considered Pugsley to be his bestest friend in the whole wide world ever. They did everything together they were such good friends. Now Bill had known Mr Peters all his life and remembered when he had been sent off to fight in some ghastly war and that, when he came home, he hadn't been very well. Some people said that he had a poorly mind and spent lots of time shut in at home because he didn't want to talk to people anymore. To help him recover from all the horrible things he'd seen, Mr Peter's mother had bought Pugsley for him when he was just a pup. From then on they were inseparable, going everywhere together. To Mr Peters, Pugsley was more than just a dog. He was true friend and, to him, behaved better than most humans did.

Struggling to get into the basket on the bike Bill put his hand under his tummy to help him.

"There's you go, lad," He said, patting him on the head as they set off downhill together.

"Faster, faster," yelled Pugsley. Bill pedalled as fast as he could. Every time they hit a bump in the road, Pugsley would come flying out of the basket and would land with a heavy thud back in the wicker tray letting out a roaring laugh.

"What's the matter?" Bill asked, hearing all the tittering coming from the front.

"It's the butterflies," Pugsley laughed, giggling like a baby. "It makes my tummy go funny when we go over a bump." He chuckled, as he encouraged Bill to go even faster.

Soon the lights of the fishing boats could be seen poking through the fog and the still waters could be heard as they gently lapped up the slipway. Coming to a halt on the quayside, Pugsley thanked Bill for his ride and in an awkward manner dismounted the bike, tumbling onto the cobbles.

"Same time tomorrow, eh?" Enquired Bill.

"As long as the weather's good," Pugsley replied wagging his stubby little tail. Waving the Bulldog off, Bill was soon gone as he pedalled off into the fog.

Freewheeling into the yard on his bike, Bill was greeted by Clive, the manager. Clive had grey spiky hair, a friendly smile, an upturned nose and tiny beady eyes that Bill thought made his friend look like a mischievous hedgehog, a nice hedgehog all the same, though.

"What do you think, eh, Bill?" Clive asked, looking up at the sky.

"Ahh… the sun will come out later," commented Bill.

Another thing that postmen were renowned for, and that's not just for wearing shorts, was their ability to predict the weather. To them, that special talent was more commonly known as the 'Postman's Nose.' Just one sniff of the air and a postie could tell what the weather was going to be for the day ahead. A postman's nose is far better than a piece of damp seaweed or a weatherman's prediction. It came in useful for knowing which coat to wear and what hat to put on when the weather turned bad.

Bill and Clive had known each other for years. Clive had been a postman for a long time before becoming the manager. He was a thoroughly decent chap and everybody thought very highly of him.

If someone couldn't come into work and they rang in to say they had a relative that was sick or poorly, he would say, "No problem. Take as long as you want, we'll sort it out later."

Or if someone wanted a day off for a friend's wedding he'd say, "Let me sort it out. I'm sure we can work something out."

After Bill had put his bike away, he joined Clive as he went inside.

"How long has you got left now?" asked Grandpa, making a joke of Clive's up-coming retirement. Clive looked down at his watch as if counting the hours.

"Too long if you ask me," he joked. Clive's retirement was a secret and no one else was supposed to know, but seeing as Bill and Clive were such a good friends, he had let him in on the secret.

Clive's hadn't really wanted to retire, but the Area Manager, who was not a very charitable man had paid Clive a visit to discuss his future. After a rather long conversation, the Area manager decided that it would be in Clive's 'best interests' if he retired.

The conversation between Clive and Bill turned towards the dogs that lived out on his round. Clive always affectionately referred to the dogs on his round as 'Bill's Dogs' because Clive thought that even though the dogs were owned by other people it was Bill that they loved the most.

"What was the name of that dog that bit your tyre so hard that it punctured it?" Clive asked trying to recall the dog's name. Bill immediately knew exactly which dog he was talking about.

"You mean Bendy!" Bill replied, with a knowing smirk.

"That's the one! Didn't he once chase you up the lane dragging his kennel behind him?"

"Yep, that's the one," sighed Bill, recalling the incident.

"That dog was completely nuts!" Clive said, shaking his head in disbelief.

"Do you know why she called him Bendy?" asked Bill. Clive shrugged his shoulders.

"Because the farmer's wife said that dog was so infuriating that it drove her round the bend!" Clive howled with laughter and slapped Bill on the back.

There were so many dog stories to tell that the two of them could have stood there all day chatting till the cows came home, but Bill had to get his round ready and Clive had to make sure all the mail was getting sorted.

The office didn't just belong to the posties though. It was home to a whole host of creatures. Bats roosted in the empty roof space above the manager's office, house martins made their nests under the overhanging eaves of the building and a family of mice lived in an old vent in the wall.

The mice weren't your everyday grey dor-mice though. They were field mice with smooth brown coats, short tails, wide eyes and big round ears. They had given up living in the fields and hedgerows long ago and, as far as Bill could remember, they had always lived in the sorting office. They had become such an everyday part of life at the office that the mice had even learned to sort the mail. Each morning after Bill had hung up his coat the mice would scurry along the heating pipes that criss-crossed the roof of the building, then slide down them on to one of the many sorting frames.

On each frame there would be a dozen mice helping the posties to sort their mail. One mouse, usually the oldest read out the address while two other mice would pick up the letter and pass it to another mouse who would be dangling by his tail from a chain of mice who were hanging from the very top of the frame.

"Morning, Bill!" they would squeak as they swung across the frame slipping the letters into the slots. You see it wasn't just dogs that Bill could hear, but also the tiny high-pitched squeaking of his little brown friends. It was harder to tell what a mouse was saying, as they weren't quite as well attuned to humans as dogs were, but being Bill he didn't seem to have any problems. With the mice helping, it didn't take long for all the mail to be sorted.

In return for their efforts, the mice would receive a crushed up biscuit. Sometimes it was a digestive or a jammy dodger, but their favourite was a custard cream. Once they had finished sorting the mail they would scamp back to their nest, carrying with them the crumbs for their babies who were tucked up tight. Sometimes Bill liked to have a peek. He would climb up on top of his frame and peer in at them through the slats of the vent.

Their nest was rather snug. It consisted of discarded rubber bands, chewed up bits of paper and the odd cancelled stamp. To help keep them cosy, Bill brought with him tumble dryer fluff from home. Tumble dryer fluff was the most sought after and luxurious of all nest building material. A mouse would do anything for it and sleeping on tumble dryer fluff was like sleeping on a floaty cloud.

The eldest of all the mice was a mouse called Ernest. He was that old that he remembered the days when they had actually been field mice, living off stalks of wheat and ears of barley. On an evening, when all the posties had gone home and the office was empty, the young mice would gather round and ask him about the old days. He would tell them of his tales of hiding from barn owls as well as weasels and foxes. The young mice were glad they didn't have to live out in a field anymore, and so was Ernest. On a morning when it was busy and all the mail came in through the door, Ernest would sit on Bill's shoulder and make sure all the mice got to the correct sorting frames. He and Bill were great friends and even Lorraine, one of the posties who worked next to Bill, had learnt to get over her mouse phobia because it meant she got a helping hand with her work.

Now although it was supposed to be a secret that Clive was retiring everyone was in on it. There had been talk of nothing else for weeks and everyone said what a great shame it was that he was leaving.

As Bill made his way along the aisles of sorting frames, somebody whispered in his ear, "How's the collection going?"

And then someone else would ask, "When's his retirement party?" While another said, "Here's a fiver," thrusting a dog-eared note into his hand. It seemed that the task of organising Clive's retirement party had fallen to Bill to sort out.

While Bill was busy sorting the mail, he thought about all the things that he would need for a party to go with a bang.

"You'll have to remember party blowers." noted Ernest who was stood on his shoulder watching the junior mice pushing letters into the frame.

"Yes, course I will," Bill replied.

"…And hats?"

"Yes, yes," Bill noted, sounding a little short.

"Now there's no need to be like that. This party planning is serious business!" Ernest said, with a stern expression. "There's also paper chains, party poppers and paper doilies so the tables look nice."

"Alright, alright. I'll make a list," Bill insisted.

"And what about food? Have you thought about that?" Ernest said, continuing to pester him.

"Lorraine…" piped up Bill.

"Yes mi' love?" she said, leaning round the corner of her frame and adjusting the glasses on her nose so as she could see better.

"What sort of food do you suggest we need for a party?"

"Ahh… I assume you're talking about Clive's retirement

party?" she said. "Well let's think, what do you need for a party, eh?" she gasped, while collecting her thoughts. "Well, you've got to have little sausages on sticks. Everyone loves little sausages on sticks, don't they?" stroking her chin as she thought, "And cheese and pineapple...then there's sandwiches with the crusts cut off... and mini pizzas...and crisps."

Bill's head began to spin at the thought of it all.

"Cheese and pineapple?" exclaimed Ernest, his big round ears picking up at what had just been said. "Ohhh... wait till I tell the others," he gasped.

Waving his hand for Ernest to be quiet, Bill struggled to listen to what it was that Lorraine was saying.

"... and jelly and ice cream...and Swiss roll...and biscuits... and..." The list went on and on and Bill wondered how he was going to manage it all.

"I can't do this on my own!" he gasped, panicking about how he was going to do it.

"Don't worry," said Lorraine putting his mind at rest. "I'll sort out the food. I'll get everyone to chip in and bring something. You just sort out the money for his collection."

"Thanks, Lorraine," said Bill, breathing a sigh of relief. He knew that he could count on Lorraine to help him out when he was in a tight spot.

Aside from the party, there was a question that had been on everyone's lips for weeks. Who was going to replace Clive? Everyone in the office was worried. They didn't know who they were going to get. Each morning when they came to work, everybody would ask each other if they had heard any news about the new manager, but all they got was a shake of the head in return. Then one morning Clive called Bill into his office.

"What's up?" asked Bill, poking his head round the corner of the door.

"Come in, shut the door," said Clive. Bill did as he was told.

As soon as he stepped inside he could tell that there was something wrong. Stood behind his desk, Clive had a worried look on his face.

"I had a phone call this morning," Clive said, looking glum.

"And?" Bill asked, wanting to know more.

Clive raised a disapproving eyebrow and let out a sigh. "It's the new manager," he said. "It's a chap called Rick Grinder. He's from head office," said Clive with a grimace.

"Rick Grinder?" replied Bill, repeating his name as if he hadn't heard right the first time.

Clive looked uncomfortable as he broke the bad news to him.

"I've not met him, but I've heard of his reputation." Clive muttered, shrugging his shoulders and screwing up his face in an unhappy way. "I heard he once made a postman wet himself, because he wouldn't let him off the sorting to go to the toilet."

"Really?" coughed Bill, almost choking with disgust.

"That's what they say," nodded Clive.

"What sort of a person is he?" uttered Bill with indignation.

Clive sat back in his chair with a miserable expression on his face.

"I wish I had some say in it, I honestly do, but I don't. From what I can gather, he's probably the meanest person I've heard of," Clive remarked.

This was not the news that anybody wanted to hear. Clive loved the people that he worked with and treated them with respect, and to hear they were getting someone like Rick Grinder worried him.

That morning Clive held a meeting and gathered everyone around while he addressed the staff.

"As you may or may not know, I am retiring shortly," Clive began. "And many of you have been wanting to know who the new manager is going to be," he said, with a sharp intake of breath. "Well I can finally tell you my replacement is going to be a chap called Rick Grinder."

A hushed silence fell upon the office as people uttered the name of the new manager with an air of disapproval. "Rick Grinder?" they whispered, looking at each other in dismay. Even the mention of his very name made people shiver with fright and recoil in horror. After the meeting, nobody even wanted to think about what was going to happen. Over the next few weeks, all the talk in the office was about the new manager's arrival.

As the date for Clive's retirement drew near, the stories about Rick Grinder got worse and worse. Somebody said that they had heard from a postman who worked on the night mail train that he had sacked an entire shift for not wearing their ties. At another office he had made a postman cry because he hadn't finished his round on time, and someone else heard that he had thrown parcels at a post lady because she couldn't fit them all in her bag. With all the terrible stories going round, nobody was looking forward to the arrival of Rick Grinder.

Chapter 5

TRUST YOUR NOSE!

Belle

I t was raining when Bill got to work. On the tin roof of the sorting office the rain sounded a hundred times worse than it actually was. All the posties shuddered at the thought of having to go out in such nasty weather. Even the mice were glad they didn't have to go out and disappeared back inside their nest to snug in.

While the posties were busy sorting one of them would poke their head out of the door to report back as to whether or not the rain had stopped.

"Bloomin' rain! Looks like we're going to get soaked," Frank, one of the postmen, grumbled.

By the time Bill went out on delivery the worst of the weather had passed. However, the roads were wet and murky and it made for an awful day out on the moor. Mist climbed through the stands of trees, and streams and brooks ran full with peaty water from the previous night's rain. As he made his way along the fern-clad lanes, Bill waved to the cows, who stood huddled in the field looking rather miserable. Giving them a cheery 'hello' he greeted the sheep with his best sheep impression, but all they did was stare back at him blankly. Even the birds, who flitted from branch to branch failed to muster a song in such awful weather.

The road led out of the valley, rising up onto the high moor. Stretching as far as the eye could see, the landscape was nothing but rough moorland grass and unforgiving bog. Suddenly, Bill saw something in the middle of the road and had to swerve to avoid hitting it. He could have sworn it was a dog, but it couldn't be. He was in the middle of nowhere and the nearest farmhouse was miles away. Bill pulled his van across the road to block the traffic and warn the other motorists.

Making his way over to the animal, he found a young border collie shaking and soaked to the skin. He had never seen this collie before and, as Bill knew all the dogs on the round he reckoned that she must have come a long way to be up here lost and all on her own. Bill bent down to comfort the young pup and gave her a reassuring stroke.

"What's your name eh girl?" he asked feeling her collar to see if there was a nametag on.

"Belle," she responded with a weak and feeble whimper. With no metal disc on her collar to say where her home was, Bill knew he would struggle finding out where she lived.

"Well, Belle, my name's Bill," he said introducing himself. "Do you have any idea where you live?"

Dazed and looking slightly confused, she struggled to remember.

"I don't know," she blurted out as she began to cry. With tears welling up in her eyes, Bill gave her a cuddle and reassured her that everything was going to be alright.

"There's a sign at the end of the lane with the name of the farm on, but I'm afraid I don't know how to read." She sobbed.

"Now, now, mi' girl, don't you worry about nothin' I'll see you right," said Bill in soothing tones.

"My owners will be worried. I didn't mean to get lost," she whimpered.

"Don't you worry about them. They'll be fine. It's you that I'm more concerned about. It looks like you been out all night by the look of things," he said, looking her over and seeing the condition her coat was in. "Have you had anything to eat or drink?"

"Only muddy puddle water," Belle responded meekly.

"Don't you worry, mi' girl, we'll soon have you sorted out," Bill said with a comforting smile.

Opening the back doors of his van he hastily grabbed some empty mail sacks and quickly made a bed for her to lie on.

"Come on girl," he beckoned, but Belle was so tired and exhausted that she collapsed right there and then on the spot. Rushing to her aid, Bill picked her up off the ground and carried her into the back to his van, laying her down on the sacks. Shuting the doors of his van, Bill jumped back in and pulled the van off to the side of the road.

Amongst the windswept heather and moorland grass Bill raced round to the back of his van to see if she was okay. When he opened up the doors it looked like Belle was about to pass out. Lying on her side motionless she had barely enough energy to raise her head, Bill had to think fast. Searching desperately through his postbag he pulled out his water bottle and raising it to her lips gently poured it into her mouth. Belle was almost too tired to take the water, but Bill mentally willed her to drink. Lifting her head ever so slightly, he tilted the bottle towards her lips and slowly she began to take the water.

"That's better!" he said with words of encouragement. After a few minutes of tender loving care, she seemed to perk up. Letting her rest for a minute, he went to the front of the van and rustled behind his seat for some dog biscuits. With only a few left he knew that they weren't going to satisfy Belle's hunger, but right now they were better than nothing.

"I knows it's not much, girl, but it's all I have for now." Holding out the biscuits on the flat of his palm, he offered them up for her to eat. Ever so gently, she placed her muzzle on his hand and gradually took them from him with her teeth. Crunching her way through a handful of biscuits she gained enough strength to manage to push herself up onto her paws.

"How are you feeling?" Bill asked.

"Better," Belle replied, licking her lips and wetting her nose with her tongue.

"But how am I going to get home?" she asked, all worried.

"Don't you worry about that," he reassured her with a loving stroke. "I'll sort that out. You just get some rest for the time being." Having been out all night, her coat was matted and covered in mud and twigs and odd things like that. Poor thing, he thought at seeing such a sad sight. Taking another mail sack, he used it as a blanket and placed it on top of her to keep her warm.

Jumping back into the driver's seat, Bill carried on with his round until he could think of a way of getting her home. With his new companion snuggled down in the back between all the parcels, spare tyres and mail, Bill chatted away to her, comforting her with soothing words.

"It's all right, girl, we'll have you home soon," he would say or something like. "Don't worry we'll find out where you live." Every so often he would look over his shoulder to check to see if she was all right. All the while Belle remained quiet. Being a lost doggy wasn't a pleasant feeling to have.

Bill pulled up at the next farm and knew that he'd be able to get some help there. Gem, a border collie who was one of the wisest dogs out on the moor, would surely know how to reunite Belle and her family. If there was one dog that was able to do it, it was going to be Gem.

Getting out of his van Bill splashed through the puddles as he ran over to an old stone barn. Sticking his head around the corner of the door, he gave a shout.

"Gem!" he yelled, his voice disappearing into the eaves of the big empty barn. From up in the hayloft, a black and white border collie poked its head over the ledge to see who was there.

"Morning, Bill," she answered back. Looking like she had just woken up from her morning nap, with bits of straw and grass stuck to her, she gave a good shake before getting to her feet.

"How can I help?" she barked down to him.

"Come and have a look at this!" Bill cried urgently, beckoning her to follow him. Gem could sense from Bill's tone that something was wrong. So, padding down the steep steps of the hayloft three at a time, she followed him outside to see what all the fuss was about. Sliding back the side door of his van, Bill presented the young pup to her. Covered with a mail sack and cowering in the back, Belle was a mess of tangled legs and matted fur.

"Hello there," she said, greeting the young pup with friendly smile.

"What's your name?" she asked. Shaking and afraid, Belle said nothing, instead she hunkered down in amongst the parcels.

"I found her out on the Whedon Ford road. All lost she was," Bill told her, recounting his tale.

"Poor thing!" exclaimed Gem, seeing the state of the upset pup.

"Her name's Belle. That's all I've been able to get out of her," replied Bill, disclosing what he knew of the young dog. "She only looks only about fourteen or fifteen months old," He noted.

"I'd say so," agreed Gem, casting her mature eye over her.

"Mind if I join you in there?" Gem asked the nervous pup. There was no reply. The sadness in her eyes said it all. Gem put her front paws up on the sill of the van and jumped into the back with her. Taking a deep inhalation, Gem drew in all those tiny invisible scents that a human nose just can't pick up.

Gem & Belle

For dogs, smells are like a fine wine or French perfume. A scent can tell so much about someone: like where they've come from, whom they've met or what they've had to eat for lunch. For a dog, they can spend hours just sniffing one trouser leg, but on this occasion Gem had a job to do and didn't have time for such indulgences.

"Mmm...I can detect a hint of heather...and grass pollen..." She said inhaling deeply as she closed her eyes. "And that smell, I know it from somewhere, wait...." It took a moment for Gem to think, as she decided which part of the moor Belle had strayed from.

"If my nose doesn't fail me, that's Northcombe Down," she concluded, opening her eyes and looking pleased with herself.

"My, my, you have come a long way, haven't you, my dear?" she said with a warm motherly tone. Gem jumped out of the van, leaving Belle curled up amongst the mail sacks.

"Don't worry, Bill, we'll soon have this youngster home. I'll get the news out straight away," confidently assuring Bill of her abilities. "She could use something to eat though. I'd let you have something from the kitchen here, but my owners have gone into town this morning and the house is locked. Maybe you'll have better luck at one of the other farms."

Dogs didn't just communicate by smell you see. Each day they had what was called the Barking News. It was where they could pass on information, catch up with old friends, and find out what was going on in the world of dogs. From farm to farm and from house to house, the news travelled far and wide across the countryside. When the weather was still, a single bark could travel a good five miles across the moor and, within pretty much a day, the news could travel across the southern half of England and, within two, every dog in the country from Land's End to John O'Groats was able to tune in to what was going on. It didn't matter if it was a dog living in a castle or stately home or one out on the street sleeping rough with their homeless companion, every dog joined in. It was a dog's duty to pass on the Barking News.

With a desire to help, Gem instructed Bill to take Belle home with him until they could find where she lived. In the mean time, she would get busy spreading the news about the lost pup.

"I'll get word through to you when we've heard something, you just sit tight till then," she told him, herding him back into his van, her collie instincts coming to the fore. No sooner had Bill pulled out of the farmyard than he saw the wise old collie racing across the fields to the very top of Signal Hill. From here she did all her barking. Letting everyone know about the lost pup.

As he carried on with his round, Bill cast a glance at Belle laid in the back amongst the jumble of mail. She must be ravenous after being out all night, he thought. Knowing that he had exhausted his supply of dog biscuits, he wondered what else he had left that he could give her. Suddenly he remembered his lunch, but very much doubted that Belle would be interested in a limp cheese and pickle sandwich or a piece of fruit.

After visiting several houses on his round and finding no one at home. Bill turned up at Lower Mansell Farm in the hope that Mrs Pemberton would be home. Lower Mansell Farm was a large stone-built farmhouse that Mrs Pemberton did her best to keep in order. However, the same could not be said for the rest of the farm. Under the control of her husband, Mr Pemberton had let the farm go. It was now a mess of run down barns and derelict outbuildings, covered with a hodge-podge of corrugated iron sheets.

Even though they were somewhere in their eighties, the couple still worked the farm. Mr Pemberton was a grumpy old man at the best of times and was almost blind, but some how he could still see well enough to drive his tractor. Mrs Pemberton, on the other hand, was a sweet, wonderful old lady who always looked after Bill whenever he came round to call. Bill wondered how she had managed to put up with her grouchy old husband for so many years, but he knew that, despite all his faults, it was her love for him that kept them together.

Knocking on the door, Bill was greeted by Mrs Pemberton herself. Opening the door, the rosy-cheeked old lady was wearing a floral dress, a red pinny tied around the waist and slippers with a pink fluffy collar that ran around the edge.

"Sorry to disturb you, Mrs Pemberton, but I've got a bit of a problem,"

"Don't worry Bill, how can I help you?" she replied, her voice full of warmth and blinking her eyes in her usual manner. He explained the story to her of how he had found Belle out on the road and how he was trying to get her home.

"Goodness me!" she exclaimed, putting her hand on her chest in sympathy. "We better take a look at this here poor mite, eh?" Casting off her slippers and pushing her feet in to her turned-down wellies, she set off to accompany Bill to his van. As he threw open the doors, Mrs Pemberton took one look at the dog, who was shivering and shaking in the back, and demanded that Belle be brought inside immediately.

With barely enough energy to walk, Bill had to carry Belle across the farmyard and into the house. In the kitchen, Mrs Pemberton set about looking for something for Belle to eat.

"Put her down there in front of the Aga," she directed Bill, pointing to one of the empty dog baskets next to the cooker. He laid her down gently in front of the oven. Feeling the warmth that radiated from the cast iron cooker, he knew that she would soon start to feel better.

Meanwhile Mrs Pemberton was busy rummaging around in her fridge, looking for something for Belle to eat, when she turned to Bill.

"You know I'd normally give her some dog food but, because she's been out all night, I think she'll need something a bit more substantial," she giggled mischievously whilst peering into the fridge.

"Oh dear!" she exclaimed, looking at Bill with a playful expression. "I'm afraid my husband will have to forgo his gammon steak today," she tittered, putting her finger to her lips. Bill thought he should really say something. He wasn't sure that Mr Pemberton was going to be too pleased when he found out the dog had eaten his lunch. Taking the steak out of the fridge, Mrs Pemberton wanted to know if Bill was feeling hungry.

"While I'm rustling this up, would you like a fried egg sandwich?" she asked. Bill wasn't going to refuse the offer. It had been a long day and knew that it would be an even later finish, and so accepted her kind offer.

The slab of meat sizzled and spat noisily as she tossed it onto the griddle. Cracking eggs into a pan, she urged Bill to take the weight off his feet and have a seat next to the burning Aga. Handing him a mug of tea, she looked down at Belle. There was mud, leaves and bits of twigs all stuck to her fur. She looked in a dreadful state.

"Here," said Mrs Pemberton, routing through one of the drawers and digging out a dog brush. "At least we can tidy her up a bit."

Pulling his chair up alongside Belle, he began to run the comb through her coat. In the warmth Belle started to come round and, after a few minutes of attentive grooming, she looked back to her normal self.

"Here we are girl," declared Mrs Pemberton, placing the juicy steak down in front of the dog. Belle's eyes lit up.

"Is this for me?" she asked in disbelief. Bill nodded and without hesitation Belle tucked into the meal. The steak was so huge that it hung off the sides of the plate and the grease dripped onto the slate floor.

"Ahh...it's good to see she's got an appetite. That's a good sign," Mrs Pemberton commented, watching the exhausted dog wolf down its meal. Bill was pleased to see that she was eating and felt he could relax a little, enjoying the warmth coming from the Aga. Mrs Pemberton passed him his fried egg butty. Biting into the thickly cut white bread, the yellow yolk poured out and ran down his chin. Moping up the oozing mess with the back of his hand, he gave Mrs Pemberton an appreciative smile. Content that her guests were happy, she took up a seat on the other side of the cooker and leant forward to stroke Belle, pleased that she could help a dog in need.

While they talked amongst themselves they were suddenly disturbed by a clunking noise coming from out in the porch. Expecting her husband home for his dinner, Mrs Pemberton anticipated his arrival. Listening to him as he struggled to take his coat and boots off, she shook her head as she heard him curse and swear. Then the door swung open and the cold air rushed in. It was Mr Pemberton. With holes in his tank top and blue baling twine tied round his waist to keep his trousers up, he ambled into the kitchen followed by their two collies, Wheeler and Wes. Now most people thought that Bill had a bit of an accent but Mr Pemberton's was so thick that even Bill could hardly tell what he was saying.

"Woz 'ee be 'aving for lunch mi' andzome?" he asked his wife. Looking at her husband, Mrs Pemberton pointed to Belle who was ravenously devouring his gammon steak. A look of horror flashed across the old farmer's face.

"Woz 'ee damn dog doin' wi' mi' dinner!" he bleated. Mrs Pemberton shot up off her chair and froze him with a look that would wither the bravest of men.

"You can have the same as Bill, fried egg sandwich, and like it!" she told him. Knowing his wife all too well, it was unwise to push things any further, and so he took his seat at the table, pulling out his newspaper. All the while moaning that his dinner had been given to the dog.

Meanwhile Wes and Wheeler wandered over to see who their new guest was. As Belle was busy tucking into her meal the two dogs stared longingly at the steak. With drool dripping from their jaws, they looked up at their mother as much to say 'Is there some for us?'

"Now come on, you two," she said, shooing them away from Belle who was still eating.

Wes sat down on the slate floor and took his place next to Mrs Pemberton. "You must be Belle?" he said to the newcomer. "We've heard all about you on the Barking News, haven't we, Wheeler?"

Wheeler being rather old was hard of hearing. "What?" barked Wheeler.

"I was just saying, we've heard of her on the Barking News, haven't we?" Wes repeated himself, this time a little louder.

"What did you say, have I been larking around?" mumbled Wheeler looking all confused. Wes shook his head.

"It's pointless talking to him, he's deaf," he moaned with a faint growl.

Giving up on trying to listen in on the conversation Wheeler settled down under the kitchen table, out of the way. When it came to meal times, Mr Pemberton was rather a messy eater and what didn't end up on his jumper usually ended up on the floor giving Wheeler a chance to hoover up any scraps. Sensing her husband's disappointment at his dinner, Mrs Pemberton threw some chips into the deep fat fryer to cheer up her husband, which brought a smile to his heavily worn face.

"Have you heard anything about Belle's home yet?" Wes the collie asked.

Now when Bill was around dogs it was all right to talk to them, but when he was in the company of other humans, he couldn't speak as people would think he was a little odd. So, scratching his ear, Bill nodded for Belle to speak on his behalf.

"There's no word yet," she blurted out. "It's all my fault, I shouldn't have gone into the woods, chasing rabbits and sniffing out new smells." She began to blub.

"Nonsense!" yelped Wes indignantly. "You're only a young pup. That's what young ones are supposed to do! How else are you going to learn about the world?" Wes barked, giving Belle a comforting lick on the side of the face. "If Bill here can't find out where you live, then I'm not a sheep dog. He's the best man I know for this job," Wes said, heaping praise on the aged postman. "He knows us dogs so well that I'm sure he was one in a previous life."

Belle laughed, managing to raise a smile.

"That's it, my girl, we'll sort you out. You just finish on up here," Licking the plate clean with her tongue, there was not an ounce of fat left on the plate when she was done.

"That's better. Well done, girl," Wes congratulated her.

As time was pushing on, Bill knew he had better get going if he stood any chance of getting his round finished by tea time. Wishing them all the best, Mrs Pemberton and Wes accompanied them out to the van. The most Mr Pemberton could do was give them a grunt as he stuffed his face with chips while Wheeler waited patiently under the table for leftovers.

Mrs Pemberton said goodbye to Belle, tickling her around the ruff. Pushing some parcels out of the way, Bill made some room in the front for her.

"You, Bill Mathers," said Mrs Pemberton patting him on the cheek, "you're a lovely man." Bill blushed.

"Here, I've got a little something for you to be going on with." Handing him a plastic box, Bill opened the lid and inside were two huge scones filled with jam and cream oozing out of them.

"Mrs Pemberton...I can't," he protested.

"Never mind all that. They're for you. Now go on," she grinned. With a toot of the horn and a cheerful wave from the window, his van was suddenly gone, swallowed by a maze of hedgerows.

Chapter 6
THERE'S NO PLACE LIKE HOME!

Gem

W hen Alex and Niall came home from school they were surprised to find a dog sat in front of the fire. Open mouthed and overcome with excitement, they were unable to speak as they stood there dumbfounded.

"Close those mouths or the wind might change!" Grandma scalded them, ushering them away from the dog with her tea towel. "Now give her some space," she ordered.

"But Granny…" Were the only words Alex could manage to get out as she pointed to the young Collie laid out in front of the gas fire. Dumping their school bags in the corner, they pleaded with Granny to be allowed to meet the pup.

"Alright, alright, but go steady," Granny cautioned them, placing her hand on Niall's shoulder to stop him from startling the dog. "She's only young and she'll scare easily," Belle looked at the children nervously.

"Come on. If we approach slowly, she'll be alright." Lowering her voice, Granny told them to edge towards Belle gradually and speak in gentle tones.

"Has Grandpa bought us a dog?" Alex enquired hopefully. Granny smiled back and shook her head.

"Sorry, no," she replied. "This here is Belle. She's lost. Grandpa found her out on his round this morning and brought her home while he goes out to do his evening collection. He's out now trying to find out where she lives."

Alex and Niall had wanted a dog for ages, but their Grandparents had said they were far too busy to look after a dog as well as a pair of excitable children.

Being ever so considerate, they sat down on the floor next to Belle and cautiously began to stroke the young Border Collie. Bill had done a good job of brushing all the muck out of her coat and, as they ran their hands through her fur, it felt like a lovely soft blanket between their fingers.

"Do you think Grandpa will find out where she lives?" Niall asked.

"I'm sure he will," said Granny sounding positive.

"But what if it takes a couple of days though?" he asked.

Grandma thought for a moment before replying. "Well, I suppose, she'll just have to stay here with us until we do find out where she lives, eh?"

Niall gave a secretive glance to his sister and she knew exactly what he was thinking. Wouldn't it be a shame if Belle had to stay with them for a few days more…or longer?

It was an exciting prospect for the children to have a doggy live with them. Sat there in front of the fireplace, the pair of them imagined all the fantastic things they could do with Belle, like taking her for walks, building dens, playing in the stream, fetching sticks and playing ball. Deep down they wanted Grandpa to find her home, but secretly they wished that she could come and live with them forever.

Having not heard any news about Belle yet, Bill was sure it wouldn't be long before one of the dogs came back with some information. He knew the Barking News wouldn't let him down and was confident that they would be able to get Belle reunited with her family. At one of the post boxes he bumped into Darcy, a Dachshund who had decided to come out without his human to take in the evening air.

"Evening, Bill," he barked as he tottered around on his thimble-like legs. "That's terrible news about poor Belle, isn't it?" he barked, as Bill emptied the box full of letters.

Darcy

"I know. Have you heard anything yet?" He quizzed him.

"No, but the barking news is red hot with chatter. Every dog between here and Cleavehampton must have heard about it by now." Bill looked anxious. Surely one of the dogs must know something.

"Don't you worry, Bill. You can count on us dogs to get things done. Gem at Merrivale Farm has the matter under control. She's a fine dog that Gem," Darcy stated, as he pranced about sniffing the grass and tearing it up with his paws. "We'll have her home before nightfall you mark my words," he yapped. Thanking Darcy for his help, Bill slammed the postbox shut and removed his keys. Noticing he had finished emptying the box, Darcy waddled over to it and cocked his leg against the base of the box.

"Oi, do you mind!" yelled Bill, "I don't want you widdling all over my box!" he grumbled.

Looking somewhat sheepish, Darcy apologised. If a dog could blush with embarrassment, he was sure he was doing so right now.

"Find a tree or something like that, not my postbox," said Bill, pointing to the hedgerow and the trees beyond. "And don't forget keep your ears open and let me know the minute you hear anything about Belle." Getting back in his van Bill merrily tooted his horn and drove off, leaving Darcy to find a tree.

Back at home Granny was making dinner with the help of Niall when Bill came through the door. Hanging up his coat on the hook, he was greeted by the sight of Belle happily laid out in front of the fire having her tummy tickled by Alex. Granny gave him a peck on the cheek and asked if there was any news on Belle.

"I'm afraid not. There's nothing been heard as yet," he sighed.

Immediately Alex piped up, "Does that mean Belle will have to stay with us if we can't find her home?" Grandpa nodded and Alex let out a little cheer.

"Does that mean that we can keep her?" Alex desperately wanted to know.

"No that doesn't mean we can keep her," said Grandpa sternly. Alex pulled a face.

"There's no need for that young lady. She belongs to someone else and we need to reunite her with her family." It had been a long day for Grandpa and, after trying to find out where Belle lived, he slumped down in the armchair looking completely worn out.

The terraced house where they lived was extremely small and with only two rooms downstairs, it was hardly big enough to swing a cat never mind look after a dog. As Niall helped Granny make the tea, Granny almost fell over Alex who was laid on her stomach busy stroking Belle.

"Grandpa?" He asked tentatively, while busy stirring one of the pans

"Yes, my handsome," He replied, sounding tired.

"What if we can't find who she belongs to? Then can we keep her?" Closing his eyes as if deep in thought, Bill rubbed his brow.

"It's not that simple…," Grandpa began to explain before Niall interrupted him.

"I mean, Alex and I would look after her and take her for walks and things," Niall pleaded putting on his best smile.

"I know you would, but there's more to looking after a dog than just taking her for walks. I mean who's going to look after her when we're all out at work?"

"Couldn't she come with you in your van?" replied Niall.

Bill smiled. "Let me tell you. There's nothing I'd love more than to have the company of a dog for the day, but I'm not so sure that work would be too keen on the idea."

Announcing to everyone that dinner was ready, Niall helped Granny to carry the plates over to the table.

"Ohh…sausage, mash an' gravy!" exclaimed Bill, chirping up and leaping out of his chair with a sudden burst of energy.

"And here's some for you, Belle," said Granny, placing down a little plate of sausages and gravy in front of her.

Tired, Belle had her head between her paws, resting, when she suddenly saw what was being offered to her. Immediately she felt much better, inquisitively twitching her nose.

Granny gave her an encouraging pat on the thigh. "Come on girl!" she said.

Belle couldn't believe her luck, she had never been this well fed in all her life. First a gammon steak for lunch and now this, sausages with gravy. It looked delicious! So joining the rest of the family, she tucked into her dinner, giving Granny an adoring look of appreciation.

Out across the moor the rain clouds had passed and the sun was now beginning to set. Twilight was a time when all the animals that had spent the day foraging and lying in the sun took to roosting in the trees or finding cover amongst the thickets of brambles and bracken. With the sun setting, a stillness descended across the land and the creatures that inhabited the dusk began to venture out. Mist formed along the river banks, pooling in grassy meadows, giving a chill to the evening air. A barn owl swooped low over the fields, searching for any rodents that took their chance with the night hunter while a fox crept stealthily from farm to farm, checking to see if there were any poultry left foolishly unguarded.

Remaining on duty, Gem had spent the whole day stood atop Signal Hill sending and receiving messages, almost making herself hoarse. It was getting late and the stars were beginning to pepper the evening sky, but still she continued with her vigil, remaining at her post. With the hills as her backdrop, she looked down upon the whole coastline, stretching west and beyond, out across the channel, out to the steel painted mountains beyond. As the pale crescent of the moon rose above the distant peaks, she felt that there was no hope left. About to give up for the night, her ears suddenly pricked up when, off in the distance, she heard a shrill bark calling her name. "Message for Gem of Merrivale Farm. I have news to follow." Gem recognised that bark as that of Holly, a wire haired terrier that lived down the lane at one of the nearby cottages

Holly the Pup

For Holly, even though her owners had named her Holly, no one ever called her by her proper name. Her owners and all the other dogs on the round called her 'Pup,' giving her the affectionate nickname because of how small she was.

"We've found Belle's home," Holly chirped up. "Her owners live at Marshgate Farm, Northcombe."

"Northcombe!" Gem growled jubilantly. "I knew the barking news wouldn't let me down." Silhouetted against the night sky she howled back as loud as she could, pleased that they'd found where Belle lived.

"Many thanks, Pup! You've done the doggy world proud. Please pass on my thanks to all the dogs involved in the effort to locate Belle's family."

"Pleased to be of service," Holly barked back, pointing her furry face to the sky. "It'll be time for a well deserved rest, won't it now?"

"No time for that we've got a young pup to get home tonight." Gem replied. With a plan in mind she knew just the dog to contact in order to help and, with no time to waste, Gem got straight to it.

"Gem calling Lightning. Gem calling Lightning, over," she hollered. The message travelled far and wide across the moors and valleys ringing through the lost hamlets, villages and solitary cottages as she repeated her broadcast until she got a response.

Darcy, the smooth haired Dachshund had retired for the evening when he was suddenly woken from his dozings. Laid out in his basket in front of the TV, he was up like a shot when he heard the call. Making a bee-line for the door, his paws scratched noisily on the kitchen floor as he flew through the cat flap, letting it bang wildly behind him. His bemused owners looked up from the TV and stared at each other.

"What on earth's got into him?" they said to each other, looking bewildered.

Pleased to help Darcy puffed up his tiny, pigeon-like chest and, with all the strength he could muster, gave his loudest yap. His tiny shrill bark echoed across the valleys and was picked up by other dogs further afield. The message, travelling swiftly from farm to farm, was soon echoing outside the window of Lightning the greyhound.

Having settled down on the sofa for the evening, Lightning was woken from his sleep. Through the open window, he heard his name being called. Fast asleep in an armchair, his owner did not stir, not even in the slightest, having spent the afternoon in the pub. Lightning knew there was no chance of him waking up anytime soon.

Sometimes his owner took him out into the fields at night with some rather unsavoury characters and made him chase rabbits and hares for money whilst they shone lights at them. Lightning didn't mind, as he loved to run, but some of the men weren't particularly nice to him and kicked and hit him if he didn't catch anything.

As Lightning's owner was rather the worse for wear, he knew that he would not be called on to go out tonight and, with the skill of a true athlete, he slipped out of the open window leaving his owner to sleep.

Running like the wind, Lightning tore across fields, bolted down lanes and leapt over brooks on his way to get to Gem. In his day, he had been a racing dog and had won many prizes, rosettes and trophies. And so he was glad to put his talent to good use, even though he was a little rusty. Soon he was sprinting up the track to Merrivale Farm and at the top of the lane was Gem waiting for him.

"Still got the magic, eh?" he grinned at Gem, while panting heavily. "Once a racing dog, always a racing dog." Lightning laughed cheerily as he caught his breath. Explaining to Gem that he had heard what was going on, he asked how he could be of service.

"I need a message delivering and you're the dog to do it," said Gem.

"Well, you've come to the right dog then," he barked, cocking his head proudly against the night sky.

"I need to let Bill, the postman, know where Belle lives," Gem told him. Relaying the address to Lightning, she made him repeat the address several times to make sure that he remembered it properly. After a drink of water from her bowl, he set out into the fading light. Guided by his nose and the lights of the villages, he knew he was getting close to Berrycombe St Martin when he could smell the salt of the sea air dancing on the breeze.

At home Alex and Niall had taken their baths and were in their pyjamas, sat on the rug playing with Belle. Tickling her tummy and getting her to do roll-overs, the two children hadn't had so much fun in a long time. Even Granny, who was warming the milk for their bedtime drinks, was coming round to the idea that having a dog might not be such a bad thing after all. Then, from the back door came a scratching sound. Granny turned to the children with a puzzled look on her face.

"What could that be?" she asked with a furrowed brow. Alex and Niall stopped what they were doing and Belle sprang to attention, her ears standing proud on top of her head. Bolt upright, she let out a series of sharp, piercing barks.

"Alright Belle that's enough!" Granny scowled at her, her ears ringing with all the noise.

"There's someone at the door," Niall guessed from Belle's telling indication.

Turning the latch, Granny opened the back door. The light of the kitchen spilled out onto the yard and there, stood in the luminous glow, was Lightning, puffing and panting, his tongue hanging out. Sensing that he was here to help, Belle leapt up from the rug and raced over to him, giving him an affectionate lick on the muzzle.

"Quick, get this poor dog a drink of water!" Granny instructed Alex.

Grabbing the old ice cream tub that was being used as a water bowl for Belle, Alex ran it under the tap. Filling it to the top with water, she hurriedly carried it over to the exhausted Greyhound and placed it down in front of him. With his head down, he drank furiously from the bowl, his tongue splashing water all over the floor.

"Go get your Grandfather," Granny instructed Niall. "He'll know what's going on," she said, shaking her head. Niall rushed upstairs and burst in on his grandfather who was in the shower. With steam billowing out of the door, he shouted at the top of his voice. "GRANDPA! GRANDPA!"

Struggling to hear what Niall was saying over the running water, Grandpa stuck his head round the corner of the shower door.

"GRANNY SAYS THERE'S A DOG DOWNSTAIRS AND

YOU NEED TO COME AND SEE HIM." Niall shouted, trying to make himself heard.

"WHAT?" Grandpa shouted back, poking the soap suds out of his ears.

"THERE'S A GREYHOUND DOWNSTAIRs!" Niall yelled. "A greyhound you say?' replied his grandfather.

"Yes," answered Niall, looking frustrated that he had to tell him three times. Grabbing a towel from the hand rail and drying himself off, Grandpa got dressed and made his way down to the kitchen to see what was going on.

"Who's this then?" Grandpa asked, not recognising the unfamiliar dog. The Greyhound stepped forward and introduced himself, offering a paw of recognition.

"I'm Lightning, and Gem from Merrivale Farm has sent me. I'm here regarding this pup," the Greyhound said, nodding in Belle's direction.

"The Barking News has located the whereabouts of this youngster's home."

As Lightning spoke, Grandpa translated what he was saying to the rest of the family and a cheer went up when everyone heard the good news.

It was late and way past their bedtime when Grandpa instructed the children to get dressed again and ordered them out to the car. It was a squeeze as they struggled to get in the cramped runabout. After some bickering and a bit of arguing, they finally decided on who was sitting where. The gangly greyhound chose to sit in the back between Alex and Niall while Granny sat up front with Belle on her lap. Her hot doggy breath blowing directly into Granny's face forced her to open the window to get some fresh air.

Like sardines squashed in a can, they set out into the night. With Belle's nose pointing into the slipstream and her ears and jowls flapping wildly in the rushing wind, she reveled in the excitement of her night time adventure.

It wasn't hard to find Marshgate Farm. As they drove up the

lane to the farm, all the lights of the house were on. Giving a yelp of delight from out of the window, Belle could smell the scent of home.

Pulling into the farmyard, a worried looking farmer stepped out from the back door. Anxiously he ran over to see who they were.

"Can I help you?" he said, bending down to talk to Bill. By now the excitement of being home was far too much for Belle and, eager to be reunited with her owner, she clambered out of the open window.

"Belle, behave yourself!" Granny protested as she tried to open the car door for her, but it was too late. Belle was already out of the vehicle.

Barking, yelping and running around excitedly in circles, she jumped up at her owner, putting her front paws up on his chest. The farmer was overjoyed to see her. Petting and tickling her and generally making a fuss, he bent down to give her a great big hug. He was soon joined by his wife and their three sons, as well as two other Collies who ran over to see Belle. Nipping playfully at her legs and tail, they barked noisily as they jumped on her back and mouthed at each other, glad to see that she was home.

"No need to ask if this is your dog?" Bill said with a smile on his face as he got out of the car. The old farmer gave Bill a hug so powerful that it almost squeezed the life out of him.

"I don't know what to say," said Belle's owner, smiling from ear to ear. Struggling to find the words to thank Bill, his eyes welled up with tears. "We were worried something had happened to her," he gasped with relief. "Me and my wife here have been in a right state, worrying about her. And my lads have been out all day looking for her." He sighed, patting Bill on the back.

Having been reunited with his dog Bill introduced his family to the old farmer. The farmer being on his best behaviour gave a little curtsy when he met Granny.

"Come in, come in," he said to them, showing them through to the kitchen.

The farmer's wife made a fuss of Alex and Niall. Giving them each a small bottle of pop with a straw in and a bag of crisps she insisted that they sit down on an old sagging, floral sofa that occupied the centre of the room. Grandpa and Grandma were treated like visiting royalty. They were served tea in the finest china cups complete with saucers and biscuits from a special tin that looked like it only came out at Christmas and on special occasions. Lightning meanwhile was made to feel right at home as Belle and the other two dogs invited him to share their biscuits and water, then gave him a tour of all the best smells in the house.

Bill explained how he had come across Belle in the middle of the road and how nobody had stopped for her. The farmer's wife gave a gasp and put her hand to her mouth in dismay.

"What's wrong with people these days?" she said, shaking her head.

One of the farmer's sons, who was lent up against the wall slurping his tea, told them how relieved he was to see Belle back. He told them how they had searched all night and day to find her and how exhausted they were. In between mouthfuls of tea and biscuits, he related the story of how he had chosen Belle from a big litter of pups. He said that he had picked her because she was the liveliest of the bunch and showed such spirit. He laughed when he told them how she had tried to climb out of the cardboard box she was in when they had gone to look at her.

"All of this has made me wonder if she is cut out to be a working dog." he said, after considering Belle's escapade.

Rushing to her defence Bill said. "She's only young yet. There's still time for her to learn." The old farmer agreed and after more tea and biscuits, funny coloured pop and some more of Grandpa's stories Granny said it was getting late and that it was time that Alex and Niall were in bed.

Again, the family thanked them for bringing Belle home safely and shook hands with Bill as well as giving him a hug. The farmers wife insisted that they didn't leave empty handed. Going into the pantry she brought out some of their own honey and gave it to Granny as way of thanks.

"Wait there a minute!" said the old farmer, as he rushed out of the room. Coming back clutching a couple of bottles of wine and a box of biscuits, he handed them to Bill.

"Here, a little something for you," he said smiling. Bill thanked him and once again shook his hand as they made their way to the door.

For Lightning, he engaged in a bit more tomfoolery rubbing noses with all the other dogs. He told Belle that next time she wanted to chase rabbits she should really think twice as it was a job best left for Greyhounds! He did however say that if she really wanted to learn how to catch rabbits then she should come and see him for advice.

Outside the back door, moths fluttered around the lamp in the lateness of the hour. Helping everyone to get into the car, Grandpa had to untangle Lightning from the seatbelt before he could finally shove him in. It would seem that Greyhounds with long ungainly legs were not devised to get into very small cars. The farmer and his family stood at the backdoor to wave them off. Belle, eternally grateful to Bill for saving her life, gave a whole series of loud, noisy barks until the farmer's wife told her to stop it and be quiet. With the windows wound right down, the two families waved to each until they were out of sight.

The journey back home in the car that evening was magical. Sat in the back, Alex and Niall enjoyed the cozy feeling of Lightning snuggled up between them, his soft velvety fur all warm to the touch, and the air rushing in through the windows. With it, it brought an enchanted smell of crisp, fresh earthiness and damp grass that made their senses tingle and come alive.

In the car the glowing dials of the dashboard gave off a secure feeling as they all joined in to sing along with the radio. After dropping Lightning off, it was well past midnight when they got home. By now everyone was exhausted and with hardly enough energy to climb the stairs Grandpa had to carry Alex and Niall up to bed. It had been a most extraordinary night and would be talked about for weeks to come.

Chapter 7
THE HUNT

Diesel

On his travels Bill came across many wondrous things. Occasionally a Stoat would dart out in front of his van, so fast that he hardly had chance to notice. Or a Buzzard would be sat on top a telegraph pole, watching intently, sometimes taking to the air to circle for hours in the rising thermals. Elsewhere rabbits would dash in and out of the hedge bottom, whilst pheasants would take ungainly to flight in a commotion of flapping wings and panicked clucking. On rare occasions, sometimes, he would find himself being watched by a solitary doe. Through a thicket he would see her staring at him, her black glassy eyes trying to make out his intentions and then, without even the merest stirring of the undergrowth, she would be gone, disappearing as silently as she had first come.

High up on the moor the enchanting call of the curlew would echo across the remote weather-beaten hills where the dark peat stained waters sprung up from amongst the rough bristle bent grass. Drinking from those same heavy waters, ponies gathered in rag-tag droves, huddling together against the strong winds of the winter months, while in summer they would roam freely amongst the purple heather without a care, gorging themselves on the tips of the heavenly scented yellow Gorse.

On this morning in question, the sawflies hung lazily in the air while swallows swooped low, picking off the haze of insects one by one. It was then that Bill caught something move from out the corner of his eye. On his left, from a well trodden track, came a fox leaping down the steep banking and on to the road before him. Bill braked. The fox took two paces and then froze, turning to stare at him with his piercing emerald green eyes. Bill thought himself incredibly lucky to witness such a spectacle. The fox broke Bill's gaze and made off up the other side of the banking, disappearing in the thick clamour of undergrowth.

Out on the roads, it was unusually busy with traffic that morning. Rusty old Land Rovers chugged along the lanes, whilst equally grumpy old men sat stoney-faced behind the wheel of their vehicles refusing to smile. It was clear to Bill that there was a hunt going on. His heart sank when he thought about the poor fox that he had just seen and prayed that it would be safe. Casting his thoughts to the deer that roamed the moor, he hoped that they too had heard all the commotion and put some distance between them and the hunt.

Pulling into Upper Compton Farm he was greeted by his doggy friend Diesel, a Heinz 57. Now some people looked down on mongrels because they are considered to be common or undesirable, but Bill didn't care because he loved all dogs the same.

Diesel had the legs of a Lurcher, the body of a Retriever and the velvety coat of a Greyhound. His fur was a beautiful grey colour, which had a fantastic sheen and, when the sun caught it just right, the colour changed to a shimmering steel blue. On his nose and tummy he had lovely soft white fur and each of his paws was the same, making him look like he was wearing little white socks. However, because he spent all his time playing in the farmyard, his paws had gone a funny green colour from all the cow poo he'd been running through, but he didn't mind. He just enjoyed the freedom to roam wherever he liked.

Diesel's favourite thing that he liked to do in the whole wide world was to fetch things. His most cherished thing to play fetch with were the lids off old animal feed tubs. Whenever Bill turned up he would go off hunting round the old fallen-down barns and sheds and come back with a well chewed lid to present to him, placing it down in front of him. Bill would throw the lid like a frisbee and Diesel would chase after it. Leaping into the air, he would do fantastic feats of acrobatics, flipping over on his back and bouncing it on his nose to catch between his jaws. But if Diesel couldn't find a lid for Bill to throw, he would search out a stick, and if he couldn't find a stick, he would bring a twig, and if he couldn't find either, he would bring a stone. That's how much he loved to play fetch.

At the end of summer when all the apple trees had dropped their fruit, he would bring a mouthful of sour tasting crab apples to deposit at Bill's feet. Picking up one of the slobbery well-chewed apples, Bill would throw it under-arm as hard as he could, along the long concrete driveway that ran up past the farmhouse. Bouncing wildly, the apple would skip over the ruts and bumps, pitching high into the air. Diesel would pounce on the apple and bite down hard on it. Looking all pleased with himself, he would then place his trophy at Bill's feet, and this morning was no different to any other, as Diesel presented him with green bug-eaten apple to play with.

"Now then, lad, get ready!" Bill announced, winding his arm up to throw. Just as he was about to let go of the apple, Daisy, a chocolate brown Labrador who also lived at the farm, came trundling out from the porch. Bill ignored Daisy and let the apple fly. Catching it cleanly, Diesel brought the apple back and placed it down in front of him. However, Daisy lunged for the apple and grabbed it in her big slobbery jowly jaws.

"C'mon give it here!" Bill demanded, as Daisy scurried off refusing to give it back. Bill chased after her and tried to wrestle the apple off her, but it was no use. She didn't want to let go.

"Why won't she give it back?" Diesel barked.

"Unfortunately, mi' lad, she doesn't know how to play properly. She's not as clever as you," he explained, while trying to prize

Daisy's jaws apart. Frustrated Diesel barked loudly, expressing his annoyance with Daisy.

All this noise brought out Barney, a rough coated Jack Russell, who also lived there. Half-blind and getting on in years, he nosed around the plant pots, and banged his head against the wall, before finally finding his bearings. Barney didn't often venture out much because of his poor eye sight. Most of the time he spent laid on his dog bed in the porch, happy to listen to life pass him by. In sympathy, Bill would give him a rub on the head while he threw the mail through the door.

It was Diesel who first noticed the stranger that had strayed into the yard and barked a warning. Bill turned around to see what all the fuss was about when he suddenly found himself confronted by one of the hunt's pack hounds. Stalking the yard, the menacing hound growled, showing its teeth and gums. The towering dog had clearly been bred for one thing and one thing only.

"Get on with yer!" Bill shouted at the dog, but the hound took no notice. It had only one thing on its mind and that was the taste of blood. Determined it was coming nowhere near them, Diesel charged the long legged hound, but it stood its ground and hunkered down as if to attack.

Barney, who had no idea what was going on, blindly stumbled straight into the path of the menacing dog. Snarling and drooling, the hound came closer to poor Barney, who was tottering around, oblivious that he was being eyed up as its next meal.

"Get back!" yelled Bill, lunging at the foxhound. The dog made an attempt to bite Bill, snapping at his leg, when Diesel came to the rescue, barking as aggressively as a well-behaved dog could. Buying time for Bill to snatch Barney off the ground and whisk him to safety Diesel barked to Daisy for help, but all Daisy did was just stand there and watch.

With all the noise going on outside, it attracted the attention of Arthur, the farmer who lived there. Stumbling out of the door, with his braces round his waist and his toes sticking through the holes in his socks, he took an immediate dislike to the canine intruder. Picking up an empty can of beans destined for the recycling, he took aim and threw the it as hard as he could at the dog. The hound let out a startled yelp, as the tin bounced off its head and flew over the wall. Arthur was that mad with the dog straying onto his property that he picked up a nearby yard brush and chased after it in his stocking feet. The dog, having never seen a human so cross before, turned tail and hot-footed it out of the yard the same way it came in, through the tangle of waist-high weeds that engulfed the far end of the farm.

Running after him and shaking the brush furiously, Arthur shouted after the dog, "Go on, get out of here!"

After plenty more shouting, he was satisfied that the dog had gone. Making his way back to the house, he cursed the sharp stones that dug into his feet, making him do a funny dance as he stood on each painful little stone.

"Damn hunt!" yelled Arthur, all irate and red in the face. Throwing his brush into a pile of junk, he stormed over to where Bill was stood.

"I've told them before about this," he complained, expressing his disgust at the hunt and shaking his head. "Breaking down hedges and attacking my livestock. I've had my fill with them," he declared in a most irate manner.

Bill was more concerned about little Barney. In his arms, he could feel him trembling. With a reassuring cuddle, he rubbed his nose up against that of Barney's, letting him know that everything was all right.

"They've been in here before with them damn dogs, 'an one of them's bitten Diesel before." Arthur grimaced, not letting up in his rant. "He's had to have stitches you know," By now Arthur's mother had come to the door to see what all the fuss was about.

"It's the blooming hunt again, Mother!" He moaned. His mother tutted disapprovingly.

"They've more money 'an sense, them lot!" she said, standing there in her blue house smock. "They should be at work, not larking round like some lord o' the manor!" said his mother, her annoyance clear to see as she pursed her lips.

"I've told them before, Mother, not to come on our land. All they do is worry the cattle," Arthur grumbled, his face now returning to its normal colour.

"Looks like this little one's alright though," said Bill, passing Barney over to Arthur. Taking the terrier in both hands, the farmer held him aloft as if he was lifting a trophy, so pleased to see that he was safe.

"Now then, lad, I don't know what I would have done if anything had happened to you. My wife would have killed me," he said.

"She wouldn't be happy I can tell you that!" his mother added, shaking her head disapprovingly at the distressed terrier. The farmer set Barney down on the ground and they watched him toddle off awkwardly in the direction of his bed. For him, it had all been too much excitement for one day and he needed a lie down.

Thanking Diesel for coming to his rescue, Bill tickled him under the chin and made a fuss of him. Diesel, pleased to be of service, rolled over on his tummy to show his appreciation.

"He likes you, that dog," noted Arthur, with a smile on his face as he watched the two of them play. Thanking him for saving little Barney and keeping the other dogs safe, Arthur and his mother said goodbye letting Bill get on with the rest of his delivery.

Running under the old granite slab bridge, water murmured as it had done for centuries, washing over the smooth pebbles that had been rounded by an age. In its slow passage, the streams had formed serene, deep pools where dogs could play and fetch sticks in the shadow of the overhanging trees and children could build dams with their friends. Downstream the trickle, became a river, carving deep, steep sided valleys dotted with pretty villages here and there. Down it tumbled, rushing over large moss-covered boulders, frothing and foaming around fallen deadwood, until it reached the ocean, spilling onto the fore shore.

Flicking through the pile of mail on his seat, Bill jumped out of his van and opened the gate to Green Gables, an enchanted house that sat tucked away on a wooded hillside with views out towards the sea. With whitewashed walls and a thick overhanging thatch, it was a place that people only dreamt of. The couple who lived there, Mr and Mrs Sampson, were lovely people, passionate about gardening. They had created a garden so beautiful that it took everyone's breath away. The path up to the house wound through a jumble of rocks, flowers and shrubs that changed with the seasons, giving a never-ending sense of wonderment. Bill loved delivering there, just so as he could stand there and admire it.

As he made his way along the gravel path that ran up to the house, he suddenly noticed something move in the bushes. He wondered if it was Mr and Mrs Sampson's dog, Puck.

"Puck, come here lad," he shouted, but there was no response. If it was Puck he would have come bounding over as soon as his name was called. It had to be something else.

Suddenly from behind a clump of flowers, a shape darted across the lawn before diving into the hedge bottom. Bill watched the shape intently and, as he did so, realised what he was looking at was a fox. Aware of his presence, the bushy-tailed animal stealthily moved between the shadows, wary of every movement and purposeful in his step. Bill swore it was the same fox that he had seen earlier that morning. With those unmistakable emerald green eyes gazing upon him, he watched as the animal skulked in and out of cover before finding refuge in a clump of bushes.

It was then, through the trees, Bill heard the unmistakable call of the hunting horn. Gripped with panic, he felt an overwhelming sense that the animal was in danger. Rushing up to the house, he banged loudly on the door in an attempt to raise the occupants.

Mr Sampson answered the door and could immediately tell something was wrong.

"Whatever's the matter, Bill?" he asked. Gasping for breath Bill explained that there was a fox in the bushes and the hunt were hot on his tail.

"Jane, Jane!" he called.

"What's the matter, darling?" came a voice, from the rear of the property.

"Looks like we've got a problem with the hunt again, dear," her husband replied in rather stern tones.

Appearing at the door in a long flowing floral gown as if she had just taken to the stage, she carried with her a cane. Mrs Sampson had been an actress in her day and was rather theatrical. Every time she spoke it was "darling" this and "darling" that. Bill found it all rather funny. He then explained to her what was going on. Listening intently to what he had to tell her, she threw arms open wide before beginning to speak.

"Well, darling, I won't tolerate them here on my property," she said in a booming voice, as if taking to the stage once more. "Where is this poor fox, my darling?" she asked, looking to Bll who pointed to the bushes.

"Come on," she cried. "We haven't got time to waste. Lead on, Macduff!" Shouting encouragement and waving her walking stick in the air.

Not wanting to be left out, Puck, the Sampson's Chow-Chow, came bounding out of the door, yelping and yapping. Running alongside the rescue party, the big ball of cinnamon-coloured fluff jumped up at Bill's side.

"Can I help, Bill, please, please?" he barked, bouncing up and down with excitement.

"Do you think you can find this fox that we're looking for?"

"Do you think I can find this fox?…Do you think I can find this fox?" Puck repeated, as he bounded around uncontrollably, leaping high into the air. "Course I can! I am a master of sniffology! This nose wasn't designed to sniff out the most minute smells this planet has to offer for nothing," he declared, his bushy tail standing all proud and erect.

"Well then, what are you waiting for?" replied Bill, and quick as a flash Puck was off, rushing ahead of them.

Racing around the flower beds he went in and out of the daisies, rooted round the lupins, and nosed his way through the catmint, it didn't take long for Puck to pick up the fox's scent. With his nose to the ground, he circled the lavender beds twice before racing towards the garage.

In the meantime Mrs Sampson hobbled along, with her husband in close pursuit, as the shrill sound of the hunting horn rang trill.

Puck

"Do you hear that, darling?" cried Mrs Sampson with her hand on her heart. "Good gracious, oh, I do hope we can save this poor little mite in time!"

Bill was the first to come across Puck. He was stood rooted to the spot with his nose pointing towards the shadowy darkness that lay at the back of the garage. Puffing and panting and dragging her poorly leg behind her, Mrs Sampson draped her arm over Bill's shoulder as she strained to see what it was Puck was looking at.

"Has he found him, darling?" she enquired, her face all hot and red.

"I think he's behind your car," said Bill, bending down to look. "It's going to be hard to get him out of there," Knowing the garage had no doors to it, he realised it was going to be difficult to keep the pack of bloodthirsty hounds from the fox.

"I don't know what we are going to do," he said, lying flat on his stomach.

"I know, I know!" announced Mrs Sampson. Then with a sudden clap of her hands as if addressing a group of actors she cleared her throat.

"Philip, I've an idea. Get me some of Puck's food from the house and maybe we can tempt the fox out with that? In the meantime you and I, Bill, shall try and figure out how we can keep this poor little creature out of harm's way,"

Bill scratched his head. He had no idea what they were going to do.

Wondering how to keep the fox safe without scaring him, the pair paced back and forth as they tried hard to think of something.

Meanwhile Puck, sitting politely on his hind legs gave a bark. "I've an idea, what if we put the food in the back of the car, and leave the boot open so he can get? Then, when he's in, we can shut the boot. Bill thought about this for a minute.

"That sounds like it might work. Let's give it a go," congratulating Puck on his brilliant idea. Puck stood to attention ruckling up his fur making him look like a miniature lion. Bill then relayed Pucks idea to Mrs Sampson.

"Oh…super, what a fantastic plan you have there," remarked Mrs Sampson having no idea that it was her own dog that had come up with the idea.

They could hear the Foxhounds getting closer. Mrs Sampson leant on Grandpa's shoulder gripping his arm tightly. "Oh, Bill, where is Philip? Can't he hurry up with that food?" she sighed, nervously looking over her shoulder for her husband.

Then, rushing into view, Mr Sampson appeared carrying with him a pouch of Puck's dog food. "Here," he said, thrusting the foil pouch into Bill's hand. Tearing open the pack, Bill squeezed the contents onto a plate as Mrs Sampson got her husband to pop the car boot open.

Bill was getting tense. He didn't want to disturb the fox and scare him off now. At the back of the garage he could hear the animal anxiously shifting about, knocking over old tins of paint and banging into ladders.

Puck gave a low subdued whine. "I think we better leave him to it now. We can watch from the conservatory, and when he's in the car, one of you can nip out and shut the boot."

Putting the plate of food in the car as directed, Bill retreated with the others as Puck did his best to corral everyone inside.

From the conservatory they could hear the lead huntsman's trumpet blare out. This time it sounded like it was only just down the lane. Mrs Sampson was almost on the verge of tears and grabbed her husband's arm.

"Oh, darling, I can't watch," she sobbed as her husband did his best to console her. Bill was sweating too. Keeping his fingers crossed, he prayed that the fox was going to make it. Puck was on all fours, making soft whimpering noises, such was the tension.

They waited and waited, and then, from round the corner of the car, the fox appeared. Everyone was on tenterhooks as they silently willed him to get in the car. Tipping his head to the breeze, the fox caught the scent of the dog food. Following his nose he stood up on his hind legs and looked in the car boot, his black wet nose twitching away furiously.

Not able to believe his luck, the fox saw the plate of food sat there, unguarded. With the same spring in his step that Grandpa had witnessed earlier that morning, he leapt into the back of the car.

"Philip, Philip go shut the boot!" ordered Mrs Sampson, who was pointing to the car furiously and doing her best to keep her voice down. They watched as her husband tip-toed stealthily across the driveway. Creeping up along side the garage, Mr Sampson silently edged his way towards the car. Then, SLAM!

A cheer went up from the conservatory as he successfully trapped the fox in the boot. For a moment the fox looked alarmed, staring out of the back window, before deciding he was much better off where he was.

"Well done," Mrs Sampson gushed, applauding her husband. Bill gave him a well-deserved pat on the back and his wife covered him with an assault of gushing kisses.

"My hero!" she commended him with her hands clasped together in an act of hero worship.

Just then the hounds came rampaging through the garden, spilling round the back of the house. Tearing up the lawn, the dogs uprooted plants and smashed pots as they searched in vain for the fox.

"Damn beasts!" roared Mrs Sampson, shaking her cane furiously in the air. "I won't be having this," she proclaimed, forcefully throwing open the door of the conservatory and marching straight out into the mass of circling hounds.

"Steady on, dear," her husband cried out behind her, but she wasn't having any of it. She was so mad that she lunged at any of the hounds that came near her with her cane.

At the gate the lead huntsman was sat on his horse, pacing up and down, when Mrs Sampson stormed down the path to give him the biggest telling off of his life. By the time she had finished with him, the huntsman's face was as red as his jacket and under Mrs Sampson's glowering gaze he called off the hounds. Blowing his horn as hard as he could, the foxhounds came tearing back over the fence one by one, watched by Bill and Mr and Mrs Sampson, while the rest of the hunt sat shame-faced on their horses. Forced to make an apology, they skulked off like naughty school children.

Mrs Sampson shouted after them, "Good riddance to unwelcome guests!"

A couple of weeks after the incident, Mrs Sampson told Bill that she had received a very apologetic letter from the hunt along with a cheque for all the damage they had caused to her property. However, the best news was that the fox whose life they had saved was now a regular visitor to their garden. Every afternoon the fox came trotting in and would help himself to the cat's food. Not minding guests at his dining table, as he was quite happy to share a bowlful of food with either Puck or Delilah the cat. Bill was pleased to hear the news and went home to tell Granny and the rest of the family. They were all glad to know that he was safe and well and had found some new friends.

Chapter 8
THE DOG SHOW

Bert

Miss Miller lived on her own. With ruddy cheeks, a drawn complexion and wiry figure, she ran the family farm that had been left to her by her father with only her dogs for help. The farm had been in the family for generations. It had over two hundred head of cattle and more sheep than it seemed possible for one person to look after, but Miss Miller coped admirably. She could do anything a man could do, if not better. She was stronger than most men half her age, but she always said that she couldn't do it without the help of her beloved dogs: Charlie, Max and Bert.

She loved her dogs so much that they went everywhere with her. Charlie and Max were border collies, who helped keep the sheep and cattle in line. Bert was a bassett hound, with big floppy ears and slobbery gums, whose sole role in life was to sleep as much as possible and get in the way whenever something needed doing.

Miss Miller's rusted Land Rover half cab was a familiar sight along the lanes. Recognisable by the fact that Charlie and Max always had their heads poking over the top or stuck out at the sides, their noses pointing into the wind, enjoying every minute of the ride. Bert, however, being a sedentary dog, was always sat up front in the passenger seat. Bassetts, renowned for their inactivity, never did anything that they didn't have to do, which seemed to be very much Bert's motto.

When Miss Miller went into town the dogs would come along with her. Leaving them while she went shopping, she would always come back to find a crowd of children and parents gathered round her truck. Petting and making a fuss of the two collies, the children loved to scratch them under the chin and stroke their soft fur. Playing to the crowd, Charlie and Max would roll over on their backs for their tummies to be tickled, and if they were really lucky, the butcher would toss them a bone each. They were happy to bask in the attention, unlike Bert, who preferred to be curled up on the front seat fast asleep. Unless there was a treat involved. Then he would stand on his hind legs with his snout sticking out of the window, doing his best to look adorable with his sad eyes and droopy face.

It had been a few weeks since Bill had last seen Miss Miller when he bumped into her at the cross roads on her way into town. Stopping to pass the time of day with her, he tossed some biscuits into the back of the truck for Charlie and Max.

"You spoil those dogs," she joked. The biscuits bounced around and skidded on the shiny metal floor of the flatbed. The two dogs, snapping wildly, did their best to chase the treats into the corners of the truck before devouring them with gusto.

"Morning, Grace," said Bill, tipping her a wink and a smile. "Do you want your post?"

"Go on, then," replied Miss Miller, as he searched through his tray of mail. While Miss Miller waited for Bill to find her mail, she suddenly had an idea.

"Say, we've got the dog show on soon. You'll have to come along and bring the grand-kiddies with you."

"Oh, definitely," replied Bill, handing her a couple of letters and a parcel that were for her.

The Withy Bridge dog show was the highlight of her year. Miss Miller lived for the show. It was the feather in her cap. She had started it many years ago, when only three dogs turned up for the first show and two of those had been hers. Now it had grown in size it had turned into the highpoint of the local social calendar. People came from far and wide to see the show. There was an agility course, an obedience section, a Best in Breed, a fun fair, and lots of stalls for people to look around.

The local Mountain Rescue Team were also invited to come along and they brought their search dogs, wearing their special red coats and booties. The Police came too. They gave displays with their Alsatians and Malinois: chasing would-be criminals, disarming them, and pinning them to the ground, as well as jumping through hoops of fire, while the spaniels sniffed out all sorts of naughty things that had been hidden in the crowd. Sometimes the Air Ambulance came to wow the crowds and landed in the field, making lots of noise. It was a real day out and everyone loved it.

"Hey I've got an idea!" declared Miss Miller with a grin on her face. "We could have a new class. How about the Postie's Favourite Dog, what do you think?"

Bill looked blankly back at her. "What would I have to do?" he asked.

"You'd judge the dogs. It'd be, like, the friendliest dog wins."

"And what if I get bitten. Then that's my tough luck, eh?" He joked.

"No, no, it won't be like that! Besides I don't know a dog that doesn't love you. You're like some sort of dog whisperer. It'll be great."

Without thinking, he said he'd do it.

"Oh thank you, Bill! The committee will be pleased. We'll put it in the programmes that we're sending out in a few weeks, and you can hand out the award at the end." Buoyed up by the good news, Miss Miller thanked him and drove off up the lane with Charlie and Max in the back wagging their tails.

Bill was quite pleased that he had been asked to judge the Postie's Favourite Dog award. Not only would there be lots of dogs there that he could pet and make a fuss of, but he knew there would be plenty of tea and cake afterwards, especially for the judges. Double yummy, he thought!

Bouncing up the lane to Merrivale Farm, he found Gem sunning herself in the porch. Reclining amongst the boots and wellies that lay strewn about, she was awakened from her mid-morning snooze by the sound of Bill's van. Yawning and stretching, she mustered enough energy to give him a friendly bark.

"Morning, Bill," she said, pointing her nose to the blue sky and sniffing at the fresh morning air.

"Guess what?" He said, hopping out of his van. "I've been asked to be a judge at the Withy Bridge dog show this year," he announced as if hardly able to contain himself.

"Congratulations," yawned Gem, her enthusiasm sounding somewhat muted.

"What's the matter? I thought you'd be pleased for me," He asked, noticing a lack of interest in her bark.

"I'm not one for dog shows myself," she remarked, scratching behind her ear with her hind leg. "But humans seem to like them enough though." Getting to her feet she gave a good shake, ridding herself of all the scuttlers and other crispy things that farm dogs pick up.

"That's better," she said with a satisfied bark. "I'm afraid, Bill, I find dog shows a bit…what's the word I'm looking for…ah, yes… degrading,"

"Really?" remarked Bill, sounding surprised.

"I'm a working dog. I wouldn't be seen dead prancing about and preening myself, like some over-groomed Poodle with a bow in my hair."

"I suppose," he said, shrugging his shoulders.

"Tell me when did you last see a dog get excited about winning a trophy?" Bill had to admit he couldn't recall an instance.

"Now a bone or something equally as tasty, that's a different matter," she added, licking her lips. "But a stupid metal trophy? Huh…sometimes you humans are as daft as those sheep over there," she barked, nodding in the direction of a field full of ewes. Anything shiny and you're instantly mesmerised." She noted dryly. Bill followed her across the yard as she walked out the stiffness in her legs. Casting her gaze on the ewes in the far field she made sure they were behaving themselves and not wandering off.

The sky was clear that morning except for a sweep of cloud. Even though the sun shone warmly, there was a chill breeze that blew down off the high moor. Taking a rest behind the wall, Bill sat down with Gem out of the wind. Stretching out on the soft grass together the pair of them bathed in the warm sun that beat down upon their faces.

"I've got a problem with this here dog show," said Bill, as he bit into his mid morning apple.

"You see they want me to judge the Postman's Favourite Dog award and…" he paused, his words trailing off into the distance.

"And?" Gem asked wondering what the problem was.

"…and the problem is, I don't have a favourite dog. I love all dogs equally…a bit like humans, really,"

"What, even the one's that give your boots a nasty nip, eh?"

"Even those," he laughed, giving a warm hearted smile.

"Well, that's very admirable of you, Bill, but I really don't think Grace Miller and Lady Norbury on the judging panel will be happy to hear that. They'll want you to pick a winner."

"I suppose," he said, letting out a reluctant sigh.

"Look at it this way, Bill. Both you and I know better. Winning means nothing to us, but humans are obsessed with it. Go along. Smile nicely. Pretend your having a lovely time and play along. Enjoy the cakes they give you… Think of it as a day out."

He knew Gem was right. He could pretend to pick a winner, but really deep down, he knew every dog was a winner.

"It'll just be our secret, eh?" he giggled to Gem, tapping the side of his nose.

The judging panel this year would be made up of the great and the good of Withy Bridge. Lady Norbury with all her fancy hats was going to be the guest of honour. She lived at Broadwood Manor with her husband who was a Lord or a Duke or something like that. Anyway, Bill carried on munching his apple while all the time thinking how he would go about picking his favourite dog.

"You see, Gem, how do I choose?" he asked, all confused. Rummaging around in his pocket, he found one last biscuit and tossed it over to her.

"Well, for starters, we don't want an angry, nasty, selfish dog, do we?" Gem remarked, chomping her way through the biscuit. "What we're looking for is a dog that's kind, has a warm personality and knows how to smile... is ready to help, enjoys playing and can get on with other dogs and humans too, oh...and one that likes having fun," she noted, thinking about the finer points that make for a fantastic dog.

"Mmm..." said Bill while munching on his apple. "I like that bit about having fun. I'm all for having fun. The more fun the better, I say," he laughed, throwing his apple core over the wall for the sheep to nibble on. "Well, thank you for your advice," he said, taking to his feet and dusting the grass off his bottom with his hands.

"I better get on. This mail won't deliver itself, eh?" thanking Gem for her advice. In return, she wished him all the best for the show.

The dog show was on a Saturday afternoon. The day arrived warm and sunny and before Bill went to work Granny reminded him not to be late. At home, Granny made sure the children were all smart and presentable. Knowing that there would be Lady Norbury and plenty of other VIPs present, she wanted her grandchildren to look well turned out.

By the time Bill arrived at the dog show, the village was already jam packed with cars and dogs. There were dogs everywhere in all shapes and sizes: on leads, misbehaving and barking at one another. It was a real doggy circus. A man in a fluorescent jacket was directing the traffic and telling people where to go when Bill pulled up in his van.

"Can I park here?" asked Bill, cheerily pointing to the entrance of the village hall car park.

"It's for those showing only," said the man.

"But I'm one of the judges," declared Bill with one of his nicest smiles. The man looked at him and then looked at his van.

"But you're a postman," he said with a puzzled look on his face.

"Yes, and I'm here to judge the Postman's Favourite Dog Award."

The man looked at him. "Postman's Favourite Dog?" he said in a disbelieving manner. He'd never heard of the Postman's Favourite Dog Award and didn't think such a thing existed. Luckily for Bill, Miss Miller turned up in the nick of time and called over to him.

"Come on, Bill, you're running late," she said waving to him. "All the other judges are here."

"See," said Bill, pointing to Miss Miller. The man then moved the cones and Bill parked his van next to all the other cars that were full with dogs being groomed, pampered and preened.

"I'm glad you've made it!" Grace chirped up, as she rushed over to meet him. Rummaging around in her handbag. She pulled out a white overall.

"Here," she said.

"What's that?" enquired Bill.

"It's a judge's coat," answered Grace, pressing it up against him for size. "There, I think that will fit you just fine," she said, sizing him up.

The show was huge. It was that big, in fact, that it had to be held in the field next to the village hall. Around the showground, dogs were being rushed from one event to another while others tackled the agility course in the main arena. Blaring out over the tannoy, a running commentary was being made on how well the dogs were doing. At the far end of the field was a large marquee for judging the best in breed, next to that, a slightly smaller tent for refreshments and handing out awards. Everybody was having a fabulous day out, wandering around all the stalls and going on all the rides.

Miss Miller hurried Bill across the field, explaining the rules about judging: there would be rosettes given to the top three dogs in each class. The first placed dog would win five giant bags of dog food. Five giant bags of dog food he thought! That would keep any dog happy.

As he was being rushed over to the VIP tent, he bumped into some of the dogs he knew from his round.

"Hello, Bill," they barked, dragging their owners enthusiastically over to see him. Doing their best to show what healthy wet noses and glossy coats they had. Rocky, a liver and cream coloured Cocker Spaniel came rushing over and shaking himself with excitement covered him in long spindles of doggy drool. With no time to stop and make a fuss of them, Bill was hurried along.

Helping him on with his judge's coat, Miss Miller raised the blue nylon rope that encircled the VIP tent and slipped under. He was introduced to Margaret from the local baker's, who was in charge of making sure everyone had everything they wanted and got to where they should be at the right time.

"I think you're all set here, Bill. I leave you in the capable hands of Margaret and I'll see you later on," said Miss Miller giving him a kiss on the cheek. "Oh... and we've still got the Police Dog Display Team and the Best In Breed to judge before you're on, so feel free to grab a cup of tea!" With that Miss Miller dashed off to go oversee the next event.

The tent was open-sided and people were milling about everywhere chatting to one another. He said a polite hello to the local Mayoress, while out of the corner of his eye he could see the Chief Inspector chatting to local councillors and businessmen.

The other judges, who were wearing white coats like him were proper canine judges – not like Bill. They knew their Maltese from Bichon Frise and rear pasterns from a hock. He felt slightly out of his depth, but didn't let his lack of experience put him off having fun. He was sure that none of them could speak dog!

Lady Norbury was the centre of attention wearing what looked like a rather expensive outfit, a big hat and matching jewellery. Grandpa didn't care for that sort of showiness. All he wanted was a cup of tea and to spend time with his family.

Tucked away in the corner of the tent all on their own were Granny and the children sipping tea and drinking pop. Bill gave them a hug and Niall was eager to show his grandfather what he had found at the back of the tent.

"Look, Grandpa," he said, impatiently dragging him by the hand to show him. There, laid out on a row of trestle tables, was the scrummiest food Niall had ever seen in his life, and it was all free!

"You can help yourself, you know!" he chirped up, with a paper plate full of sandwiches, crisps and cakes. Bill looked down at his plate.

"You don't have to eat it all at once, you know," he said, pinching a handful of crisps from him.

"And look what else they've got," Niall pointed enthusiastically. Arranged on various stands were bowls of trifle, profiteroles, chocolate mousse, gateaux of every kind, and more sorts of cream than Niall knew existed. Even Grandpa's mouth was watering.

"Can I have some please?" asked Niall, looking longingly at the desserts. Bill saw that none of the sweets had yet been touched.

"I think it's best if you finish what you've got first," he said advising caution. "Maybe later, after I've finished judging, we can all have some pudding, eh?"

Granny was so pleased to see Grandpa in his judge's outfit that she made Alex and Niall stand with him while she took a photograph. Then she got Niall to take a photo of her stood proudly with her husband.

Soon it was time for him to do the judging and Margaret, the lady in charge, took him into the main marquee and introduced him to the man with the microphone who was doing the compering. He asked Bill his name and made some jokes about dogs not liking postmen, which made all the crowd laugh.

"What are you looking for in a dog?" he asked him.

"One that doesn't bite!" Bill cheekily replied, and everyone laughed some more.

Soon the show started and everyone paraded into the arena with their pooches on leads. Bill already knew quite a few of them and gave them a wink of recognition: There was Maggie and Mabel, a pair of black Labradors who were sisters that lived at Pipers Park. Then there was Tarn, a Corgi who lived with Miss Ellis, a lovely lady, Rusty, a tan coloured terrier who could never stop barking, Lucky, an aged working dog, who had been entered for the show by mistake and Beaumont, a Great Dane, owned by Professor Nicholls, whose son had brought him along for the day. Even Bill's next door neighbour, Joan, had come along with Kurry, her Airedale terrier. All told, there was some thirty dogs, all hoping to be crowned top dog.

Bill found it difficult to concentrate in the arena with all his doggie friends barking away and wanting to say hello. He wished he could chat to them like he did normally, but couldn't risk giving away his secret in front of everybody. Stood in a line across the back of the show ring, the dogs and their owners patiently waited their turn while he and the compere made their way down the line.

Stopping by each dog Bill bent down to ask for a paw, in return he would give them a good stroke and tickle around the ear. The compere followed him around and seemed to like making jokes at the expense of some of the dogs. Bill didn't like it. Just because they were dogs didn't mean they couldn't understand. They had feelings too.

"Look at this dog here," shouted the compere at Beaumont, the Great Dane. "You'll need a saddle for this one. It's as big as a horse…ha, ha, ha!"

Beaumont took exception to this and let out a loud bark, asking for Bill to come closer. "Who is this idiot that you've got with you?" he muttered under his breath.

"He's the compere," whispered Bill, trying not to be heard.

"Well you can tell him from me that his jokes are as stale as his breath," Bill did his best not to laugh, as he turned round to face the man.

Once he had finished meeting all the dogs, he scribbled down a few notes on a piece of paper so he could remind himself of all the key qualities that he admired in a dog: kindness, an affectionate nature and a waggy tail. It was a tough decision to choose a favourite dog. All the dogs had been extremely friendly towards him and there had not been one single growl or snarl amongst them. If he could, he would have given them all a rosette for being such nice doggies. This judging malarkey was a lot harder than it looked, especially when all of them were his favourite.

The compere announced that the results would be given out shortly on the winners' podium by the VIP tent. Everybody clapped politely, showing their appreciation for Bill and all the dogs on show. As everybody filed out of the main marquee, Granny waved to him to get his attention.

"Phew!" he said, wiping the sweat from his brow as he came over to see her. "That was hard."

"You did ever so well, don't you think?" Granny remarked, prompting the children to applaud their grandfather's efforts.

"And you do look extremely smart in your white judge's coat.

Even Mrs. Robbins commented on how smart you looked, didn't she?" The children nodded.

"Gosh, that was difficult," agreed Granny. "I don't think I could have picked a winner out of that lot. They were all such lovely dogs, weren't they?"

"I liked the one with the big bushy curly tail." Alex added.

"I liked the one that had the funny wrinkled face," said Niall, referring to Honeysuckle, a Chinese Shar-Pei.

All of this wasn't helping him make his decision. He didn't want any of the dogs to feel left out if they didn't win, but how was he going to choose?

At last the moment had come and couldn't be put it off any longer. Margaret escorted him outside to the winners' podium where the compere, the expectant dogs and their owners were waiting for him to announce the results. Bill gulped. All eyes were on him now. Watching him from the VIP tent, Granny along with Lady Norbury and the rest of the dignitaries, waited to find out which dog would be crowned winner of the Postman's Favourite Dog Award.

"Right then, Bill, have you got the results?" the compere asked, sticking the microphone in his face. The tannoy made a nasty whistling sound and he stammered nervously.

"Erm…err…" he muttered, fumbling in his pocket for the piece of paper that he had written down the names of the winners on.

Just then he heard Bernard, a beagle, let out a loud bark. Grabbing the attention of all the other dogs, they swivelled their heads around to see what he was barking at.

"Have you seen the desserts and puddings they've got in there?" he declared, his wet nose pointing in the direction of the V.I.P tent. "They've got my favourite, trifle and chocolate mousse." Bernard could almost taste it.

When they saw all the sweets on offer, the dogs suddenly forgot all about winning the Postman's Favourite Dog Award and were more interested in what puddings there were. Barking like a choir of street hounds, they howled to be set free. No stupid metal trophy or bag of unappetising dog food was ever going to compete with a selection chocolate gateaux and delicious desserts!

Bill could see what was going to happen. Trying to buy some time, he pretended that he'd lost the bit of paper with the names of the winners, in the hope that the dogs might forget about the puddings, but it was too late. Their heads were full of mischievous thoughts.

"Black Forest gateaux!" exclaimed Katie, a cocker spaniel, who was wagging her tail furiously.

Pulling on her leash, her owner shouted for her to stop being so naughty, but it was too late. Katie was far too strong for the old leather lead and the leash snapped. As Katie had made a dash for the VIP tent, all the other dogs wanted to follow. Overwhelming their owners and breaking free of their leads, the dogs went surging across the show ground with just one thing on their mind. All Bill could do was stand there and watch, his mouth wide open as the dogs raced past him.

Lady Norbury let out a scream as the excited dogs came charging towards her. The Mayoress froze in terror, while the councillors in their suits panicked, and the judges fell over each other as they tried to escape out the side of the tent. The Chief Inspector, relying on his years of Police training, thought that his authoritative voice would quell the situation, but the dogs thought otherwise.

"HALT!" he yelled sticking out his gloved hand. The dogs just ran straight past him, knocking him to the ground. Getting to his feet, the Chief Inspector looked around for his hat and feeling rather embarrassed he realised his wig was missing too. Searching round desperately for his hairpiece, he watched on in horror as Mitty, a Pekinese, attacked it thinking it was a rat.

"Give it back!" shouted the Chief, as he chased after his wig, but Mitty thinking it was all a game, headed in the direction of the tent to join in all the fun.

It didn't take long for everything in the tent to descend into chaos. There was cream, custard and blancmange flying every-where as the dogs leapt onto tables, licked at bowls, and chomped into gateaux's. With cream on their chops and cake stuck to their noses, they were in sheer doggy heaven. Lady Norbury let out another great big scream.

"SOMEBODY HELP ME!" but it was too late. A bowl of custard came flying in her direction and covered her head to toe in the thick, yellow, gloopy goo. As it dripped from the brim of her hat, she blubbed helplessly as one of the dogs happily licked custard from her skirt.

Wiping cream from his face, the Chief Inspector blew his whistle furiously, but none of the dogs paid any attention. They just carried on making a mess. People were slipping and sliding on the wooden floor, struggling to get to their feet. The Mayoress was an unrecognisable mess of trifle, blancmange and glace cherries. Nobody had ever seen such mayhem at a show. All the VIPs were rolling around on the ground, their nice suits and fancy clothes all covered in various sorts of gunk.

Even Granny and Niall were splattered with the mess. Niall couldn't stop himself from laughing. He had never seen so much fun before in his life. Hiding behind Granny, Alex had yet to be touched by the mess.

"You're covered in it," she laughed pointing at Niall, but it didn't take long for her to get her comeuppance, as a large bannoffee pie came flying towards her, hitting her square in the face. Niall laughed some more.

Granny wasn't pleased. "Let's get you two out of here," she said as the dogs ran amok in the tent. Granny and the children staggered out of the tent and over to Grandpa who was busy watching the carry-on.

"Well, it looks like you've had some fun?" he laughed, looking them up and down.

"Never mind us, go sort that mess out!" Granny snapped, pointing to the dogs who were busy misbehaving themselves. When Bill saw that look on Granny's face, he knew it wasn't time to hang around.

"I'll go and see what I can do," he hastily added, as he rushed over to help.

The owners were doing their best to round up their naughty dogs, but it was no use. When a dog has the taste for jelly and custard, the only thing they're interested in is filling their tummies and they won't listen to a word being said.

Bill couldn't bear to see the VIPs, sliding around the floor, knee deep in cream and custard. The owners were struggling to round up their dogs so, Bill gave a few sharp whistles and the dogs stopped what they were doing.

"There's Bill!" the dogs barked, turning around. With another whistle and a pat on his thigh the dogs came racing over to see him and sat around him staring adoringly up at him.

"Good dogs," he said, heaping praise on them while their owners looked on flabbergasted.

"How did he do that?" they asked.

Someone in the crowd whispered. "I've heard he tunes in to his inner dog,"

"Maybe I should try a bit of that?" someone else muttered.

Just then Bill heard a cry.

"My hero, my hero!" he knew that voice anywhere. It was that of Lady Norbury. Rushing over to him in her high heels, clutching her hat and covered head to toe in custard, she gushed at what masterful control he had over the dogs.

"You've saved us from those terrible beasts!" She declared wrapping her sticky arms around him in praise.

"What's your name, my good man?" she asked.

"Bill," he replied.

"Tell me, how did you learn such a marvellous skill?"

"I'm a Postman. I can talk to dogs," he declared proudly.

"You must tell me how you do it?" she enquired, pressing him for his secret. He explained in the best way he could.

"All you have to do is be kind. You see, dogs can feel kindness," he stated quite simply.

"Well, that is an amazing talent you have there, Bill." she said, praising his heroic actions. Then looking about as if she had misplaced something, she suddenly shouted out aloud.

"Where's the Chief Inspector? Has anybody seen the Chief Inspector?" she demanded. Everyone looked blank.

"SOMEBODY GET ME THE CHIEF INSPECTOR!"

Bill wondered what was going on. He wasn't in trouble was he? Then, from out of the crowd, staggered the Chief Inspector, his smart uniform completely covered in whipped cream and missing his wig.

"How may I be of service, Ma'am?"

"This man here."

"Yes…"

"He's saved us from this motley bunch of unruly mutts. He deserves a medal or something."

"Yes, Ma'am," replied the Chief, bowing his head.

"Well, see to it that he gets one," she ordered.

"Yes Ma'am," he said, bowing his head once more. Dispensing with the services of the Chief Inspector, Lady Norbury waved him off, as she wanted to know more about Bill.

"Tell me, Bill, how long have you been a postman?" Bill cast his mind back, but before he had chance to answer she had something to ask of him.

"Say, would you care to accompany me to my car? she asked. Holding out her hand for him to take Bill steadied her as she walked back to her car. With every step she took custard splurted out of the side of her shoes. Introducing Granny to Lady Norbury she insisted that she give Granny and the children a lift home. Granny was over the moon and Alex and Niall were extremely pleased as they got to sit in the back of her shiny chauffeur-driven car.

Leading the way with his van, Bill took the long way home through town, just so Granny and the children could wave to all their friends from the back seat of the car.

Some weeks later he had to attend a special presentation at the Police Station, where he got to meet the Mayoress and the Chief Inspector again. They gave him a nice certificate to say thank you for a job well done and for sorting out all the mess. Bill didn't want to go, but Granny insisted. After a lot of arguing, he finally decided to go when Granny told him there would be plenty of tea and cake for him.

So, Bill attended the presentation. He said thank you in all the right places, had his picture taken for the local paper and got to drink lots of tea and help himself to as much cake as he wanted. Granny was so pleased that he had his picture taken with the Mayoress and Chief Inspector, that she had the picture put on top of the mantelpiece and showed everyone who came round to visit.

Chapter 9
SORRY YOU'RE LEAVING

Lottie

The day of Clive's retirement had come. After many years of faithful service it was his last day in charge at the office. Bill had got up extra early to make sure he had everything that he needed for the party. Granny had made two lovely cakes for him to take to work. One was a triple-layer chocolate cake and the other was an extra thick sponge cake filled with lots of lip-smacking cream and jam. Both he and the children had been under strict instructions by Granny not to touch them as they were for the party. She had been watching them like a hawk to make sure that no one pinched a slice.

Stacked in cake tins, Bill carefully loaded the cakes onto his bike. Struggling in the dark to tie them to his basket, he gave them a good tug to make sure they wouldn't fall off.

On his way to work he passed the newsagents. It was far too early for Pugsley to be up. Looking up to the darkened bedroom above the shop, he knew that Pugsley would be fast asleep. Dreaming of a hundred and one ways to cook Mackerel, or Twenty Best Bone Dishes by G.Nash. Bill didn't blame him one bit. Given half a chance, there were some mornings when he would rather be tucked up in bed than out delivering mail in the wind and the rain.

When he arrived at work, Tom and Tina were stood outside taking a break: Tina was leant up against the wall, and Tom had a cup of tea.

"What a night we've had!" she said to Bill, grinning from ear to ear.

"Have you done everything I asked?" Bill enquired, as he hopped off his bike.

"Come and see for yourself," as she beckoned him to follow her inside.

"I think you'll be pleased with what we've done," added Tom, puffing out his chest proudly.

Once inside Bill was greeted by the mice. Sliding up and down the heating pipes, they begged him to come and see what they'd done.

"Bill, Bill!" one of the younger mice squeaked, desperate to tell him what they had been up to.

One of the older mice put a paw to his lips silencing him. "Shhh, it's a secret!" he said.

"Wow!" Bill sighed as he walked into the canteen. "What can I say? I'm lost for words."

From the roof hung streamers and all sorts of colourful bunting. Balloons bobbed around the ceiling and sparkly dangly things were festooned around the walls. There was also a big banner saying 'Happy Retirement' strung across the windows. They'd even turned the pool table into a big banqueting table with lacey tablecloths to put the food on.

"You've really outdone yourselves" He said, congratulating them. Tina began to blush.

"It dosen't look half bad." she giggled, resting her head on Bill's shoulder and pretending to be all puffed out.

Ernest, the eldest mouse, ran up Bill's leg and climbed onto his shoulder to survey their efforts.

"We worked all night to help put up the decorations," he squeaked in his ear. "Some of us even tied streamers to our tails to help.

"I must say, I'm very impressed," commented Bill, looking at their work.

"Let me show you!" announced Ernest, leaping from Bill's shoulder like an Olympic gymnast. Landing on the pool table, he then disappeared down one of the pockets reappearing seconds later on the other side of the table from a different pocket.

"What do you think, will Clive like this?"

Stunned by their hard work, all Bill could do was nod as he stood there open-mouthed.

Suddenly the door was flung open and in marched Lorraine, carrying plastic tubs and boxes stacked as high as her head.

"Can someone give me a hand, please?" she asked. Rushing to her aid, all three of them helped unload the boxes from her and put the goodies out on the table.

Ernest, who was at a loose end, busily sniffed his way around the boxes, his whiskers twitching at all the fine smells he was picking up. Then, from one of the boxes came a aroma that was instantly recognisable to him. Smelling like old socks, he immediately knew what was inside the box.

"You're not going to believe this," he squeaked. "There's a cheeseboard!"

An audible murmur went around the mice. "A cheeseboard!" they whispered excitedly to each other.

Ernest wasn't the only one who was on the lookout for treats. Bill was too. Examining each container and shaking them, he sneaked a look inside each of the boxes. One box particularly intersested him.

"Chocolate millionaire shortbread!" he said, drooling.

Lorraine slapped him playfully on the back of the hand. "Now think on. These are for everybody, not just you!" Pretending to look all hurt, he rubbed his hand in the hope of some sympathy.

"Don't come that with me," Lorraine scowled at him, knowing that he was putting it on. "And get these mice out of here! Otherwise they will eat the lot!" Shooing Ernest off the buns he disappeared down one of the pockets and escaped out of the bottom of the table.

The rest of the mice didn't hang about either. Seeing the displeasure on Lorraine's face, they knew she wasn't for messing. Bill called after them, reassuring them that he would make sure that he would put some cheese aside for them. Ernest and the other mice scurried back to the nest for safety, telling the young mice what a wonderful surprise was in store for them.

As the posties piled through the door they each handed in their contributions that they had made to the party. Some had brought egg sandwiches with the crusts cut off, others homemade pasties, and then there were the scotch eggs, sausage rolls and crisps, not forgetting the buns, biscuits and jelly, which were top of the list of scrummy food.

Grandpa, being in charge of the collection for Clive's retirement, took the presents that they had bought for him and put them upstairs in a safe place ready for the presentation later on.

When Clive arrived for work everyone acted as if nothing was going on. There was hardly any chatter. The mice were busy hiding and everybody got on with the sorting.

"Morning, Bill," said Clive, as he made his way to his way to his office.

Not wishing to make arouse suspicion, the posties kept their heads down and carried on sorting.

Once Clive was out of earshot, Lorraine whispered over to Bill, "Do you think he knows?"

Sucking his lip thoughtfully, he replied. "I'm not sure... but knowing him... I'm sure he's already onto us."

There was a buzz going around the office. Once Clive was out of the way, the conversation turned to that of the party. It was all they had been looking forward to for weeks. Bill put the word out for everyone to make their way up to the canteen as quietly as possible. With everyone upstairs, he knocked on the door of the manager's office and went straight in. Clive was at his desk relaxing.

"So this is it, eh, my surprise party?" Clive smiled knowingly.

"How did you know we had a surprise party planned for you?" asked Bill.

"I've got ears!" Clive laughed. "No one can keep a secret in this place," he said, getting up from his desk and walking round to shake hands with Bill. "I'd like to say it's been a real pleasure working with you all these years,"

"The pleasure's been all mine," Bill replied, shaking his hand enthusiastically. "Now, if you don't mind, me and the rest of the staff would like to invite you to share with us a token of our appreciation."

"Why not, eh?" agreed Clive, patting him on the back and loosening his tie. Bill escorted him upstairs to the canteen and, when they reached the top, he paused.

"After you" he said, inviting Clive to open the door.

"SURPRISE!" Everyone cheered as he walked through the door. Whistles blew, party poppers exploded, streamers flew through the air as people sprayed silly string everywhere. Afterwards it was hard to tell that it was Clive under all that mess. Looking like some colourful snowman, he wiped away the streamers from his face and laughed. Everyone crowded round to slap him on the back, shake his hand and say their thankyous, as well as wishing him all the best. Clive even got kisses off all the Post ladies.

Struggling to be heard over everyone talking, Bill climbed on a chair and tapped at a glass to get everyone's attention.

"Can we have a bit of quiet, please?" he shouted. Finally, everyone settled down and at last Bill was able speak.

"As you know, it's Clive's last day here today and I'm sure

everybody here would like to wish him all the best…" He then turned to Clive who was stood by his side.

"…and by way of thanks, we've had a little whip round and got you a few things as a leaving present." Reaching down he presented him with a huge bouquet of flowers. It was so big that Clive could hardly be seen under the mass of brightly-coloured blooms.

"These are for your wife. For everything she's had to put up with. All the early morning phone calls, and late night knocks on the door."

"I'm sure she'll be delighted," he said, accepting the flowers on her behalf and thanking everyone for their generosity.

Now Clive had grown up on the moor and loved walking. As he was such an avid rambler, everyone had clubbed together to get him some books on walking as well as some vouchers towards a new pair of walking boots. One of the ladies had very kindly knitted a pair of matching bobble hats for him and his wife to wear on their hikes. Taking an instant liking to them, Clive decided to wear his there and then. He was so overwhelmed by all his gifts and the love shown to him he had to wipe a tear from his eye and his voice went all wobbly. Bill got a chair for him, so he could sit down and compose himself. Then instructed everyone to tuck into the food.

It was the biggest party anyone had ever seen. No one could ever remember a party like it. There was so much food on the table that it was straining under the weight of it all. The mice had even come to say their goodbyes too.

While everyone tucked into the spread, Clive looked nervously at the clock. It was getting late and he knew that the people of Berrycombe St Martin and outlying districts would be waiting on their mail, but no one seemed inclined to leave the party. However, Clive had already made arrangements that would encourage the posties back to work.

"Right everyone," he yelled over the din. "For those who make it back in time for lunch, there will be a free drink and nibbles at the pub across the road."

Bill had never seen a group of posties move so fast. Offering a free drink to a postie was like giving a dog a bone. Grabbing handfuls of food, the posties, stuffed as much as they could into their pockets, and rushed downstairs to get on with the sorting.

Meanwhile Grandpa picked through the leftovers, taking cheese for the mice and filling a carrier bag with meat for all the dogs on the round. Looking over his shoulder to make sure no one was around. He even stuffed a couple of extra slices of millionaire's shortbread in his pocket just for himself.

Ralph

Out on his round, the dogs were pleased to see Bill. Sniffing out the leftovers from the party, Ralph, an English Bull Terrier, leapt into his van. Ralph looked terribly mean with his snub nose and aggressive stance, but he was ever so friendly. He would lick your face, give a paw, do rollovers.

"Get out!" ordered Bill, showing him the door. Ralph looked puzzled. He couldn't understand why he was being ordered out of the van. After all, he was only being friendly.

After giving Bill a big lick on the face, he jumped out of the van, leaving muddy paw prints all over his shorts and jacket. Bill sighed, but couldn't be mad at Ralph for long because he was such an affectionate dog and that odd looking nose of his made him look ever so cute.

"Here you are," he said, holding out a slice of cured ham for him. Ralph sat down politely and, shuffled around excitedly on his bottom, wagging his tail furiously. It was unusual for a dog that was normally so unruly to have such a delicate manner when it came to food. Taking the piece of meat ever so gently from his hand, Bill praised him.

"That's a good lad," he said, giving him a pat on the head for being so well behaved. Ralph, licking his lips, let out burp and gave Bill a face full of hot, whiffy dog breath.

"Is there any more?" he asked, looking hopeful. Bill had to explain to him that he had to save some for the other dogs on the round.

"Oh well," shrugged Ralph before turning tail and making off up the garden path, to roll around on his back and play with his well-chewed football.

At Greater Tythe Farm, Bill had to stop to unlock the gate, which was always closed on account of Bendy. The maddest, baddest dog that Bill had ever known. However, with the passing of years, Bendy had become more likeable and friendly towards people. The was because the son, taking over the running of the farm from his parents no longer kept Bendy locked up in his kennel or shackled to a chain. Bendy was now free to spend his days as he pleased, which included wandering the fields, smelling the flowers, rambling down the lane to meet other dogs and lying in the sun doing absolutely nothing.

He had become so relaxed that he no longer got worked up by postmen coming into his yard and was even quite pleased to see Bill when he turned up. Bendy was a Border Collie and, with his age, his fur had started to grey. His coat no longer had the sheen of youth and big tufts of fluff were starting to sprout out in all sorts of unusual places. Around his eyes the fur was more noticeably white and his nose was beginning to dry out as old age crept up on him.

When he said 'hello' on a morning and rubbed his nose against the back of Bill's hand, his age became evident by the roughness of his snout. Bill was also aware of Bendy's rather awkward gait, as his arthritic hips no longer kept up with his aspirations of vigour. Bill didn't mind one bit though. It was nice just to be able to show Bendy some affection rather than being chased up the track by him.

This morning Bendy was laid out in the rough grass, sunning himself when Bill turned up in his van. Looking up as if just being disturbed from a lovely dream, he struggled to his feet in order to greet him.

"Morning, Bill," he said, sneezing with all the pollen from the grass.

"Have I got something for you!" Bill declared with excitement. Getting out of the van he showed him the bag of cured meats. Even an old dog could still muster a twinkle in the eye when offered such a treat as this. Lolloping over, Bendy pushed his muzzle into the bag and took a deep breath.

"Could I try some of that salami, please?" he barked. Bill routed around in the bag and pulled out a couple of slices for him. Wolfing them down, Bendy did a little dance as the spiciness made his eyes water.

"Too hot, too hot!" he cried, looking for a puddle to take a drink from. Sticking his head into a hollow he gulped down a couple of mouthfuls of ditchwater.

"That's better," Bendy groaned with relief. "Could I try something a little less spicy, please?"

"Course you can," replied Bill, as he searched in his bag for something that might be better suited to Bendy. As he did so he felt something sharp stab him on the bottom. Recoiling with surprise he fell into the van dropping his bag of doggy treats on the ground.

With a lot of hissing, flapping of wings and feathers, an angry goose attacked him from behind. Pecked all over with a hard, orange bill, he shoved the nasty bird away with his feet, quickly shutting the door of the van.

With feathers filling the cab, he stuck his head out of the window to see where his bag of treats were. The irritable goose then stuck its long neck through the window and tried to peck Bill in the face.

"Bloomin' geese!" He fumed quietly to himself. Then with a tap-tap-tap…tap-tap-tap coming from the back of his van he looked to see what it was making all the noise. Peering into his mirror he was shocked to see five angry looking geese pecking away at the back of his van.

"Get off!" Bill shouted, shooing them away. Distracting them for a second they stopped what they were doing.

Bill knew he had to pick up the bag of meat that he had dropped; otherwise, none of the other dogs on his round would get a treat. Nervously pushing open the door he tried to retrieve the bag when the geese spotted him.

"Honk…honk…honk…honk," they went, making a beeline for him with their sharp pointy beaks. Jumping back into the van the geese hissed and honked wildly.

"Bendy, can't you do something?" Bill asked. Bendy looked at him, then looked at the bag of treats on the ground, and then looked at Bill again. This was a real dilemma for Bendy. He could have a whole bag of tasty meats all to himself, or he could help Bill by returning the bag to him. Bendy gave him a big toothy grin and then laughed to himself, imagining lying in the sun dining handsomely on a fine selection of meats.

About to pick up the bag and make off with it, Bendy was suddenly gripped by his conscience. I can't eat this all myself, he thought. What about all the other dogs on the round? They won't get anything if I eat it all.

Bendy shook his head and growled like he used to do when he was an angry caged dog. Then, with the athleticism of a young Collie chasing his first sheep, he turned tail and charged the geese.

"Be gone with you, you noisy pests!" He snarled, recalling his younger days when his most ferocious bark was saved for the postman. The geese scattered like dandelions on the wind and scurried cowardly towards the empty milking sheds for cover.

"Thanks, Bendy," said Bill, thanking the old dog as he hopped out of his van to retrieve the bag.

Bendy gave an embarrassed smile. "Hmmm…. yes… thank you," he barked, ashamed that the thought had ever crossed his mind to run off with the bag. While the geese sat in the shed, cowardly calling names, Bill handed over some more of the meat as a reward to Bendy.

"Here you are, lad. This is for being such a helpful dog." Underneath all that fur, Bendy was blushing.

"I can't," he protested.

"No, I insist," said Bill, holding a piece of ham out in front of him.

"No, no," Bendy replied, shying away from the gift, but he couldn't refuse as Bill held it mere inches from his nose. Accepting that there was no other way out of the situation, Bendy gobbled down the ham.

As Bill drove back up the track, the geese came out from their place of hiding and chased him up the lane. Tap, tap, tap, they went on the back of the van door. He looked at them in his mirror and shook his head.

"Bloomin' geese!" he moaned.

Chapter 10

MR GRINDER ARRIVES

Lupin

Monday morning came around far too soon. Wondering what the new manager was going to be like they hoped that he was nothing like the terrible stories that they had heard of him.

Cycling into the yard, Bill was greeted by what could be best described as a 'bit of a scene'. Colin, who brought the mail down from the main sorting office was stood there in the middle of the yard being shouted at by a short, angry, little man. Bill who had never set eyes on the man, could only presume it to be the new manager, Mr Grinder.

"What's going on?" he asked everyone, who had gathered outside to see what the all commotion was about.

"It's the new manager," replied Tina, who was trying to earwig. "He says that Colin's late in bringing the mail down."

Bill looked at his watch. "Doesn't Colin get here at this time everyday?"

"Yeah, that's what we tried telling him, but he wouldn't listen," Tina answered.

"Well, hasn't someone tried to sort this out?" asked Bill, realising the situation could get out of hand. Nobody came forward to help.

"We're putting bets on how long it'll be before Colin knocks him out," piped up one of the posties. Bill knew that he had to step in.

"Leave him to it, Bill. If he knocks him out he'll be doing us all a favour," Frank, another postie, chirped up, but Bill ignored him. Squaring up between the pair, he waited for a break in the argument before stepping in.

Rick Grinder was an extremely short chap. He was that small that you could say he was sparrow-like in stature. Barely coming up to Bill's shoulder, he had a shaved head, a pair of wire rimmed glasses, a scowl that would make a baby cry and more fake tan than was strictly necessary, which made him look like an orange. All those stories about him being mean and horrible to postmen instantly rang true. He looked like the sort of chap that would sell his own granny if it meant getting ahead in life, and according to the posties on the night mail train he had actually done such a thing! He had sold his granny to a take away pizza firm and now she was working as a moped delivery rider for them.

Bill sighed. He wished that Clive was still the manager. This sort of thing would have never happened if he was still in charge.

"Can I help?" asked Bill, trying to step in. Colin, the driver looked at him.

"Can you tell this idiot what time I get here?"

"Don't you call me an idiot!" Rick Grinder roared, bouncing up and down on his tippy toes.

"Idiot," the driver sneered under his breath.

"What was that? I'm warning you, I'll have you on a charge. I'll have you sacked!" Rick Grinder shouted.

"Now, I don't think we need to go that far," Bill remarked. "I think it'll be best if we leave Colin to unload the truck himself, eh?"

he said, trying to soothe Rick Grinder's temper and persuaded him to go back inside.

"Don't worry, I'll find out who your boss is and I'll have you sacked!" he yelled, wagging his finger in Colin's direction.

By this time, everybody inside had stopped what they were doing and had come out to watch.

"What are you lot looking at? Get back to work!" he yelled, the veins in his neck bulging. Everyone hurried back inside. In all the time Clive had been the manager, not once could Bill ever recall him losing his temper, and certainly not shouting at anyone.

As they walked back up the yard, he took the opportunity to introduce himself.

"I'm Bill, by the way," he said, smiling and holding out his hand for him to shake. Rick Grinder stared blankly back at him. How odd, thought Bill. What sort of a person doesn't want to shake hands and be friends with somebody? Bill went to put his bike away.

"Stop! What's that?" barked Rick Grinder, pointing to his bicycle.

"It's my bike," he replied, showing off his pride and joy.

"That's not your bike," he exclaimed, running his beady eye over the bike. "That bike belongs to me!"

Bill froze on the spot. "But I've had this bike for years. Clive gave it to me." He said trying to explain, but he was rudely interrupted by the manager.

"I don't care who gave you it. That's company property and I'm seizing it!"

With a glowering expression, Rick Grinder stormed over and snatched the bike from him. Bill was that shocked, he couldn't speak.

"Consider this bike confiscated! It will be locked in my office until I have the time to arrange for it to be disposed of!"

Scratching his head Bill blurted out. "But what about Pugsley? What's he going to do?"

Rick Grinder turned around and gave him a withering look. "Pugsley? Whatever or whoever a Pugsley is, I don't care," he sneered. "That's not my problem is it? Just get in there and get your sorting done." Pointing to the door.

As Bill got on with his sorting, all he could think about was Pugsley sat on the street corner, waiting for his lift down to the harbour. Bill felt sad. He loved letting Pugsley sit in the basket. How would he explain to the poor little Bulldog that he couldn't give him a lift anymore?

Inside everyone was in a sombre mood. Rick Grinder had only been at the office two minutes, yet the whole atmosphere seemed to sour behind him. As they watched him wheel Bill's bike towards his office everyone stopped and stared.

"That's Bill's bike," Someone piped up.

"So it seems, but it belongs to me now!" Rick Grinder snapped back. No one dared speak. They were far too afraid to say anything.

Locking himself away in his office, Rick Grinder sat behind his desk and quietly seethed away to himself. He'd already taken an instant dislike to the posties of Berrycombe St Martin. Their happy, helpful attitude had already annoyed him greatly and, to cheer himself up, he sat there thinking of new ways that he could make their lives a misery. His favourite thing that he liked to do when he was feeling down was to think horrible thoughts. That cheered him up no end.

Getting out of his chair he strolled over to the window overlooking the sorting office floor. As he stood there watching the posties busily working away, he looked down at Bill's bike that was propped up underneath the window. Stroking the leather saddle he thought of the many ways in which, he could have the bike destroyed. Conjuring up a whole host of images, he imagined a tank crushing it under its tracks, or chopped into a million pieces by a junkyard crusher, or melted down in a vat of molten steel. Inside him, he could feel a warm satisfied sensation rising in the pit of his stomach as he thought about his evil deeds.

Watching the staff from behind the blinds of his office, he listed all the ways in which he disliked them. The fat ones, the thin ones, the short ones, the tall ones, the ones that were old, the ones that had a smile on their face, the ones that weren't up to the job. Rubbing his hands together, he smirked to himself, taking great enjoyment in the knowledge that he was about to make their lives as miserable as possible.

Once the sorting was finished Rick Grinder called everybody over for a meeting. So he could introduce himself and outline his plans that he had in store for them.

Dragging their heels, everyone gathered around. Stood there in his black pin stripe trousers, orange shirt and orange tie, he tapped at his clipboard with his pen. An uncomfortable silence spread around the room as he made everybody wait for what he had to say.

"As you may or may not know, this place has been on Head Office's radar for sometime and I have been sent down here to sort this place out," he began. "I have spent the morning going over the figures, and it is as I suspected," he said, adjusting the glasses on his nose. "Quite frankly, it tells me that you lot are a lazy bunch of good for nothing postmen and women." Not mincing his words, he took the posties by surprise. They had never been spoken to like this before, and Lorraine wasn't standing for this.

"How dare you!" she fumed, speaking up for everyone. "We work just as hard as anyone else."

"And you are?" replied Rick Grinder, looking over the top of his spectacles.

"Lorraine Fish," she answered, sounding irritated that she had been addressed in such a manner. Standing on the balls of his feet, Rick Grinder began to bounce up and down, a sure sign that he was getting angry.

"WELL, MRS. Fish," he said, "I hate to say, but the figures don't lie, and here at Berrycombe St Martin you seem to be a rather slovenly lot."

This caused immediate uproar in the office.

"What a damn cheek!" Frank, one of the postie's shouted out, whilst another at the back of the room shouted, "What a load of rubbish!" and someone else yelled, "Go back to head office!"

Rick Grinder cast an his gaze around the room, one that he had been practicing in front of the mirror at home for some time.

"I see we have one or two rather immature individuals in here," he stated, looking all smug with himself. "But, now that I have your undivided attention. I can share with you how bone idle you really are." Holding a piece of paper in his hand Rick Grinder waved it about in front of everybody.

"Here are the figures and it tells me you lot here are only one hundred percent efficient, and in my books that is not good enough."

Shocked at what he was hearing Bill spoke up. "What's wrong with being one hundred percent efficient?

"Quite frankly, we could get chimps or robots to do your job." He said breathing on his glasses and polishing them with his tie.

"I'd like to see that. A chimp driving a van," someone muttered and a roar of laughter went up in the office.

"SILENCE!" shouted Rick Grinder. "This is MY meeting and I have some new rules that you lot will be adhering to from now on!"

Everybody looked at each other. New rules, everyone thought, this couldn't be good.

"Firstly," he declared, "that damn infernal noise that you call the radio will not be tolerated anymore. As from tomorrow, it goes in the bin."

A low rumble of discontent emanated from around the office as Frank muttered something rather rude under his breath.

"Secondly, there will be no jokes, no laughing, and strictly NO FUN."

No one could believe what they were hearing. The whole office thought he was joking, and burst out into another fit of laughter.

"I SAID...I SAID... NO LAUGHING!" shouted Rick Grinder, trying to make himself heard. "Laughter is inefficient," he stated, all stony-faced. "The process of telling jokes loses valuable sorting time. For every joke you tell, we lose nine seconds of sorting time.

"Now on to my third point: HAPPINESS," he said, casting a suspicious gaze around the room. "If you are happy, then your mind is not on the job. At head office, we have conducted several studies into the problems connected with being happy and we have found the root cause to be fun. Now if we can stop people from having fun then we can improve efficiency."

At which point Rick Grinder produced a flip chart and, turning the page over, revealed a big graph.

"Here we can see the causes of fun and happiness." He pointed with his laser pointer.

"And here we can see productivity." Feeling that the staff weren't really engaged with his presentation, he looked to some way of getting them involved.

"You," he said, looking for a volunteer and pointing to Russell, the youngest postman in the office. "Come here and read this for me."

Russell wasn't sure he wanted to do it, but felt he had no choice but to do as he was told. Making his way up to the front, he stood next to the flip chart looking suitably unimpressed.

"Can you read the bottom line for me?" asked the manager

"Causes of fun," said Russell.

"And the rest…," Rick Grinder demanded.

"Number one: Family. Number two: Playing games. Number three: Outdoor activities."

"Now you see all these things that we have just mentioned impact badly on business." Said Rick Grinder.

Around the room Bill could see everyone scratching their heads. It had even got him wondering why it was so wrong to have a lovely family? Frank immediately put his hand up.

"Yes," said the manager pointing to him.

"I have a question."

"Ahh I'm pleased that someone is showing an interest in my presentation. Good, go ahead," he continued.

"How is it me having a family is bad for my job?" asked Frank.

Swelling with pride, Rick Grinder puffed out his chest. "I'm glad you've asked that. Now does anyone have any idea in what way having a family can be undesirable for the business?"

No one put their hand up. The posties couldn't believe what they were hearing. They thought the man was mad.

"One of the many factors of a family being bad for business is that those who have children will find themselves from time to time being called on to look after sick, miserable, whining, whinging children, and if there's one thing I can't stand, is a whinging child.

Everyone looked at each other. Nobody could believe what they were hearing.

By now no one was listening to a word he was saying, as he was talking that much rubbish, but still he went on. "Those of you here who also play sport may also want to reconsider your choice of game. Rugby, football, hockey are all sports to be avoided." He said, illustrating his point by showing them on his graph.

"Those of you who MUST play a sport, may I suggest you consider safe sports such as bowls, croquet or tiddly-winks, something where the risk of injury is greatly reduced…Oh, but if you are going to play tiddly-winks, may I suggest you wear suitable eye protection."

As he finished talking, Russell asked if he could go back and join the others.

"No, stay standing. I haven't finished yet," he ordered him as if talking to a dog.

"It is my mission in life that Berrycombe St Martin sorting office to be known as the most efficient office in the country! One hundred percent efficiency is not good enough. I want this place to be two hundred percent efficient. Let me set out my vision for this," he said, turning another page on the flip chart.

"From now on you are all going to take out two rounds each." There was a gasp of disbelief from the office.

"We can't manage that," Bill replied. "We don't have the time."

"May I suggest you start running," grinned Rick Grinder.

Bill looked around at his colleagues. "There's no way that Charlie can run, I mean, he's nearly seventy already."

"Well, maybe he should consider whether or not this is the job for him?" Rick Grinder answered back.

"It'll kill him if he has to run round!" Bill protested.

Not a flicker of emotion showed on Rick Grinder's face, but, secretly on the inside, he was doing loop the loops and cart wheels. The more old and infirm posties he could get rid of the better it would be.

"You see what I want to do is mould you into the leanest, most efficient machine possible. By the time I've finished with you all, you'll be eating, sleeping and dreaming of letters."

There was a stunned silence as nobody could believe what they had just heard.

"Now, if you will excuse me, I have work to be attending to." And with that, he disappeared into his office.

Everybody stood there in disbelief, thinking they hadn't heard him right.

"What does he mean by happiness and fun being bad for business? Is there something not right with the man?" asked Frank, shaking his head. "And what's all this about whinging children?" he wanted to know.

Incensed by what she was hearing, Lorraine let her thoughts be known on the matter. "The only thing that this man cares about more than himself is money." she said stating her case. "All we can do is show him that we are not going to stoop to his level of mean-ness and carry on doing our jobs the best we can!"

"I agree," added Bill. "We can't let our customers down, now can we?"

"And the dogs!" added Russell who was as fond of the dogs on his round as Bill was.

"That's right, and the dogs!" Agreed Bill.

Chapter 11

A MOUSE PARADISE

Gypsy

While everyone was busy getting their rounds ready, Rick Grinder decided to stick his head out of his office. Striding up and down the rows of sorting frames he glared menacingly at the posties.

Pausing for a moment he removed a pencil and note-pad from his top pocket and stood behind Bill watching him. Licking the end of the pencil, he began to jot things down, all the time whilst looking at his watch.

"What's he doing?" whispered Lorraine from round the corner of her frame.

"I think's he's seeing how fast we sort," he replied, trying not to be overheard. However, Rick Grinder's hearing was especially keen and he had already heard what they were saying.

"I'm here to get more work out of you miserable lot and this little notebook tells me how efficient you are!" With everyone worried, they put their heads down and started sorting as fast as they could.

Busy making his calculations Rick Grinder suddenly noticed something move on Bill's frame.

"What's that?" he asked.

"What's what?" Bill replied.

"That!" he shrieked., "I just saw something move."

"Oh that, that's a mouse,"

"MICE! WE'VE GOT MICE IN THE OFFICE!" Rick Grinder squealed, jumping ten feet in the air and landing in the arms of the nearest postie. "GET THOSE INFERNAL THINGS OUT OF HERE!" he demanded, wrapping his arms round Tom's neck and clinging to him like a baby.

"But they live here, Bill tried explaining.

"NOT ANYMORE, I'M GETTING THE EXTERMINATORS IN!" he shouted all red faced.

Groaning under the strain Tom told him he couldn't hold him anymore and thought he was going to drop him.

"THEN PUT ME DOWN SOMEWHERE!" he insisted.

Tom was about to let go of him when Rick Grinder screeched out loud, "Not on the floor! Not on the floor! I don't want to share my space with those vermin." Doing as he was told Tom dumped him on top of his frame, leaving him in a crumpled heap.

Taking offence at being handled in such a rough manner Rick Grinder barked orders to those around him, "I WANT THESE MICE OUT OF HERE, GET RID OF THESE MICE NOW! DO YOU HEAR ME?"

Everyone stopped what they were doing. Rick Grinder refusesd to move until he was absolutely sure there were no more mice about. Bill politely asked the mice to go and hide while they did their best to coax the manager down off the frame, promising he'd be back later to look after them.

Sweating and with his knees trembling, Rick Grinder clambered down off the frame. Making his way back to his office he made it known that he would make it his personal goal to get rid of all the mice from the office.

"I'll have traps set for them all!" he grimaced as he twitched and shook nervously. "And poison!" he yelled from over his shoulder.

"Did you hear that?" said Lorraine.

Bill shook his head in disbelief. "I won't let him harm a single hair on any of those mice's heads," he uttered, as he thought of how best to keep the mice safe.

He had to act fast. There was no telling what Rick Grinder might do. An emergency pest controller could be there within the hour with a van full of traps and poison. Wracking his brain, he suddenly came up with a plan. Underneath the sorting office was a basement. Nobody ever went down there, but Bill knew he would find exactly what he was looking for there.

Putting his shoulder to the door he gave it a shove. The room was covered in a tangle of spiders' webs and an inch layer of dust, a sure sign that nobody had been down there for years. Brushing the cobwebs from his face, he cast his eye over the years of accumulated junk.

From where he stood it looked like a treasure trove just waiting to be explored. He picked his way through the jumble of boxes and, there in the corner of the room, he found what he was looking for. Piled up in a heap were a stack of old delivery pouches. Picking one up, he turned it over and to his surprise found that it had never been used and looked brand new.

Racing back upstairs with the pouch under his arm Bill made sure that Rick Grinder was nowhere to be seen before he climbed back up onto his frame. Tapping the vent where the mice lived Ernest stuck his head out.

"It's okay, Rick Grinder's in his office," he whispered "Look, I haven't got time to explain, but I've got a plan," he said, patting the canvas pouch that was slung over his shoulder. Ernest looked worried. The lives of all the mice depended on him and he couldn't let them down.

"It's terrible," exclaimed Ernest. "All the mice are worried sick about what's going to happen to them. They're petrified that they are going to be caught in traps or worse…" Ernest gulped.

"Well, that's why you're coming with me. I just need you all to get in here," he said, opening the flap on the bag.

Ernest looked at it. "Is that your plan?" he said in a less than enthusiastic tone.

"Look I haven't got time to argue. Just get all the mice in here and I can sort everything out later."

Understanding the seriousness of the situation, Ernest knew that Bill had their best interests at heart and disappeared back inside the vent.

The nest was in chaos. There was wailing and blubbing as mice darted this way and that. For Ernest, it was time to take charge. Coughing loudly he cleared his throat.

"Right. Listen up, mice," he said addressing them in confident and assured manner. They stopped what they were doing and sitting up took notice.

"I know that this is not a very nice time for us. This nest has been our home for more seasons than most of us can remember. We have watched many Christmases come and go, with parcels stacked up as high as the ceiling, but now our lives are in peril and we must put our faith in Bill. He has always looked after us and made sure that no harm has ever come to us. We must leave our nest, or run the risk of being caught by the dreaded pest controller." As Ernest stressed the urgency of the situation, there was silence amongst the mice.

"I need every mouse, to get whatever they need to take with them and be ready to leave in the next few minutes." It was a hive of activity as the mice collected together their families.

Outside Bill was waiting for them with the pouch to transport them to safety. There was a tussling of soft furry coats as the mummy mice emerged clutching their babies tight to their chests.

"We need two orderly lines up against the vent," Ernest announced, getting everyone ready for the big move.

Seeing that the mice were ready to leave, Bill held the pouch open.

"Go, go, go!" yelled Ernest, patting each of the mice on the back as they leapt off the vent and into the pouch. Landing with a soft thump in the bag, the old satchel filled up quickly as the mice jostled to make themselves comfy.

"How's it going?" asked Lorraine, eager to hear how the move was progressing.

"Nearly there," replied Bill, peeking inside the vent to see how many were left.

Inside Ernest was checking off the mice as they exited the nest.

"Buttercup, Florence, Max, Rupert, Ruth, Teddy...Phew," he called out aloud as he checked them off one by one. Then he heard the call of a young mouse in distress.

"Help, help!" squealed Chloe, finding herself stuck between the slats. Seeing the young mouse in desperate need of help, Ernest ran over to her and tried shoving her through the vent, but Chloe wasn't moving.

"I think I've eaten too much cheese," she cried as she remained stuck.

"Don't worry, I'll get you out," Ernest said, trying to reassure her, but as hard as he tried, Chloe wasn't for budging. Worried that Chloe was would be left behind Ernest turned around, and with his shoulder wedged against her bottom began to push.

"Mmmmph...," he groaned. Then, with a sudden pop, she went shooting out of the vent like a cannonball, landing in the pouch with a thud.

"At last," Ernest sighed with relief.

"Are we all done in there?" asked Bill, aware that Rick Grinder might be back any minute. Checking there was no one else left in the nest, Ernest dived into the overflowing sack of mice. Lorraine begged him to let her see the mice.

"Awww…how cute?" she cooed putting her finger into the bag so she could feel how soft the mice felt.

Bill laid the pouch down in his trolley, tucking it in amongst all the others so there was no way Rick Grinder was ever going to find them. Not unless he did a spot check.

As he wheeled the trolley through the office, Norman the head postman came rushing down to see Bill, all red faced and out of breath.

"Bill, Bill!" he gasped, trying to get Bill's attention.

"Rick Grinder's on the phone. He's arranging for the pest controllers to come out this morning. You'll have to get the mice out of here before they arrive." Bill smiled and, looking around to make sure that Rick Grinder was no where in sight, he motioned for Norman to take a closer look.

"Here," he whispered, bending down to lift up a tray of mail. Underneath the tray was the mice. Looking up at him with their round black eyes and big ears, Norman couldn't get over how adorable they looked.

"How could anyone want to harm them? It's beyond me," he said, shaking his head. "You better get them out of here quick just in case he decides to come out of his office," he said. Not having to be told twice, Bill made a hasty dash outside, hiding the bag in his van.

It was a while before one of the mice was brave enough to stick his head out of the post bag.

"Psssst…psssst…is it safe to come out now?" he asked.

"I don't think Rick Grinder will find us out here," Bill replied, pulling the van over and taking in the wondrous views of the purple heather. The mice pushed their way out of the bag, breathing deeply on the fresh moorland air.

"Have you ever seen anything like it?" they gasped in delight.

Most of the mice they had never left the confines of the office, let alone experienced anything like this.

"Can't we live here?" one of the young mice asked. "It's so beautiful."

"It is, my dear," Ernest replied, sighing deeply. "But the winters are harsh and the food can be scarce up here," he told them. "It looks lovely now, but it is a hard life for a mouse when the snows come. Even the ponies struggle to find enough food for themselves." Realising that Ernest was talking sense, the young mouse put her ambitions aside.

With the mice sitting comfortably on the dashboard Bill carried on with his round. As he drove along, the mice bounced up and down giggling wildly as they went over the bumps in the road, catapulting them off the dash and into the pile of mail. They were enjoying their day out so much that they had forgotten about losing their home.

Cosy Nook Cottage belonged to Mr Robinson, an elderly gent who lived on his own with his most trusted companion, Gypsy, a Maltese terrier. Now some people like to over-preen Maltese terriers by putting bows in the hair and doing all sorts of silly things to them. Some even go so far as to blow dry them so that the poor dog ends up looking like a walking carpet. But Mr Robinson didn't like any of that faff. He liked a dog to be a dog, one that he could go for a walk with, that could chase balls and fetch sticks, not one that wanted to win dog shows.

Gypsy spent most of her days curled up on Mr Robinson's lap, keeping him warm. It was Mr Robinson's favourite thing, sitting there in his high back chair, reading to his furry companion. Mr Robinson was such a avid reader that many of the books he had read several times, to the point where Gypsy could recite them off by heart. Any book where there was a dog involved, or where the dog was the hero, got her paw of approval.

It was just after lunch when Mr Robinson took up his book again. Distracted for a moment he noticed Gypsy's ears begin to twitch as she heard something that was beyond the range of human hearing. Leaping from his lap she raced across the lounge and jumped onto the window ledge, slipping and sliding about as her claws scratched at the paint work. Barking for all she was worth she raced back and forth like a wind up toy. Mr Robinson not being as sprightly as he once was had to ease his old bones out of the chair. Hobbling over to the window, he went to see what all the commotion was about.

"What's wrong, girl?" he asked, looking out of the window.

"There's nothing there," he added, but Gypsy couldn't be persuaded otherwise. Relying on her doggy senses she ran out of the room and began scratching, begging to be let out of the door.

"Hold on, girl!" Mr Robinson called after her as he tottered on behind. Then, from over the hill, Bill's van appeared.

As soon as the door opened, Gypsy shot off up the drive.

"Wait up, girl!" he called after her as he struggled to keep up. Seeing Bill parked at the top of the drive she rushed headlong to meet him.

"Hello, girl," he said, greeting her in his usual manner, but Bill sensed that she wasn't herself that afternoon. Normally Gypsy was a mild mannered pleasant dog and was always well behaved, but today she was acting like a dog gone wild.

"I don't know what's got into her," shouted Mr Robinson to Bill, as she growled and showed her teeth. Chasing up the drive after her, Mr Robinson shouted at her to heel, but she completely ignored her master's voice. Then one of the mice poked their head out of the van window and Gypsy went berserk, spitting and snarling like an angry human.

Unable to control her instinctive nature, seeing a mouse had set her off in a wild frenzy and all she could think of was chasing mice!

"Grrrrrr….let me at those mice!" grizzled Gypsy, gnashing her teeth.

"Get down, you bad girl!" shouted Mr Robinson, scolding her and grabbing hold of her roughly by the collar.

"I'm so sorry, Bill," he apologised, wrestling to hold on to his own dog. Intrigued to see what was making all the noise, the mice came to take a closer look at the angry terrier.

"Wait a minute. Isn't that a mouse?" Mr Robinson asked, surprised to see a mouse sticking its head out of the van.

"Not just the one mouse," said Bill proudly. "Take a look." Bill invited him to take closer look and, poking his head inside, Mr Robinson was surprised to see a bunch, of happy mice smiling back at him.

"Good grief!" he gasped. "What are you doing with all those mice?"

"I saved their lives," Bill said proudly. "They used to live at the sorting office. That was, until the manager threatened to put traps and poison down."

"Traps and poison, what a beastly thing! What sort of a person is he?" Remarked Mr Robinson disgusted by the whole matter.

"Not a very nice one," added Bill.

"Well, he sounds thoroughly disagreeable to me." Dumbfounded by the situation, Mr Robinson picked Gypsy up so that she could see the mice. Having calmed down, she was now a little less boisterous, but she was still growling at the mice in a disagreeable manner.

"Less of that!" Mr Robinson snapped, telling her off for her less-than-friendly behaviour. "These poor mice have lost their home and here you are barking at them and being uncharitable." Gypsy looked ashamed by her behaviour and let out a whimper.

"I should think so, now you apologise to these mice," Mr Robinson lowered Gypsy down to see the mice and cautiously they stepped forward to meet their first ever dog. Curiously Gypsy began to sniff at the mice and one of the young mice who had been collecting flowers from the moor offered one to Gypsy as a gift.

"Here you are, I have a present for you," she said. Gypsy sniffed and licked the young mouse in return. As Gypsy only had paws and no hands to receive the offering the little mouse leapt onto Gypsy's nose and ran up onto her head tucking the bloom behind her fluffy white ear.

"I think you've found a friend there," exclaimed Mr Robinson with delight.

The conversation then turned to what Bill was going to do with the mice and where they were going to live.

"I'm going to take them home with me," remarked Bill. "But I haven't got anywhere to put them."

Mr Robinson frowned as if he was thinking. "Hang on a minute. I think I might have just the thing for you." Inviting Bill to follow him, they headed down the path towards the garage.

At the end of the drive stood an old wooden garage. Putting Gypsy down on the ground, Mr Robinson did his best to pull the door open.

"It's a bit stiff, Bill. Can you give me a hand?" Without hesitation, Bill offered his assistance. While they were struggling with the door, Gypsy took the opportunity to get better acquainted with the mice.

Pulling themselves up on her tight curls the mice clambered eagerly onto her back. Sat a top of her like a jockey, she gave them a ride round the garden. Being a true dog Gypsy couldn't help but run around in furious circles, getting herself all giddy. Clinging on for dear life, the mice squealed with delight. Gypsy ran so fast that some of the mice lost their grip and went spinning off into the flower bed. Getting to their feet, they clambered out looking somewhat dishevelled, but wearing big silly grins on their faces.

Eventually, after being able to push the door open, Bill and Mr Robinson were confronted with a garage filled with junk. Piled high there were cardboard boxes, old bikes, bits of cars, moth eaten curtains, deck chairs and a wide selection of odd lengths of wood.

"What is it we're looking for?" Bill asked scratching his head.

"I'll know it when I see it," Mr Robinson replied, wading through the waist-high sea of unwanted junk. Picking up various objects he examined them for their worth and then discarded them, tossing them over his shoulder. Then, as if striking gold, Mr Robinson erupted with an exuberant cheer.

"HURRAH!" he yelled.

"Have you found what you we're looking for?" enquired Bill.

"Come here, come and see this!"

Squeezing his way between the boxes Bill finally made his way over to where Mr Robinson was. "What is it?" He asked. Poking out from underneath a blanket, all Bill could see were shiny bits of plastic.

"What is it?" Grandpa asked.

"Ahhh…all is about to be revealed. Are you ready?" asked Mr Robinson as he held the edge of the blanket in his hand.

"TAH-DAH!" Whipping off the blanket as if unveiling a plaque, Mr Robinson begged for Bill's thoughts.

"What is it?" To Bill, it looked like nothing more than a tangled mass of see through tubes, pipes and drums.

"This here, my friend, is Hamster City. The last word in luxury when it comes to rodent accommodation," he stated. Bill stood there looking puzzled, wondering what to do with it.

"My girls kept hamsters when they were younger and I knew we had it here somewhere. You can let the mice have it for their new home," he suggested.

Having no better plan Bill agreed to take it. Mr Robinson then explained to him how to put it all together while he loaded it into the back of his van.

When he got home he couldn't wait to show the children the surprise he had in store for them.

"What have you got there?" asked Granny as she watched him parade through the house on his way to the shed. Bill just tapped the side of his nose and told them it was a secret. Alex and Niall were intrigued as to what it was their Grandfather was up to and hovered around expectantly as he came and went from the shed.

"Can we see?" they asked, trying to get a glimpse of what he was up to.

"Don't be so nosey. You can see when I'm ready," he said, closing the shed door behind him to keep their prying eyes from seeing.

"I wonder what he's up to?" said Alex, looking wistfully out of the kitchen window at her grandfather beavering away in the shed.

"Beat's me," replied Granny, who was stumped as what he was up to.

Some ten minutes later, Grandpa strode purposefully back into the house.

"What have you been up to?" asked Granny. Remaining tight lipped, Bill invited everyone to follow him out to the shed.

"I smell a rat, Bill Mathers," observed Granny as she made her way across the yard, ducking for the clothesline.

"I think you'll find it's a mouse, darling. You smell a mouse!" Bill laughed to himself. Granny had no idea what he was on about. She thought he was just being funny.

Stood like a circus ringmaster about to announce his next fantastical act, he made Granny and the children wait.

"C'mon, let us in, we want to see what you've got in there," Niall moaned impatiently. Taking a bow and pretending to take off his imaginary cap, Bill opened the door to the shed.

"WOW!" exclaimed Niall upon seeing what it was that his Grandpa had been up to.

"THAT'S AMAZING!" commented Alex, taking it all in.

"Are those mice?" asked Granny curiously. Bill nodded.

There in front of them was a mass of twisted tubes, drums, pipes, domes, and balls and inside were all the mice running around. Niall was lost for words. All he could do was point, while Granny looked at her husband with an air of disapproval.

"What?" he said, shrugging his shoulders innocently. "Rick Grinder was going to have them K-I-L-L-E-D," he said, spelling out the awful word so as not to upset the mice.

"He wasn't, was he?" Sniffed Granny in a disbelieving manner.

"He was," said their grandfather. Granny put her hand to her mouth as she gasped in horror. Suddenly she wasn't so cross with him when she found out what could have happened to the mice.

"Look," said Bill, wanting to show the family just how cute the mice were.

"This is Ernest. He's the eldest mouse," introducing the mouse to them.

Popping his head out of one of the plastic tubes, Ernest stood on his hind legs and held out his tiny paw to shake as way of thanks. Alex and Niall took it in turns to offer their finger for the mouse to shake followed by Granny.

"My, he is a very civilised mouse, isn't he?" she said, impressed by his manners.

"This is wonderful," gushed Ernest, looking round at his new home.

"It's better than anything we could have imagined. We love it, thank you, Bill," he said, heaping praise on his friend. Not only did they have miles of tubes and pipes to run along, but they had water bottles and food dishes for them to feed from. Another bonus was that inside the shed was a tumble drier, which blew lovely warm air onto the mice's new home. Providing them with more tumble drier fluff than they could ever want. Thankful of their new home, all the mice gathered round and let out a tiny cheer.

Chapter 12

GRANDPA BLOWS A GASKET

Maggie & Mabel

Rick Grinder had been in charge of Berrycombe St Martin sorting office for only a few weeks, but he had already made a lasting impression on the staff.

"Have you seen this?" chirped up Charlie, the oldest postie in the office expressing his concerns to Bill. "In all the years that I've worked here, I've never seen such a mess," he grumbled, brushing his white wispy hair across his head.

Bill looked at the mountain of mail that surrounded him.

"Look at it," Charlie groaned, pointing to yet another round that had not been delivered. "It's a sad day when we haven't got enough posties to deliver the mail," he grumbled.

Bill had to agree. He'd never seen such a sight. Even at Christmas, the busiest time of the year, things had never been this bad.

"Clive wouldn't have let this happen, you know," said Charlie, voicing his displeasure.

Bill agreed. Since Rick Grinder had let his computer take charge, things had got worse not better.

"It wouldn't be so bad if we still had the mice here, at least they'd help us out," muttered Charlie with regret.

Just then Lorraine stuck her head over the giant pile of mail.

"What are we going to do Bill? We can't go on like this?" she said, but Bill wasn't going to give in so easily.

"Never mind, if we all dig in we can get through this," he said, rolling up his sleeves and picking up a handful of letters. "Right, let's get to it, eh?" he said, trying to lift the flagging spirits of his friends. "Let's show this Rick Grinder just how good the postmen and women of Berrycombe St Martin are."

Sorting as fast as he could, the letters flew from his hands like a mouse after cheese. With just the slightest of glances, he knew which letter went where. Bill was like a walking A to Z. As he read each address he conjured up a mental picture in his head of the house, the pathway up to it, the people who lived there, the names of the children, even down to the names of their pet goldfish, his memory was that good.

Sorting that fast, sweat was starting to bead from his brow and his ears burnt bright red as he tried to get rid all the extra heat.

"This sortings thirsty work, eh?" he said, turning to Charlie. "How about a cuppa?" Charlie agreed and disappeared upstairs to make everyone a cup of tea.

It wasn't long before Rick Grinder showed his face. Swaggering round the office with his clipboard and pen, he stood directly behind Bill watching him.

"Mmmm…" he muttered as he tapped away on his calculator. "Passable, but I want more out of you," he sneered.

"You need to be working faster," admonishing Bill for what he saw as a lack of speed.

"But I can't go any faster," Bill replied.

"I don't want excuses," he scowled. "Excuses are for those who aren't up to it."

Bill didn't like letting anyone down and so, focusing all his energy, he tried to sort even faster than he already was.

Lorraine didn't like the sound of what was happening. She was worried for Bill. Looking over at him she could see that he was starting to go bright red in the face and wasn't sure how long he could keep it up.

"Bill slow down. You'll make yourself ill," she begged of him.

"Nonsense!" snorted Rick Grinder, who was breathing down his neck. "You could do with taking a leaf out of this man's book," he snapped, telling her to get back on with her work.

"But you're going to make him poorly," Lorraine pleaded, trying to appeal to his better nature. But it was no use. Rick Grinder didn't have a better nature.

"Faster! Faster!" he yelled.

Lorraine was really worried for Bill. Noticing the colour drain from his face, she rushed to his side to steady him.

"What do you think you're doing?" Rick Grinder demanded to know.

"Get back to your sorting frame," he snapped.

Ignoring him, Lorraine took Bill by the elbow to catch him, but it was too late. Totally exhausted, he collapsed, falling off his stool and banging his head on the floor.

"Bill, Bill!" Lorraine cried anxiously as she crouched down beside him.

Gently slapping him on the face to try and bring him round, Bill lay there in a giant pile of letters. He was now beginning to mutter all sorts of strange things.

"Get this man back on his feet and get him back on his frame," demanded Rick Grinder who stood over Lorraine glowering at her.

"What's wrong with you? Can't you see he's not well?" Lorraine snapped back. Just then Charlie came down from the canteen with a mug of tea and stumbling across the scene, rushed over to help.

"Get out o' the way, man!" he yelled, barging past Rick Grinder and knocking him flat on his back, sending his clipboard and calculator flying through the air.

"Here, have a sip of this," said Charlie, bending down to let Bill have a drink, but it was worse than they thought. He was that worn out that he couldn't even manage a drink.

"He doesn't look good, does he? I think we better get him home," Lorraine shouted for the other posties to help.

By now everyone had stopped what they were doing and had gathered round to see what all the fuss was about. After finding out that Rick Grinder had made Bill poorly, some of the posties got rather angry and suggested what they would like to do if they got their hands on him. Sensing that he was not welcome, Rick Grinder scuttled back to his office.

Rushing around in a panic, everyone lent a hand to help lift Bill onto an old wooden mail cart, which they used as a makeshift stretcher. Then, wheeling him out to the loading bay Charlie was ready, waiting with his van.

"Easy boys, watch his head," Charlie instructed, as they lowered him into the back of the van. Lorraine jumped in with him to make sure he was okay.

It was early when Granny heard the knock at the door. Alex and Niall were already dressed in their school uniforms having their breakfast when they looked up to see who it was. Even Granny was surprised when she heard the knock at the door.

"Who's that?" she asked. Drying her hands on her pinny and putting the toast down, she went to answer the door. Alex and Niall did their best to listen in to what was being said but, as the kitchen door was closed, it was hard to tell who was talking.

"Who is it? What are they saying?" asked Niall.

"Shush! I can't hear," said Alex, waving her hand at her brother to get him to shut up. There was an awful commotion in the hallway, along with the sound of someone arguing.

Bursting though the kitchen door, Alex and Niall were taken aback to see their grandfather being helped in by two posties. One of the posties, a thin old chap, had his arm wrapped around their grandfather's shoulder, while the other postie, a lady, was carrying Grandpa's jacket and pouch with her.

"Put him down over there," Granny said to Charlie, pointing to the armchair.

"I'm fine, I'm fine, I can do it myself," Bill moaned, but there was no point arguing with Granny who insisted that Charlie help him. Lowering him slowly into the chair, Bill let out a sigh.

"That's better," he said taking the weight off his feet.

"That makes two of us," winced Charlie as he stood up to rub his back. "I didn't think I'd have been able to carry you any further. You're some weight!"

Charlie was almost seventy and was thin as a griddle with hardly an ounce of fat on him. His face was covered in a multitude wrinkles where time had left its mark, but he carried with him a smile that not even the passing of years could erase.

No longer interested in his breakfast, Niall was more concerned about his grandfather.

"Ahhh… I've just blown a gasket, nothing serious," Bill added. Just then Charlie recognised the children.

"It's Niall isn't it?" he asked. Niall looked bemused as he didn't recognise the old postie.

"When I saw you last, you were nothing but a tiny bundle o' joy. My, how you've grown!" he said, ruffling the hair on Niall's head in an affectionate manner.

"And this one," Charlie remarked, turning his attention towards Alex. "My, you're a handsome young maid, ain't you, mi' dear?" he laughed.

"This is your Uncle Charlie," said Bill, introducing them to him. "It must be some years since you've last seen these two, eh?"

Charlie nodded. "Aye, that it be."

"Is your dad still on the boats?" Charlie asked, sweeping his thin grey wispy hair across his head. Alex nodded shyly. Aware that they were nervous of the stranger, Charlie turned his attention back to their grandfather.

"Anyway, what are we were going to do about this Rick Grinder?" he grumbled, shaking his head. "I mean how are we ever going to sort all that mail with just the few of us?"

"Beats me Charlie, I've no idea," Bill answered, shrugging his shoulders.

Making sure he was comfy, Granny plumped the cushion up behind him. Being polite, she offered Charlie and Lorraine a cup of tea, but they declined knowing they had to get back to work.

"Can't we get the mice to come back?" asked Lorraine. "They really helped with the sorting and I kind of liked seeing their cute little faces around the place."

"Mmmm…they certainly did help us sort a lot of letters didn't they?" agreed Charlie, stroking his bristly chin.

"But what about all the traps and poison?" Niall cried out, alarmed by the idea of putting the mice back into harm's way. "Won't they get hurt?"

For a moment everyone looked puzzled as they tried to figure out what to do. Then Charlie clicked his fingers.

"Wait, I've got it! I'll get Stella, the cleaner, to get rid of all those traps when she's sweeping up and Rick Grinder won't even notice a thing! Then the mice will be able to wander round with impunity."

"Impunity? What's impunity?" asked Niall with a puzzled look on his face.

"It means they can do whatever they want, love," said Lorraine.

Taking a minute to mull over their plan, Bill came up with a suggestion. "Why don't I go and ask the mice right now?" he said, trying to get up out of his chair.

"Oh no you won't. You'll sit there and rest," Lorraine ordered him.

"Nonsense," argued Bill but, as he tried to get out of the chair, he collapsed again.

"See. Lorraine's right. You'll do nothing of the sort. It's bed for you," said Granny who stood in front of him with her arms crossed. Charlie laughed.

"Better do as you're told, eh?" he smirked. Leaving him to get some rest, Granny thanked Charlie and Lorraine for bringing her husband home and led them to the door to see them out.

After spending the rest of the day in bed, Bill felt much better. Taking a sip of orange juice from the jug that Granny had left for him, he wondered what he was going to do. Alex and Niall were at school and Granny was at work. He thought he might take it easy. He could read a book, listen to the radio and maybe have the odd biscuit or two.

It wasn't long though before he heard something rustling and felt the bedcovers move beneath him. Sitting bolt upright in bed and looking over the top of his book he was surprised to see the mice pop their heads up from underneath the covers.

"How did you get in?" he asked surprised to see them. Ernest explained that they had squeezed themselves under the gap in the back door and had pulled each other up the stairs using their tails as mountaineering ropes.

"Very clever," noted Bill, looking impressed.

A few of the baby mice wanted to come along to wish him well, bringing with them some tumble drier fluff. They thought that Bill might appreciate some extra fluffiness seeing as he was poorly. They'd also found a discarded toffee that had fallen down the back of a chest of drawers in the shed. Before presenting their gift to him they had all given it a lick trying to get the worst of the fluff from it.

He thanked them for their generosity and was happy to accept their gifts, but said he would save the toffee for later, as he wasn't really feeling that hungry.

Bounding over the duvet, Ernest climbed up onto Bill's chest and swung himself into his pyjama pocket.

"Say, this is snug. I could get used to this," said Ernest, testing it out for size. "I'm glad to hear that you're better now," he squeaked. "One of the mice overheard what had happened to you this morning. He said that you're in a bit of a pickle down at the office?"

"It's that Rick Grinder, he's got us working like robots. There's no break from it," he muttered gloomily. Ernest shook his head.

"I've always said there's no point to life if you can't stop to smell the cheese," he said, resting himself on the lip of Bill's pyjama pocket.

"Funny you should mention robots," Ernest smiled, digging around in his fur as if looking for something. He then handed him a piece of paper.

"Here, have a look at this," Ernest grinned.

Unfurling the paper Bill took his time to look at it. Not sure what to make of it, he turned it around and then turned it around again. Looking at it some more, he began to scratch his head.

"Do you think this will work?" he asked studying the plan.

"Course it will," the little mouse replied confidently.

A smile crept across Bill's face.

"You just leave it to me. Give us a couple of days and we'll have it ready," Ernest, looked rather pleased with himself. Swearing him to secrecy, Ernest folded up his plans and tucked them back into his fur.

"In the meantime, you just rest up," he said, bidding him farewell and gathering the rest of the mice together to get on with their secret work.

Chapter 13

THE MOUSE-A-TRON

Kurry

O ver the next couple of days Bill watched with anticipation at the comings and goings of the mice as they made their way to and from the shed. Occasionally Ernest would come to visit Bill, asking his permission to use some of Granny's things. Bill would ask how things were going, but Ernest always remained tight lipped about the project.

Peeking out from behind the curtains he watched as they carried in a plastic funnel, an old fashioned meat grinder, a colander and even Niall's telescope. It didn't stop there. Parading across the yard they dragged with them the entire contents of the glove drawer. Bill's fingerless work gloves, his furry winter ones, a set of yellow washing up gloves, Granny's best white dress gloves, Niall's crocodile mittens and Alex's pink gloves, the one's with the stretch fingers. Even though Bill had seen Ernest's plans he couldn't make head nor tail of it. All he could do was stand there scratching his head.

Next door lived Auntie Joan's dog, Kurry. An Airedale terrier, he was a mass of tan and black curls with two distinct black eyes that peered out from underneath all that fuzz like two lumps of shining coal. Kurry was a likeable dog – once you got to know him – but he didn't take well to strangers. If someone came to call at the house, he would get all out of sorts and start to bark. Auntie Joan would have to be strict with him and put him out in the back yard to calm down.

It just so happened that this morning the repair man had been and, to stop Kurry from nipping at him, Auntie Joan had shoved Kurry out in the yard to behave himself. As he lay there, dozing on the back step Kurry could hear the comings and goings from over the other side of the fence.

There was a lot of banging going on and, struggling to sleep, Kurry let his displeasure be known.

"Keep it down!" he barked, raising one of his bushy eyebrows in disgust. The noise suddenly ceased.

"Ahh… that's better," he sighed to himself, pleased that he had made his voice heard. Placing his head down on his paws to rest, he was just dozing off when the racket began again.

"What the blazes?" he growled, sitting bolt upright with his hackles raised. Letting them know he meant business, Kurry let out a series of sharp barks. "I won't tolerate this. Just who do you think you are?" he snapped furiously. The trouble was that Kurry was not very tolerant. Anytime somebody did something that he didn't like, he got all nippy and unpleasant, just like he did with the repair man.

"I say!" he barked over the fence, infuriated that someone should dare disturb him. "I'm trying to sleep here and, whoever you are, you're making an awful lot of noise," he barked, but there was no reply.

"The cheek of it!" he growled, getting himself all worked up that nobody was listening to him.

Frustrated that no one was paying him any attention, he tore around the yard in a furious manner, growling and whining. Standing on his hind legs he tried to get a glimpse through the fence of what was going on. With one eye closed he did his best to squint through a small, circular hole, but all he could see where various household objects disappearing into the shed. Then, spotting a tiny inch gap at the bottom of the fence, Kurry tried sticking his head through.

"Hello! Hello, I say. Who's there? Can you hear me?" he howled.

Seeing the wet nose of an Airedale poking under the fence, all the mice could do was giggle in response. By now Kurry's desire to know what was going on had got the better of him and he let out a series of long painful howls. All this unwanted racket brought Auntie Joan out to see what was going on.

"What's got into you?" she wanted to know as she stormed out into the yard, mop in hand. By now Kurry had got himself into such a tizz that he was glued to the spot, his nose tipped towards the heavens howling like a banshee.

"Stop that! Stop that at once," Auntie Joan demanded, but Kurry's nosiness had got the better of him.

"What's got into you this morning?" she demanded to know, chasing him away from the fence with her mop, but Kurry was too wound up to listen. Naughtily he bit the head of the mop, shaking it between his teeth furiously. Fed up by his bad behaviour, Auntie Joan grabbed hold off him by the collar and scolded him, telling him off for his unwanted outburst.

All this noise hadn't gone unnoticed. Bill getting out of bed, stuck his head out of the window to find out what all the commotion was about.

"What's going on?" he asked, leaning out of the window to get a better view.

"It's Kurry," she declared. "I don't know what's got into him, but he won't stop barking. He seems to be attracted to something on your side of the fence."

"Ah! That'll be the mice," Bill said.

"Mice?" gasped Auntie Joan in a panic, thinking she would be over run.

"You know the ones I told you about the other week, the ones we saved from the office," he explained trying to put her mind at rest.

"Oh yes. Those mice," she recalled, sounding a little more relieved.

"Well, they're busy working on a secret project for me."

"A secret project?" Joan said sounding impressed.

"Yes. Let me come down and show you," he said, putting on his dressing gown and inviting her to see what the mice were up to.

It had been a few days since the mice had started work on their secret project and it was so hush-hush that even Bill hadn't been allowed to see it.

"If you wait there a minute, I'll go and see if we're allowed to have a look," he said, as he opened the gate between the two properties.

Knocking on the shed door Ernest came out, dressed in a white lab coat, a pair of goggles and carrying some rolled up plans underneath his arm.

"How can I help, Bill?" he asked, making sure the door was closed behind him so they couldn't see in.

"I was wondering if we could possibly have a look at your... err... 'thing'?" he said struggling to find the right words to best describe Ernest's new invention.

"Mmm..." Ernest replied, scratching his whiskers and dusting the sawdust from his shoulders. "It's not really ready yet," he admitted.

"It doesn't matter, we don't mind if it's not finished," Bill said.

Ernest thought about whether of not to let them see his secret contraption, but as Billl had asked nicely, he gave in to his request.

"You'll have to bear with me," Ernest apologised, inviting them to follow him into the shed.

On seeing the mice beavering away, Kurry's natural hunting instinct kicked in and he got all carried away with himself, having to be restrained by Auntie Joan.

"Don't be so naughty," she said, taking hold of him by his collar and pushing his bottom down onto the ground to get him to sit. Ernest looked at Bill as much to say: why did you have to bring him in here? But Ernest recognised something in Kurry that might come in useful later on.

"Are we ready for a demonstration then?" asked Ernest.

Bill and Auntie Joan were presented with a mass of gears, pulleys and levers attached to a wooden framework.

"I give you the Mouse-A-Tron Five Thousand mobile sorting machine" announced Ernest. Bill stared on in wonder.

"Wow, you've really out done yourself. What does it do?" he asked.

"It sorts mail," Ernest replied, as if the name of the machine wasn't obvious enough.

"Can we see it working?" Bill eagerly wanted to know.

"All in good time, all in good time," replied Ernest, motioning with his paws for them to be patient.

"I say, it does look something special," Auntie Joan added as she tried to work out what each individual part did. Aware of their keen interest, Ernest then proceeded to show them the finer points of the Mouse-A-Tron Five Thousand.

The contraption was built around a yard brush, which acted as the central support and on the bottom were roller skates. From there all manner of sorting aids were connected to the main frame. At the very top of the sat Granny's colander, from which the grab arm from Niall's toy excavator had been taken. It then dropped through to the funnel below, which queued up the mail ready for the pulley system which was powered by a mouse wheel.

"Hang on, wait a minute, I recognise that mouse wheel from somewhere," exclaimed Bill. "Isn't that the one from hamster city?"

"The very same," winked Ernest, tapping the side of his nose.

Then from the mouse wheel a selection of gears and levers sprouted so the mice could control how fast the pulley worked. Dotted with pegs, the pulley was a borrowed clothes line and, set equal distances apart, it allowed the pegs to hold each letter individually as it ran through the machine. Next was clever bit.

This was where the mice's sorting knowledge came in. After seeing each letter flash by in front of them, the mice (sitting in chairs taken from Alex's dolls' house) could push a button, and the letter would be plucked off the washing line by a rotating-hand wheel. And from there the letters would be sorted to the correct round. All pretty impressive stuff, eh?

"What can I say?" said Bill lost for words. "Does it work?"

"Does it work?" Ernest laughed shouting over to one of the other mice. "Maurice, select first gear and feed in some letters."

Bill, Joan and Kurry watched open-mouthed as the gadget whirred into motion with a pleasing hum. From a pile of discarded mail, the Mouse-A-Tron grabbed a handful of letters and dropped them into the colander at the top. Even running in first gear, the letters slipped through the system so quickly that they were barely visible to the naked eye. Soon the machine was firing letters out like bullets. Ernest turned to his gathered audience.

"You find the test satisfactory, I presume?" Amazed by its complexity and baffled by its brilliance, Bill stood there in his dressing gown admiring its ingenuity.

"Remarkable, truly remarkable," he gushed with admiration.

"I take from that resounding success that we can put the Mouse-A-Tron into full service, eh?" enquired Ernest, modestly understating his own brilliance. Auntie Joan was so overcome by the display's inventiveness that she needed a sit down.

"I never knew mice were so ingenious," she said, taken aback by the whole demonstration. "But how are you going to get it to the sorting office?"

Ernest had already got that in hand, but right now he wasn't going to disclose his secret.

That evening after a busy day of doing nothing, Kurry was sat on top of the steps watching the moon rise and appreciating the wonder of the universe, when suddenly he heard a scuffling sound. Silently, a small oval shaped dog biscuit slid underneath the gap at the bottom of the fence.

His curiosity aroused, Kurry got up and went over to investigate. Sniffing the biscuit cautiously, he heard a voice call from over the other side of the fence.

"Pssst! There's more where that came from," Now Kurry couldn't see who it was that was doing all the talking, but he wasn't about to start barking down the neighbourhood when there was the possibility of more treats. Kurry put his nose to the fence and gave a good sniff.

"It's me, Ernest," came the tiny voice. squeezing himself under the gap at the bottom of the fence he dusted himself down. Carrying with him another dog biscuit, Ernest looked up to find Kurry towering over him.

"I have a proposition for you," he announced placing the biscuit down in front of the lively Airedale. Kurry was all ears.

"We require your dog walking skills," stated Ernest.

Kurry was puzzled, he didn't know what he meant by dog walking skills. Shaking his head as if to say he didn't understand, he waited for Ernest to explain things further.

"Be here tomorrow night at ten-thirty and bring your lead with you. Oh... and there'll be more biscuits." With that, Ernest disappeared back under the fence leaving Kurry to chomp away on his biscuit. Not exactly sure what it was that Ernest wanted from him, he didn't mind as long as there was a steady supply of biscuits involved.

The following night Kurry made sure he was ready early. Sat on the back step with his lead in his mouth, he waited for a signal from Ernest. At ten-thirty on the dot, a biscuit silently slid under the fence and a voice told him to come through. Leaning on the gate he pushed the handle down with his nose and the gate swung open.

"Down here," came a voice from the darkness, as one of the

mice waved to him to follow him into the shed. Poking his button-like nose round the corner of the door, he found the mice getting the machine ready for its first proper test. Ernest wandered over to greet him.

"Good evening, Kurry," said Ernest. "I see you've brought your lead with you. Well done, lad."

Dropping his lead on the floor and panting with excitement, Kurry enquired what it was that they wanted him to do.

"I'm glad you asked that," said Ernest.

"We require someone to tow the Mouse-A-Tron to the sorting office," he explained."And in order to do so, we must do it in disguise, and this is where you come in."

Kurry listened attentively to what Ernest had to say.

"Our plan is to hide our contraption in plain sight. We will disguise it as human. We'll attach your lead to it and you will be able to pull it along. To any casual passer-by, it will look like a dog being taken out for a walk by its owner. But we will know better!"

Kurry looked at the Mouse-A-Tron and looked back at Ernest. There was no way he thought that thing was ever going to pass for human.

"But it looks nothing like a person," he barked, letting his feelings be known.

"Duly noted," Ernest replied. "Can we have the camouflage team, please?" he called, clicking his tiny paw-like fingers together.

With that, a group of mice came abseiling down from the ceiling on lengths of parcel string. Securing one of Granny's hats and a wig to the colander they applied some lipstick, foundation and false eyelashes that they had borrowed from Granny's cabinet and heaved her best raincoat on to the Mouse-A-Tron with the use of more string.

"It still looks like a heap of junk, but now it's a heap of junk wearing a hat and coat," barked Kurry, belittling Ernest's best efforts.

Undeterred by his canine friend's lack of vision, Ernest called for the lights to be turned off. "There, what do you think?"

To Kurry, in the darkness, half squinting, the Mouse-A-Tron did sort of resemble a person.

"It might work," he said.

"Course it will," replied Ernest enthusiastically. All that was left to do was to secure and tie Kurry's leash to the Mouse-A-Tron and they were ready to go.

Clambering on board, the mice ran through their final pre-walkies check list before giving their thumb's up to Ernest.

"Right, Kurry. Ready when you are," Ernest shouted through a megaphone that he had fashioned from the end of an ice cream wrapper.

Kurry took a few tentative steps forward, taking up the slack in the lead, and the Mouse-A-Tron slowly lurched into life.

"More speed, please," called Ernest. Slowly the Airedale picked up the pace and the Mouse-A-Tron gently rolled up the passageway and out onto the street outside. Hauling himself up to the very top, Ernest directed his four-legged friend from his elevated position on top of Granny's hat.

To any passerby walking along in the darkness not paying attention, Kurry and his mechanical master looked just like any other dog walker out for their evening stroll.

"What if we get spotted?" yelped Kurry nervously.

"Just smile politely and keep on walking," Ernest yelled down from his perch.

Everything was going swimmingly as they made their way towards the office. Negotiating parked cars, they crossed the road and were almost there when they hit a snag. The pub next door was still open!

To avoid being seen, they would to have to cross the road twice, taking up valuable time. Ernest looked down at Kurry.

"Push on, lad," he called out, waving him on with his paw. "We'll take our chances and, if someone spots us, well..." Ernest shrugged. Kurry was doing his best to look like he was enjoying his evening stroll, but secretly he was shaking on the inside. What would they do if someone spotted them, he thought? There was no point worrying now.

Approaching the bright lights of the pub, they thought they had got away with it, when a gentleman came stumbling out onto the pavement almost knocking them over. Kurry gave a sharp warning bark. Staggering to his feet, the drunken man regained his composure and coming face to face with the Mouse-A-Tron, struck up a conversation.

"Hick... Good evening, gorgeous," he said introducing himself, as he leered at the made-up Mouse-A-Tron. Taking hold of its gloved hand, he then kissed it.

"Whatzzzz yer name, my love?" he enquired slurring his words, but there was no reply from the Mouse-A-Tron.

"Ohh woz up...? Is you shy, my dear?" he drooled. Ernest knew they were in big trouble and shouted down to Kurry to run as fast as he could. Not having to be told twice, Kurry broke into a sprint and shot off down the street. In the dash to escape the gloved hand of the Mouse-A-Tron recoiled so hard that it slapped the drunk squarely in the face.

"Serves you right!" Ernest yelled at the man as he clung on for dear life.

Whizzing into the yard at full speed, Kurry pulled tightly on the lead with his teeth, stopping the wayward machine from running away with itself.

"Phew. That was close," sighed Ernest, somewhat dazed. Feeling that it was now safe to come out, the mice who had been sat in the colander left the Mouse-A-Tron by sliding down the belt attached to Granny's coat. When they reached the ground, they found Kurry shaking in fright.

"I thought we'd been rumbled," he whimpered with his knees knocking.

"Me too," replied Ernest, steadying himself against the wheel of a roller skate.

Once they were feeling better, Ernest asked for volunteers to unlock the door to the sorting office.

"Right. We need someone who can squeeze under the door and unlock it from the other side," he said. Three brave mice stepped forward.

"Well done, well done," he congratulated them, patting them on the back. "According to our sources, the traps are all gone and there is no more poison on the premises. But be careful!" he warned.

The three mice pushed themselves under the door, their tails waggling and bottoms wiggling as they pressed themselves flat to the ground. Then with a flash they found the light switch and, after a couple more minutes of awkward clunking, the door opened.

"Marvellous," cried Ernest applauding their efforts. Kurry, sticking his nose in the gap, pushed the door wide open. Towing the Mouse-A-Tron into the office, they set it up in front of one of the sorting frames. Taking off its coat and hat, they revealed the impressive invention in all its glory.

Ernest shouted for everyone to take their places. The mice all crawled into position. One team of extremely fit mice got into the wheel at the bottom ready to power the contraption and the mice who were doing the sorting clambered up the framework into the viewing gallery. While at the top, two mice fired up the grab crane and feeder basket (otherwise known as the colander.)

"Ready when you are!" shouted Ernest as Kurry stood by his side watching. The crane arm dropped down to pick up its first pile of letters and, retracting the grab bucket slowly, it rose upwards with a handful of mail between its jaws.

The pulley system was soon up to speed and, as the letters dropped out of the bottom of the colander, they were picked up by a speeding peg. In the viewing gallery, mice pulled levers and pushed buttons sending letters this way and that. Then the gloved hand of the sorting wheel picked up the appropriate letter and threw it into the correct pigeon-hole on the sorting frame. The whole process only took a matter of seconds from start to finish.

"What do you think, eh? asked Ernest of his curly haired companion.

Kurry let out a howl of admiration.

"Mmm…that's just what I thought," he chuckled, twirling his whiskers with satisfaction. "I think we can increase our sorting rate, eh? Feed in some more letters," Ernest said, shouting up to the mice who were running the crane and grab bucket.

Soon the Mouse-A-Tron was running like clockwork. Even Kurry was helping feed letters into the machine with his mouth, confident that no one would mind a bit of dog drool on their mail.

A few hours later just as they were nearly finishing a red light started to flash accompanied by a loud buzzing sound.

"Quick, shut it down!" ordered one of the mice who knew that a flashing red light is never a good sign.

Making a hideous racket the Mouse-A-Tron came to a grinding halt with a sickening judder. Rushing to see what was wrong with it, the mice were all over it within seconds, testing springs, checking pulleys and measuring tension with their micrometers.

"What's the matter up there?" Ernest called out as he sat on a pile of rubber bands with a well-deserved thimble full of tea. The mice looked blankly back at him as they struggled to get to the bottom of the problem. Pouring over Ernest's blueprints they tried to track down the source of the stoppage. Ernest looked at the clock on the wall. It read a quarter past one. There was no reason to get worried, Rick Grinder wouldn't be in for another few hours. Then one of the mice who was studying the drive system found something.

"Over here," she called. "Look at this." There, jammed between the teeth of the gears, was a lump of tumble drier fluff.

"How did this get here?" asked the mouse as she removed the fluff. From up above, on the inspection gantry, a tiny squeak could be heard.

"Sorry," came the voice of Chloe, one of the baby mice who had hidden herself away to come on this great adventure. "I didn't mean to drop it. I just brought it with me to keep warm," she apologised, trying to make up for her mistake.

"Never mind," noted Ernest. "Send the little monkey down to me." The other mice helped Chloe down off the machine and Ernest looked after her, providing her with an acorn cup of tea and some rolled oats to nibble on, which the mice had borrowed after burrowing into Granny's porridge box.

Satisfied that everything was in working order, they fired up the machine and it purred into life.

"Let's not have any more stoppages, eh? We want to be out of here before Rick Grinder turns up," said Ernest spurring them on. Within the hour the mice had sorted all the mail and were ready to leave. Sliding the hat and the raincoat back on to the Mouse-A-Tron they turned off the lights and quietly slipped out of the back door unnoticed.

Making their way home with Kurry leading the way, they were suddenly stopped in their tracks when a police car pulled up alongside them.

"A bit early for walking your dog, isn't it?" said the officer, winding down his window and addressing the Mouse-A-Tron. Kurry froze and the human imposter jerked to a halt.

"Grrrrreally?" growled Kurry, putting on his best human voice so it sounded like the Mouse-A-Tron was really talking. The officer looked down at his watch.

"I suppose not, eh?" he commented with a shrug of the shoulders. "Are you on your way home?" he asked.

Now although Kurry could make a few words sound human, he definitely couldn't speak human. To have an entire conversation with a person who couldn't speak dog was a whole different matter. Thinking fast he let out a doggy sneeze and taking his cue from Kurry, Ernest had one of the mice pull the hand of the Mouse-A-Tron up to its mouth so it looked like it was the Mouse-A-Tron sneezing and not the dog.

"Bless you," the officer replied. "Sounds like you've got a nasty cold there. Anyway, I shan't keep you any longer I've got villains to catch." Wishing the Mouse-A-Tron a goodnight, he drove off. Ernest poked his head out from underneath the hat.

"Were getting good at this aren't we?" he said. Kurry didn't see the funny side of it and just wanted to go home for a lie down.

When the posties arrived at work the next morning they were overjoyed to see all the mail had been sorted. With not a wrongly sorted letter to be seen anywhere, all the rounds were ready to go out. Everyone was now curious to see what Rick Grinder would say when he came in. They didn't have to wait long to find out.

"Where's the mail? We haven't got any mail!" he shouted when he saw there were no letters to sort. "We've been robbed," he yelled frantically.

Norman, the foreman then politely tapped him on the shoulder.

"I think you'll find it's already been sorted, sir," he said, pointing to the posties who were busy getting their deliveries ready to take out. Rick Grinder was speechless.

"How…what…I mean…what the blazes?" he spluttered, unable to comprehend how the mail had been sorted so fast. Norman smiled sweetly at the Manager, not saying a word about the mice and their marvellous invention.

Rick Grinder knew there was something afoot, but he had no

idea what was going on. These posties are playing with me, he thought.

"Just you wait..." he muttered under his breath as he stormed off to his office to ponder what had just happened.

Chapter 14

WHO'S GOT THE BISCUITS?

Lightning

It had been a couple of weeks since Bill had received his knock on the head. Now that he was feeling much better, he was busy keeping his customers happy as well as making sure that any lost dogs were returned to their owners, and upside-down sheep were turned the right way up.

Upside-down sheep were a well-known hazard out on his round. While nibbling on tender shoots of grass, an over-enthusiastic ewe or ram could get carried away with themselves and roll over on their side. And no matter how hard they tried, they just couldn't get back up.

Bill could never get over how silly they were. Instead of helping each other out, they were quite content to munch away and ignore their floundering companion. So, with their feet thrashing around in the air, it was left to Bill to turn them the right way up.

Back at the office, things were unusually quiet. Rick Grinder hadn't shouted at anyone for at least three days and it was well over a week since he had last thrown a parcel at one of them. The posties thought that it must be one of two things. Either he was sickening for something, or he must have something really mean up his sleeve. As was the case with Rick Grinder, it turned out to be the latter.

Arriving at work one morning, Bill was surprised to find everyone stood outside, huddled together. Bill wondered what was going on.

"What do you think he's up to?" asked Frank.

"Beats me," replied Bill, his breath steaming up in the cold morning air.

Young Russell, who was scared of Rick Grinder, asked Lorraine if he could hold her hand.

"Course you can, love. Come here," she said, putting her arm around his shoulder and giving him a hug. The posties were chatting amongst themselves when Rick Grinder interrupted their conversation.

"SILENCE! We'll have no talking here," he hissed. Afraid of his terrible temper, everyone stared down at the ground not wanting to make eye contact with him. Looking at his watch, Rick Grinder snapped his heels together and began to address the staff.

"Right," he said, with arms folded behind his back and his chest puffed out. "Some of you will be wondering why I have asked you to wait outside this morning" he said.

"It has come to my attention that some of you are carrying dog biscuits with you. We have had a new rule sent down from head office. As from today, it is an offence to feed any dogs. So from now on there will be no more petting dogs. Do I make myself clear?" The posties looked at each other with puzzled looks on their faces.

"What do you mean no more petting of dogs?" Charlie replied with a mystified look on his face.

"You heard me," replied Rick Grinder. "That means no interaction between postal staff and dogs. Is that understood?"

No one said a word. It sounded like a stupid idea and it was clear from the look on everyone's face that they thought so too.

"…and if anyone doesn't understand the policy then I have the rules right here," Rick Grinder pulled the rule book from out of his pocket.

"It states…" he said reading out aloud, "…that if a dog approaches you, you should not engage with it and you should not attempt to deliver to the property. The mail must be brought back to the office. Anyone caught so much as petting a dog will be liable to severe disciplinary procedures."

"Yeah, but you can't stop a dog wanting to sniff your leg, can you?" someone piped up.

"And what about all the dogs at the farms I go to?" asked Bill sounding confused. "I'd have to bring ALL the mail back."

A peel of laughter erupted from the posties at the thought of Bill not being able to deliver any of the mail. This angered Rick Grinder no end.

"You're not here to think, Bill Mathers. You're here to do as you're told," he glowered at him. "Besides… I HATE dogs! I really, really HATE dogs!" he growled as if to emphasise his point. "Dogs are vermin and they should be put down!" he said with a dastardly grin on his face.

Bill shuddered. How could anyone want to harm a dog, he thought?

Rick Grinder continued with his rant. "The flea-ridden balls of fluff do nothing but bite postmen and leave dog mess for people to stand in, the filthy creatures," he said, getting all worked up.

"Let me explain the reason why I have got you all out here this morning. I have reason to believe that certain individuals here are feeding dogs with biscuits and other edible treats."

Bill gulped and looked around nervously.

Scowling at them as if to emphasise the serious nature of the subject, he then reached into his pocket and pulled out an odd-looking piece of equipment.

"This has been sent down to me from head office," he said holding up the object for everyone to see.

"This is the Acme Dog Biscuit Sniffer. It will detect anyone hiding dog biscuits on, or about, their person," he said.

Bill began to feel uneasy as Rick Grinder showed it off to everyone.

The biscuit sniffer was made of plastic and had a pistol grip like that of a toy gun. On top was mounted a moulded dog's head with big flapping ears, a bulbous nose and snarling teeth.

"What this piece of equipment does…" Rick Grinder explained, "…is, with an array of sophisticated electronic sensors mounted in the nose, it can detect even the most minute traces of dog treats or biscuits!" Proudly he showed it off to everyone. "It can even tell if you have come into contact with a dog biscuit in the last twenty-four hours. It doesn't have to be on your person. It's that sensitive," he enthused as he continued to explain the full workings of the Acme Dog Biscuit Sniffer. "You see, when a biscuit is detected, it triggers an alarm, which makes the sniffer's nose flash red. Its ears will also flap up and down and a deep growling sound is emitted as way of an alarm."

Bill knew he was done for. He had with him, tucked in his postie's bag, a brand new box of un-opened doggy treats. The ones with a crunchy shell and the extra–meaty-goodness in the middle that all the dogs went mad for. Bill didn't know what to do. He couldn't get rid of them as Rick Grinder would spot him. His only hope now was that the Acme Dog Biscuit Sniffer wasn't as good as Rick Grinder had made it out to be.

Stood quite a way down the line Bill watched as Rick Grinder slowly made his way along checking for any hidden dog biscuits. Standing in front of each postie he held the device inches away from them and swept their entire body making sure that he hadn't missed any treats.

The first few posties passed the inspection with no problem and then Rick Grinder moved on to Russell.

"I'm not going to find anything unwanted am I?" the manager

asked. Russell shook his head nervously. Then, holding it at arm's length, Rick Grinder proceeded to waft the Biscuit Sniffer over him like a magician waving his wand. Suddenly the device sprang into life. Letting out a fearsome electronic growl the red bulb on its nose flashed red and its ears flapped up and down like a dog with its head stuck out the car window. Poor Russell immediately burst into tears.

"I'm sorry, Mr. Grinder, please don't sack me!" he pleaded, throwing himself at the mercy of manager.

On his knees Russell begged him not to get rid of him and handed over his stash of homemade dog biscuits, the ones that he had made specially in the shape of hearts and bones.

Displeased that he was abusing the no dog biscuit policy, Rick Grinder singled him out and made him stand on his own.

"I'll deal with you later," he said.

Moving down the line, Rick Grinder slowly inched his way closer to Bill and the Biscuit Sniffer went off again. This time it was Tom. Going through the same awful scene, he ordered him to join Russell who was stood on his own.

It was then Bill's turn to be frisked. Knowing full well that there was nothing else to do, he had to come clean. Rick Grinder stood directly in front of him looking him straight in the eye. Just as he was about to run the device over him, Bill stopped him.

"Could you hang on a second please?" he asked, raising his finger and delving into his bag.

"Ah…here we are," declared Bill, rummaging around his bag. Stood to attention, he proudly presented Rick Grinder with a box of un-opened dog biscuits. All Rick Grinder could do was stare open mouthed.

"Would you like one?" asked Bill shaking the box in front of him. Rick Grinder's face turned from spray-tan orange to red.

Snatching the dog biscuits, Rick Grinder threw them on the ground and jumped up and down on them.

"See this?" he shouted. "This is what I think of your dog biscuits!" Everyone looked at each other wondering if Rick Grinder had lost his mind. "Get over there!" he fumed, pointing for him to join the other two. "Just you wait…I'm going to make sure that you pay for this," he said.

As Bill made his way over to join Russell and Tom, the rest of the posties gave him a round of applause for standing up to Rick Grinder.

"Well done, Bill," they cheered. "That's shown him." Even though Bill knew he was going to get into trouble, he didn't mind as he knew he was doing the right thing.

Sat in the manager's office waiting for Rick Grinder to turn up, the three posties wondered what was to become of them. Poor Russell was so worried that he was going to lose his job, he couldn't stop shaking. Bill put his arm around him.

"Don't worry, lad. It'll be alright." he said, trying to reassure him.

"What do you think he's going to do with us, Bill?" Tom asked looking uneasy.

"Well, he's not going to sack us, put it that way," he answered. "Can you imagine trying to sack someone for carrying dog biscuits with them?" he laughed.

Hearing that, Tom looked a little more relieved and the colour returned to his face.

The door swung open and in walked Rick Grinder. Watching him suspiciously the three of them wondered what their fate was going to be.

Without saying a word, he sat down behind his desk and took off his glasses. Leaving them in suspense, he slowly breathed on the lenses. The only sound was that of Russell sobbing.

"Well, gentlemen," he began as he leaned back in his chair enjoying the moment. "It seems to me that you have fallen foul of company policy," he added, shuffling a handful of papers in his hands and placing them down on the table in front of him.

One by one he read through the papers, adding to the already tense atmosphere. Then taking in a deep breath, Rick Grinder spoke.

"Carrying dog biscuits on your person is a serious offence," he said calmly, taking great pleasure in what he was doing. "Are you aware of this?"

The three posties shook their heads in reply.

Pursing his lips and pressing his fingers together, he looked at them, then opened the top drawer of his desk. Reaching down, he brought out a thick, leather-bound, maroon-coloured book.

"This here, gentlemen, is the full, version of the mail carrier's rules and regulations. Has any of you, seen a copy by chance?"

Russell shook his head and Tom replied that he hadn't seen it either.

Rick Grinder opened the book and flicked through, searching for the right page. "Ahh…here we are," he exclaimed, adjusting the spectacles on his nose as he began to read aloud.

"It states under article nine, sub-section four, paragraph three of the revised mail carriers code that it is forbidden for a post person – or post persons – to engage in the nourishment, dispensation or provision of foodstuffs for consumption by any said animal of canine origin." Rick Grinder looked up from the book with a satisfied smile. "I think that is quite self-explanatory, don't you, gentlemen? And I'm sure that none of you are going to argue with me and tell me you weren't carrying dog biscuits with you, are you?" Rick Grinder leaned back in his chair and looked the three postmen.

"Before I spoke to you, I have just been on the phone to the Area Manager. We were debating what action I should take." Rick Grinder then leaned forward in his chair.

"Now for you and you," he said nodding to both Tom and Russell.

"…it was suggested that I give you both a written warning." The pair of them glanced at each other with a sigh of relief.

"However, for you, Mr. Mathers, as you were carrying such a large amount of dog biscuits on you, I have something entirely different in mind."

Flicking through the various bits of paperwork, Rick Grinder got Russell and Tom to sign their names at the bottom of each page and told them that they had to behave themselves in future.

"Right, you two are free to go," he said.

"Thank you, Mr. Grinder," said Russell apologising to him as he left the office. The two posties closed the door behind them, leaving Bill sitting there.

"Well, well, well," gloated Mr. Grinder, revelling in the fact he had got Bill on his own.

"Let me tell you something. Customers aren't bothered about seeing a happy smiling face. They don't want to know your name, and they certainly couldn't care for your so-called kindness," he chuckled away to himself in a repugnant manner. "Anyway, enough of this small talk. We're here to discuss your breach of the rules." Rick Grinder got up out of his chair and walked round his desk.

"To be quite honest, if I had my way, I would get rid of you right now," he stated. "But regretfully, I can't do that. However, for what time you have left here in my employment, I am going to make your life as difficult as possible." Rick Grinder, taking time to enjoy the moment, sat down on the edge of his desk in front of

Bill. "After taking everything into consideration and talking to the Area Manager, I have come to the decision to remove you from your regular delivery and put you on a town round where I can keep a closer eye on you. How's about the Town Hill round? That should do you for size, eh?" he said with a wicked smile.

The Town Hill round was the hardest round in the office and Rick Grinder knew that. It had the most houses, the steepest streets, the most steps to climb and received the most mail. Even the youngest and fittest posties struggled to complete the Town Hill round.

"You'll allow me to say goodbye to the dogs on my round, won't you?" said Grandpa.

"Ha!" laughed Rick Grinder. "I'm afraid not. You'll be starting your new round tomorrow," he smirked, with delight, ushering Grandpa out of his office.

Chapter 15

THE COMPLETE WORKS OF A DOG

Ted

With autumn approaching, the leaves on the trees were beginning to turn and accumulate in large drifts along the sides of the lanes. A sure sign that Christmas was not far away. For Gem at Merrivale Farm there was no let-up in the work. There were always troublesome sheep to round up no matter what time of year.

After coming back from an early morning trip with the farmer on his quad to get the sheep ready for market, Gem decided to take a well-deserved break. Lying in the porch relaxing with not a wayward ewe in sight, she watched as Bill's van bounced up the lane towards the house. Pulling into the farmyard with a flurry of fallen leaves dancing in its wake, Gem got to her paws to welcome him.

"Morning, Bill," she barked loudly, full of the joys of a cold clear autumnal morning. The van came to a halt in front of the old farmhouse and out stepped a young girl. It was Karen who did Bill's round when he was off. Gem thought nothing more of it and, after getting a stroke from Karen, went back to sleep.

The following morning Bill's van came sweeping into the yard and, again, out stepped Karen. Gem was confused. Bill never had two days off in a row, not unless he was sick or on holiday. And if he went on holiday, he always told Gem beforehand.

"Where's Bill?" she barked, but it was useless. Karen, the post lady, didn't speak dog. Trying to look as appealing as she could, Gem playfully dropped her ball at her feet in the hope that she might tell her where Bill was, but no luck. The post lady got back into her van without so much as a by-your-leave. Gem was starting to get concerned. What could have happened to Bill she wondered?

When Karen turned up on the third day, Gem definitely knew that something was wrong. Lying on her back, showing her tummy, she tried her best to distract Karen. Hoping that it would give her owner, the farmer, time to come to come to the door and collect the mail. Then, if the post lady got talking she might reveal what had happened to Bill.

"C'mon you daft dog," Karen teased as she stepped over Gem ignoring her. There was only one thing left for it, Gem would have to give her fiercest bark, like she did when there was an intruder sniffing around the farm.

"Grrrr…woof, woof…woof, woof, woof," she howled, making as much noise as possible.

Now Gem wasn't prone to any unnecessary barking and, the minute the farmer heard her bark like that, Mr. Cranbrook was straight out of the door to see what was going on.

"What's the matter, girl?" he asked, stumbling out of the door and looking around bewildered. "It's only the post lady. What's got into you?" he remarked. "That's not like you," he said, giving Gem a funny look for interrupting his breakfast. But it didn't matter because Gem had engineered the situation perfectly. Immediately Mr Cranbrook, struck up a conversation with the post lady. While Gem sat by his side listening attentively to every word that was being said, she hoped that she might get to hear some news about Bill.

The two of them talked about the weather. The post lady asked how this year's lambs were doing and they chatted at great length as to how their children were getting on, but there was no mention of Bill. Gem was disappointed. Saying goodbye to the farmer the post lady got back in her van and drove off, leaving Gem still none the wiser as to Bill's whereabouts.

She knew it wasn't like Bill to disappear without telling her. There was the possibility that he was sick, but her doggy sixth sense was telling her that it was something more, something was not right. With her nose twitching she knew there was only one thing for it. She was going to have to take to the Barking News to find out.

Desperate to find out what was going on, Gem was eager to climb Signal Hill, but the farmer had a busy afternoon planned for her, grading lambs for market and moving some of the older ewes in off the moors. And not only that, when she had finished with the sheep, there were the children to fetch from school. She would have to wait till later before she could get to the Barking News.

Now the reason Mrs Cranbrook required Gem's presence on the school run was because, as well as being able to keep unruly sheep in order, Gem could also keep excitable children in line.

Pulling up at the school gate, all three of Mrs Cranbrook's children were stood there waiting for her. Piling into the back of the old Land Rover the aged Border collie made a fuss of them all, wagging her tail and giving each of the children a lick on the face as a reward for being such good friends.

On their way home the children played their usual game of catch with Gem in the back of the Land Rover. Tossing her well-chewed ball back and forth between each other, they tried to get her to catch, but for some reason Gem seemed decidedly uninterested.

"What's wrong with Gem?" asked Mrs Cranbrook's eldest daughter, Josie, who noticed the collie's lack of interest. "She doesn't want to play."

"She's not sickening for something, is she?" enquired her mother, who was busy concentrating on driving.

"Maybe she's eaten something?" piped up Charles.

"Mmm…maybe," noted their mother suspiciously.

However, Rachel the youngest knew that it was nothing of the sort. She had just turned seven, but like Bill she too had the magic in her and could hear what dogs were saying. Putting her arm round the collie to comfort her, she leaned in close to listen to what she had to say.

"What's the matter girl?" she asked. Gem gently rubbed her muzzle against the side of her face and let out a series of low-pitched barks that no one else heard.

"Mum…" Rachel called out from in the back.

"Yes love?"

"Gem wants to know what's happened to Bill, the postman."

Letting out a giggle her two elder siblings laughed at her and their mother gave her a strange look from up in the front.

"Is that so?" her mother said, but Rachel could tell from her mother's tone that she didn't believe her.

"It's true!" she protested.

"Don't be silly. Dogs don't talk," her brother teased her.

"Yes, they do!" she answered back, reacting angrily.

"No, they don't!" he laughed, poking fun at her some more.

Sensing that there was trouble brewing, their mother interupted. "Now come on, you lot. Let's not have any falling out in the back there."

With the cautionary warning from their mother. Charles gave up teasing his sister.

"See," smirked Rachel proudly. "Dogs do talk."

Charles pulled a face and shook his head as if mocking her.

As they made their way back home along the twisting lanes, Gem grew agitated and began to bark loudly.

"What's the matter with her now?" asked Mrs Cranbrook straining to see what was going on in the back.

"She wants the window opening," said Rachel, picking up on what Gem was saying.

"Open the window then, eh ,love?" their mother asked Charles.

Begrudgingly doing as he was told, Charles slid the window open and Gem stuck her head out into the oncoming rushing air. Slowing down as they came through one of the many small hamlets Gem spied a Manchester terrier being walked by its owner.

"Hello there," Gem barked. "Do you know Bill the postman?"

The terrier shook its head. "Sorry, our postman is called Don," the terrier replied.

Gem reluctantly sighed. "Oh well, never mind. Thank you for your help."

With the children niggling each other and the dog barking away in the back, Mrs Cranbrook wished she could be home. So putting her foot down, the old Land Rover coughed away as they made rapid progress along the lanes.

At the next village, Gem spotted a pug who was wandering about the village green with his nose to the ground, sniffing out the best smells that an old bench had to offer.

"Excuse me," Gem barked most politely. "Could you tell me, is Bill your postman?"

The pug thought for a moment. "Bill, Bill…," he muttered to himself as he tried to recall who his postman was.

"It is rather urgent that you remember," said Gem, trying to jog the pug's memory as Mrs Cranbrook started to pull away down the road.

Wishing to help, the pug tried to keep up with the Land Rover and chased it through the village. Putting her foot down, Mrs Cranbrook suddenly spotted the pug in her wing mirror running alongside the vehicle.

"I say what's wrong with that dog?" she asked her children, looking to them for an answer. "It seems to be chasing us."

"It's Gem. He wants to talk to her," Rachel told her.

"Really, dear. Dogs don't talk," her mother replied.

Rachel wasn't going to bother arguing. She knew she was right. Finally, as they reached the outskirts of the village, the pug managed to recall the name of his postman before he ran out of breath.

"Frank, it's Frank, the name of my postman," he barked at the disappearing vehicle. Gem, thanking the little pug for his efforts, shook her head disappointedly.

Fed up with getting nowhere, Gem pulled her head back inside the vehicle and lay down next to Rachel on the torn vinyl bench looking all out of sorts.

"I did hope to have heard something about Bill by now," she whimpered, sounding all down in the mouth. Rachel didn't know what to do. There was nothing that she could say that would raise Gem's spirits. All she could do was give her a loving stroke.

When they got home Mrs Cranbrook went round to the back of the Land Rover to open the door for the children. As she did, Gem sprang from the door, racing off without telling them where she was going, such was her desire to know what had happened to Bill.

"Well, what's got into her?" Mrs Cranbrook exclaimed, watching Gem dart across the farmyard and leap over the wall into the neighbouring field.

Gem had only got one thing on her mind. Racing to the top of Signal Hill, she let out a bark that rang through the dry valleys of the combes and across the heather clad moorland in the hope that her message would reach the small town of Berrycombe St Martin.

"Calling all dogs," she howled. "Does anybody know the whereabouts of Bill the postman? I'm desperate to hear how he is."

Three farms away Ted, an Australian shepherd dog, replied. Despite being named an Australian shepherd dog, Ted had never been further than the local cattle market, never mind Australia.

"Woz' be going on, mi' lover?" Ted answered in his best West Country accent.

"It's Bill, the postman," she replied. "I'm worried about him. I haven't seen him for the last three days and I think something's wrong. I would be most appreciative if someone could help me find out how he is."

"Funny," Said Ted, his bark echoing back through the Combes. "Now you come to mention it, I thought I hadn't had my usual biscuit when the post came this morning. Now don't you go worrying about a little thing like that. I'll make sure that the message gets passed on and I'm sure we'll have a reply in no time, eh. How about that?" Ted could always be relied on to help out and his comforting words eased Gem's worried mind.

That evening Gem could not settle. Pacing back and forth in front of the fire the logs popped and crackled as everyone sat around watching TV.

"What's wrong with that dog tonight?" Mr Cranbrook demanded to know, shaking his head disapprovingly. "She's done nothing but skulk around the house all evening and get under my feet!" he added, shovelling another biscuit into his mouth and making loud slurping noises as he drank his tea.

"Really dear?" countered his wife with displeasure in her voice.

"I know. It's off-putting, isn't it?" Mr Cranbrook answered back, thinking that his wife was referring to the dog's behaviour.

"No, I'm on about you," said his wife poking him in the ribs. "Do you have to make such a disgusting sound when you drink your tea?"

Mr Cranbrook looked aghast that his wife should say such a thing. "I don't make noises when I drink," he protested, looking most indignant that he should be accused of such a thing.

Josie, their eldest daughter, looked up from her book that she was reading. "Yes, you do, Dad. You sound like a pig," she stated, before turning her attention back to her book. Charles and Rachel laughed at their sister's comments.

Feeling hurt by what his family had said, Mr Cranbrook sat there on the sofa nursing his tea, afraid to take a drink on account of what they might say. Conscious of his own behaviour, he only took a sip when he thought his family weren't watching, and even then, he stuck his little pinkie finger out just to over-compensate.

All this worrying was doing Gem no good. Having nearly worn the carpet through with all her pacing, she poked her nose through the gap in the curtains. Stood on her hind legs, she looked out of the window, but there was little to be seen against the darkness of the night sky. Expectantly she thought she might hear something, some news of Bill, but the only sound was that of the cattle bedding down for the night and the lonely clang of a gate banging against a post in the wind.

It was getting late and the children had gone to bed. After watching the weather forecast for the day ahead as all farmers do, Mr Cranbrook switched the TV off. Making sure the house was all locked up, he put Gem out for the night. Her main job at night time was to keep watch over the farm and see off any intruders. If any wrong-uns wandered in, looking to steal something, she would sound the alarm by barking as loud as she could to wake Mr Cranbrook.

Usually she slept in the warmth of the hayloft above the old barn on big soft bundles of straw, but tonight, because she wanted to keep an ear open for any news of Bill, she chose to sleep out in the cold of the open tractor shed. There wasn't much in the way of comfort amongst the tangle of machinery. With no doors to stop the wind from blowing in, Gem bedded down on some old plastic feed sacks. It wasn't pleasant, but it was all she had and it would have to do.

As much as she wanted to stay awake, it was impossible. Fighting to keep her eyes open, she soon found herself drifting off and, as the night wore on, the weather closed in and a fine drizzle blew in off the hills. Waking up in the dark, she found herself covered in a damp blanket of moisture. Her coat all stuck together, tangled and smelling like week old washing, she wished for morning to arrive, but daylight was still hours away. With nothing heard, there was only one thing for it and that was to go back to sleep.

Morning arrived quietly at Merrivale Farm. Low cloud shrouded the house and outbuildings in a thick, oppressive atmosphere and the grey brooding skies, heavy with rain, stifled even the slightest of sounds. Around the farm everything was wet and damp. Rusty bits of machinery dripped with the constant exposure to the damp air, and the overgrown tufts of grass that poked up in sporadic clumps lacked life and vigour as their energy retreated back into the earth. Such was the ebb and flow of the seasons.

Gem rose stiffly from her bed, her old rheumatic bones suffering in the damp conditions. There was no point her climbing Signal Hill this morning. All communications would be suspended in such bad weather. Staggering across the farmyard to the house, Mr Cranbrook opened the front door and let her in. As she made her way into the kitchen he looked at her with a dubious expression.

"I hope you've calmed down after last night's carry on?" he said, airing his disapproval at the dogs behaviour of the previous evening. Gem was far too tired to answer after her night in the tractor shed. Besides, she did not have the energy or desire to be wandering off anywhere else. With the scent of bacon on the grill and a bowl of food, Gem was quite happy to rest in the warmth of the kitchen for a while.

Mr Cranbrook, like all farmers, was awake before the rest of his family, having all sorts of things to attend to on the farm, like fences that needed mending, sheep that needed feeding and cattle that needed mucking out. It was up to Gem to join him on his morning chores.

No sooner had she closed her eyes than Mr Cranbrook was cajoling her to join him out on the rounds. As unwilling as her old body was, she forced herself to jump onto the back of his quad. Speeding along the lanes, the constant drizzle robbed her of what heat she had and soon she was shaking. But like all hardy collies, she knew that it wouldn't last long. In a minute or two she would be off chasing sheep around the field, and she would soon warm up again.

Jumping off his bike, Mr Cranbrook hoisted a feed sack onto his shoulder and poured it out in a long line across the field. The sheep gathered round him. Gem chose to stay put. She was far too tired to join him. Resting on the back of the bike, she thought she heard something over the idling of the engine. Pricking up her ears, her head darting this way and that, she tried to make out where the noise was coming from.

Above the constant puttering of the bike's engine, she could swear she could hear a dog barking somewhere off in the distance. Leaping off the bike, she wandered over to the far side of the field away from all the noise and listened carefully. In the distance, she could hear the faintest of yelps. It was Holly the Pup!

"Hello, Pup, it's Gem," she barked back excitedly. "Have you got any news for me?"

From the cottages down the lane, Holly's tiny yelp came bouncing back. "Yes. Apparently, a bulldog by the name of Pugsley has replied to your message," Holly responded, telling her what she knew.

"And…" Gem snapped back, eager to know more.

"It's not good I'm afraid. Bill's been taken off the round."

"What do you mean, he's been taken off the round?" she answered, her ears all pointy and her nose twitching.

"It seems the new manager found him carrying dog biscuits and, as a punishment, has put him on a town walk."

"What? You mean he's delivering on foot?" Gem replied, sounding all puzzled.

"Yes."

"All because he was carrying dog biscuits with him?" she added, unable to believe that humans could be so mean.

"Yes," Holly barked back, frustrated with all the questioning.

"Well, when's he coming back?"

"No one knows," Holly yelped. "According to Pugsley, the bulldog, it could be a permanent thing."

Gem was horrified to hear such news. The thought suddenly passed through her mind that she might never see her friend ever again, and her heart sank.

"We can't have this! We've got to do something about it!" she growled angrily.

"Like what?" Holly answered back, wanting to know more.

"I don't know. I'll think of something though."

Just then Mr Cranbrook interrupted their conversation with a shrill whistle and beckoned for Gem to join him by his side. Gem thanked Holly the Pup for her news, and obediently returned to her master's side as they set off to check on yet more sheep.

Gem's mind wasn't on rounding up sheep that morning. She had bigger things to worry about. The sheep, clearly recognising that something was wrong, could tell she wasn't her normal self. Usually she was snapping at their heels and making them pick up the pace as they moved from field to field, but this morning she was content to let them wander aimlessly.

At lunchtime, while Mr Cranbrook went inside to tuck into the leftovers from last night's dinner, Gem took herself off to the hay-loft to think. How could she get Bill back? she wondered. While she was lying there wondering how she was going to do it, suddenly she had a brainwave. I know, she thought, I'll start a petition! Excited by her new idea, she bounded down the steps of the barn and out into the farmyard.

"Ted, Ted!" She barked trying to get the attention of the Aussie shepherd dog, who was busy having his afternoon nap. Over the years, Ted had grown bored of rounding up sheep and thought the whole sheep-herding thing was a bit overrated. Preferring to sleep rather than to chase energetic ewes about, he left it to Barney, a young collie with a bit more life in him, to take over duties.

"What be happening, my handsome?" Ted blearily answered back with a yawn.

"Have you heard the news about Bill?"

"I'm aware he'z been taken off the round, yezzz," stated Ted, lazily drawing out his words and wishing he could go back to sleep.

"Well, I'm going to get him reinstated, do you hear!"

"Just how do you plan on going about that, then?" came his response, while being side-tracked by a fly landing on his nose.

"I'm going to get a petition going," Gem answered back, all pleased with herself for coming up with the idea.

"A petition!" scoffed Ted, never having heard of a dog do such a thing. "Who's going to write it, you?" he chuckled.

"Yes!" replied Gem indignantly.

"Just in case you didn't know, us dogs can't write," he barked back, as if stating the obvious.

By now the fly had got the better of him and was taunting Ted at will. Getting to his feet, the unhurried hound snapped at the thin air as he tried to catch the annoying fly with his mouth.

Gem wasn't going to be put off by Ted's less than enthusiastic comments, but it wasn't till after their conversation that she wondered just how she was going to go about doing this. She had never written before and looking at her paws she saw she had no thumbs, which would make holding a pen impossible. Maybe I could hold the pen with my mouth? she thought.

Trotting back inside, Gem rooted around the hallway looking for something to write with. There, underneath the phone table, she found a pen, and picking it up between her teeth, she hunted around for some paper to write on.

Stacked at the side of the table were a pile of old newspapers belonging to Mr Cranbrook. He kept them so he could study the form of race horses and place bets over the phone. However, Mrs

Cranbrook did not know about his little secret and, if she ever found out, she would be furious that he was squandering their hard-earned money on useless old nags. Gem, knowing that he kept some spare paper between the pages of the newspapers for his racing notes was sure she would find some there. Ever so gently with her nose, she pushed the stack of newspapers over and there, hidden amongst everything, was a blank sheet of paper.

Concentrating as hard as she could, she took the pen in her mouth. Tilting her head to one side, she began to move the pen slowly over the paper. At first the paper slipped about underneath her and she had to hold it still with her paw, but after a while she got the hang of it and started to make shapes and lines on the page. Gem stood back to inspect her efforts and looked at her first attempts at writing. She was very impressed with what she had done, but somehow it didn't quite resemble what humans called writing.

Just then Mr Cranbrook casually walked in to make one of his secret phone calls to the bookmakers and found the newspapers scattered on the floor. With the pen in her mouth, Gem stood there looking guilty.

"Who's made all this mess!" he demanded to know, grabbing hold of the piece of paper that Gem had her paw on. Studying it hard he saw that it was covered in all sorts of funny marks, like a child's painting. He looked at it and then back at the dog astounded.

"It can't be…!" he exclaimed clutching his head in his hands. "What's wrong with my dog?" He cried out looking heavenward for an answer.

"Why can't I just have a normal dog that rounds up sheep?" The farmer said, kicking the newspapers as they shot up in the air. Gem thought Mr Cranbrook was blowing this out of all proportion. She was sure that there would be plenty of nice people out there who would love to have an articulate dog as a pet, but obviously not Mr Cranbrook. Realising that she would have to wait till later to write her petition, she scurried off outside leaving Mr Cranbrook to calm down.

That evening after dinner Gem padded upstairs and poked her nose round the gap of Rachel's bedroom door. Pushing the door ajar with her nose, she wandered in and laid down on her tummy next to Rachel who was busy colouring in. Rachel could see Gem was looking down and cocking her head to one side, she asked her what the matter was.

"I was trying to write a petition," Gem replied glumly.

"A petition, what for?" Rachel wanted to know.

"You know Bill, the postman? The one that delivers here?"

Rachel nodded.

"Well, he's been taken off the round and moved to one in the town."

"Why have they done that?" she asked.

"It seems they've got a new manager who hates dogs and they found Bill carrying dog biscuits. Apparently, it's a new rule that you can't feed dogs anymore."

Not liking what she heard, Rachel screwed up her face.

"Sounds like a rubbish rule to me," she said, agreeing with Gem. "I tell you what. I'll help you write your petition."

Gem's face lit up and her ears stood on end. "Would you?" she begged, her tongue sticking out of the side of her mouth excitedly. "That would be brilliant, because I'm not very good at writing yet. I tried earlier, but Dad got all mad with me," Gem admitted.

"Don't worry." Rachel added. "I've just learned to write joined up at school."

Gem gave a jubilant bark. "Well, what are we waiting for, then?" Gem rushed over to the printer and pulled out a wad of paper with her mouth. Her tail wagging, she placed it down in front of Rachel and they set about writing Gem's petition.

Chapter 16

WHO'D HAVE THOUGHT...

Mauler

The following morning Gem stood at the front door with the petition in her mouth. Saying her goodbyes, she told Rachel not to worry and that she would be gone for a few of days. Hoping that Mr Cranbrook would not to be too cross for leaving him with all the sheep and cows to look after. Eager to get going, she started out across the farm yard when Rachel called her back.

"Gem, wait. Don't go. At least not without something to eat." Rachel rushed back inside the house and came out holding a little package. "Here, I've got something for you," she said, presenting Gem with a couple of pork chops wrapped in greaseproof paper. Gem thanked her but wasn't sure how she was going to carry them, since she was already holding the petition in her mouth. Rachel realising this then disappeared inside once more and this time she came out carrying her school satchel.

"Here, you can have this," she said, emptying out the contents and instructing Gem to put her paws through the straps. Doing as she was told, she stepped into the loops and Rachel tightened them up, making sure the bag was secure. Tucking the petition and chops inside for safe keeping, she gave Gem a final cuddle.

"Take care. Good luck," she said, wishing her friend all the best for the trip. Gem returned the sentiments, giving a paw and an excited bark before making her way across the rutted farmyard and jumping the wall of the adjoining field.

She had a long journey ahead of her. Gem knew that Bill's round stretched further than the horizon and then some. It was going to take her a couple of days to cover all the farms and cottages that he delivered to, but she was determined to get all the dogs on the round to sign her petition.

It didn't take long for her to bump into her first dog. Laid out, fast asleep, at the bottom of the lane in amongst the weeds and milk crates was Ted. Gem gave him a gentle bark so as not to startle him. Bleary-eyed, he looked up from his bed in the bottom of the hedgerow and yawned.

"Gem, what are you doing here?" he said with a look of surprise.

"I've come to get your signature on my petition."

"You've come to do what?" he muttered, licking his nose with his tongue and trying wake himself up.

"I've come to get your signature,"

Ted shook his head in disbelief. "You've written a petition?" he said, sounding all flabbergasted.

"Yes," sighed Gem, who was getting a little frustrated by Ted's lack of belief.

Technically she hadn't written the petition, but she didn't have time to explain to him that her human friend had done it on her behalf. Diving into her knapsack to retrieve it, she pulled it out with her teeth.

"Here, seeing as you're the first dog I've bumped into, you can have the honour of being the first to sign it,"

Ted looked amazed. "I don't believe it! I knew you were a smart dog, but this? This takes some beating."

Gem didn't have time to waste and, knowing that she had lots of other farms and cottages to visit, she hurried him along.

"Come on Ted, I need you to put your paw print on this," she said, unravelling the petition and laying it flat on the ground.

"What do you mean?" asked Ted.

"I mean, get some dirt on your paw and stand on it, like this," she said demonstrating to Ted what she wanted him to do. Doing as he was told, he dabbed his paw in some muck and made his mark on the clean, white sheet of paper.

"There!" he declared, taking a step back in order to admire his work. "I've got to hand it to you, girl. You've certainly done an handsome job," he barked, full of admiration for Gem.

"I'd be first to admit I didn't think you were going to do it, but I take it all back. I'll get on the Barking News straight away and let every dog between here and Highampton know that you'll be coming," he added, puffing up his chest with importance knowing that he had a job to do.

"Don't you worry, old girl. I'll make sure there'll be board and lodgings wherever you need them. No door shall be closed to you," he assured her.

Slipping the petition into her bag, Gem gave him her best doggy smile and, rubbing noses, bid him farewell. As she trotted off down the lane, Ted shouted after her, "I'll let everyone know you're coming. Take care, mi' lover!"

Gem returned a cheery bark and a sharp wag of the tail before finally disappearing round the bend in the lane.

The weather was on her side. The scattered cloud provided enough cover to make the going easy and a light breeze blew in from the sea, keeping her cool under all that fur. On her travels she encountered all manner of obstacles. She found herself fording streams, climbing steep-sided combes and negotiating her way through thickly covered undergrowth. But there was also time to enjoy herself too. She chased butterflies through the meadows while the tall grass tickled her nose. And from time to time she stopped to take a rest in the shade of an old wall, as well as hitching rides on passing pick-ups with other farm dogs.

Her adventures gave her opportunity to finally meet the dogs that she knew by name only from the Barking News. At one house, she bumped into Pipin, a black and white spaniel.

"From the sound of your bark and the way it carries on the wind I thought you were going to be a springer or a clumber." Pipin was flattered by Gem's comments that she thought he was much bigger than he actually was.

"I'm afraid I'm only a regular cocker spaniel," he confessed.

"There's nothing wrong with being JUST a regular cocker spaniel," Gem told him. "There's many great cockers that's helped the police sniff out all sorts of naughty things," Gem told her, making the little cocker feel better about himself.

"I suppose you'd like me to sign your petition?" smiled Pipin, wagging his tail with his new-found confidence. Surprised that he knew about her petition, Gem asked him where he had got his information.

"Ted let me know about half an hour ago that you'd be on your way. It's a real shame about Bill being taken off the round, isn't it?" said Pipin.

Pipin

While the black and white spaniel signed the petition, her owner who had been watching the two dogs from out of the window stumbled up the path towards them.

"I say, Pipin, what are you doing?" asked his bemused looking owner, who wanted to know what was going on.

Pipin looked over at Gem. "Don't worry, she can't understand a word of dog, but she is a very sweet old lady all the same."

Gem pushed the petition towards the friendly old lady with her nose.

"Well what do we have here?" she said, picking the petition up out of the dirt. Squinting as she tried to make out the words, she did her best to read it, although her eyesight was rather poor.

"We the undersigned…," she said, reading aloud and tracing the words on the page with her finger. "…request that Bill, being such a kind and thoughtful postman… and friend to all dogs be put back on his old round." She peered over the top of the petition to look at the two dogs.

"What a noble cause," she said, noticing the smudged paw prints at the bottom of the page.

"Ohh look, Pipin…you've done a fine job of signing it," she said, admiring Pipin's paw mark. "I must say, I do miss Bill, too. What a terribly nice chap he is," she noted. "And all those biscuits he gives you, eh?" she said giving Pipin a wink.

"I tell you what, let me get my pen." And with that the white-haired old lady toddled off inside, coming back having signed the petition. Gem was rather pleased with herself that she had got her first human signature.

"I think what you're doing is wonderful. Tell me what's your name?" the old lady asked.

Gem barked out her name aloud, but, knowing that the old lady couldn't speak a word of dog, she wouldn't be able to understand.

"How sweet!" The lady applauded politely, pretending to know what she was saying. "Here, I've got a little something for you." Rummaging around in her cardigan pocket, she brought out a sausage roll.

"I was going to have this for my tea, but seeing as you've got a long way to go, I think it would be better if you have it instead." The old lady bent down and slipped it into Gem's satchel for her.

"That's for when you get hungry," she said, giving her a fond wink and patting the bag.

Gem travelled all day collecting signatures. When she got to the next farm or house, a dog would be sat outside waiting for her with their paw ready to stamp Gem's petition.

"Good old Ted!" barked Gem, knowing that he had been busy spreading the word. The news about Gem's petition had travelled far and wide, and it wasn't just the dogs who wanted to sign it, but their owners too.

"It's wrong what they've done to Bill!" one farmer exclaimed.

"They should reinstate him immediately," another said.

"Why would they want to do such a thing to a person as kind as Bill?" one farmer's wife added. Page after page was filled with doggy paw prints and human signatures. Gem never thought that her petition was going to do this well.

At the next farm, all was quiet. A tall stand of sycamores cast shadows down on the high stone wall that encircled the property, and in the yard rusted cars lay abandoned with weeds growing out of them. Gem paused, unsure as to whether to go any further. There was a strange stillness about the farm that told her doggy senses that something wasn't quite right.

"Hello?" Barked Gem cautiously, but there was no response. Tentatively she made her way towards the property. The drive was made of hard packed earth and under the trees grew a profusion of garlic, its pungent scent hanging heavy in the air.

Built of chiseled stone, the large windows were shuttered to the daylight by heavy curtains that made the house look even more un-inviting than it already was. Gem approached the house cautiously and, as she turned the corner, she was suddenly bowled over and knocked off her feet by something unseen.

"RUFF, RUFF, RUFF," came the frenzied bark, as she felt a

sharp pain in her leg. Gem recoiled and using her speed put some distance between her and her attacker.

Turning around to look, she found an angry rottweiler pulling at his chain and baring his teeth. Gem looked down at her front paw. She had been bitten! The black fur on her leg was matted from the blood that was trickling down her shin, turning the white fur on her paw red.

Gem, not having the time to tend to the wound, was instinctively on her guard in case she was attacked again. Straining on his chain, the large dog let out a series of threatening barks, with saliva spitting from his mouth.

"Can't you read? Are you blind?" He shouted, pointing his snub round snout at a faded sign that hung from the gate post. "It says no trespassing, private property!"

"Sorry, I didn't see." Gem apologised. "I've just come to…"

Without having time to explain herself, the angry rottweiler interrupted her.

"I don't care what you've just come for," glared the rottweiler, his veins bulging in his neck as his collar pulled tight around his throat.

"Get out of here. This is my yard!" he yelled.

With her tail between her legs, Gem turned around and limped back towards the gate, when suddenly she felt the urge to confront the hateful dog.

As she turned around and hobbled back to the farmhouse, Gem was spotted by the irate dog. Running down the drive, charging towards her, the rottweiler bared its teeth.

"What do you want? I've told you before!" he growled furiously, about to pounce on her. When all of a sudden, the lumbering dog reached the end of his chain and found himself abruptly brought to a halt.

"Nrrrrrrrff," was the noise the rottweiler made as the chain pulled tight around his neck. Finding himself flat on his back, staring up at the sky, Gem stood over him.

"Are you alright?" she asked.

"Do I look like I'm alright?" the rottweiler growled grumpily, his collar almost choking him.

"There's no need to be like that," said Gem, looking concerned for the upturned dog. "Do you need a paw?" she asked.

All the stunned dog could do was groan in response.

"Here, let me help," Gem offered.

"I'm alright!" the short-tempered rottweiler barked back.

"You don't look very well," she replied, watching him gasp for breath. "I could undo your collar with my teeth, but you'll have to promise not to bite me." The rottie thought about this for a minute. Not having much of a choice, he agreed to Gem's terms.

Reaching around the back of him she nimbly unbuckled the collar with her teeth and he shook himself free. The lumbering dog got to his feet.

"Hmmmpff," he groaned sounding most displeased.

"What's the matter? I thought you'd be happy to be off your chain," stated Gem.

"It's my job, I'm supposed to be angry," he roared.

"Who told you that?" Gem asked feeling the full force of his resentment.

"My owner."

"Your owner?" she exclaimed in disbelief. "Well, frankly, he doesn't know what he's talking about. Don't you know that a dog's main aim in life is to be happy and make humans happy? It's an unwritten doggy rule."

As she spoke to him, Gem noticed a patch of rather sore skin around his neck where his collar had been digging in.

"That looks painful," remarked Gem, inspecting the wound.

"What does!" he snapped back sharply.

"That horrible scar around your neck."

The rottie wandered over to one of the old wrecked cars that was lying about and, standing on his hind legs, examined himself in the cracked wing mirror.

"Oww," he squealed, shocked to see his injuries. Then, a tear welled up in his eye.

"Don't worry," barked Gem, trying to comfort him. "We'll get you sorted out. Isn't there something inside that we can put on it, like antiseptic?" she said thoughtfully.

The rottweiler nodded, but, unable to hold back the emotion, a flood of tears came running down his face. Gem tried to cheer him up with a reassuring lick and a sniff of her nose, but he was too upset even for that. Instead she followed him over to the house.

Still blubbing the rottie pushed the front door open with his nose and invited Gem inside. The house was dark, apart from a small chink of light coming from a gap in between the curtains.

"Let's have some light in here," Gem declared, tugging at one of the moth-eaten curtains. Pulling on the faded old material, the curtain pole suddenly gave way and came crashing down sending a billowing cloud of dust up into the air. All around, light flooded into the room revealing the true state of the house.

Everywhere there were unwashed pots and pans, old newspapers piled up on tables and scattered across the floor, were a whole raft of unopened letters.

"Doesn't your human tidy up?" asked Gem looking at all the mess. The sad looking rottweiler shook his head.

"Never mind," smiled Gem. "Let's get you cleaned up."

The fearsome attitude of the angry rottie had disappeared and now he looked at her with sad-puppy-dog eyes.

"I'm sorry, I didn't mean to bite you," he whimpered. "It's just all I've known since I was born, is how to bite people," he blubbed, sounding sorry for himself.

"Let's not worry about that now, eh?" Gem replied. "Besides, I don't even know your name. Mine's Gem," she said, introducing herself.

"I'm Mauler," he replied.

Gem raised her eyebrow. "Really, that's quite a name, isn't it?"

"I know, I don't like it either. My owner gave it to me," sensing Gem's surprise at hearing such a menacing name.

"Where is your owner, by the way?" Gem enquired, looking round the deserted kitchen.

"He's out working. He steals cars to make money."

"That's no way to make a living," Gem frowned.

"That's why he makes me scare people away. All the cars outside are stolen and he doesn't want anyone to know."

Gem felt sorry for Mauler. She could see by the condition of his coat that he wasn't very well looked after or cared for.

"And he beats me with a stick," he added. When Gem heard that she could feel her blood beginning to boil, but there was no use in getting angry, as it didn't make things any better.

Rooting around in one of the cupboards, she came across a tin with a red cross on and pulled it out into the centre of the floor where she could see better.

"Here we are. Let's see if we can find something in here to put on that wound."

With her mouth she removed an old rolled up tube of antiseptic from the tin and, holding it firmly on the floor with her paw, she used her sharp pointy teeth to twist the cap off. Standing on the tube she placed all her weight on her paw and, slowly, the strong-smelling pink cream flowed from the tube. Catching it on the end of her nose, she rubbed the antiseptic into the wound that had cut deep into Mauler's skin.

Mauler cried out and let out a whimper. "It hurts," he winced.

"Don't worry, it will soon be better," Gem said, trying to soothe him.

"What about you though?" he asked looking at the cut on her leg where he had bitten her.

"I'll get round to that in a minute. Let's get you sorted out first," she said, doing her best to comfort him. While she tended to his injuries, Mauler asked her a question.

"Gem…," he uttered tentatively.

"Yes?" she replied.

"Can I come with you? It doesn't matter where you're going. It's just I don't want to live here anymore."

Gem thought about it for a second, about all the complications of where Mauler would live. She knew there was no way she could leave him there, in the hands of someone who beat him.

"Alright," Gem answered. "but first we'll have to get ourselves sorted out here."

Mauler was over the moon that Gem said he could join her. It didn't matter that he didn't know where he was going to be living tonight. He was just glad that he was not going to have to live with his mean-spirited owner anymore.

Gem put a bandage around Mauler's neck and got him to hold one end while she tied a knot in the other with her teeth. Then she dabbed some antiseptic on her own leg. Mauler laughed at Gem.

"You've got a pink nose!" he giggled.

Gem looked at her reflection in the tin lid. "So I have!" she remarked, doing her best to rub off the antiseptic on an old towel that hung from the back of a chair.

"I've been wondering," said Mauler. "Why are you carrying a bag?"

"It's a long story," she told him. "And I haven't really got time to explain. Right now we need to get out of here."

They had a long journey ahead of them and Gem didn't want to waste anymore time, just in case Mauler's spiteful owner turned up. This got her thinking. Looking at her knapsack, she wondered if she had enough food for the both of them. Mauler was a big dog, and she was sure that the pork chops and sausage roll were not going to be enough to keep them from both going hungry.

"What's in the fridge?" she asked.

Mauler nosed the door open and inside was a gone-off bottle of milk and a half-eaten block of cheese covered in mould. Gem turned her nose up at the contents.

"Looks like we'll have to try our luck elsewhere," she said, letting out a low moan.

Time was getting on and Gem knew that they would have to leave soon in order to find shelter for the night.

"Are you ready?" she asked. Mauler looked nervous.

"What's the matter?" she enquired, seeing Mauler's knees beginning to knock together.

"I…I…I've never been out of the yard," he stammered.

Gem smiled sweetly at him. "What, never?" she remarked sounding amazed. "There's nothing to worry about, trust me," she said, trying to calm his fears. "It's an amazing world out there. There's nothing to worry about."

Winking, she pulled open the front door with her paw. Mauler hesitantly made his way down the steps behind her. When they got to the top of the drive, Mauler stopped.

"What's the matter?" Gem asked.

"I'm scared," he whimpered. Gem turned around and sat down next to him.

"I know it's scary for you, but there is so much beauty out there," she told him as she described the flowers that grew in the hedgerows, the animals that lived in the countryside, as well as all the amazing people there were in the world. She told him about her home and where she lived, promising him that she would find him a home as good as hers. When Mauler heard about Gem's family, he too wished he could experience the same love that she was describing. All this talk was just what he needed. It gave him the courage to turn his back on the old farmhouse and make a new start.

With new-found determination, Mauler trotted along behind Gem even though he still felt a little bit shaky on his legs. As they made their way through the fields Gem explained to him that she was getting all the dogs and humans to sign her petition to reinstate the postman.

"What? A postman?" Mauler barked sounding surprised. "But aren't dogs supposed to hate postmen?"

Gem laughed at his inexperience of the world. "That's a lie perpetuated by humans. Bill's a really nice man. He brings us biscuits and he can talk dog too."

"What, he can hear what we're saying?" replied Mauler sounding amazed.

"Yes, you see, people who are kind, and have lots of love inside of them, have all sorts of amazing abilities."

Mauler had never heard of this before and, although it sounded bizarre, he trusted what Gem was saying.

Stopping off along the way, Gem picked up some more signatures for her petition. Everybody wanted to meet Gem and make a fuss of her and Mauler too. Mauler had never been stroked before and loved the feeling of a warm, caring hand running over his shiny coat. He was so happy, being stroked, that he thought if he was a cat he could quite happily purr right now.

Every where they went people lavished gifts on them, sausages, chews, pork pies, everything that Gem liked. She tucked them in her bag for later, and with her new-found friend they crisscrossed the parish boundaries, collecting more paw prints and signatures. At one church they took a drink from the font while there was a service on, and at the village hall, they sneaked into a Women's Institute meeting to 'borrow' a couple of slices of cake that were sat looking neglected.

It had been a long day and Gem was feeling tired. Looking over at Mauler, she could see he was shattered. Mauler had never travelled that distance before in his life and looked like he could fall asleep right there on the spot. Looking around for somewhere to sleep they found a stable with a horse who had its head sticking out of the open door.

"Good evening," said Gem, introducing themselves to the

chestnut coloured mare. The horse whinnied in response, blowing a raspberry and tossing its mane in the air.

"My friend and I were wondering if we could possibly spend the night in your lovely warm stable?" The horse looked at them both.

"Aren't you the dog that's trying to get the postman his job back?" The mare enquired.

Gem nodded, staring up at the tall animal.

"I heard from my owner's dog that you might be coming this way," said the horse, flaring its nostrils and pulling back its gum to give a smile. "I would be honoured to have your company for the night. My name's Primrose, by the way."

With a loud thud the lower half of the stable door flew open as the mare kicked it hard with her hoof. Mauler and Gem scampered inside.

Primrose, Gem & Mauler

"Here you are. There's some fresh straw for you to lie on," she said, clearing a neat little space for them. The two dogs laid down on the soft warm hay and Gem unpacked her bag of goodies.

"I'm not sure we've got anything in here that you would like, but you're more than welcome to help yourself to whatever's here." Gem had all sorts of treats that she had been given and, as she re-moved them from her bag, she laid them out in front of her on the straw. There were even a couple of odd apples that had somehow worked their way into her bag.

"Apples?" barked Mauler. "Whoever gave us those? Since when have dogs be known to like apples?" he asked.

Gem shrugged and offered them to Primrose. "Would you like these?" she said.

Primrose looked delighted by the offer.

"May I?" she asked. Gem nodded. She was sure that Primrose would much prefer a tasty-looking apple to a bunch of dried up old grass to chew on.

With her head lowered, Primrose bit the apple in two and, munching noisily on it, the juice ran down her chin. Gem kindly offered the chops and sausage roll to Mauler. He was a big dog and she knew that he would easily polish them off. Setting aside a couple of pork pies for herself, she then settled down in the straw.

The evening light was fading and it was getting dark inside the stable. Sharing out the last of the food she had been given, the three friends settled down for the night. Lying there awake, Primrose asked Mauler how he came to be with Gem. Mauler was at first reluctant to say and let out a low whimper.

"I've run away from home,"

"Oh, I am sorry to hear that," said Primrose, neighing with sympathy. In the dark, Gem snuggled up closer to him. It was scary being somewhere strange with companions that he hardly knew.

"Are you alright?" asked Primrose.

Mauler tried to put on a brave face, but he couldn't hold back any longer and began to cry.

"There, there," whispered Primrose, stroking him with her nose to comfort him. "Get some sleep and I'm sure things will look better in the morning."

Mauler was exhausted and overcome with emotion. Before long he was fast asleep, snoring away next to Gem.

They were awoken the next morning by the birds singing outside.

Through a gap in the door, a narrow beam of light cast a golden glow across the floor. Gem yawned and looked over at Mauler who was still fast asleep. She didn't really want to wake him, but as she had the rest of her petition to get signed, she couldn't afford to lose precious time.

With a gentle nudge Mauler stirred, licking his nose lazily with his tongue. With the two dogs now awake, Primrose staggered to her feet letting out a great squeal followed by a long whinny.

"Morning," she said, brimming with joy for the day ahead. Pushing the top half of the stable door open, her breath steamed up in the cool morning air.

"Looks like it's going to be a good day for a ride," she commented, hoping that her owner would arrive soon to take her out. Gem rooted around in her bag to find something to eat. Sharing the last few chews they had been given they offered Primrose the stale piece of cake they had picked up from the Women's Institute, which she heartily tucked into.

Shaking the straw from themselves, they ventured outside to take a drink from the trough. The water was cold and took their breath away. Slurping away, they splashed it everywhere and were soon ready to go. Thanking Primrose for her hospitality, they set off up the rough cinder track together and, as they trotted along, Mauler asked Gem a question.

"Gem... where am I going to live?"

Gem had been thinking hard about this. "I haven't quite figured that one out yet…," she said. "…but if we can't find you anywhere to live, I'm sure you can come home with me and live with my family. They're nice people and wouldn't see a dog without a home."

Mauler was no longer an angry, bad-tempered dog. In fact he was quite sweet and cuddly once you got to know him. Gem was sure that she wouldn't have a problem finding him a new home. After all, he would make someone an adorable pet.

Mauler loved the idea of coming to live with Gem. He imagined lots of cuddles and strokes, as well as having the company of humans who would love and care for him.

"Perhaps I could become a sheep dog?" he barked excitedly.

"There aren't any rottweiler sheep dogs that I know of," Gem noted, screwing up her nose trying to think hard.

"Well, just because you don't know of any doesn't mean I can't be one,"

Gem had to agree with him. "Maybe you could be the first Rottweiler sheep dog. Who knows? There's always someone who's got to be the first at something," she mused.

"I might not be able to run as fast as a collie but my bark might come in useful," he growled happily at the thought of becoming the world's first rottweiler sheep dog.

"I must admit, that is quite a bark you've got there. I'm sure the sheep will do as they're told if *you* tell them," she admitted. As they bounded along together Mauler was all pleased with himself at the thought of becoming a sheep dog and having a new home.

Chapter 17

THERE'S NO PLACE LIKE HOME

Lucky

Having spent the morning going door to door gathering lots more signatures the two dogs decided to take a rest in the next village. Looking for a nice cool stream to drink from, they spotted an old man sat on a bench. Having never seen the two dogs before, the old man thought they were lost and so beckoned for them to come over.

"Hello, you two," he called over.

"Who us?" Mauler barked back, sounding all surprised. The old man winked at them and patted the bench next to him.

"Come on!" he called, waving them over. Always one to say hello, Gem scampered across the road followed closely by Mauler, who tagged on behind. The two dogs sat down politely in front of the old man.

"Now then you two, I haven't seen either of you before. What are you doing here?" the old man said, putting his book down. Gem didn't know what the old man wanted but he had a kind smile and looked like the sort of person who would want to help them.

"Now, then, what's your name?" he asked, with a twinkle in his eye. Gem gave a cheery bark, introducing themselves.

"My name's Tom," replied the old man as Mauler did his best to look adorable by offering him his paw to shake. Stroking his chin, the old man wondered where they had come from.

"I've never seen you two round here before. Are you lost?"

"We're not lost. We're on a mission," Gem barked, reaching into her rucksack for the petition and dropping it into his lap.

"What's this? What have we got here, then?" the old man questioned them, as he dug around in his shirt pocket for his reading glasses.

"A dog with a petition, eh? Now that's not something you hear of every day," he chuckled. Casting his eye over the dog-eared sheets of paper, he smoothed them out and quietly read it to himself.

"Well," he exclaimed, after reading Gem's petition. "I was wondering what had happened to Bill," he said, looking up at the dogs after studying their petition. "Let me tell you what, seeing as Bill was such a good friend, I'll sign your petition for you."

While signing the petition the old man told the two dogs of how he used to have a dog of his own. "Candy was her name," he said. "She was a lovely dog. Cocker spaniel, she was. Bill used to bring her a biscuit every day and she'd sit here on the step, waiting for him," he remarked wistfully, thinking back to the past.

"Oh, they were great friends," he said recalling happier times.

Gem was sure that she could recall that name from somewhere, then it dawned on her, the Barking News. Candy had always been a regular on the evening wire, telling stories and passing on the daily news.

"She was a sweet dog," Tom said fondly, as he tickled Mauler behind the ear. "Anyway I'm being rude," he chirped up. "I'm forgetting my manners. I'm sure you two would like a drink, wouldn't you?" Getting up from his seat, he beckoned for them to follow him inside the house.

The kitchen was small and doubled up as a dining room with a large table in the middle. Motioning for them to take a rest, the old man clattered around the kitchen cupboards, as if looking for something.

"Let me see, where is it?" he muttered to himself, with his head stuck beneath the kitchen sink. "Ah-ha, here it is!" he exclaimed, standing up and proudly showing off a dog bowl.

"This was Candy's, I knew it would come in useful one day!" Running the bowl under the tap he filled it to the top with water till it came slopping over the sides and placed it down in front of the two dogs, who thirstily lapped up the cool fresh water.

"I suppose you'd like something to eat as well?" asked Tom, opening the fridge door and sticking his head inside.

Mauler couldn't believe his luck. His old owner only ever fed him occasionally and sometimes not at all. Some nights he had to go to bed with a hungry tummy. It hadn't been very nice living with someone that was so cruel.

"Let's see. What would you like?" the old man asked, turning to the two dogs. "We've got sausages or a bit of steak?" said Tom, sounding somewhat disappointed that he didn't have much to offer his guests, but that didn't bother Mauler one bit.

"Did you hear that?" gulped Mauler excitedly. "He said steak!" Mauler had never had steak before in his life and the very idea of it had him wagging his tail madly from side to side and thudding loudly on the stone floor.

"I tell you what. Seeing as you're my guests, why don't we have both."

Mauler nudged Gem excitedly. "Can you believe it, we're going to get sausages AND steak?" he said.

Gem let out a low whimper so as the old man could not hear. "Don't get too excited," she cautioned him. "Our host seems very nice, so I don't want you doing any of that jumping up or impatient scratching or nipping that that you get from some dogs. Do you hear?"

Mauler tired from his day's travels stretched out excitedly. With his head to the ground and his bottom up in the air he gave a bark to say that he would behave. "Anything you say, Gem," he answered solemnly.

While the old man was cooking the meal, the two dogs decided to have a wander round the house and make themselves at home. Downstairs in the other room was the lounge. It had a small two-seater sofa, a TV, an armchair, and next to that was a table full of photographs.

Gem sauntered over to have a look, enjoying the soft feeling of carpet beneath her tired paws. She poked her nose around and peered at the photographs on the occasional table. They were all of the old man and his dog, a liver-and-cream coloured spaniel.

"Look at this!" she barked, getting Mauler's attention. "That must be him with Candy," she whispered, so as not to be heard. "I tell you, there's not a single photo of him with another human be-ing in."

"Poor man," Whined Mauler, feeling sorry for Tom. "He must have loved her," he noted, as they stood staring wistfully at the photos.

There were pictures of them playing frisbee together, another of them sharing a picnic with each other, one of them on a nice walk and another of Candy splashing around in the ocean with a ball in her mouth. Then Gem suddenly noticed something.

"Look at that," she said, pointing with her nose. There in front of the hearth was an empty dog basket.

"Oh, dear," exclaimed Mauler. "He must really be missing her."

"Mmm...I know." Gem sighed as she sniffed the basket. "There's barely a scent left on it."

"Let's be especially kind to him. He deserves it. Maybe we could play fetch with him after dinner, eh?" Mauler suggested. Although they were on a tight schedule, Gem agreed. They couldn't possibly turn their backs on an unhappy human. It's what dogs had been put on this earth for, to cheer people up.

Candy

"He seems such a nice man, do you think he can talk dog?" Mauler asked. Gem shook her head.

"No. He'd be able to hear us straight away if he could. It takes a special person to be able talk dog. Not everyone can do it," she replied.

"Yeah, but he seems to have really loved his dog. He must be able to?" Mauler barked back.

"It's not that easy for humans. There's only certain ones who know how." Gem elaborated, "You see, those humans that can talk dog are very much like dogs themselves. They love everything and everyone."

"What, even the nasty people like my old owner?" Mauler asked of her.

"Even them," she smiled. "The thing is, people think it's really hard to talk dog, but it's really very simple. All you have to do is get along with each other. It's just humans make it so difficult for themselves. They sometimes struggle to love," said Gem. Mauler was amazed by how simple it was. He thought, if only everybody knew how easy it was, then dogs and humans the world over could be talking to one another, and what an interesting place it would be! Just then the old man called them through for dinner.

With a heavenly smell wafting through from the other room, the two dogs rushed into the kitchen, tripping up over each such was their eagerness to eat. On the floor in front of them were two dinner plates with the most appetising meal they had ever seen. Each of them had a juicy piece of steak that had been cut up into cubes specially for them and even the sausages had been cut down the middle and split in half. As the steam rose up, the two dogs stared adoringly up at Tom.

"What do you think of that?" asked the old man, seeking a response. The two dogs howled joyously and ran over to him, licking and nuzzling him on the back of his hand as way of thanks. Encouraging them to tuck into their dinner while it was still hot, Tom watched contentedly as they noisily licked at their plates and chased their dinner round.

It didn't take long for the Gem and Mauler to polish off their lunch and, while they waited for the old man to finish his, they sat politely by his side grinning from ear to ear.

"Did you enjoy that?" he asked clearing away the plates. Their delight was plain to see as their tails wagged back and forth in sheer pleasure.

Thrilled to have the companionship of his four legged friends in the house, Tom bent down to give the dogs a friendly tickle when he noticed the bandage on Mauler's neck. Pulling back the cotton dressing he was shocked to see such a horrible scar.

"Who did this to you?" he demanded to know with a stern look upon his face. Mauler put his head down looking all out of sorts, worried that he had done something wrong.

"Don't worry, lad, you're not in trouble," he said running his hand over Mauler's soft coat to try and reassure him. "I don't know who did this to you, but they don't deserve to own a dog. If you were mine, I'd look after you better than anyone else."

Suddenly Gem's ears pricked up and her eyes flashed green as she realised that Tom might want to be Mauler's new dad.

Gem wished there was some way that she could tell Tom that Mauler didn't have a home, but she was stuck. He didn't speak dog and there was no way in which to communicate with him. The old man bent down to examine Mauler more closely.

"Mmmm…" he muttered, as he looked at the wound. "It looks nasty. What was it? Your collar too tight, eh, lad?" he asked. Checking for any other injuries it occurred to the old man that he didn't know Mauler's name.

"Seeing as I don't know your name, I'm going to call you Toby. You look like a Toby to me," he said as he stood back to admire the thickly set dog.

"What do you think, eh?" he said, asking Gem for her opinion.

Gem let out three sharp barks of agreement. "I like Toby. It's much better than Mauler," she replied. "It's far more…what's the word I'm looking for…ah, yes, dignified. Yes, that's it, dignified. What do you think?"

Mauler smiled. "Toby, mmm…I like that," he added, allowing his chest to swell as he felt out his new name for size.

Digging a glass bowl out of one of the kitchen cupboards, the old man went over to the sink and filling it with warm water added some antiseptic. Spreading a towel on the table, he motioned for Mauler to jump up.

"Come on, Toby, let's have you up here," he said, encouraging the dog to use the chair to get up.

"Did you hear that?" giggled Mauler. "He called me Toby!"

"Woof…woof… pleased to meet you, Toby," Gem laughed. The two dogs found Mauler's new name highly amusing.

Gem watched as Tom prepared to treat the wound on Mauler's neck. Tearing off a wad of cotton wool, he dipped it in the bowl of warm water.

"Ooowwww…Ooowwww…Oooooooww," howled Mauler as the antiseptic stung. Tom's hands worked gently as he tried his best not to cause the dog any discomfort, but even so Mauler couldn't help but let out a low whimper.

"Oowww… it hurts," he cried to Gem. Standing on her hind legs and propping herself against the table, Gem rubbed her nose against his whispering words of encouragement. "Be brave now. It won't take long," she barked, but Mauler couldn't help but cry. It hurt that much.

Watching the old man take care of Mauler, Gem could see how much he loved dogs. Deep down inside she hoped that there was some way in which Tom could adopt him and give him a new home.

"Hold steady, Toby," said the old man, his soothing voice putting him at ease. "There, all done now!"

After he had finished, Mauler tried to get to his feet but his legs felt all wobbly. The old man did his best to help him down off the table. Putting one arm under his tummy and another under his bottom he took his weight as he helped him down.

"I think I need a lie down," said Mauler, looking pale as he wandered into the front room for a rest.

"Now, is there anything I can do for you girl?" Tom asked Gem. Gem who was sat there patiently, raised her paw to show him her wound. After everything they had been through, it felt like such a long time since Mauler had bitten her on the leg.

"C'mon, then," said Tom, patting the table with a smile.

Being a sheep dog, she athletically jumped up onto the table without needing any assistance.

"That's my girl," said Tom, praising her dexterity. While the old man cleaned out the wound, he took his time to find out more about Mauler.

"Tell me where did you come across Toby?" he asked her. Although she knew the old man couldn't understand what she was saying, she played along, barking every time he asked a question.

"I know that Toby has been mistreated…," he said, shaking his head sadly, "…and I can tell he's not been fed properly either" he said, dabbing her leg with cotton wool.

"You know what?" he whispered, moving closer to Gem so as not to be overheard. "I'm in two minds whether or not to let Toby go home. In fact I'm thinking of looking after him myself."

Gem let out a jubilant bark. "Thank goodness!" she declared as if her prayers had been answered.

"To tell you the truth," said the old man relating his story to Gem. "I haven't really felt the same since my Candy passed away. I'm sure Toby's company will do me the world of good and I'd bet he'd love to have someone care for him."

Gem gave a double bark of joy. She couldn't wait to tell Mauler she'd found him a new home. Tom finished dressing the wound on Gem's leg and, tying a little bandage around it, he taped it up so it would stay in place.

Getting off the table, Gem hopped down off the chair and scampered through into the living room where she found Mauler laid out in Candy's old basket.

"GUESS WHAT?" Gem excitedly barked.

"What?" replied Mauler, looking sorry for himself.

"Tom, the old man, wants this to be your new home,"

Mauler's ears pricked up and his eyes became wide. "Really?" he said, unable to believe what he was hearing. "He wants to be my new dad?" he barked.

Gem nodded, her tongue sticking out of the side her mouth as she panted excitedly.

"No, seriously?" he asked her, making sure she wasn't having him on.

"Yes. Tom wants this to be your forever home!" Gem barked back.

Mauler was so overjoyed that he forget all about the pain in his neck. Unable to contain their excitement, the two dogs began to play fight, tumbling around on the floor together.

"I can't believe it!" he kept saying over and over again, as they rolled about on the carpet pretending to bite each other. "I'm going to have a new dad!" he barked.

Finally, the pair calmed down and Mauler gave Gem a great big slobbery lick on the side of the face.

"Thank you. I'm so glad we met. I would have still been tied up on that chain if it wasn't for you."

Gem blushed. "It was nothing. Any dog would have done that for you," she barked modestly.

"Not everyone," replied Mauler, as he rolled around on his back giddily, over the moon about his good news. "But what about the petition? Don't you still need my help?" he said, rolling back on to his tummy.

"Don't worry about that," Gem reassured him. "I think we're nearly done. Besides, I think Tom needs you more than I do right now."

Just then Tom popped his head round the corner of the door, carrying with him a black and white checked blanket. "I didn't know if you were cold, so I brought this for you." Bending down Tom lay the blanket over Mauler, tucking him into the dog bed.

It was time for Gem to leave but, before she went, she wanted to pass on all her years of doggy knowledge to him.

"Remember, the sole purpose of a dog is to keep humans happy," she said, looking him straight in the eye. "And make sure you take Tom for walkies everyday, so he stays fit and healthy. And don't take the ball back to him every time he throws it. Make sure you give him some exercise too…" Gem barked, imparting her wisdom, "…and let him tickle your tummy. You know that tummy tickling makes humans feel good. It does something funny to their brain. Oh…," remembered Gem as if almost forgetting. "…and maybe you can teach him to how to speak dog. After all, it only takes some unconditional love." After dispensing her advice Gem turned to make for the door.

"Wait!" Mauler called after her. "Will I see you again?"

"Course you will," she replied. "I expect to hear from you on the Barking News."

"Don't you want to play fetch with us before you go?" Mauler asked.

Gem turned to look at Mauler. "I'd love to, but I think you need to rub your scent on him and let him know that he's loved. I'm sure we'll have plenty of time to play fetch in the future." With that Gem scratched at the front door with her paw, signalling to Tom that she had to be on her way.

When Gem arrived back at the farm, there was no one to be seen. The place was deserted except for the cows in the shed who had their heads down busy munching away. She knew that Mr Cranbrook must be out in the fields working and, with the Land Rover gone, she guessed that Mrs Cranbrook had gone on the school run.

Gem was exhausted from all her adventures and needed a lie down. Standing on her hind legs, she pushed the door handle down with her nose and, putting all her weight on her paws, the front door swung open. Making her way in, she gave a tentative bark to see if there was anyone home, but there was no reply. Wandering through the empty hallway and into the living room, she lay down in front of the fireplace. She was tired beyond words and immediately fell asleep with her rucksack on.

Gem was woken with a jolt when Rachel came rushing into the room to greet her.

"GEM!" she cried out aloud, throwing herself on the floor and giving the dog a big hug. Rubbing the sleep from her eyes with her paw, she gave Rachel a big lick on the side of the face and rolled over on her back to have her tummy tickled.

"Urrgh!" giggled Rachel, wiping the dog drool from her face. "How did it go? Did you get any signatures?" she asked, reaching into the rucksack to find Gem's petition. Flipping through the pages of signatures and paw prints, she was amazed at how many dogs and people had signed it.

"Gosh! You have done well," she exclaimed. Then she noticed the bandage on Gem's leg.

"What happened to you?" she asked, looking all concerned. Gem was far too tired to go into all the details but told her that a nice old man called Tom had bandaged it up. Rachel could see that Gem was exhausted and decided not to bother her with questions right now, so she let her go back to sleep. Just then Rachel's mother stuck her head round the door.

"Oh, I'm glad to see Gem's back. Your dad will be pleased. Those sheep have been causing him no end of problems while she's been away," she added.

Rachel raced over to her mother to show her all the signatures on Gem's petition. Her mum looked at her with a puzzled expression.

"Tell me," she said. "How did you know what Gem wanted you to write?" she asked, looking all baffled.

Rachel looked at her as if to say it was simple. "I told you I can speak dog," she said proudly.

Her mother shook her head in disbelief, but there was no other explanation for it. There was no other way she could have done it.

At dinner that evening, Gem was the guest of honour at the table. She was held in such high regard that they had even cleared a place at the end of the table for her. Recounting her exploits, Rachel translated for her. She told them all about Pipin, her night spent in the stable with Primrose and how she had hurt her leg. She even told them about Mauler, and how he had been mistreated and how a lovely old man called Tom had given him a new home and that Mauler was no longer called Mauler but had a nice new name, Toby. She told them about all the lovely people they'd met and all the food they'd been given as well as the cake that they 'borrowed' from the Women's Institute.

"That's some tale," Mr Cranbrook declared, sounding somewhat dubious about her story, "...and I'm sure while she was busy getting the petition signed, she met some flying pigs as well," he scoffed in disbelieving manner.

Gem gave a sharp bark to Rachel.

"Dad," said Rachel. "Gem says that you shouldn't leave your racing tips lying around in the hallway as somebody might find them."

Mr Cranbrook nearly choked on his dinner when he heard that.

Cocking her head inquisitively and looking at her husband, Rachel's mother wanted to know what Gem meant by 'racing tips.'

"Err…I…I… don't know," coughed her father, covering his mouth with his hand and trying to stall for time while he thought of an excuse. "I mean… you don't really believe a dog, do you?" he stuttered as he looked for excuses. "Since when can dogs talk?" he said dismissively, putting his head down and staring at his plate.

Mrs Cranbrook looked at her husband disapprovingly.

"Well, I was going to let your dad have the last piece of pie," she said to the children. "But seeing as Gem has done such a wonderful thing of trying to help Bill, I think she should have it!"

Mr Cranbrook didn't say a word. He didn't want to risk Gem saying any more about his gambling habits, just in case he should get in more trouble. Making an excuse that he had to check on the cattle, Mr Cranbrook sneaked away from the table, while the rest of the family spent the evening listening to Gem's incredible tales.

After they were all done eating, they got down from the table and Rachel's mother turned to her. "Darling, just how is it you can hear what Gem is saying?" she asked with a suspicious look in her eye.

Rachel gladly answered for her. "It's easy," she said. "You've just got to have lots of love in you, right up to here," she exclaimed, standing on her tippy toes and marking the top of her head with her hand.

"Yes, darling, I see," was all her mother could say as she gave her a bemused look.

It was a couple of days before Gem had recovered enough strength to make the climb to the top of Signal Hill. That evening as the light faded across the western horizon and the chatter of the dogs in the valleys below could be heard sparking into life, Gem took to the Barking News. There were Jack Russells, border collies and every other sort of dog busy divulging the day's events when she interrupted the ebb and flow of the conversation. As soon as the other dogs heard that she was on the barking news, they all wanted to wish her well, congratulating her on all her hard work.

"What a fine job you've done," they barked, as they passed on their regards. Acknowledging their praise, Gem heartily thanked everyone who had supported her over the last couple of days.

Down the lane Holly the Pup chirped up. She had an important message to relay to Gem.

"I've a message from a rottweiler named Toby," she barked, her tiny voice ringing shrilly. "He says all is well and that he loves his new owner very much and that he loves him back..."

Inside, Gem felt a warm glow at hearing such good news. "That's wonderful," she barked back, before being quickly interrupted by Holly once more.

"... he says he is now the happiest dog in the world," Holly replied.

"Tell him, Pup, it was a pleasure and I enjoyed our adventure together... and don't forget to pass on my love."

Holly acknowledged Gem's message and asked if there was anything else she wanted to add. Suddenly Gem remembered something that she had almost forgot.

"Can you put the word out, Pup, that we'll need a volunteer to deliver the petition for us?"

"Right-o!" the tiny terrier barked back.

Signing off from the Barking News, Gem made her way back down the hill to take a rest. Nosing her way through the dying bracken, her journey home was made a little easier knowing that back at the farm Rachel had put aside a nice juicy lamb chop for her dinner. With the anticipation of a tasty snack for supper, Gem quickened her pace and made her way home for a well deserved rest.

Chapter 18

DOGS, DOGS, EVERYWHERE!

Rusty

There was a knock on the manager's door. Rick Grinder looked up from his computer with a stiff glare, annoyed that he had been disturbed.

"Come," he said, not even bothering to look up from his desk. The door opened and there stood Norman, the senior postman.

"You've got a visitor to see you, Mr Grinder," he said.

"Yes, yes…alright, show them in," he replied waving his hand dismissively, frustrated that he had been distracted.

"Right you are, Mr Grinder," Showing their guest in, Norman left the visitor in the company of the manager.

Barely able to tear himself away from his computer, Rick

Grinder looked up from his desk to see who was there, but there was no one to be seen.

Hello?" he called out, puzzled. "Hello…hello, who's there?" he said with a mystified look on his face. He was then greeted by a deep woof that seemed to come from out of nowhere.

"What was that?" Rick Grinder asked himself as he stood up to see what was making all the noise.

"A DOG!" he exclaimed, as he looked down from the other side of his desk.

"Why is there a dog in my office?" he demanded to know, but Norman had already disappeared. Peering over the edge of his desk, he was surprised to see a squat, thickly-set bulldog sat staring back at him.

It turned out that it was Pugsley. When Pugsley had heard that Gem needed a volunteer to deliver the petition, he was first to step forward. It was the least he could do for his friend Bill.

Sat in the middle of the manager's office, Pugsley looked up at the orange-faced little man who was stood staring back at him. "What's wrong, have you never seen a dog before?" he quipped.

All Rick Grinder could do was stand there looking slack jawed.

"Has your mother ever told you that your face will stick like that, if you stand there too long?" Pugsley remarked, sick of being starred at. "Anyway," Pugsley barked. "I've come here to deliver this."

Picking up the rolled-up petition that he had been carrying with him, he dropped it on the floor in front of the manager. Rick Grinder stroked his chin.

"Hmmm…" he muttered. Fearful that Pugsley might bite him, he clung nervously to his desk. "Stay back do you hear!" he shouted at Pugsley, as he edged his way gingerly towards him. Pugsley rolled his eyes. He had no intention of giving the manager a nip even though he was tempted to.

"What have we here?" Rick Grinder smirked, as he bent down to pick up the rolled up piece of paper. Tearing off the ribbon that it was tied up with, he tossed it over his shoulder and unfurled the petition, holding it at arms length.

"What's this?" he muttered.

"We, the undersigned request that Bill, being such a kind and thoughtful postman and friend to all dogs be put back on his old round." Rick Grinder couldn't be bothered to read any more and looked at Pugsley with contempt.

"What poppycock!" he declared tossing the petition to the ground without even giving it a second thought. "That man just isn't up to the job. He's too slow! All this helping people and being kind is not productive! Profits is all I care about!"

Then, realising that he was having a conversation with a dog, he let out a shriek. "Look at me! I'm talking to a dog. I must be losing my marbles," he laughed to himself. "I'll end up like that demented old postman, Bill Mathers!"

Pugsley looked on helplessly. How could he just dismiss their petition out of hand so easily? All Gem's hard work, all the dogs who had stamped their paw print on it and all the humans who had signed it too. Pugsley, not wanting Gem's efforts to be in vain, let out a series of loud barks as he tried to get Rick Grinder to reconsider.

"Do be quiet, you useless hound," Rick Grinder snapped back, trying to silence him and shoo him away. "Besides, I'm the manager round here. I say what goes!" he snorted, but the short, round bulldog was not going to be put off so easy.

Scamping round Rick Grinder's side of the desk, he jumped up onto his chair and, mustering all his strength, leapt on to the table.

"Whooaaa!" shrieked the manager, taken aback by the dog's feisty spirit. "Don't you even think of biting me!" he yelled, fumbling around for something to protect himself with. "Besides, if you do, I'll see to it that the dog warden has you put down!" he yelled.

Pugsley was tempted to show him his teeth and scare him some more, but that wasn't going to help the situation. Instead Pugsley snatched the petition from Rick Grinder's hands and shook it wildly, hoping to get him to see how much people wanted Bill back on their round.

"Give me that," snapped Rick Grinder, pulling it free from Pugsley's slobbery jaws. "I tell you what I think of you dogs and Bill Mathers, for that matter."

And with that, he tore the petition into tiny little pieces and threw it into the air, scattering it like confetti.

"There," he sneered gleefully. "That's what I think of your petition,"

Pugsley imagined himself sinking his teeth into Rick Grinder's leg and making him cry like a baby, but not wanting to get into any trouble, he thought better of it. There was no other choice, he was going to have to leave and come up with another plan. Letting Rick Grinder revel in his short-lived victory, he marched out of the office with his tail held high, but not before he had decided to cock his leg and water the corner of Rick Grinder's desk.

"Get out of here! Get out, you filthy little beast, do you hear?" screamed Rick Grinder, trying to shoo him out of his office.

It didn't take long for word to get back to Gem. With a hastily arranged Barking News, the message travelled through the town like wildfire.

"Did you hear?" one dog would say to another as word spread, "that Rick Grinder has torn up Gem's petition," to which, they would shake their heads in sheer disbelief and howl in indignation. Along the back streets, all down the harbour and all up the hill to the very top of town, the message flew in a hurry. Dachshunds yapped in disbelief, irked Imo-Inus paced back and forth frustratedly, and seething shar peis ruffled their noses with displeasure. This was not on. No one could be allowed to treat the dogs and Bill this way. Something had to be done.

Back at the farm, Gem was busy herding the cattle when Ted, the Australian shepherd dog reported back to her.

"Gem, Gem, is you there, mi' handsome? I've got some urgent news for you." Although she was busy helping Mr Cranbrook, the pressing nature of Ted's message demanded that she leave him to deal with the cattle on his own. Mr Cranbrook, now used to Gem's erratic behaviour, just shook his head as he watched her jump over the wall and race off across the fields.

Not even half way up Signal Hill, Gem could hear Ted's bark quite clearly from across the distant valley.

"What's the matter?" she barked, returning his call.

"You know that Rick Grinder?" he said, with a disparaging tone evident in his bark. "He's only gone and torn up your petition."

"What?" cried Gem in disbelief.

At first she didn't know whether to cry or bite Rick Grinder on the bottom, but she wasn't going to let Rick Grinder get away with this.

"Is there anything I can do for you, mi' lover?" Ted asked.

Gem thought for a minute before replying.

"Don't worry, Ted. We may be down but we're not out. I'll think of something. Prepare yourself to receive an E.B.N."

Now an E.B.N stood for Emergency Barking News and it was a message of the highest priority. It was that important that when a dog heard an E.B.N, they had to stop what they were doing immediately and pass on the message and be prepared to act if needed.

"Stand by for a transmission within the next twenty-four hours," she instructed him before signing off.

Ted had never sent out an Emergency Barking News before and, knowing that he would soon be called on to command hundreds of dogs into action, he thought he better get organised. So, dragging his bed out into the porch, he stockpiled a large box of dog biscuits by his side in order to keep his strength up and paced back and forth across the farmyard like a sentry awaiting his orders.

Meanwhile, when Gem got back to the farm, she found Mr Cranbrook in a right old state. A drove of young bullocks were refusing to do as they were told. They were crashing hedges, stomping down walls and trampling crops, leaving a trail of destruction behind them.

"Gem, Gem, I need your help!" Mr Cranbrook yelled, struggling to catch his breath as he ran up the lane after them.

Finding it impossible to run in his wellies, Mr Cranbrook was quite a sight as he flailed around uselessly trying to keep pace with the stampeding animals. Seeing him in such distress, Gem knew she had to help out.

"Don't worry!" she barked as she flew past him in a blur, her fur sleek to her body with the pace she was carrying. "I'll sort these bullocks out!" she growled, as she shot past him. With Gem on the scene, Mr Cranbrook got a chance to take a breather. Bent double and gasping for air, he watched as Gem raced ahead of the pack to cut them off.

Reaching the top of the lane before the lumbering animals had chance to escape, she blocked their path so they could not make it out onto the road. With lots of snorting, tossing their heads and kicking the air, the young bullocks charged up the lane.

"You lot!" she barked, trying to get their attention as they rushed towards her. "Stop right now!" But the bullocks ignored her and came at her, their heads lowered as if about to toss her over the hedge with their horns.

"What are you going to do?" The first bullock mooed threateningly. "You're only a dog. We can trample you like you're nothing," they snorted, laughing amongst themselves. But Gem was not to be deterred. Standing her ground, she looked them in the eye and in her mind she made herself bigger than a thousand buses stacked one on top of each other.

"Grrrrrrrr…Grrrrrrrrr," she went with her meanest growl and saliva dripping from her fangs as Gem showed them her gnashers.

Seeing her sharp teeth, the bullocks suddenly had second thoughts about running her down. "Maybe this is not such a good idea," said the bullock who had been leading the charge. Coming to a halt in a cloud of dust, the over-enthusiastic animals began to look rather sheepish.

"Ahem…," said one of them, coughing embarrassingly, as they stood in the lane with nowhere to go. "I don't like the look of those teeth. They look a bit sharp… a bit pointy. Don't you agree?" one said to the other.

Gem stopped growling and even she was quite amazed at the effect she had on the troublesome cattle. Finding it funny that she had put a halt to the bothersome bullocks, she secretly laughed to herself at the thought of the bullocks thinking she was a big bad dog, when really she was only just pretending.

"Well, gentlemen," she barked. "If you would like to turn around and make your way back down the lane please, the farmer will be waiting to escort you back into your field." Even though the cattle had been naughty, it did help to say please and thank you, as she found things got done much easier if you did. At least that's what her mother told her when she was a young pup, and it seemed to have worked out for her so far in life.

As the bullocks filed into the field one by one, Mr Cranbrook came running up the lane, puffing and panting, looking somewhat dishevelled from all the exertion. Stopped in his tracks, he watched as Gem politely showed the animals into their field.

"How did you manage that?" remarked Mr Cranbrook, all red in the face and pushing his cap back on his head as he breathed in and out heavily. "I don't know what I'd have done without you. I take it all back, all my grumbling. Please forgive me?"

Gem gave a happy bark as Mr Cranbrook rummaged around in his pocket for a doggy treat.

"Come here, you deserve it," holding a biscuit in his hand. Gem gently took it from him as Mr Cranbrook gave her well-deserved tickle around the ruff to show his appreciation.

That evening, while everyone was having dinner, Mr Cranbrook recounted the day's events to his family about the problems he had with the unruly bullocks. Gem meanwhile was laid out underneath the kitchen table, her thoughts elsewhere. All she could think about was ways in which she could help Bill get back on his old round.

As she lay there listening to Mr Cranbrook sharing their mornings exploits with the bullocks, suddenly an idea occurred to her.

'Mmmm...what if?' she thought. Keeping her thoughts to herself, she took herself off to settle down in the barn for the night and think about her idea some more. Snuggled down in the soft warm hay, she thought about what had happened with naughty bullocks and, while she was thinking about it, she came up with a fantastic plan. Excited to tell the other dogs about it, she knew she would have to wait till morning as no one would appreciate a hound howling in the middle of the night and waking everybody up.

After breakfast and helping Mr Cranbrook out in the fields, Gem finally got the opportunity to take to the Barking News. While Mr Cranbrook had his mid-morning cuppa and his usual sneaky peak at the racing results, she silently skulked out of the door without being noticed. Making for the top of Signal Hill, Gem put the call out.

"Gem calling Ted. Gem calling Ted!"

Without hesitation Ted instantly responded to the call. Having hardly had a wink of sleep all night he knew that sending out an Emergency Barking News was serious business and had been ready to receive a message at any moment.

"What is it, mi'girl?" he barked back.

"Tomorrow morning, at first light, I want every dog between here and Berrycombe St Martin to be outside the front gates of the sorting office."

"What time's that?" Ted barked, not being able to tell the time.

"Before the sun comes up and the cock crows...," she added, making sure he understood.

"What should I be telling the dogs you need them to do?"

"Nothing, nothing at all. All I need is for them just to be there...," Gem replied. Ted was puzzled that there wasn't any more information, but he didn't argue as he was sure that Gem knew what she was doing.

"...and make sure that you let every dog know that this message is an Emergency Barking News of the highest priority. We've got to get Bill back on his old round!"

Ted got straight to it. Barking out his orders to all the other dogs at the neighbouring farms, he told them that this was Emergency Barking News of the highest order and it was imperative that it was passed on with the utmost urgency to every dog that they knew.

Down the lane Holly the Pup was busy barking for all she was worth. Chasing every car with a dog in the back, she ran after them until the dog inside had got the message. When Pugsley heard the news, he made sure that every dog that came into the paper shop accompanied by their owner was made aware of the situation.

"This is of utmost importance," he barked in his sternest of tones, underlining the serious nature of their objective.

That night the whole of the two counties came alive to the sound of dogs barking. People couldn't sleep because of all the racket being made. Lights were being switched on and people could be heard shouting at their dog to tell them to be quiet. In all the small towns and villages that peppered the hills of the South West of England, neighbours were leaning out of their bedroom windows wondering what on earth was going on.

"Have you heard that racket?" they asked each other as they scratched their heads looking all bleary eyed. "What is that infernal noise?" they wanted to know as they peered out into the night bewildered.

On farms, slippers were being thrown at dogs to try and shut them up and farmers were forced from their beds to see what was going on. Trudging downstairs in the middle of the night with a torch, they made their way outside to see what all the fuss was about. There they would find their dogs straining to be let off their chain or set free from their run. Some dogs bolted as soon as the front door was opened, disappearing into the night, leaving a confused farmer to stand there in his dressing gown.

On a quiet country lane, a policeman was sat in his car he when he saw a dog run by. Thinking it was a little peculiar to see a dog on its own in the middle of the night, he wound down his window when he saw another run past, and then another. Knowing that something was going on, he got on his radio to report back to base.

"Err…..come in, control. Over," he said. The radio crackled with static while he waited for a reply.

"Control, over…go ahead."

"I seem to have some rather odd…," the officer hesitated, unsure of how best to describe what was going on. "…errr…we seem to have some rather strange dog behaviour going on tonight." There was a silence while he waited for a response.

"Nineteen Fifty Two, have you been drinking? The sergeant wants to know."

The officer didn't know what to say. There was no point in responding. Instead, he just stared blankly out of his window as he watched more dogs run by.

Across the two counties, dogs took to the back lanes as they made their way to Berrycombe St Martin. At first it would be one dog on their own. Then he or she would be joined by another and then another until there was a small pack, then that pack would join up with another pack, and then that pack became bigger until, by the time they got to Berrycombe St Martin, all the roads leading into the town were filled with dogs and they were just one giant pack.

The whole town was now wide awake by this time. All the yelping and barking had brought people out onto the streets. Stood on their doorsteps they watched the strange procession go by. There were mothers and fathers in their dressing gowns, children in their pyjamas. Some people had gone so far as to feed the dogs as they passed by and somewhere in the middle of it all was Gem with Ted and Holly the Pup by her side.

"Now think on," Gem barked to the assembled pack of dogs as they flowed through the streets towards the sorting office. "This is to be a peaceful protest. We are here to support Bill and, in doing so, we will conduct ourselves like all true dogs should. We will not stoop to the level of humans with their fighting and nastiness. We will show them how to behave properly and respect one another." A large bark went up from the group of assembled dogs as they let out a loud cheer.

By the time they had got to the sorting office, the dogs were over a thousand strong, and Bill struggled to get to work through the vast sea of dogs. There were all kinds of dogs there. Some he had never even seen before, like an Entlebucher mountain dog, a komondor, a Nova Scotian duck-trolling retriever, and some that he had no idea what breed they were, but somehow they all knew him.

"Hello, Bill!" they barked, licking him all over and wanting to give him a paw. He was taken aback by the level of support he received. Even the mice had come along to see what all the commotion was about. Riding on dogs' backs, the mice cheered and whistled, waving to everybody as if it was some giant carnival. By the time Bill arrived at the gates of the sorting office, Gem had managed to nose her way to the front of the pack.

"Morning, Bill," she said. "Quite a turn out, eh?" nodding to the assembled dogs.

Bill was touched by the show of strength that the dogs had put on for him. "I'd really like to thank you for all your support," he said, addressing the vast sea of dogs.

"I heard about the petition," Bill sighed with resignation. "It's a shame it didn't work out... but never mind. This turnout will show Rick Grinder that his behaviour is unacceptable and he can't do this."

There were so many dogs that not only did they block the entire gateway to the sorting office, but they blocked the main road through the town. Down the street they heard a truck beeping its horn. It was the truck with all the mail on from the main sorting office. Having abandoned his vehicle, the driver made his way up to the gates where Bill and Gem were stood.

Bill explained to him that Gem and all the other dogs were trying to get him reinstated on his old round, and that their previous attempt, a petition, had been unsuccessful. So now they were trying something new, a doggy sit-in.

By now the rest of the posties had turned up for work and had heard what was going on.

"We're not going in," they said to Bill. "Enough is enough.

This Rick Grinder has to learn that people are more important than money and petty rules."

Just then a car could be seen flashing its lights and beeping its horn as it pushed its way through the crowd of dogs. It was Rick Grinder.

"Get out of my way!" he shouted as he jeered and spat at the dogs from his car window. The dogs didn't know what to make of him. They had never met somebody as dislikable as him before. Pulling up in front of the office gates, he threw open the car door and stepped out shaking his fist at the dogs.

"Go on, get out of here!" he bellowed, waving his shoe at them as if threatening them with a kicking.

"What's the meaning of this?" he growled at Bill in an officious tone.

"It's a doggy sit-in," replied Bill, as all around him were gathered Gem, Ted, Holly the Pup, Little Staffie, Diesel, Rusty, Lucky and all of the other dogs from his round. Even Mauler had come along to support him.

"I knew you'd have something to do with this," Rick Grinder snapped at Bill. Runnning his hand over his shaven head he desperately tried to think of a way to get rid of them. "You're going to have to tell them to move," he said, glaring at Bill.

"I can't," Bill answered back.

"Why not?" seethed Rick Grinder.

"Because they can think for themselves, and they know what you're doing to us is wrong. I can't make them change their minds."

"Arrghhhh!" screamed Rick Grinder, unable to control himself as he jumped up and down. "Look, I want these dogs gone within the next ten minutes and you lot back inside, or else…," he sneered, casting his gaze at the rest of the posties who were huddled outside.

"Or else what?" said Bill.

"Or else you'll be sorry," he snapped. Getting back into his car he revved the engine and began beeping his horn. Driving at the dogs with no thought for their safety, they had to jump out of the way so he didn't run them over.

"Gosh, he's rude isn't he?" barked Diesel. "I don't suppose he wants to play fetch with us?"

"No, but I will" And with that, Bill threw his cap for Diesel to chase.

In his office Rick Grinder stood looking out of the window. There were dogs as far as the eye could see. They were dogs sat on top of walls, dogs sat on top of lamp posts, dogs sat on top of pillar boxes, wherever there was a space there was a dog, all with a thousand shiny eyes looking back at him. Under his breath, he quietly cursed the dogs.

"Those dratted mutts," he sneered.

With no sign of the posties coming back to work, and the truck with all the mail on still stuck half way down the street, Rick Grinder picked up the phone to ring the Area Manager.

"Hello, good morning, sir…," went the conversation as Rick Grinder did his snivelling best to explain the situation.

"What's that?" came a loud voice from down the other end of

the telephone. "What do you mean there's a thousand dogs blocking the entrance to my office?" he shouted.

Holding the phone away from his ear, Rick Grinder could still hear the Area Manager shouting at him from three feet away. He was that annoyed.

"Sorry, sir," said Rick Grinder, doing his best to apologise.

"I'll be straight down there," the Area Manager snapped back at him, sounding rather displeased.

"I...I... don't think there will be any need for that, sir," Rick Grinder grovelled. "I can sort this out on my own." But, before he had chance to explain, the phone had been slammed down.

An hour later, Bill and the rest of the posties suddenly had their attention drawn to a big black car, honking its horn and pushing its way through the gathering of assembled dogs. There was only one person it could be: the Area Manager.

Leaping out of the way for fear of being run over, the dogs took cover as the black car stopped for no one. Swinging into the yard, out stepped the Area Manager with his briefcase in his hand.

"Good morning, sir," said Rick Grinder, doing his best to crawl up to his superior. "There was really no need to come down at all, sir. I had the problem all in hand,"

The Area Manager surveyed the scene. Placing his hands upon his hips and sweeping back his lank greasy hair, he looked at Rick Grinder with contempt.

"Really, is that so? I sent you down here to sort these lot out, Grinder, not to cause me more problems… and what are these dogs still doing here?" he snorted, venting his frustration.

"It seems that they won't leave until I have reinstated one of the postmen on his old round," he snivelled as he tried to explain the situation. "Apparently the dogs are particularly fond of him, sir. They even delivered a petition, which I ignored."

"Well done, well done," the Area Manager commended him as he thought how to get rid of the dogs. "Tell me, Grinder, which one of these posties is the one in question?"

"That one there, sir," said Rick Grinder, singling Bill out. "I took him off his round because I found him carrying dog biscuits on him."

"Dog biscuits?" blurted out the Area Manager. "Don't they know the rules? They can't carry dog biscuits with them."

Rick Grinder slithered up to the side of the Area Manager as he tried to explain himself. "You know what these posties are like, sir: lazy, inefficient, insubordinate," he said, trying his best to creep up to his boss.

"Mmmm," agreed his boss, flattening his greasy hair back against his head. "Well, leave it to me, Grinder. I'll sort these damn infernal posties out, once and for all." And with that the Area Manager sucked in his stomach and marched over to where Bill was stood.

"You!" he shouted angrily at Bill. "What the blazes do you think you're doing, holding up my mail!"

Remaining calm, he explained that this was none of his doing, but it was entirely that of the dogs.

"You expect me to believe that!" he grunted in an off hand manner. "Next, you'll be telling me dogs can talk."

"They can," Bill replied.

The Area Manager laughed hysterically. "Tell me, what does this dog here have to say for itself?" he said, pointing to Gem who was sat politely by Bill's side. Bill looked down at Gem.

"Well, girl, what have you got to say to the Area Manager?" he asked.

Gem let out a bark.

"She says you're far too mean and greedy, and you should learn to be more dog."

"More dog?" the manager gloated as if he knew better. "More dog?" he repeated, unable to control his laughter. "Did you hear that, Grinder? This mutt here says I should be more dog."

"Very funny, sir. Very funny," noted Rick Grinder, applauding his boss.

By now the whole of Berrycombe St Martin had been brought to a standstill. The thousand-strong pack of dogs had blocked all the roads coming into the town and no one could get to work. Cars, buses and lorries were stuck going nowhere, and even the local news had sent a TV crew to report on the incident. The posties were enjoying all the fun too. Sat outside the gate, they were sharing their sandwiches with the dogs and, needless to say, Little Staffie was busy nosing his way around everyone's lunch box to see who had the tastiest treats on offer.

Unaware of the TV crew filming him, the Area Manager turned to Rick Grinder and did his best impression of Gem.

"Look at me: I'm a dog, I can talk!" he said, putting on a silly voice and pulling a stupid face. It didn't stop there. He continued to take the Mickey out of all the dogs and began to do a silly walk to accompany his impression.

"Woof, woof, woof, I'm a dog!" he said in his most ridiculous voice. However, Rick Grinder had spotted the TV crew and tried to get the Area Manager's attention.

"Ahem…sir….sir…," he coughed, tugging at his boss's sleeve.

"What?" his manager snapped back, spinning around on his heels.

"There's a TV crew filming you"

Coming to his senses, the Area Manager suddenly pretended to be all grown up, straightening his tie and flattening down his hair.

"Why didn't you tell me?" he hissed.

"I tried, sir, but…" Rick Grinder said, trying to calm him down.

"But nothing. Now you've made me look a fool on national TV"

Outside the gates, the dogs had formed an almost impenetrable barrier, stopping anyone from entering or exiting the building. Not a single letter had been sorted, and the Area Manager was looking at his watch, knowing that if they didn't get the mail into the building soon, there would be no deliveries going out that day.

"Look…," he whispered over his shoulder to Rick Grinder. "I'm going to make my way down the street and I'm going to drive that truck full of mail back here."

"But you can't drive a truck, sir," Rick Grinder added.

"How hard can it be?" he said, throwing his hands in the air. "Watch me."

Striding towards the gathered dogs with his briefcase in his hand, he shouted at the hounds to move. "Come on, you stupid mutts, get out of my way."

Lopez who had come with his favourite dolly to chew, ruckled up his nose in disgust. "I don't like him. He's not very nice, is he?" he barked to the others. Meanwhile Mauler, who was wearing his new collar with his name tag that said Toby, tried to get Gem's attention.

"Gem, Gem," he barked. "Can I bite him…please? Just for old time's sake," he said, pleading to sink his teeth into the Area Manager's behind.

"No. This is a peaceful protest. You may only defend yourself if you are attacked," Gem replied, giving her strict instructions.

The Area Manager stood in front of the assembled group of dogs and looked at them in disgust.

"Move!" he shouted, but not a single dog budged. The throng of dogs was too thick for him to step through. Desperate to get the mail into the office, he lost his temper and lunged at Holly the Pup, the smallest dog there. With his shiny shoe he kicked her as hard as he could, and Holly went sailing through the air. Whimpering in pain, she landed with a heavy thud and all the other dogs gathered round her to see if she was alright.

"Right, that's it!" growled Mauler. "I'm not standing for this."

And with that, he bit the Area Manager on the bottom, taking the seat out of his expensive trousers.

"Arghhhh, you little…" he shouted as he leapt into the air with his red and white striped underpants showing through.

"Toby!" barked Gem, using Mauler's Sunday-best name. Mauler turned around, looking rather red-faced.

"I told you about that: no biting," Gem reminded him.

Mauler was all apologetic. "I'm sorry," he replied with his head hung low. "I was only trying to protect the rest of the dogs," he said, trying to justify his actions.

"Never mind," smiled Gem, knowing that even though she didn't approve of it, the Area Manager had got what was coming to him.

By now the Area Manager was hopping mad and threw his briefcase at the dogs in frustration. Diesel who had been sat there quietly, minding his own business, suddenly saw the briefcase come flying through the air and, Diesel being Diesel, thought it was a game of fetch. The briefcase bounced and landed on the ground, narrowly missing one of the dogs. Rushing over to where it had landed, Diesel picked it up by the handle. Running back with it in his mouth, he tried returning it to the Area Manager.

Seeing Diesel come bounding towards him with the briefcase in his mouth was enough to put the wind up the Area Manager. Thinking there was another dog about to bite him, he threw his hands in the air and turned tail, running for the safety of the office. All Diesel wanted to do was give the man his briefcase back. Screaming like a baby, the Area Manager ran straight past Rick Grinder and dived through the office door, locking it behind him, leaving Rick Grinder stuck outside.

By now the dogs had got bored with all the hanging around they were doing and went to sit on top of the Area Manager's car. Having left his car door open, they even took it upon themselves to have a little lie down on his expensive upholstery. Leaving the car full of dog hairs, mucky paw prints and a smell that would take weeks to get rid of.

All this carry-on hadn't gone unnoticed and had been caught on camera by the local news crew. As the reporter finished his piece for that evening's news, the police turned up.

"What's going on here?" they asked, using a police alsatian as a translator. Managing to come to an understanding between the dogs and the posties, they got all the traffic moving again and everything got back to normal. The dogs all went home and the posties went back to work.

That evening, gathered around the TV Granny and the children watched as their grandfather made a surprise appearance on the news. They could hardly contain themselves when they saw the headlines and the Area Manager doing his best impression of a dog at the top of news.

"Gosh," Granny declared, seeing her husband on the television. "I didn't know you knew that many dogs," she said, sat on the sofa with her cup of tea.

"Neither did I," he answered, sounding all surprised.

"Where did they all come from?" asked Alex.

"Beats me," replied Bill, shrugging his shoulders.

Trixie

He wasn't the only one surprised by the turnout of all the dogs. In living rooms all up and down the north coast, owners spat their drinks out when they saw their dog appearing on the local news. Owners looked in disbelief at each other. How on earth had their little Trixie ended up on the local news, they wanted to know? With a suspicious eye, they looked at their dogs mystified as if to say, how…what…where! They couldn't understand it. But the dogs just smiled at their owners, and rolled over on their backs to have their tummies tickled. All their owners could do was shake their heads in a bemused fashion and wonder just what it was that their dogs got up to when they weren't around.

Chapter 19

DOGGY DELIVERY

Bryn

Christmas was just around the corner and things were starting to get busy at the sorting office. Everyday more parcels came through the door and to keep their spirits up, Stella, the cleaner, cooked everyone a giant breakfast to keep them going. However, one person who was not entering into the festive mood was Rick Grinder.

From the window in his office, he watched as the posties trudged out of the gates laden down with parcels. Gone for the whole day and not to return until after dark.

"Good. Good. That's what I like to see…," he muttered to himself, rubbing his hands together. Then, from out of the corner of his eye, he spotted Bill. His trolley weighed down with parcels.

"My, my, you have surprised me, Mr Mathers. I thought the Town Hill round might have finished you off by now, but no. Your resilience is impressive," he remarked, stroking his calculator in his top pocket as if it were his favourite pet.

Now at this time of year most people are thinking about buying gifts for their loved ones or helping someone out who is less well off, but no, not Rick Grinder. He was dreaming of some strange Frankenstein-like experiment, where he could create a postman with eight arms, like that of a spider so they could sort faster. Or crossing a postie with a cheetah in a test tube so they could run faster. With his head full of all sorts of strange ideas, he suddenly came over all sentimental for a moment when he thought about his dear old Granny, wondering what she would be doing on Christmas Day. Then he realised she would be out delivering pizzas on her moped and his heart soared.

"Ahh...," he sighed contentedly, "my Granny. Still out earning money, even on Christmas Day," Just for a second, he thought he felt a tear well up in his eye, but dispelling such an idea, he realised it was just a bit of dust.

At home with the Mathers family, there too was a feeling that Christmas was on its way. While people fought in supermarkets over the last bag of walnuts that no one was ever going to eat, the mice and the children had done an extremely good job of decorating the tree. Swinging from baubles and using the tinsel to abseil down, Granny had to tell the mice off as she thought they might have the tree over with all their messing about.

Alex and Niall were extremely excited at the thought of what Santa might bring them and had spent the last few weeks writing out a Christmas list. Top of that list was a dog. Later, over dinner that evening, Bill asked how their list was going.

"So, what have you asked Santa for, then?" Their Grandpa wanted to know.

"I've asked him for a dog," said Alex.

"A dog?" gulped Bill, nearly choking on his food and raising an eyebrow. "What about the mice? Aren't they fun enough?" he asked.

Alex shrugged. "I suppose," she admitted reluctantly. "But you can't take a mouse out for a walk or play fetch with them, can you?"

Grandpa looked up from his meal. "Course you can. You just pop your mousey friend in your pocket and, hey presto, there you go! And what about the mouse ball, eh? Maybe you could put some string on it and pull it along behind you?"

Niall burst out laughing at the thought of walking down the high street with a mouse on a lead.

"See, your brother thinks it's funny," he laughed, pointing to Niall with the end of his fork. "Besides, I'm not sure Santa can get a dog in his sled, and I know it's not legal to wrap one up as a present!" smirked Bill, tucking into his dinner. "What else have you asked Santa for?" he asked.

Putting her knife and fork down, Alex began to count on her fingers as she recalled her Christmas list.

"A colouring book, felt tip pens, a teddy…," she went on.

"Oh well, we'll just have to see what Santa brings, eh?" noted Bill, giving Granny a knowing wink.

"And what would you like?" He asked, turning to Niall.

Niall thought for a moment before responding. "I think I'd like a dog too," he added.

"Really? Are you sure you wouldn't like a new football, or a metal detector or something like that?"

Niall shook his head. He was adamant he wanted a dog for Christmas.

Grandpa gave a sideways look to Granny, knowing the children would be disappointed this year as there would be no dog in their Christmas stocking.

The following morning at work, Rick Grinder was feeling especially nasty and wanted to see Bill in his office.

"Ahh…glad you could see me," slimed Rick Grinder in his most snivelling tone. Wrapped up in his hat and coat ready to go out, Bill stumbled into his office.

"Since you've been on the Town Hill round, I have been watching you," said Rick Grinder, with his back to him looking out of the window. "I see you going out of those gates every morning…, and how shall I put it…," he said, pausing to find the right words. "Quite frankly, there is no other way of saying it. You're just too slow."

"I'm no slower than any of the others," Said Bill, trying to defend himself.

"Hmm… I'll be the judge of that," Rick Grinder replied as he turned around to consult his computer. "I've been running through my figures and it says here that you are half an hour late everyday."

"It's only half an hour," Bill replied.

"HALF AN HOUR, HALF AN HOUR!" screeched Rick Grinder, barely able to control himself. "Let me tell you. I didn't get where I am today by pretending half an hour didn't matter," he said, banging his fist on the table. "So this morning, I'll be timing you."

"Timing me!" Bill blurted out.

On his white board behind him, Rick Grinder pulled down a map of the town. "See this," he said, pointing to it with his laser pen.

"This is your round and I expect you to be here at ten o'clock. I shall be following your progress in my car. Do I make myself clear?"

"What do you mean?" asked Bill.

"What do I mean? Wah, wah, wah!" wailed Rick Grinder, pretending to cry like a baby. "I mean you better pull your finger out and hurry up, or you'll be out of a job. That's what I mean! I expect to see you at the first check point in half an hour, so you better get going," he snapped, pointing to the door.

Bill looked at his watch. Crikey, he thought, that doesn't give me much time. Setting off from the office, he broke into a steady jog hoping he would be there by the time Rick Grinder turned up. With his bags overflowing, Bill puffed and panted and went all red in the face, as he struggled to keep to the tight schedule.

Looking at his watch, he saw he was already running late for his first stop. Oh, dear, he thought, Rick Grinder won't be happy, as he tried to pick up the pace. By the time he had reached the end of street, he could see Rick Grinder waiting in his car for him.

"Sorry I'm late. I had a lot of parcels to deliver," said Bill apologising.

From the comfort of his car, Rick Grinder took his clipboard and made note of how late he was. "I don't want to hear excuses, I just want you to be on time," he remarked grouchily. "You've got twenty minutes to make it to Sycamore Walk," he snapped, starting his stopwatch again.

"Really?" Bill replied.

"Standing here, arguing with me, is only wasting your time," Rick Grinder wound his window up and drove off at speed, leaving Bill to chase after him.

Making his way along Sycamore Walk, Bill thought he could hear his name being shouted, but not seeing anybody about, he thought he was hearing things. Then, as he reached the brow of the hill, he could see Rick Grinder watching him from a distance with a pair of binoculars. Shouting at him through a megaphone.

"Move it. Move it. Come on, pick up the pace, Mathers," he growled as the tinny voice wafted along the street. Bill was astonished. He couldn't believe it. A megaphone?

Rick Grinder was still shouting at him through the megaphone when he reached him.

"Is there really any need for that?" Bill asked.

"Course there is. Think of it as a motivational tool," he said, blasting out poor Grandpa's ears and letting everyone within a one hundred feet of him hear their conversation.

Holding the megaphone to him, Rick Grinder told him he would drive alongside and shout encouragement at him. Bill tried to say that it was not really necessary, but Rick Grinder insisted.

"It's my job!" he grinned joyously. "I'm here to make sure you give me two hundred percent, and nothing less!"

News of how badly Bill was being treated soon spread through the town's dog community. Cockapoos leaned over garden gates to see what all the noise was about. Labradors took a minute out of their busy schedule of licking their bowls clean to see what was going on, and Afghans, who were being preened in grooming parlours, put their arduous beauty regimes on hold to waft their long flowing coats in disgust. Soon news reached Pugsley who was busy sorting the evening papers.

"Have you heard?" said one whippet who had come into the shop with his owner. "That Rick Grinder's making Bill run around his delivery."

Pugsley stopped what he was doing. "What?" he declared, as if his ears were deceiving him. "Right! That's it!" he snarled fiercely, his stumpy tail wagging with displeasure. "I'm not having anymore of this. We're going to help him out."

And with that, he picked up one of the newspapers in his mouth and tore it up in disgust, shaking it violently until there was nothing left of it. Mr Peters, the newsagent, was taken aback by his dog's behaviour, and a customer, who had stopped by the shop, looked at Mr Peters, agog.

"I've never seen your Pugsley behave like that before. What's got into him?"

"Beats me," replied Mr Peters, scratching his head, looking just as puzzled as the customer.

Halfway round, Bill was so tired that he couldn't run anymore. His feet hurt. His legs ached and his back was so sore that he had to walk the rest of the way. Unhappy with his performance, Rick Grinder had got fed up and had gone back to the office to put his feet up while he waited for him to finish.

It was nearly tea time when Bill got back to the office. Soaking wet and fit to drop. He was so tired that he could hardly stand and had to prop himself up against a wall.

"Ahh...you made it at last," declared Rick Grinder, removing his feet from his desk and beckoning him to come closer. "Let me tell you something," he began. "You're an old man and let's be honest," said Rick Grinder, looking him up and down, "You're not in the best of shape, are you? Why don't you make this easy for yourself and resign?"

"Resign? What for? I love my job and all the dogs I meet!" Watching him bouncing up and down on his tippy-toes, Bill could see Rick Grinder was getting angry.

"There's no easy way to put it," he said, clearing his throat and straightening his tie. "You can either retire, or I'll have you running up and down every hill this poxy little town has to offer, till you come to me begging to resign."

Now Bill was an extremely tolerant person and, as much as he liked to help people out, he wasn't going to be bullied by this man. So, thanking Rick Grinder kindly, he turned around and marched out of his office.

By the time he made it home, Pugsley was already sat outside waiting for him.

"Hello, Pugsley. What are you doing here?" he asked, looking worn out.

"I've come to talk to you," he barked as he followed Bill in through the door. When Granny saw the state of her husband, she insisted that he sit down immediately and plied him with plenty of hot tea to keep his strength up. Not forgetting the little bulldog, Granny turned to Pugsley to inquire if he would like a drink.

"Would you like a saucer of tea, my dear?" she asked.

"Please, Mrs Mathers, as long as it's wet and warm, I don't mind." he barked politely. Placing the saucer of tea down in front of him, Pugsley lapped away furiously at the warm milky tea, splashing it all over the rug.

"Mmm…that was good," he noted thanking Granny for her hospitality.

Kicking off his boots and pulling off his socks, Grandpa bent over and found that he had some rather nasty blisters on his feet.

"Let me get you some water to soak them in," said Granny, taking the washing-up bowl from the sink and pouring in some hot water.

By now, the mice had come in from the shed to see how Bill was. They too had heard the news. All afternoon there had been nothing but dogs barking over fences, shouting across the street and stopping one another in the park as they told each other about Bill's plight. Wanting to make sure he was alright, the mice sat around the edge of the washing up bowl dangling their tiny feet in the water as they listened to what was being said.

"Look Bill," said Pugsley. "This whole thing with Rick Grinder, it can't go on. He's treating you worse than a dog. You're one of the nicest, kindest people I know, and that's not just to us dogs, but to humans too, and I think it's about time that he recognised that. So… I have an idea that might help you out."

Pugsley got up on his hind legs and, with his front paws on Grandpa's chair, he whispered to him. After a discussion between the two, Grandpa agreed to Pugley's plan.

"What was all that about?" Granny asked when the bulldog had left. Bill tapped the side of his nose and winked. "Just you wait and see!" he said with a knowing smile.

A few days later, Grandpa arrived at work as normal and, after taking off his coat, got on with his sorting.

"Morning, Mr Grinder," he said, whistling a happy tune to himself as the manager walked past him.

"Err…morning?" replied the manager hesitantly, suddenly conscious of Bill's cheery happiness. Immediately Rick Grinder's brain whirred into motion, there must be something going on he thought.

Why was he so happy and cheerful, especially after he had been so horrid to him? It didn't compute and Rick Grinder's suspicious mind went into overdrive as he tried to figure out what Bill was up to.

"Don't forget, Mathers, I'll be coming out with you again this morning," he added, trying to bring Bill's happy mood down, but it didn't seem to work.

Instead, he just carried on whistling. This really got on Rick Grinder's nerves. How could someone, who he had been particularly nasty to, still be so cheery? He began to feel uneasy about the whole situation and wondered what was going on.

When it came time for Bill to go out on his round, he gave a loud knock on the manager's door.

"Just thought I'd let you know I'm ready to go now," he said cheerily.

Rick Grinder hopped up from his desk and put on his rain coat. "Now remember, you've got half an hour to make it Victoria Square," he said sharply. "I'll be waiting for you in my car."

With his trolley loaded up with Christmas cards and presents, Bill was making his way down the street when he heard someone whistle to him.

"Over here!" came a bark from down a dimly lit alleyway. It was Pugsley and all his doggy friends. Checking the coast was clear and Rick Grinder was not following him, he slipped down the side street to join him.

At Pugsley's request, there were some thirty dogs all stood in the shadows ready to help, some with newspaper bags slung over their backs.

"Well, what do you think?" remarked Pugsley, looking all pleased with himself. Bill cast his eye over the happy band of dogs.

"What a fine bunch of eager-looking hounds we have here. I'm sure they'll make great post dogs," he declared, inspecting the line of regimented pooches.

For the ones that didn't have a newspaper bag, Grandpa handed out some spare pouches that he had brought with him. To make things look more official, he gave each one a hi-viz vest, just the thing for their first doggy delivery.

"You see this lot," Pugsley said with his paw over his mouth so as not to be heard. "These dogs are the elite, the best of the best. I hand picked them myself through a rigorous selection procedure that I devised."

Bill nodded impressed by Pugsley's efforts.

"Firstly, I made them carry an extra heavy bag of Sunday papers up the hill to test their stamina. Then, to demonstrate their skill, I left them with a can of dog food and a tin opener. Those that managed to open the can made the cut."

Bill was taken aback by the extent to which Pugsley had gone to in order to prepare the dogs for their covert mission. "Well, I suppose we better get on with things, eh? Rick Grinder will be waiting for me," said Bill looking at his watch.

"Dogs," barked Pugsley preparing them for action. "You heard the man. Let's get this show on the road."

Lining up in front of Bill, the highly trained canines were eager to put their newly acquired skills as post dogs to the test.

Unloading the contents of his trolley, Bill split the bundles of mail down. First up was Bryn, a hard-bitten cross terrier who had spent many years chasing rats for a living.

"Right, Bryn," Bill directed him. "You've got number one Accommodation Road here." The bushy-whiskered dog barked to say that he understood and grabbed the letters in between his jaws.

"Oh and don't forget this parcel," he added. The parcel was much bigger than Bryn and it was far too big to fit in his bag.

"Look, what if we put your letters in your pouch and you carry the parcel with your mouth?" Bryn barked back to say that he would give it a go. With the letters secured in his pouch and clutching the box with his teeth he set off down the road.

Up next was Dhupa, a Tibetan mastiff. Strong and standing tall, she had two pouches slung either side of her thick-set body like a pony with saddlebags.

"I'll be able to take more than one house." She said.

"It's not too much, is it?" asked Bill, but she was insistant.

The mice who had tagged along now saw this as the perfect opportunity to go for a ride.

"Can we come along?" squeaked Ernest.

"Why not? The more the merrier," Dhupa replied.

"Make sure you behave yourselves and give Dhupa a hand if she needs it," Bill instructed the mice. The dogs queued up excitedly in front of him all desperate to help and soon he had emptied his pouches of all the mail.

"Not bad, eh?" commented Pugsley. To him it was just like any other day at the newsagents, but this time, instead of sorting out paper boys, it was dogs.

Bryn meanwhile had trouble getting the attention of the people who lived at number one. He found that his paw was far too soft to knock on the door and even his scratching wasn't loud enough to be heard. So, putting the parcel down, he clambered on top of it and with an explosive burst of energy jumped for the doorbell, pressing it with his nose. 'Ding-dong' it went.

When the owner of the house came to the door, she was puzzled to find no one there. About to close the door, she heard a sharp little bark as Bryn tried to grab her attention. Lowering her gaze, she was pleasantly surprised to find a small terrier stood on her doorstep.

"What do we have here?" she enquired, bending down to see what Bryn wanted. "My goodness!" she declared. "You've brought my parcel."

Bryn gave a couple of extra barks to say just how much he enjoyed delivering her mail.

"Is this for me?" she enquired picking up the parcel. "How sweet," she gushed, full of praise.

The lady was so taken aback, by Bryn's cuteness and uniform that he was wearing, that she had to get a photo of him with her phone.

With all the mail delivered, the dogs had to go into hiding while Bill met up with Rick Grinder. Disappearing behind hedges and hiding behind bins, the dogs made themselves scarce while Pugsley took to posing as one of the reindeer, which formed part of someone's Christmas decorations on their front lawn.

When Bill reached Rick Grinder, he was sat in his car listening to the radio and taking a break. He tapped on his window. Taking him by surprise, Rick Grinder leapt out of his seat spilling red-hot coffee all over himself.

"Argggh!" he screamed, jumping from the car and holding his trousers away from him so it didn't burn him.

"Quick, take them off." suggested Bill, taking out his hanky and trying to dab the front of his trousers for him.

"What do you mean, take them off?" Rick Grinder yelped, as he hopped madly about on the pavement.

"They'll burn you!" said Bill with a sense of urgency in his voice.

Now all morning there had been passers-by going about their business -- either shopping, taking a stroll or rushing to work -- when suddenly they were confronted by this odd and rather bizarre spectacle. There, in front of them was a fully grown man, yelling and screaming and grabbing at the front of his trousers in a peculiar fashion.

"What's wrong with him?" asked one lady to another, who was pulling her shopping trolley along behind her.

"Beats me," answered the other. Cocking her head to one side, trying to work out what was going on. "Maybe he's got a ferret stuck down there or something," she reasoned. The other lady took another look and shrugged.

"Take's all sorts, I suppose," she remarked flatly. Then, shaking their heads they both went their separate ways, wondering what it was that they had just witnessed.

Meanwhile Rick Grinder was still hopping and dancing around on the pavement like some uncontrollable idiot.

"Owww…it hurts!" he winced.

Having considered all other options, there was nothing else for it. Doing as he was told, Rick Grinder took off his trousers in full view of the public.

"I bet you planned this, didn't you!" he sneered accusingly at Bill.

By now the dogs, who were hidden behind bushes, lamp posts and parked cars, had to put their paws to their mouths in order to stop themselves laughing.

"Tee-hee," giggled Pugsley, as he did his best to remain still whilst posing as a Christmas reindeer.

"Here let me help you," offered Bill, taking hold of his trousers.

"Get off me, you fool," Rick Grinder shouted showing his displeasure. There was nothing else for it, stood there in his underpants, Rick Grinder was going to have to go home and get changed.

Once he had sped off the dogs came out from their hiding places.

"Now I wasn't expecting that," Pugsley remarked. Barely able to believe what they had seen the dogs fell about laughing.

"I couldn't have planned it better myself if I had tried," said Bill, astonished by the whole incident.

By now the dogs had all gathered round and, having enjoyed their brief time as post dogs, wanted to help out some more.

"There's no point sending them home, not after all the training they've had," Pugsley noted.

"I say we carry on helping out," one of the other dogs piped up.

Bill had to agree. Now that they were fully fledged post dogs, why not let them carry on? For the dogs it wasn't like work really. It was more like fun. Pushing letters through a letterbox was a bit like chasing a stick, but rather than it being a stick, it was a letter.

Around town word spread fast about the post dogs, and everyone wanted to come out and see them. As they raced up driveways, people cheered them on and gave them a biscuit in return for dropping off their mail. To which, the dogs would proudly wag their tail and give a paw. The customers were so pleased with the dogs that they wanted to see them as a permanent feature. But Grandpa said once was enough, as they had far more important work to do in looking after humans.

Chapter 20

CHRISTMAS IS SUSPENDED

Barney

I t was Christmas Eve and it had been raining for days. Since there was no sign of it stopping, the dogs hunkered down in their baskets turning their noses up at the very notion of a walk when suggested by their owners. Out on the moors and hills, the ground underfoot was like a bog and ponies huddled together against the grey slate-tinged sky in small ragtag groups.

The long days of summer were now gone. The hum of insects and the idle thrum of tractors was just a dim and distant memory of what had been. All life yearned desperately for the return of the sun. Rivers ran swollen with water, coursing through valleys it rang out with a thunderous roar as the torrents washed away trees and ate away at the banking. Water voles could only pray that their homes wouldn't be destroyed while otters had taken to higher ground, leaving the riverbank for the temporary safety of the woods and fields beyond.

Even though it was Christmas and most people had finished work for the holidays, there were still those who had to labour on regardless. For the farmers there was no let up. The cattle still had to be mucked out and the sheep that were still out on the high moor had to be fed. But that was life on the land. They had to accept whatever nature threw at them. It was the same for the posties too. Still in their shorts and with their collars turned up against the weather, they went out to deliver the last minute parcels and presents, whatever the weather.

On the television they had been predicting for days about an upcoming storm. Alex and Niall's father had made sure that his boat was tied up securely in the harbour and that all his equipment and nets were lashed down. As the wind blew and grew in strength, the waves drove hard against the cliffs and harbour wall, filling the air with a thick salty spray. The inclement weather brought an added bonus for Alex and Niall: they knew that the bad weather meant their father would be joining them for Christmas. Aware of this, Granny made sure there was extra bedding ready and fussed around the house getting everything organised for when Grandpa came home from work, insisting that Christmas couldn't start without him.

At the newsagent's, Pugsley and Mr Peters were open as usual waiting for the final edition of the papers to turn up.

"Have you ever seen anything like it in all your years?" he commented gloomily to Pugsley. Meanwhile the paper boys and girls looked like drowned rats.

"Come in, come in," he said, ushering them in through the door.

Offering them a towel to dry themselves on, Mr Peters handed out the bags of sweets to all the paper boys and girls as a way of thanks for all their hard work throughout the year.

By now the papers were well overdue and Mr Peters looked at his watch all concerned. "What's happened to those papers?" he said to Pugsley as if expecting a reply.

No wiser as to their whereabouts, Pugsley just shrugged and stuck his nose to the glass as he continued to watch the rain outside.

Huddled by the steamed-up window, the paper boys and girls stared at the water rushing by.

"I've never seen rain like this. Do you think the papers will turn up?" asked one of them. Mr Peters peered out of the window. Weighing up whether or not to send the children home, he watched for what little movement there was out on the street before finally making up his mind.

"Right, that's it," he declared. "I'm not sending you out in this. If the papers do turn up, then, tough. They'll have to wait!"

The children cheered. No one wanted to go out in this rain. As they left to go home Pugsley came out to see them off. Once he was quite satisfied they were home safely, he stepped back inside to shake off the water, covering the magazines and Mr Peters in spray.

"Pugsley!" Mr Peters shouted in disgust. "Look what you've done!" pointing to the water-soaked periodicals. But Mr Peters couldn't be mad at Pugsley for long. He was far too cute for that. Taking hold of the towel, he rubbed Pugsley dry and as he did so the stocky little bulldog began to laugh.

"Stop tickling me!" he giggled. Seeing that his most favourite companion in the world was enjoying himself so much, he couldn't help but tickle him some more. Losing all sense of himself, Mr Peters rolled around on the floor making funny noises and pretending to be a dog.

"Merry Christmas, Pugsley," he said.

"Merry Christmas," the bulldog barked back.

At which point the bell above the door rang and in walked Mrs Armitage for her morning paper.

"Sorry. Am I interrupting something?" she said, looking all put out.

Taken aback by the sudden intrusion, Mr Peters picked himself up off the floor and acted as if nothing had happened.

"Morning, Mrs Armitage," replied Mr Peters, trying his best to keep a straight face. "We were just… we were just…" he said struggling to find the words to explain himself. He knew then that there was no way she would be able to understand and that sometimes you just had to let your inner dog come out and play.

Meanwhile at the sorting office, everyone had turned up extra early so they could get home and spend more time with their families. Begrudgingly Rick Grinder had agreed to allow the posties to put up a tree. But had drawn the line at lights on account that it would be using unnecessary electric.

The posties were busy sorting the last of the Christmas cards and presents when the telephone rang.

Rick Grinder rushed to pick it up. "Hello, Berrycombe St Martin sorting office."

"Hello, Mr Grinder," came the voice down the phone. It was Karen, the post lady who was covering Grandpa's old round. "I'm not feeling very well. It must be something I ate, but I won't be able to come into work this morning," she said, apologising for the inconvenience she knew it would cause.

"Can I ask what's wrong with you?" he enquired.

"I've been sick… a lot," she replied.

"Hmm…how much is a lot?" he wanted to know as he sat perched on the edge of his desk biting his nails nervously. "Is that just a little bit, a couple of times, or more than twice?" he grilled her, probing her for more information.

"A lot!" Karen snapped back.

"I know it's a big ask but…" said Rick Grinder, winding himself up to something more, "but we're really stuck and you'd really be doing us a favour if you could come in and just take out a bit of mail."

"Mr Grinder, I'm poorly, I can't," Karen stated.

"Not even the tinseyest-winceyest bit?" he said, his fingers barely touching as if measuring out the tiniest of amounts.

"No, not even that!" she answered him back, before wishing him a Merry Christmas and putting the phone down on him.

Left holding the phone, Rick Grinder suddenly realised he was stuck. The mail had to go out, but there was only one person in the office that knew the round and that was Bill. There was no way he was going to go grovelling to him, not after he had made a fool of him on TV and made him take his trousers off in public. Besides he had banned him from driving and there was no way he was going to ask for help from him.

Rick Grinder thought for a minute and wondered just how hard it could be to go out and stick a couple of letters through a few doors? If a postie could do it, then so could he! Marching out of his office he announced to everyone that as Karen wasn't coming into work, he would be taking Bill's old round out. Everyone looked at each other dumbfounded.

"Rick Grinder's going to do Bill's round?" they said with disbelief. "Does he know where he's going?" the posties whispered.

Norman, the senior postman, gently took hold of Rick Grinder by the arm and pulled him to one side.

"Excuse me, Mr Grinder, I heard what you were saying about taking Bill's round out on your own and I'm not so sure that's a good idea, sir," he said, trying to be as polite as possible so as not to offend him.

"Nonsense! How hard can delivering a few letters be?" he replied, all sure of himself.

Norman bit his bottom lip as he thought how best to get him to reconsider.

"It's not that easy, sir. It's not just like looking at a map. You see there's all sorts of little out of the way places and short cuts where you could get lost," he said, trying to be as tactful as possible.

"Ridiculous!" Rick Grinder crowed, shunning Norman's well-meaning request.

Norman was worried about him being out there all on his own.

"Have you thought about asking Bill?" Norman enquired. "It is his round after all and, I mean, it wouldn't hurt would it?"

Rick Grinder gulped uncomfortably. It looked as if he was having second thoughts about going out on his own. Whispering from out of the corner of his mouth so as not to draw attention to himself, he quizzed Norman about the particulars of postal work.

"Surely anybody can do it, can't they?" he said discreetly.

Norman looked awkward. "It's not that…" he sighed letting his words trail off. "…it's just…"

"Just what?" Rick Grinder demanded to know.

"You'll get lost." Norman stated plainly.

Mulling over his predicament, Rick Grinder pursed his lips together while he came to a decision.

"If I put that Bill Mathers back on his round, it will look like he's won, won't it? And I'm not letting that stupid, dog-whispering idiot win."

"It's not about winning, sir. It's about you being safe and getting the job done," Norman tactfully reminded him.

"I'll have you know, I wasn't voted the most efficient Manager five years running for nothing!"

"That's as may be, sir, but I strongly advise you to reconsider. Bill could quite easily do it. You could then sit in your office, where it's nice and warm and put your feet up. Now wouldn't that be better, sir?" said Norman, trying to make the prospect of staying in the office look more attractive.

Outside the weather had not got any better. In fact it looked to be getting worse. From the window of his office, Rick Grinder watched as the rain blew sideways across the yard. Wrinkling up his nose he wondered if he had made the right decision to go out, but there was no way he was backing down now.

The weather wasn't any better for dogs either. With no great desire to venture out in such inclement conditions, there was not a solitary murmur to be heard on the Barking News. All was quiet. Holly the Pup was snuggled up in the kitchen in her soft, warm basket. Ted, the Australian shepherd dog, was fast asleep, out of the way of any sheep. Little Staffy, as always was looking for something to eat, and Lopez was watching expectantly as his human wrapped the presents. Wondering if Santa was going to bring him another Rudolph or a dolly, as the ones he got last year he had already chewed to bits.

Elsewhere, Gem woke up to the sound of rain hammering down on the barn and the predictable drip, drip, drip of water as it found its way in through the gaps on the roof. As much as she wished she could go back to sleep, she knew she had to get up and go help Mr Cranbrook with the animals. With her usual enthusiasm she bounded down the steps of the hayloft and ran across the farmyard, splashing through the puddles, pushing the front door open with her nose.

In the hallway the smell of cooking permeated the house. Gem sniffed the air excitedly. Bacon... Sausages too! Gem never got to taste a cooked breakfast, the only thing she ever got were the leftovers, the odd bit of bacon rind, a gristly half-chewed sausage or whatever the children did not want.

Squeezing her head through the gap in the door she pushed it open with her nose and made her way into the kitchen.

Mr Cranbrook was leant over the cooker when he suddenly became aware of a presence in the room.

"Ahh, there you are girl," he sighed holding a frying pan in one hand and a fish slice in the other. "Woof, woof," barked Gem.

"Shhh...quiet!" said Mr Cranbrook, putting his finger to his lips and pointing to his family asleep upstairs. "It's not Christmas yet. I know, but seeing as we've got the place to ourselves we might as well enjoy the peace and quiet, eh?" He winked knowingly.

"Here you are, girl," he said, holding out his hand to Gem. There between his thick, calloused fingers was a sausage! She couldn't believe her luck.

"For me?" she said with a soft whimper of thanks.

"Merry Christmas, girl," he said, giving her a wink. Gem gently took the sausage from his hand and Mr Cranbrook gave her a pat on the head in return. Taking it away, she lay down under the table and carefully bit it into smaller pieces using the side of her mouth and paw to hold it.

"Go steady, there's more to come," Mr Cranbrook told her. Leaning over the cooker with his back to her, the pan sizzled and popped as yet more sausages and bacon were being cooked.

"These are just for us!" he declared, with a big grin on his face as if letting her in on a secret that only the two of them knew about.

Cracking a few eggs into the pan and putting on some toast, Mr Cranbrook took a couple of plates out of the cupboard and put them on the side ready. While she waited for him, Gem went to fetch him that week's racing news from out in the hallway. Carrying it through in her mouth, she placed it down at his feet.

"Oh... thanks, girl," he said, giving her a smile and putting it down on the table for him to read later.

Sliding the contents of the frying pan onto the plates, he picked one of them up and put it down on the floor in front of her. When Gem saw what she was getting, her eyes lit up.

"Now, careful, this is hot!" he cautioned her. Having cut it up into little pieces for her, there was toast, eggs, bacon, beans, tomatoes and sausage, all the good stuff that she never normally got. Gem was in heaven. She had never had a full cooked breakfast all to herself before.

While Mr Cranbrook read the paper and tucked into his breakfast, she got down to hers. With her rough tongue she licked at the yellow yolk that had spread itself across the plate and chomping away on the toast she made funny little noises with her throat as she tried to swallow it. Staring admiringly at Mr Cranbrook, she looked up at him with a trickle of egg yolk on her nose.

"Come here, girl," he said, licking his thumb then rubbing it off and wiping it on his trousers.

"That's better," he chuckled, shaking his head.

Several cups of tea later, Mr Cranbrook put down the paper and gazed outside.

"I don't like the look of that out there, eh, girl?" he frowned, knowing that at some stage he was going to have to go out and see to the animals. "Oh well, suppose we better get on with it, otherwise it'll never get done," he sighed, resigning himself to the fact that they had to go out into the teeth of a howling storm. Pulling on his wellies and big green over trousers, he slipped on his coat and pulled his cap tight making sure that it wouldn't blow off.

"C'mon then!" he gestured to Gem, beckoning for her to join him. With a full tummy, Gem staggered to her feet as she got up off the slate floor.

Outside on the bike, the rain blew hard against her face and stung at her eyes. Squinting into the prevailing weather, she tucked herself in behind Mr Cranbrook as they battled the elements, his head lowered with a look of grim determination.

In places the lanes were almost impassable. With drains blocked there was nowhere for the water to go. The puddles just got bigger and bigger. Even Mr Cranbrook was unsure as to whether or not risk going through the flood water. As they scooted along the back lanes, they did their best to avoid the branches that the raging southwesterly had blown down. Torn branches were strewn across the roads and it wasn't long before they were stopped dead in their tracks by a felled tree. There, lying across the road was a slender old beech, its sinuous grey trunk blocking the road ahead.

"Looks like we're going to have to get the chainsaw," Mr Cranbrook shouted, trying to make himself heard above the bellowing gale. Gem nodded and licked at the water that was dripping from her snout. There were still sheep out in the fields that needed feeding and they couldn't be left, so, turning the bike around, they headed back to the farm to get the chainsaw.

As Rick Grinder drove along the exposed moorland roads, the wind buffeted the van from side to side and the rain lashed down so hard that the windscreen wipers struggled to keep pace with the deluge. The van full with last minute parcels.

"Pah!" sneered Rick Grinder in contempt of the weather. "I'll show these posties that there's nothing to it," he said, following the directions given to him by the sat nav. "I'll be back in my office with my feet up in no time!" he confidently chuckled to himself. The sat nav then directed him to turn off the main road and down a tiny little side lane.

"In two hundred yards you have reached your destination," the voice announced. Peering out into the gloom Rick Grinder looked around to see where this supposed house was. All he could see were trees.

"Where is this infernal place!" he shouted, banging his fist on the steering wheel.

The lane led down into a steeply sided valley. Cut into the hillside, flanked by moss-covered walls and ancient trees on both sides, it was only wide enough for one vehicle at a time. Rick Grinder was getting stressed. Driving further down the lane he continued to look for the house when the voice of the sat nav spoke up. "You have passed your destination. If possible make a u-turn." came the calm voice.

"Arrgggh!" yelled Rick Grinder, standing on the brakes and thumping the horn. "Where is this wretched place?" he yelled, putting the van into gear and reversing back up the hill. Staring out of the window, he looked for some sort of dwelling or house that could possibly resemble the place he was looking for. Then, set amongst a thicket of trees, he saw a small white cottage poking out of the gloom.

"At last," he snarled. Rushing out into the rain, he ran up the gravel path towards the house.

Kizzy

"Woof, woof, woof, woof, woof," barked the dog from behind the door.

Having total disregard for all dogs, Rick Grinder opened the letterbox and looked inside. There behind the door, jumping up and down excitedly, was Kizzy, a black and white spanier. Now I suppose you're wondering what a spanier is, aren't you? Well, it is in fact a spaniel crossed with a terrier, just in case you didn't know.

Kizzy's owners, Mr and Mrs Deerhart, had bought her when she was just a pup and had been told that she would grow up to be a spaniel. As with all dogs, when they're young they all look the same and you can't tell one from the other. So, when Kizzy turned up at the Deerhart's looking as cute as possible, it wasn't until she started to grow that they noticed that she didn't quite look how a spaniel should. She had tiny legs, a small body, big floppy ears and a long spaniel-like tail. But that didn't matter to them as they loved her all the same, whether she was a spaniel, a terrier or somewhere in between.

Whenever Bill came to the house, Kizzy would rush up to him and lick him on the hand. He would give her a biscuit and in return she would roll over to have her tummy tickled, and if she got too excited sometimes, she'd wee herself, and sprinkle him like a fountain.

Anyway, this morning Kizzy had heard the postie coming up the path and was excited to see who it was. Expectantly jumping up behind the door she was hoping it was going to be Bill, but unfortunately, it was the disliker of dogs, the kicker of canines: Rick Grinder.

Laughing to himself, he positioned the mail on the lip of the letterbox and, waiting for the right moment, watched as Kizzy bounced up and down. Then bang...! Firing the mail through the box as hard as he could, he hit the young spanier square in the mouth. There was a stunned silence from the otherside the door and then some hushed whimpering.

"Ha-ha!" Rick Grinder sniggered, all pleased with himself before disappearing down the garden path.

Mrs Deerhart, who had heard what had happened came rushing to the door.

"I saw what you did! What sort of a human being are you?" she shouted, waving her mail at him. However, Rick Grinder was as pleased as punch at his shameless antics.

"Come back. I want your name," she called after him, but Rick Grinder didn't care.

Speeding off down the lane, he jumped in and out of the van as he delivered the next few houses.

"Hello postie, Merry Christmas!" said one of the customers, wishing him well, but all Rick Grinder could do was scowl back at them.

"What's so MERRY about Christmas?" he replied in a decidedly un-festive mood.

When Rick Grinder reached the next village, people were already looking out for the postie. Hopping out of the van, he hurriedly opened the back doors and was greeted with a great rumble when the entire contents of the van fell out on top of him, knocking him to the ground.

"These infernal parcels!" Rick Grinder grumbled.

Getting to his feet and clambering out from underneath the mountain of boxes, he vented his anger on the parcels, kicking them and throwing them into the van, such was his temper.

"That can't be Bill," commented one old man to his wife who was watching out of his window at Rick Grinder's antics.

"Why's that, dear?" his wife enquired.

"Well, he seems awfully bad-tempered and he's kicking the parcels all over the place."

"Really?" said his wife coming through to see. "Mmm," she remarked with an air of disgust. "That's not Bill, he would never do such a thing. The sooner we get him back, the better we shall all be!"

After Rick Grinder had finished having his tantrum, he got back in his van and realised that he still had a stack of mail left to deliver. There was no way he was going to get all this mail delivered on time. There was only one thing for it, he thought, Christmas was going to have to be suspended.

As he sped along the lanes, missing out house after house, he threw the mail into the back of the van along with all the presents too.

"Ha! They'll just have to wait," he laughed, knowing full well that there would be some upset children and adults about.

In cottages and houses, children were stood at the window eagerly waiting the arrival of the postman, but all Rick Grinder did was sneer at them as he flew past in his van.

Missing out whole villages he drove as fast as he could, forcing cars off the road and tooting his horn at dog walkers as he covered them in muddy ditch water.

As morning turned to lunchtime and then to afternoon the rain had not let up. Muddy water poured out of the fields and streams and rivers ran swollen, raging with unstoppable power. Churning and heaving, the water boiled and crashed sweeping away anything that got in its path, washing away bridges and even threatening homes with flooding.

Dropping down into one of the many valleys, Rick Grinder's progress was suddenly brought to a halt by a swollen ford. Angrily he got out of his van and began cursing his luck. Facing the dilemma as to whether to carry on or not he looked around for something to test the depth of the water. Finding a fallen branch he poked around at the edge of the murky water.

The thickly stained waters swirled around the stick setting forth spinning eddies into the fast flowing currents. Gurgling and groaning like a living being, the water reached halfway up the gnarled branch as he considered his options.

"Ha!" he scoffed, puffing out his chest with pride. "A piffling little thing like this won't stop me," he declared.

Getting back in the van, he reversed up the road to give himself enough of a run up. Then, putting his foot down raced down the lane. Hitting the water he created a bow wave that shot up in front of him. Keeping his foot down on the accelerator he urged the van on.

"Come on, you useless automobile. I've seen kiddies' pedal cars with more power than this!" he raged.

However just as he reached the middle of the ford, the water began to rise up over the bonnet and rush into the footwell, filling up with cold, murky water. Screaming as his feet began to get wet, he pressed the accelerator all the way down to the floor, but it didn't make a blind bit of difference. The van shuddered, coughed then suddenly stopped dead in the middle of the river. The lights went off and Rick Grinder was left there, all alone with nothing but silence and the sound of surging water around him.

Chapter 21

A SHINING LIGHT

Tiny

All the shops had closed for the evening and the streets were quiet. Everyone had gone home to spend Christmas Eve with their families. Behind every door and window lights were shining brightly and people were having fun.

At home Alex and Niall were waiting patiently for their grandfather to finish work. Sat around the telly with their Dad, Granny had allowed them to open the Christmas treats early. On the table were dishes full of nuts, crisps and all sorts of other goodies that Granny had put out to help themselves to. Niall had even saved a few cheese footballs for the mice, sneaking them into his pocket. After all, it was the season of goodwill to all men and Niall was pretty sure that extended to mice too.

Back at the office Bill was shaking the worst of the rain off his jacket when Norman approached him looking rather worried. Straight away Bill's inner dog began to twitch. He could sense something was wrong.

"What's the matter, Norman? You got a problem?" he asked.

Norman stroked his chin anxiously. "It's nearly five o'clock and Rick Grinder hasn't come back yet," he said, looking up at the clock on the wall.

Bill knew this didn't sound good. "Has he not rung in or anything?"

Norman shook his head. "No, but we've got customers from all over the round ringing in to say that they haven't had their mail yet. What are we going to do, Bill? Something's happened to him." he said sounding worried.

Joining Norman in his tiny office, Bill picked up the phone and rang around a few of his old customers on his round.

"Hello…is that Mr Finnegan? This is Bill… the postman. Could you tell me if you had any mail today, or at least seen the postman at all?"

Desperate to hear of any news, Norman leaned over Bill's shoulder to listen in.

"… What's that… you haven't?" said Bill. After thanking Mr Finnegan for his time, he rang round a couple of his other customers who he thought might be able to help.

"Hello, Mrs Taphouse? It's Bill. Yes, Bill…your old postman," he explained. Again he asked if she'd seen any sign of the postman and, after replying that she hadn't, she told him that she was still waiting for some of her Christmas presents to arrive. He thanked her for her patience and said he would do his best to get them to her. The story was much the same elsewhere.

However, there had been a few sightings of Rick Grinder and, when Mrs Deerhart recounted what had happened to Kizzy, Bill shook his head in disgust.

"What sort of a person does that to a dog?" he tutted, agreeing with her.

After a few more phone calls, Bill thought he had narrowed it down to where Rick Grinder had been seen last.

"He's somewhere between Keens Hill and Frampton Bishop," he said, tapping the side of his nose and giving Norman a sly wink.

"How do you know that?" Norman asked, looking puzzled.

"Well, Mrs Deerhart lives at Winsford Mill, she saw him this morning, and old Tom Price who lives at Steppes Farm also saw him, but Pete Levy at Warren Cross hasn't seen anyone all day. He must be stuck somewhere between Keens Hill and Frampton Bishop."

"Well I'll be!" exclaimed Norman, impressed with Bill's detective work. "But what are we going to do? I can't go out looking for him. I'll have to stay here and look after the office in case he turns up," said Norman reluctantly.

"What about you? You could go?" he said, looking at Bill hopefully.

"I can't go! I'm not allowed to drive, if you remember," he replied. Stumped as what to do, Bill then had a sudden flash of inspiration.

"I know!" he exclaimed with a mischievous look on his face. "Just you wait here and I'll be back in a minute."

Bill disappeared leaving Norman scratching his head wondering what he was up to. Standing on his tip-toes with his face to the glass, Bill peeked through the blinds of the Managers office.

There, underneath the window, propped against the wall was his old bike. It seemed like Rick Grinder hadn't got round to scrapping it, after all. Testing the door, Bill found that it was open and creeping into the office took a moment to be reunited with his old bike.

Squeezing the tyres, he pulled at the brakes and finally, gave the whole thing a good shake. He was ready to go. Wheeling his bike down the corridor he shouted to Norman to come and see.

"What do you think?" he called out.

Norman did a double take. "You can't go out on that. It's pitch black and throwing it down out there."

Bill laughed. "Are you sure you?" Norman said looking concerned."You don't have to go out. I mean, after all, he's not been very nice to you, has he?"

Putting his coat on and zipping it up tight, Bill looked at him.

"I know he's been pretty awful, but he's still a human being, isn't he? What sort of person would I be, if I didn't help?" Norman agreed.

Outside it was tipping it down. Throwing his leg over the cross-bar, he hopped on the bike and set the crank turning. Pedalling along the damp streets, the raindrops caught in the bike's headlight making for a temporary distraction to what was going to be a long night. It was then, rounding the corner of the high street that a four-legged silhouette came into view. Bill recognised that dog anywhere.

"Pugsley!" he shouted. Distracted from his business, the rotund little bulldog looked up.

"Bill! What are you doing here? Shouldn't you be at home with your family?" he asked.

Bill nodded, "Yeah, but we've got an emergency."

"What sort of emergency?" Pugsley asked, shaking the rain from his coat and pricking up his ears.

"Rick Grinder's gone and got himself lost."

"Oh dear." barked Pugsley.

While Bill explained to his canine friend that Rick Grinder was out somewhere beyond Keens Hill, Pugsley, stared longingly at his bike.

"Any chance a chubby old bulldog like me might be allowed to come along for a ride, just for old time's sake?"

"Be my guest," said Bill. "But won't Mr Peters want to know where you are?"

"He's watching TV with a box full of chocolates all to himself," barked Pugsley, looking up at the light coming from the window above. "I'm sure he won't notice if I'm gone for an hour or two." He tittered in a way that all mischievous dogs do.

"Well, what are we waiting for then?" Bill replied, glad that his old cycling pal was coming to join him.

It was tough cycling into the wind and rain, but that didn't deter the pair. Sitting in the basket, Pugsley helped pass the time by listing his most favourite things that he liked about Christmas.

"Christmas pudding. I love Christmas pudding!" he declared. "Especially if it's covered in Brandy butter," he howled in delight, licking his lips.

"…and pigs in blankets, too," he cooed.

While listening to Pugsley ramble on, Bill thought about all the things that made Christmas special for him.

"What about peace on earth, haven't you forgotten that?" Bill reminded him, tucking his head in low against the wind.

"Oh yes, of course. Peace on earth," barked Pugsley over the howling gale. "That's a given. It's the only way to go," he said, screwing up his little face to protect his eyes from the stinging rain.

The light on the front of the bike cut through the heavy cloak of darkness, illuminating their way along the narrow winding lanes. Above them the heaving branches groaned and whistled as if taunting them, but it didn't put Bill off. Listening to his inner dog, he ignored the haunting noises and forced his aching muscles to go on. Pugsley joined him too in his defiance of the weather. Howling at stones and pebbles that scuttled along in the water filled gullies at the side of the road. Giving his biggest and bravest bark as he tried to chase them off. "Ruff, ruff, ruff," he went.

In return Bill gave him an affectionate pat on the head, to show his appreciation for his efforts. "Well done, lad!" he said, acknowledging that Pugsley was doing his best to keep their spirits up.

From the top of Keens Hill the road wound down and down, twisting this way and that before finally reaching the ford at the bottom. As they sped down the hill at terrific speed, they came to a screeching halt. The sound of river was so loud that it could be heard over the din of the storm.

"I don't like the sound of this." said Bill, listening to the water rushing by. Dismounting, they walked towards the river in order to get a better look.

The bike's light cast a long beam out into the darkness and in the shadows, it caught the shape of cresting waves as they surged down stream. Bill could hardly believe it. He knew the road so well and normally the water was that shallow you could walk across it without getting your feet wet. Making low moaning sounds it rumbled and shook, as it carried with it all sorts of hidden debris and rocks.

Wondering what to do, Bill looked down at Pugsley.

"I'm afraid there's only one thing for it. We're going to have to walk down stream and see if we can cross there."

The once gentle stream was now swollen beyond all recognition. The banks of the stream were no longer visible as the flood waters spilled out onto the fields beyond, forming lakes and marshy puddles. With damp feet and damp paws, the two of them trudged through the soggy pastures pushing the bike along with them. The cattle and the sheep that had been left out in the fields to brave out the storm looked on bemused at the two companions as they tried to make sense of what a human and a dog would be doing out on a night like this.

At home Granny had anxiously been looking at her watch and knew something was wrong when she heard the phone ring. Answering it, she found that it was Norman on the other end. Recounting the tale of how Rick Grinder had gone missing, he told her how her husband had gone to find him.

"What, in this weather?" she replied sounding horrified. "On his bike?" she gasped. Aware that something was wrong, her son who had been happily watching TV immediately leapt from his chair and ran over to reassure her.

"It's alright, Mum. I'll go help," he said trying to offer some assistance, but Granny, putting her hand to the phone and covering the mouthpiece, told him that under no such circumstance would he do such a thing.

"There's no one that knows those moors and lanes better than your Dad," she told him, before apologising to Norman for the interruption.

Norman assured her that he would let her know as soon he heard any news.

Meanwhile, leading the way, Pugsley sniffed out a safe route for them to follow across the fields. Being as it was so dark, he stopped every few paces to give a reassuring bark and to let Bil know where he was.

"Good lad!" Bill shouted back to his friend. Tramping through the water-logged fields, Bill was beginning to find the going slow. Up to his knees in mud and not wanting to waste any time, he encouraged Pugsley to push on.

"Keep going, lad!" he shouted, as he struggled to pull himself out of the thick, boggy mud.

With his nose to the ground Pugsley routed this way and that, sticking his snout into all sorts of interesting smells as he picked a way through the soggy fields. In amongst everything, he could smell rabbits, foxes, deer and all sorts of other small rodents. He wasn't bothered that it was raining or that it was muddy. He loved it. It wasn't often that he got to go out on such an adventure and take in such interesting smells.

Then, coming to a halt, he stopped dead in his tracks. Having a good sniff, it seemed that he had come across a scent that seemed out of place. Snuffling around with his nose, he investigated it some more.

"Woof, woof, woof," he barked excitedly. Listening intently, Bill could tell by the tone of Pugsley's bark that he'd found something.

"What is it, lad?" he said, dumping his bike in the long grass and rushing over to his side. When he got to him, Bill found Pugsley rooted to the spot. With his nose to the ground, his curly tail pointed as straight as a curly tail could ever point.

"I've smelt that smell before," Pugsley declared, baring his teeth and growling with displeasure.

"What is it…a stag?" Bill speculated.

"No, it's Rick Grinder," barked Pugsely, wagging his tail with satisfaction.

"Are you sure?" asked Bill.

Pugsley threw him a disapproving look.

"I'll never forget the smell of that aftershave of his!"

Bill then asked him if he thought he could find him.

"Just you wait here and I'll be back in a minute," he barked. The self-assured bulldog then scampered off into the night with his nose firmly planted to the ground.

With water dripping from his cap, Bill stood under a tree for shelter. It wasn't long before his patience paid off when off in the distance he heard frantic barking sounds coming from somewhere downstream. He knew that Pugsley must have found him.

Making his way along the banking as fast as he could, he stumbled across Pugsley who was covered in mud, his nose twitching and pointing to an old tree that had been washed down by the river.

"Look, there!" barked Pugsley. Bill strained to see anything in the dark. All he could make out was a tangle of branches and various bits of debris that had washed up against the fallen tree.

"I can't see anything. Are you sure he's there?" asked Bill, leaning further out into the river to get a better view.

Frustrated Pugsley barked back, "Look! There's your van sticking out from between all those branches."

Squinting hard Bill could just make out the shape of his van: submerged with its nose down and bottom up in the water.

"Rick, Rick!" He shouted, trying to get the manager's attention. There was no response and Bill feared the worst, but he wasn't giving up. He kept trying. After much shouting and yelling, Rick Grinder's pale face appeared from at the window.

"Rick, Rick, are you alright?" He asked, but there was no reply, he was far too shocked to answer.

"He doesn't look good," noted Bill. "There's only one thing for it. We're going to have to rescue him." Pugsley looked up at him in disbelief.

"If it hasn't occurred to you, Bill, we haven't got any rope. And I hate to be the one to break it to you: that neither of us will be coming out of there alive if we go in after him,"

Bill scrabbled around in the dark, trying to find something that he could lay his hands on, a stick, a bit of nylon cord, but there was nothing. As the water surged by, it was obvious that it was flowing far too fast to risk going in.

"Look, there must be a dog round here that can help us?" suggested Pugsley, doing a little dance as he tried to keep his feet out of the rising water. "You must know of at least one?"

"I do, but we're never going to get hold of them in this weather, are we?" Bill replied.

"Well, we'll have to give it a try. There's nothing else for it. I could put out an Emergency Barking News."

Out of all options and with no way forward, Bill agreed to give it a go. Pugsley reassured him that everything would be fine and that he wouldn't be long. He just needed to find some higher ground. Before setting off to help he gave Bill a good rub against his leg, just to show him how much he loved him.

Pushing his fat little bottom through the gaps in hedgerows, Pugsley waddled as fast as his short legs would carry him and soon he reached the top of the valley. Taking a minute to catch his breath, he let out a series of barks in hope that someone might hear him over the driving wind and rain.

"Calling all dogs, calling all dogs: this is an Emergency Barking News. We require assistance with a trapped man." On a night like this he was not sure that there would be any dogs out there to hear him, but he gave it a go all the same. He repeated the message in the hope that at least one dog would hear him.

Up at Drue Farm, Ted, the Australian shepherd dog had been put outside for the night after stealing the best part of Mrs Rouse's turkey that she had put aside for Christmas Day. Laid in the porch with a tummy full of bird and sleeping off the worst of his indulgences, he wasn't sure if he was dreaming when he heard a dog barking. Cocking his head to listen, he thought he was hearing things. But there, unmistakably, in the distance, was a dog howling away.

"Well, blow me. If that's not a dog out there on the Barking News and in this weather too!" he exclaimed, sounding all surprised. Staggering to his feet, he sploshed across the muddy farmyard to hear better what was being said.

"Must be desperate if they be out on a night like this," he grumbled to himself as the wind whistled round the out buildings and blew through the power lines like a banshee. Taking shelter behind an old stone wall he hid out of the rain and the worst that the storm had to offer.

"This be Ted. Who is that?" he said, barking as loud as he could in an effort to be heard over the howling gale.

"This is Pugsley. I have an Emergency Barking News," came the barely audible reply. "I'm with Bill the postman and we're trying to rescue a person that's trapped in the river."

"Bill, have you got Bill with you?" Ted asked shocked to think that Bill would be out on an evening such as this.

"That's right," replied Pugsley. Ted knew he couldn't let Bill down, not after all the strokes, petting and biscuits that he had received over the years.

"Don't you worry. We'll have this sorted out. You can rely on us dogs," came his reply as he rushed off into action.

Glancing up at the weather, Ted didn't hold out much hope of being able to raise another dog on an evening like this. As the wind blew and the rain soaked through his thick matted coat, Ted cleared his throat and let out the biggest howl of his entire life, hoping that it would be heard all the way across the moors and to the Combes beyond.

Being as it was Christmas Eve and such terrible weather, he

half suspected that most dogs would be safely tucked up inside having their tummies tickled while their owners were sat watching TV. However, luckily for Ted, Holly the Pup, who was desperate for a widdle and had slipped out of the back door, when she heard Ted calling across the fields. Tearing herself away from sniffing where next door's cat had been rubbing itself up against the plant pots, she responded to Ted's call.

"Ted, is that you?"

"Yes mi' lover. It be me. I'll make this quick," he hurriedly explained."This is an Emergency Barking News. Bill the postman is in trouble and I need the help of every dog you can muster, down by the river as soon as possible."

"The river?" barked Holly thinking she hadn't heard him correctly.

"Yes, the river, mi' dear, and don't delay." And without any further instructions Ted signed off.

Up the lane at the next farm lived Gem. Holly was confident that it wouldn't take long to raise her and so setting about barking she began to transmit the message.

"Gem," she yelped, her tiny voice getting lost in the storm. "We have an Emergency Barking News." she yapped.

While waiting for a response Holly sat patiently under the light of the back door as the sound of carols rang out from inside the house. As the church bells tolled over in the next village, she waited and waited, but still no reply was forthcoming.

"Gem, where are you?" she squealed in desperation. Getting in a tizz, she anxiously ran around the yard a few times as she tried to think of what to do. After a few minutes of silliness, she decided that it was no use, and that she would have to go and see her in person.

Scamping down the path that ran between the cottages, she turned out onto the lane and set off running as fast as her little legs would carry her. Barking as she went, she ran all the way up the road without stopping. It didn't take long for her to reach Merrivale Farm and when she got there she found the farmhouse with its lights on.

Running up to the front door, she let out a series of barks as she tried to grab Gem's attention, but it was no use. The TV was on that loud that there was no way Gem was ever going to hear her over all that noise. There had to be a way to get Gem's attention. Running round to the back of the house she found herself in luck.

There in the back door was a cat-flap, just the right size for a wire-haired terrier to squeeze through. Pushing herself through the pint-sized hole, she suddenly found herself in the kitchen. All on her own she wondered what to do next. With the sound of laughter coming from the room next door, she followed her instincts and headed for where all the noise was.

Bounding into the room like a supercharged dynamo, she took everyone by surprise. Mr Cranbrook almost spat his tea out when the white and tan ball of fluff flew into the room.

"What the heck is that?" he spluttered, taken aback by the animal that had just invaded his living room.

"It's Pup from down the lane," exclaimed Rachel who was laid out in front of the fire with her pyjamas on watching telly.

"I know it's Pup," her father blurted out. "But what's she doing in my house?" he demanded to know.

Charging around the room and jumping up on everybody putting muddy footprints everywhere, Gem urged her to calm down.

"What is it, Pup? What's got into you?" she barked trying to rein in Holly's excitement. Out of breath and with her tiny pink tongue hanging out, the terrier tried to explain herself.

"It's a…it's a…a…," she said, barely able to get her words out.

"Slow down. Take a deep breath," Gem instructed her.

Doing as she was told she composed herself before finally managing to get her words out. "It's an Emergency Barking News," she gasped in between breaths.

"An Emergency Barking News?" Gem replied sounding surprised. "But it's Christmas Eve. Are you sure?" she enquired.

After her run up the lane Holly was too tired to speak and all she could do was give a simple nod.

"Maybe if we give her a minute to catch her breath, she might be able to tell us some more," said Rachel, getting up on to her knees.

As the border collie paced back and forth in front of the fire, Rachel's mother wanted to know what was going on. Explaining that something serious was going on, Rachel told her that no dog would send out an Emergency Barking News on Christmas Eve, not unless it was urgent.

"Do I need to phone the police?" her mother wanted to know, getting up from the sofa and putting down her drink.

"I don't know." answered Rachel. "It depends on what Pup here's got to tell us."

The wire haired terrier rested for a while and, after Rachel's brother had given her a party sausage from the fridge, she had recovered enough energy to be able to speak.

"Ted sent the message," explained Holly. "He wants us to meet him down by the river. It's Bill the postman…"

"Bill!" exclaimed Gem sounding all worried. "What's wrong? What's happened to him?" she asked, the concern evident in her bark.

"Bill's fine," replied Holly. "But there's someone stuck in the river." That was as much as Holly could recall.

"Well, there's nothing else for it," barked Gem. "It's an emergency. We'll have to go."

By now Mr Cranbrook was looking thoroughly bemused by all this barking that was going on, and to further add to his confusion was that his daughter seemed to regard the fact that two dogs talking to each other was an everyday occurrence. Getting up off the sofa, he demanded to know what was going on.

"Look, dear," he said to his wife. "What's wrong with these bloomin' dogs?"

"You'll have to ask your daughter. She seems to be the one in the know," she calmly replied, finding her husband's irritation amusing.

Exasperated, and with his arms open wide as if to say what was going on, her father demanded an answer.

"Well, Dad, it's like this…," she began. It didn't take long for Rachel to explain that there was a dog emergency and that all the other dogs had to help out.

"It's the rules," she said. Her father shook his head in disbelief.

"Am I the only one round here that doesn't seem to think that dogs can talk?" he ranted, venting his frustration. Not saying a word, his family looked at him disapprovingly. Being grumpy at Christmas was not allowed.

By now the two dogs were scratching impatiently at the front door, howling to be let out. Realising that he'd get no peace till he did, Mr Cranbrook lifted the paint-encrusted latch and the two dogs burst out of the door with a turn of speed that he'd rarely seen from an animal, never mind a dog. Scratching his chin Mr Cranbrook couldn't help but wonder if there was something in it, that dogs could talk.

Running across the fields Gem barked over to Holly, her short little legs going nineteen to the dozen as she tried to keep pace with the border collie.

"Look," barked Gem. "I'm going to find Bill. I need you to muster as many dogs as possible, I've a feeling we're going to need some help," she said, listening to her doggy instincts.

Following Gem's instructions, Holly peeled off and made a bee-line for the nearest house: jumping five-bar gates as if she were a show dog and leaping ditches without so much as getting a paw wet.

At the first house she came across, she found the back door open and rain blowing in. Wondering why it should have been left open on such an awful evening she cautiously entered, nosing her way through the kitchen and into the dimly lit hallway. She soon found herself confronted by a pair of lifeless human legs hanging over the end of the sofa. Timidly she looked around and there laid out in front of the TV was Lightning.

"Pssssst…psssst," went Holly as she tried to get his attention.

Lightning's velvety ears pricked up as he looked round. "Pup!" he said with a soft low bark, so as not to be heard. Getting up, he trotted over to her.

"You could have got yourself in trouble," he told her, nodding his head in the direction of his owner who was asleep on the sofa. "Lucky, he's had a few drinks…," Lightning whispered, "…but if he'd have been awake, he might have hurt you, or worse still, sold you to someone for money."

"Sorry, I had to come. It's an emergency," she said apologising. Hurriedly she explained to him that Bill was in trouble and needed their help.

"But it's Christmas Eve?" Lightning said sounding surprised. "Who goes out on Christmas Eve?"

Having already explained this to Gem, Holly shrugged. She didn't have time to recall the whole story again. Instead she told him that they had a dog emergency on their paws and that they needed the help of every dog in the area.

"I was going to put out an Emergency Barking News," she told him. "But the weather's terrible and I don't think anyone will hear me over the wind and rain. We'll have to go door to door instead," Holly told him.

Agreeing to help Holly raise some more volunteers, Lightning trotted outside with her. Looking down at her, and without wanting to be rude, Lightning wondered how a little dog like her was going to keep up with him. Holly had already thought of that.

Hurtling through the darkened skies, Holly clung on to his back. There was no way a terrier could ever keep pace with the sheer speed of a greyhound.

"Are you alright up there?" he asked as his long-striding legs covered the ground rapidly.

Holly couldn't speak. She was doing her best to hold on and not be thrown off as she clung to the loose ruffles of skin on the back of his neck with her teeth.

Bounding past a row of cottages and houses, Holly gave an

urgent bark to any dogs that might be listening. All this commotion outside caught the ear of a bored labradoodle named Bob. Sticking his head up at the window, he peered out into the darkness.

"This is an Emergency Barking News," yelled Holly as they raced past. "We need your help. Bill the postman is in trouble down at the river!"

"What, Bill's in trouble?" Bob barked back, sounding all concerned. "I'll be on my way," he told them as Holly and Lightning pressed on into the night.

Looking at his owners who seemed to have settled down for a cosy night in, Bob proceeded to do his best impression of needing to be let out for the toilet. crossing and uncrossing his legs and pacing back and forth until his owners got the message that he wanted to go out.

Bob

Not far down the road lived Tarn with her owner, Miss Ellis. Now, when Bob saw the lights were on at her bungalow, he instantly decided to leap over the gate and bound across the lawn where he found Miss Ellis sat in the front room with Tarn on her knee watching TV and knitting.

"Tarn!" he barked through the thickly glazed window, but it was useless. The glass was far too thick for him to be heard. Then, from out of the corner of her eye Tarn spotted Bob breathing heavily on the large picture window, making big slobbery marks on the glass.

Unable to answer him as she didn't want to raise the suspicion of Miss Ellis, Tarn used her doggy sixth sense to ask him what he wanted. Gently leaping from her owner's lap, she excused herself and padding across the soft, luxuriant carpet headed for the back door.

Tarn was a very lucky dog. She had a dog flap all of her own, installed at the behest of Miss Ellis, so Tarn could come and go as she pleased. Poking her head out of the flap Tarn found Bob sat outside waiting for her in the rain.

"What's going on?" Tarn asked trying her best to avoid the worst of the weather that was blowing in.

"It's Bill. He needs our help," Bob told her, shaking the rain off his head.

"At this time?" Tarn replied sounding all surprised. "What's he doing out on a night like this?" she wanted to know.

"Beat's me," answered Bob. "A terrier riding on the back of a greyhound just came by my place minutes ago, telling me that they had an Emergency Barking News and that Bill was in trouble down at the river."

"Really?" Tarn enquired, feeling the fire inside her rise. Without a second thought, she pushed herself out of the dog flap headfirst, leaving it flapping wildly in her wake. "We better get going. It must be serious," she barked, shaking the rain from her dry coat.

"I've never heard of an Emergency Barking News on Christmas Eve before," she added with an excited tone to her bark. Without even pausing to put on her Tartan overcoat that Miss Ellis always made her wear, Tarn followed Bob down the lane as they rushed to help. Along the way wherever they came across a house with a dog, they stopped and barked up at the window to pass on the news. Soon dogs from all over the valley were rushing to the aid of Bill.

Chapter 22

DOGS TO THE RESCUE

Dhupa

The rain continued to pour down as Pugsley and Bill sat curled up underneath an old hazel tree for shelter. While waiting for help to arrive, Pugsley pushed himself in between the flaps of Bill's jacket and, pressing his paws into his stomach, he padded around as he struggled to get comfy.

"Are you done in there?" asked Bill peering down into his jacket. Two glistening yellow eyes came staring back at him.

"Don't be so fussy," Pugsley replied. "I'm trying to keep you warm!"

As they sat there, leant up against the tree shivering, they heard off in the distance a lone bark echoing through the leafless boughs of the deep valley.

"Over here!" Bill shouted, trying to make his position known. The barking grew louder. Then from out of nowhere he felt a soft nose prodding him in the back and turning around he found it was Ted.

"Hurrah!" he cheered, taking hold of Ted by the scruff of the neck and giving him a big hug. "Good to see you, old boy," he said expressing his relief.

Meanwhile, Pugsley was stuck inside Bill's jacket. Keen to make Ted's acquaintance, he pushed his head out of the top of Bill's jacket and frantically clawed his way out to rub noses with the Aussie.

The two dogs introduced themselves, sniffing madly at one another. Carried away by the moment, they broke out into a play fight as they tried to establish a bond together.

"Stop that, you two, we haven't got time for that sort of business!" Bill snapped, chastising them for frolicking around while they pretended to bite each other. Doing as they were told, the two dogs sat bolt upright and, as they did so, they heard the bark of another dog approaching.

"I know that bark anywhere!" exclaimed Bill, getting to his feet. "That'll be Gem." Within two shakes of a dog's tail, he could soon make out the white ruff of a border collie, as it leapt over logs and skirted its way along the river bank.

"Over here, girl," he called out, patting his thighs in order that she could locate him.

Jumping up on her hind legs, pleased to see him, she pushed her muzzle into his face to rub her scent on him.

"I'm glad to see that you're alright. Pup told me that you were in trouble," she barked as she made a fuss of him.

"It's not me. It's Rick Grinder," Bill explained, as the rain trickled down his face.

"RICK GRINDER!" growled Gem, unable to believe her ears. "What's he done now?" she wanted to know.

Pugsley kindly offered to show her. Padding his way to the water's edge, he pointed with his wet, drippy nose towards where the van that was stuck fast against a tree. Gem shook her head in dismay. Gingerly dipping her paw into the water she briskly pulled it out, letting out a sharp yelp.

"Brrrrr, that's cold…" she whined. "We'll have to get him out of there soon, otherwise he'll catch his death," she said, with urgency in her bark.

By now the news of the emergency had got around and more and more dogs were turning up every minute to help. Spotting Holly and Lightning, Gem bounded over to see the pair.

"I'm sorry to ask you this," she blurted out. "But I need you to go back up to Merrivale Farm."

Lightning looked shattered at the very thought of the idea, but knew he couldn't refuse as it was an emergency.

"I need you to get hold of Rachel," Gem instructed. "She's the only one, apart from Bill, that can understand us. Tell her to get her father to bring his tractor and some ropes with him and meet us down here."

Holly nodded to say that she understood and, without a moment's hesitation, they set off back up the hill. Lightning, racing at break neck speed, made rapid progress as Holly clung to his back, her teeth and paws digging in as she did her best to hold on.

Gem's focus now shifted to that of Rick Grinder. Peering into the darkness she could see that he was slumped over the steering wheel.

"Don't worry, we'll soon have you out of there," she barked at him, but the only response she got back was a limp handed wave. Gem knew she had to act fast if she was to prevent the worst from happening. All the time the water was getting deeper and deeper and at any minute the van could be washed away and him with it.

Scrutinising the pack of dogs that had turned up she spotted Victor, a big black, shaggy Newfoundland. Now Newfoundland's were renowned for their fantastic swimming abilities as well as their special webbed feet and Gem knew that Victor would be just the dog for the job.

"Victor!" she barked over the din of all the other dogs barking. As with all laid back Newfoundlands, they never rushed anywhere and Victor was certainly no exception. Taking his time he ambled over towards her with his big pink tongue lolling out of his mouth and drool dripping from his jowls like a giant slobber chops. Joining her down by the water's edge, he asked in his deep, resonant, bass-like bark what he could do for her.

"Do you think you can swim out to that van and bring back the man that's trapped inside?" she said pointing with her nose. Victor thought for a moment while he weighed up the situation.

"Yes, but I'll need some help," he said bluntly. "The water's flowing far too fast for me to hold my position. We'll need to make a chain so that you can hold on to me from the bank."

"A chain?" replied Gem with her head cocked to one side, exhibiting the curious nature of a border collie.

"Yes, a chain of dogs," he said as he began to elaborate. "If one dog holds on to my tail, then the other holds on to his and so on and so on then we can make a chain all the way out to the van. That way you'll be able to hold on to me so I don't go floating off downstream." Gem didn't know quite how this was going to work, but what Victor was saying seemed to make sense.

Jumping onto an old tree stump, Gem cleared her throat to get the attention of the dogs.

"Quiet, please!" she barked trying to settle down the pack of excitable dogs. Once they finished their yapping, they gathered round her in a semi-circle as they listened to what she had to say.

"Out there, we have a human trapped in a van…," she informed them as they listened intently. "…and, even though he has not been very nice to us dogs and other humans, we must put that behind us now. Our main aim is to get him out of the water before the unthinkable should happen," she explained.

"Victor here has kindly volunteered to be lead dog. He will swim out to rescue the trapped man, but in order to do so he requires us to make a dog chain."

"A dog chain?" chirped up Bob, a labradoodle having never heard of such a thing.

"Yes," replied Gem. "a dog chain! Victor will require someone to hold onto his tail as he swims out, and then another dog will hold onto the tail of the preceding dog, and so on and so forth," she explained, "until the chain reaches far enough out that we can rescue the man trapped inside the van. That way none of us go floating off downstream and the chain will be secured here on the bank." The dogs looked at each other.

"We've never heard of a dog chain before," they said, as they chatted idly amongst themsleves.

"Look!" Gem snapped. "We don't have time to waste. I need all of you dogs to line up behind Victor, NOW! And take hold of whoever's tail is in front of you as you enter the water."

With nothing else better to do on a wet and windy Christmas Eve, the dogs agreed to help out.

"Beats sitting at home watching TV, doesn't it?" mumbled Bob with a mouthful of Victor's tail clamped tightly between his jaws.

Entering the water, Victor waded out into the river till the water was up to his tummy. With the next dog following on behind they started to swim out. One by one the dogs entered the water, each with the proceeding dog's tail grasped firmly in their mouth.

"That's it, keep going," Gem instructed them from the bank. The chain arced out into the middle of the river and, as the last few dogs entered the water, Bill held onto the tail of the last dog so they didn't go floating off. Up to his knees in water, Pugsley was worried that Bill might go head first into the water. So latching onto his coat tails with his teeth he swung from the bottom of Bill's jacket, his paws thrashing wildly as he struggled to reach the ground beneath him.

Victor meanwhile had reached Rick Grinder and was desperately trying to free him from the van. Barking encouragement at him, Rick Grinder was too weak to climb out under his own steam and Victor didn't have enough strength to pull him out of the window on is own.

"Gem!" he barked over the swirling noise of the swollen river. "I need your help." Gem had been busy directing operations and now she was the only dog left that could help. Glancing down at the raging water she knew she'd be washed away if she jumped in on her own.

Her only hope was to jump the gap that lay between the fallen tree and the riverbank and then make her way out along the tree to the van. The gap was a good car's length. She might have been able to clear such a distance when she was younger, but now, being as she was no spring chicken, she wasn't sure that she could manage it. She looked down at the raging water and then looked back at Rick Grinder's pale face: she had no choice.

Gem took a run up and went for it. As Bill watched her leap into the darkness, he prayed that she would make it. Sailing through the air, her body outstretched she cleared the raging waters landing roughly on the end of the great, torn stump. Clawing her way up on to the trunk and pushing with her hind legs for all she was worth, the dogs praised her as she pulled herself up on to the log. Bill let out a sigh of relief, glad to know she was safe. Letting them know she was alright, Gem gave a jubilant bark before picking her way through the twist of branches to where the van was wedged.

When she reached Victor she found him holding onto Rick Grinder by the scruff of the neck and refusing to let go. Instantly without thinking she dived in through the window of the van and licked Rick Grinder on the face. Knowing that she had to get him out of there she pulled at the door handle with her teeth. With a clunk, the door slowly opened, and Rick Grinder floated out into the rushing water.

Victor, momentarily letting go of Rick Grinder, pushed him clear of the wreckage using the time-honoured tradition of doggy paddle to keep him afloat. Once they had him clear of the van Gem barked over to Bill.

"Right, Bill, pull us out."

Waist deep in water and with Pugsley holding onto his coat tails, Bill gradually began to drag the dogs out in the reverse order that they had gone in. As each dog made it back to dry land they gave themselves a thorough shaking covering Bill head to toe in filthy brown water.

Last but not least Victor made his way back up the bank, up to his tummy in water he dragged with him the limp body of Rick Grinder.

"Is he alive?" Bill shouted, as he came charging through the waters to come and see. Grabbing him by his jacket, he dragged him from the frigid waters and onto the muddy bank for safety.

"Rick, Rick," he shouted, as he tried and get some response from him. Unable to open his eyes, Rick Grinder let out a low moan.

"Thank God!" shouted Bill, relieved to know he was still alive.

Just then Gem let out a bark. It was Mr Cranbrook with his tractor. From a distance they watched at the slow progress of the tractor as it made its way down the valley and across the boggy fields towards them. Riding high in the cab with her father was Rachel and sat alongside was Holly and Lightning.

"Good girl, I knew you could do it," said Bill congratulating Gem, as he rejoiced at the sight of help on its way.

Climbing out of the cab and jumping off the steps, Rachel ran over to where Bill was huddled over Rick Grinder trying to keep the worst of the weather off him.

"The dogs told us you were here...," she said, garbling her words so fast that she could hardly speak. "...and we've brought everything with us that you asked," shouting as her voice got lost in the wind.

"Good girl," replied Bill giving her a pat on the back.

Following on, not too far behind, was her father. With his torch flashing in the darkness, the dogs ran around him in circles, barking madly and urging him to hurry up. Stumbling across them in the field, Mr Cranbrook leant over his daughter's shoulder to check on the condition of their patient.

"How is he?" he asked, bent over looking at him.

"Not good," Bill answered back grimly.

"Don't worry. We've got the Air Ambulance on its way. It should be here any minute now," he said.

Taking the blankets that they had brought with him, Mr Cranbrook and his daughter wrapped Rick Grinder up and made him warm. Once he was tucked up safely the dogs snuggled up by his side, keeping him warm as they patiently waited for help.

"Here, looks like you could use one of these too," said Rachel's father, placing a blanket around Bill's shoulders. As dogs and humans gathered around Rick Grinder's limp body, they prayed that he would pull through.

"I hope he makes it," Gem quietly whispered, letting out a low whine as she pushed her head under Bill's armpit to get a better view.

"Me too," Bill replied. Then, as if their prayers had been answered, the colour seemed to flood back to Rick Grinders face as he struggled to open his eyes.

"I'm sorry, Bill...," he moaned, reaching out, feeling for his hand. Bill took hold of his hand to reassure him and rubbed it to keep him warm.

"It's alright, you save your energy," He told him, but it was no use. Rick Grinder had to unburden himself.

"I've been awful to you, all of you, especially the dogs," he confessed. "All my life I've chased money thinking it would bring me happiness…," he said, his voice trailing off as he fought to retain consciousness, "…and now I realise none of it is worth it. None of it!" he said as if pouring scorn on his whole life's work.

"All I know is that kindness and love are the only things in life that matter…," he said, grabbing hold of Bill's hand tightly and squeezing it for all it was worth. "…and it really doesn't matter whether you're human or not, or that you've got four legs…or whatever… we are all here on this tiny rock just to all get along," he said, giggling as if drunk on some new found elixir of life.

Barely managing to open his eyes, he gave Gem, who had been standing over him, a weak, but feeble stroke.

"Hello, my friend," he said staring into her deep green eyes and playing with the fur on her ruff. Lowering her head, she gave him an affectionate lick on the face, and for the first time in what had been a very long time, a genuine smile crept across Rick Grinder's face.

Rachel looked over at Bill. With a wink of acknowledgment, they both knew what was going on.

"Looks like he's found his inner dog, eh?" Bill chuckled. Relieved that he was feeling better, Rachel gave a contented smile and pulled the blankets tight under his chin to keep him warm while some of the dogs howled with appreciation.

"Thank you, thank you, all of you," Rick Grinder blurted out, as he experienced an upwelling of emotion and the tears ran down his face.

After he had been loaded on to the Air Ambulance, the group huddled together as they shielded their eyes from the rotor wash that beat down upon them. Once all the noise had died down, Mr Cranbrook turned to Bill.

"You've had some day, haven't you?" he said with a smile. Bill was too exhausted to speak. Instead, Mr Cranbrook put his arm around his shoulder and gave him a great hug.

"C'mon, we better get you back to the house and dried off. You look like something that's been dragged out of a bog!" he noted, trying to make light of the way Bill looked, covered head to toe in mud.

While Rachel and Bill walked back to the house with the rest of the dogs in tow, Mr Cranbrook followed on behind in his tractor, pulling Grandpa's battered old van with him that he had dragged from the river.

Concerned that her family had been gone a long time, Mrs Cranbrook was busy staring out of the window awaiting the return of her husband, when off in the distance she spotted the flickering lights of the tractor.

"At last," she sighed with relief, as her two remaining children played happily in front of the fire. However, as she looked closer she could tell there was something that wasn't quite right about the animals that were making their way up the lane towards her house.

"Are those sheep, dear?" she asked of her children. Popping their heads up at the window, Josie and Charles tried to make out what it was their mother was looking at.

"I don't know, they don't look like sheep to me, Mum," replied Charles.

"Mmmm...they don't look like sheep to me either," his mother added dubiously.

Intrigued as to what they were, Josie pressed her face to the glass to get a better look. "That's because they're not sheep," she replied. "THEY'RE DOGS!" she gasped with surprise.

"Dogs?" her mother blurted out in disbelief. "They can't be dogs. What would that many dogs being doing out on a night like this?"

Stood at the door ready to greet her husband, Mrs Cranbrook was taken aback when a pack of wet dogs trooped into the farmyard busy barking and chasing each other around.

"Who do all these dogs belong to and where have they come from?" She demanded to know. Josie and Charles weren't interested in their mother's concerns. They were far too excited to go out and meet the dogs. Rushing out to greet them they went out in their wellies and pyjamas to play.

"What are you doing? You'll get yourselves all filthy!" their mother snapped, trying to call them back in, but Josie and Charles were having far too much fun petting and stroking all the dogs to listen to what their mother was saying.

The dogs were pleased to see the children, but they were even more pleased to see a warm, inviting farmhouse. Without the chance to say anything they rushed straight past Mrs Cranbrook and into the house. Letting out a terrific shriek, she threw her hands in the air, not knowing what to do with so many dogs in her house. Once inside the dogs plonked themselves down wherever they could find space: leaving big muddy paw prints on all the furniture, the carpets, and – to make themselves feel even more at home – they shook themselves off all over Mrs Cranbrook's lovely clean, white walls. All Mrs Cranbrook could do was stare on in horror.

Running across the farmyard, Rachel distracted her mother from what was going on in the house.

"Mum, Mum," she yelled, as she sploshed through all the puddles. "Guess what?" she said, all giddy with excitement and out of breath.

"What?" replied her mother with her arms folded looking slightly cross.

"You'll never believe me, but...," she gasped, her hands waving about as she began to talk. "...the dogs held each other's tails in their mouths and then made a chain to swim across the river... and then they saved a man's life... then we kept him warm with our blankets... then a helicopter came to take him to hospital...," she blurted out, not knowing what to tell her mum first. Seeing that Mrs Cranbrook was going to need a minute to take all this in, Bill stepped forward apologetically.

"Please, Mrs Cranbrook, allow me to explain," he said.

Bill was Mrs Cranbrook's favourite postman and, as she had not seen him for such a long time, she soon forgot about all the dogs being in her house and gave him a big sloppy kiss on the side of his face.

"Come in, come in," she urged him, taking hold of him by the arm and escorting him inside, leaving her husband to empty the van of all the soggy parcels.

"Look at the state you're in! How on earth did you get like that?" she wanted to know while busy fussing around him. "...and I think your uniform could do with a wash...," she insisted, wagging her finger at him. "Have you rung your wife yet? I bet you haven't, have you?" she questioned him.

Bill had barely chance to get a word in edgeways before she spoke again.

"Here, while I'm running you a bath, you can ring your wife and let her know that you're alright," she said pushing the phone into his hand.

It was late when he rang home. The phone had hardly chance to ring when Granny picked it up.

"Hello, mi' dear," said Bill sheepishly, thinking he was going to be in big trouble, but instead Granny immediately burst into tears.

"Thank God, I was worried sick about you," she cried.

"Please don't be mad at me…," said Bll, trying to apologise for his lateness.

"Mad… mad?" wept Granny down the phone. "I'm not mad at you. I'm just glad you're alright," she said through the flood of tears.

Bill explained to her that, with the help of the dogs, they had saved Rick Grinder's life and rescued all the undelivered Christmas presents from the water. Granny wasn't too bothered about the Christmas presents, but she was extremely pleased to hear that he had saved somebody's life and, as a reward, she said she would cook him his favourite dinner of egg and chips when he got home.

Putting Alex and Niall on the phone, they told him how they had both been really worried about him and thought that they might never see him again. After he had apologised several times to them, he said that he would tell them about how the dogs pulled Rick Grinder from the river and how the helicopter took him to hospital, which they couldn't wait to hear.

Bill could hear Mrs Cranbrook calling from upstairs to tell him his bath was ready. So saying goodbye he told them not to worry and that he'd be home in time to spend Christmas morning with them.

After having a good soak Grandpa came down stairs and was amazed to find dogs draped all over the house. On the stairs, in the hallway, in the living room and in the kitchen: there were dogs everywhere drying themselves off and licking themselves clean.

Wearing some of Mr Cranbrook's old clothes that his wife had picked out for him, Bill took a seat at the kitchen table while Josie passed him a steaming hot mug of tea.

"That's better," remarked Mrs Cranbrook with a satisfied air, pleased that Bill was looking a little more presentable. After having got over the shock of having a whole load of dogs in her house, she got busy with rustling up a hearty supper for everyone.

Seeing as it was Christmas Eve and Mrs Cranbrook had already prepared the meal for the following day, she thought they might as well have Christmas early and stuck the pigs in blankets and some of the other trimmings in the oven to cook. Pugsley was extremely pleased when Mrs Cranbrook tossed him one of the hot sausages wrapped in bacon.

Meanwhile Gem, who was exhausted from everything, was just happy to lay in front of the Aga and let the heat creep into her old bones.

"Well done," barked Pugsley, congratulating her as he licked the last of the bacon fat from the floor. "I'd have never been able to jump that gap between the river and the tree: you know, you were amazing," he barked.

Underneath all that fur, Gem was beginning to blush. "Stop it, any dog would have done the same," she replied coyly.

"Ahh... but you helped another human being, that's special," noted Pugsley with a burp.

As Mrs Cranbrook served out Christmas dinner, Bill looked over at Rachel and Gem.

"I don't know what I would have done without these two," he said. praising their efforts. "They were fantastic," he said, raising his mug of tea to toast them.

Her father, appreciative of his daughter's help, gave her a rub on the back to show just how proud of her he was. "Didn't she do well?" he grinned with a big, beaming smile across his face.

As they sat around tucking into their supper of roast potatoes, stuffing, bread sauce and all the trimmings, talk turned to what they were going to do with the heap of soggy parcels that were stacked up on the floor. Mr Cranbrook looked at the pile of undelivered Christmas presents that were drying out and shook his head.

"Seems a shame that they won't get delivered," he mused.

"I don't mind taking them," replied Bill, with a casual shrug of the shoulders.

"You must be joking: look at the time, it's nearly midnight!" exclaimed Mr Cranbrook, almost choking when he heard his suggestion.

"But people will be waiting for them," replied Bill.

"You can't go out in that, have you seen the weather out there?" said Mr Cranbrook shaking his head. "Besides the roads are flooded and it's still blowing a right old gale out there," argued Mr Cranbrook, trying to dissuade Bill from going out.

"I know, but I've at least got to try," he said. "Could I borrow your tractor?" he asked Mr Cranbrook.

Well, when he heard that Bill wanted to use his tractor Mr Cranbrook started coughing as if something had got stuck in his throat and went a funny colour in his face. Mr Cranbrook's tractor was his pride and joy and the thought of someone else borrowing it made him feel uneasy, but his wife thought otherwise.

"What a good idea, eh, dear? That way everyone will still get their presents," she commented, but Mr Cranbrook thought otherwise. Stammering and trying to think of some excuse for Bill not to use his tractor, he came out with all sorts of old drivel to try and put him off.

"Err…I…I don't know, love, it's awfully complicated to drive…," he said to his wife. "…I mean, what with all those gears, an' all that," Squirming nervously as he fidgeted awkwardly in his chair.

"It's not complicated at all, Dad," chimed up Charles. "You let me drive it all the time."

Mr Cranbrook shot his son a withering glance and muttered something under his breath that his wife didn't quite catch.

"Oh, don't worry, I've driven tractors before," said Bill, trying to put Mr Cranbrook's mind at ease.

"See, what did I tell you," said Mrs Cranbrook confidently. "Everything will be fine, dear," she assured him, pouring some more gravy on his supper. "Think of all those happy children when they find out that Santa's been to call," Mr Cranbrook daren't say a word. He knew it was unwise to go against his wife's decision and so, accepting what fate may bring, he handed the keys over to Bill.

Bill was so hungry that he got two thick slices of white bread and put it all together to make one giant sandwich. Biting into it he let the bread sauce and gravy run down his chin. Impressed with his creation the Cranbrook children copied him, insisting it was the best sandwich they'd ever tasted. Even Mrs Cranbrook made sure the dogs got something, letting them have the leftovers and the roasting tin to lick out for good measure.

When it came time for Bill to leave Mrs Cranbrook gave him back his uniform that she had washed, while outside her husband helped him to load the parcels onto the sheep cage on the back of the tractor. Just big enough to hold a few lambs and a couple of ewes it made an ideal hod for carrying parcels. Once stacked with all the presents, Mr Cranbrook threw a tarpaulin over them to keep them dry, lashing it down tightly so they didn't get wet.

Pugsley wishing to thank the family for their hospitality, expressed his gratitude to Mrs Cranbrook by standing up on his hind legs and giving her a paw. Gem didn't want to be left out and pushed through the tangle of children's legs to see Pugsley off. Coming over to have a good sniff they rubbed noses with each other and Pugsley said that if she was ever in town she should let him know and he would make sure he had a nice piece of fish waiting for her.

"Aww...how sweet!" gushed Mrs Cranbrook, delighted to have shaken paws with Pugsley. The rest of the dogs showed their appreciation for the family by way of a chorus of contented barks and much wagging of their tales as they trotted out into the night, heading off in all different directions as they made their way home.

"Come on you!" said Bill, looking down at Pugsley. "We haven't got all night. We've still got this lot to deliver," he said, pointing to the hod full of parcels. Giving Pugsley a helping hand, he lifted him up and pushed him into the cab. As Bill climbed the steps up into the tractor, Pugsley stuck his head out of the door and let out a final bark of thanks to the Cranbrook family. Gem, in response, lifted her muzzle to the night sky and let out a long, drawn out howl as if echoing her wolf like ancestry.

"Stop that, Gem, stop that at once!" Mrs Cranbrook scolded her, putting her hand to her ears. "I've heard enough barking for one day!"

Mr Cranbrook looked on nervously as Bill started up the tractor. Stood in the doorway he watched as the old machine spluttered into life.

"Watch out for flood water!" shouted Mr Cranbrook anxiously, his hands cupped to his mouth as the rest of his family huddled in the porch out of the rain.

"Don't you worry," replied Bill, leaning through the gap in the back of the cab. "I'll have it back here as soon as I can and without a scratch on it." Even though Bill had sworn to say he'd look after the tractor, Mr Cranbrook couldn't help but feel a teensy bit nervous about letting someone else drive it.

Waving till they were out of sight, Bill and Pugsley chugged along the lanes, bouncing up and down on the seat like yo-yos. By now the rain had eased and the wind was not so strong. They made their first stop to deliver a packet. Aware that it was the middle of the night and that most people had gone to bed Bill did his best not to wake anyone up as he popped the parcel in the shed outside. Writing them a note to say how sorry he was that their parcel was late and a little damp, he hoped that they would understand and asked if they didn't mind that he helped Santa out this year with delivering all the presents.

As they travelled the lanes across the moors, Pugsley looked out at the night sky in the hope that he might see Santa on his sleigh. By now the storm had passed and the sky was beginning to clear revealing the universe in its true majesty.

"It's an amazing world," sighed Pugsley, wistfully looking up at the stars and the outstretched arm of the Milky Way.

"It certainly is," replied Bill, echoing his friend's sentiments.

"Do you think there's other people out there, celebrating Christmas like us?" he asked, looking up at the stars. Bill laughed.

"I'm sure there are, but I doubt they're having Christmas. There probably just up there living peacefully together like we all should," Pugsley nodded, letting out a somewhat sad snuffle.

"What's up, lad?" asked Bill, wondering why Pugsley was feeling so down.

"I wish everyone could be just a little bit more dog and get along with each other," he whimpered.

"Don't worry, lad," said Bill, pulling him tight against his chest and giving him a cuddle. "One day, lad. One day," he assured him, giving him a kiss on the flat of his brow. Pugsley looked up at him and gave him a heart-warming smile.

All along the combes and valleys, people were woken from their slumbers by the sound of a tractor roaring up to their house. Wondering what was going on, they blearily rubbed their eyes as they looked out of their bedroom windows, only to find Bill stood on their doorstep with a parcel under his arms.

"Bill, what are you doing?" they shouted down to him. "Don't you know it's the middle of the night?" they said.

Bill cheerily waved back up to them. "I know, but I'm here to deliver your presents!" he replied in his loudest whisper.

In farms and properties all across the moors, lights were being switched on and kettles put onto boil for cups of tea as people came downstairs to welcome Bill into their homes. Everyone found Pugsley adorable and when he carried their parcel in for them they wanted to reward him with a treat. They offered him the carrots that had been left out for the reindeer, but Pugsley, even though he knew that carrots were lovely and helped you see in the dark, couldn't help but turn his nose up at them when he saw an uneaten mince pie.

Asking Pugsley if he would like a mince pie was a bit of a silly question. Licking his chops, and with his stumpy little tail wagging furiously, he soon found himself the lucky recipient of more mince pies than he could dream of. As they travelled from house to house, Pugsley wanted to know why Father Christmas left so many mince pies uneaten, but after his fifth mince pie Pugsley soon knew why.

"Cor...I feel sick," he barked, pawing at the door of the cab to be let out. Stopping the tractor immediately, Bill let him out to get some fresh air. Disappearing behind a hedgerow Bill switched off the engine as Pugsley sounded decidedly unwell. Pugsley came wandering back looking rather unsteady on his feet and a little green round the gills.

"Is it time to go home yet?" he asked Bill, sounding rather poorly. Taking pity on him, Bill wrapped Pugsley up in one of the lovely warm blankets that Mr Cranbrook had left in his tractor and let him sleep while he delivered the last of the presents.

It was still dark when they arrived back in Berrycombe St Martin. Dropping Pugsley off at home, he watched as the portly bulldog snuck in through the back gate and waited till he saw he was safe.

All of Berrycombe St Martin was asleep when Bill drove up the street; that was, all except for one house. Guided by the light that shone brightly from the windows, he parked the tractor directly in front of his house. The mice who had been hanging by their tails from the fairy lights in the window rushed to tell Granny that he had arrived home.

By the time Bill had got out of the cab, the whole family was waiting for him on the doorstep. Not having slept a wink, Granny and her son were still dressed, but Alex and Niall were stood there in their night clothes. For Bill it was a glorious sight to behold. Hugging and kissing them all, Granny ushered everyone inside out of the cold. She was so over the moon that her husband was home safe that she couldn't stop crying, and Alex and Niall's dad had to get her to sit down while he went and made her a cup of tea.

Bill was so tired that he flopped down, right there and then, on the sofa.

"That's better," he said wearily as his grandchildren sat next to him on the edge of the sofa.

"So I suppose you want to know what happened, eh?" he said to his grandchildren as they nodded. "Well, it all began like this...." he started to say, but he was so tired he dozed off mid sentence and was unable to complete his story.

He slept right the way through the whole of Christmas Day and didn't wake up until it was tea time. Instead of Christmas dinner with all the trimmings, Granny had made egg and chips for everyone. As they sat around the kitchen table tucking into their dinner, Bill declared it was the best Christmas dinner he'd ever had.

"Who needs presents when you've got a family as wonderful as this!" he cheered, raising his mug of tea in a toast.

"I agree," chuckled Granny, giving him a kiss.

EPILOGUE

Well, I suppose you want to know what happened to Rick Grinder and the Area Manger, don't you?

It turned out that the Area Manager had been filmed by the local news crew kicking dogs and had to go to court to answer for his rather unpleasant behaviour. After reviewing the evidence, the Judge thought it best that he be given community service and sentenced him to eighty hours as a dog poo warden.

That wasn't the end for the Area Manager though. After Head Office heard what he had been doing, how he had been so uncaring to the staff that worked for him, they demoted him to postman and, as a punishment, they made him fold empty mail sacks until he knew how to treat people and animals properly.

As for Rick Grinder, he never came back to work. After being rescued from the river by the dogs, he had a change of heart and wanted to do something positive for society. So, he opened his own Disco Dancing Dog Grooming Salon where he pruned and preened pouches to within an inch of their life. In his salon he played disco music, which the dogs all loved, and had a glitter ball hanging from the ceiling. While he trimmed and sheered, he danced around on roller boots, such was his flair for dog grooming. Everyone came from miles around just to see him work.

And he never counted a penny of his money in his life again. Instead, he took in sick and abandoned dogs and looked after them till he could find a new home for them. He even found a home with Bill for a young Staffordshire Terrier, which Granny and the children were extremely pleased about.

In Berrycombe St Martin, Head Office decided to make Tina the new manager and things went back to the way they were when Clive was in charge.

As for Bill, Tina put him back on his old round and all the dogs were overjoyed to see him back. Each of them wagging their tails in ecstasy when they heard the news. Every day he would bring them a dog biscuit, safe in the knowledge that there would be nobody watching over him with a dog biscuit sniffer ever again.